BETWEEN TWO WARS

Aaron Dryden

Inspired by the incredible true story of my great-grandfather

Charles Young Watson

Contents

Chapter 1

The Farmhand

The sun was only just lifting over the horizon, but Charles had already beaten it. The paddocks shimmered in the early light, filled with the lowing of cattle and the sigh of wind through the grass. Alone on horseback, a slender stockman moved the herd with practiced ease.

He rode as though born in the saddle. Every shift of his weight, every press of his knee, turned the horse as if it were an extension of his body. The herd bent to his will, steers flowing like water with the faintest nudge. Charles leaned forward, whistled, and the horse surged ahead. For a moment, boy and beast moved as one.

Up close, his youth betrayed him. A baby face, still patchy with stubble, gave away the truth; he was no more than sixteen. Yet his fearlessness told another story, years of hard chores, loyalty to the farm, and a stubborn refusal to falter.

Then came the call, sharp and familiar across the paddock. "Charles, it's time to get moving!"

He reined in, turning toward the sound. His foster mother's voice carried across the fields, pulling him back to the homestead. Charles had left the Townsville orphanage at eight, the city nothing but a blur of fenced in yards and church bells. Here, on the farm, he had found family. To him, they were simply Mother and Father.

He closed the gate, trapping the herd in the field, and walked his horse back to the stable. There was no rush; after all, it was the summer holidays.

Charles banged through the back screen door, its wire mesh rattling against the frame. The door opened straight into the kitchen of the small two-bedroom homestead. It was quaint. His family were not wealthy; if they had been, they wouldn't be living in Woodstock, a rural town in North Queensland.

Sure, Townsville was only forty-five kilometres away. Now, in January 1917, you could make that journey on the Great Northern Railway in an hour and a half. But with all the work to do on the farm, Charles rarely saw anything resembling real civilisation. Since leaving the orphanage, Townsville remained the only place outside Woodstock he had ever known.

He grabbed a bowl of porridge from the kitchen bench where his mother had left it waiting. She stood in her apron, stirring tea leaves in the billy before setting it on the brick hearth, the fire crackling below. Charles took a seat at the end of the table in the living room, just off the kitchen, where his father already sat with the latest edition of The Townsville Daily Bulletin.

From his spot opposite, Charles could see only the front page. Two bold black headlines jumped out at him. The first read, *Gallipoli Casualty Lists*.

To Charles, Gallipoli already felt like a lifetime ago. He wondered why, after more than eighteen months, it would still make the front page; and why it had taken so long to learn who hadn't come back.

In his naive young mind, Gallipoli still meant adventure and heroism rather than tragedy. He thought of it as a tale of mateship and courage, not loss and misery. That was how he and his schoolmates, Billy Carter and Frankie Doyle, spoke of the war, an exciting path to glory and new experiences. Frankie, though, often tempered their enthusiasm. He seemed to see something the others did not.

A squealing whistle from the billy pierced Charles's ear as his mother pulled it off the hearth in the background. The sound broke his focus for a moment, but curiosity drew his eyes back to the page. The next headline caught him immediately, *Conscription Debates*.

It was clearly a continuation of the arguments that had divided the nation before the October 1916 referendum on compulsory military service. Charles knew the Labor Party had pushed for it, and that it was narrowly defeated by a 51% *"No"* vote. What puzzled him was why the Australian Imperial Force couldn't find enough men willing to volunteer for what surely seemed the adventure of a lifetime.

He was so absorbed in the thought that he didn't notice the chair beside him scrape across the crooked timber floor, or his mother taking a seat. Lost in his own musing, he muttered under his breath,

"Cowards."

Though quiet, the word seemed to echo through the small kitchen. Apart from the tinkling of his mother's spoon tapping the teacup and the occasional bang of the window shutters catching the wind, the room was silent.

His mother's eyes flicked nervously toward him. Clearly, his father had heard as well; he lowered the newspaper, revealing a face roughened by years under the Queensland sun. The thick beard, the streaks of grey cutting through black hair, the deep lines, skin leathered; all signs of a man hardened by the land. His piercing brown eyes fixed on Charles as he spoke in a low, steady voice.

"What exactly do you mean by that, Charles?"

Charles froze. The hairs on his neck stood up. His father's calmness frightened him more than anger ever could. He realised, too late, that the very kind of man who filled their small town he'd just called *"coward."* The teaspoon stopped. Even the wind seemed to vanish, total silence.

He knew he had to answer. And though his father intimidated him, Charles had never been one to shy away from speaking his mind. Finally, he said,

"Well, I mean... how does our country get into a position where it needs conscription? Don't we have enough able men willing to fight for our kingdom?"

His mother gulped. This had clearly been a topic of conversation at this table before. Charles knew his father was among those who could have volunteered. He didn't think of him as a coward, far from it. To Charles, his father was a strong man, hardened by years of running the farm and teaching him everything about this harsh life.

His father took a slow breath, composed himself, and crossed his arms. Then, in a voice low but firm, he said, "Our kingdom? You think men volunteer to fight for a crown; or for a king they'll never meet? That war's on the other side of the world, boy. Europe's fight, not ours. They're just using us for cannon fodder."

He paused; eyes fixed on his son. "Don't be quick to call men cowards, lad. Some of them have already given the King more than he has any right to ask."

Charles always loved to snap back. Maybe it was his youthful mind speaking before it thought, but all he managed to say was,

"But isn't that what loyalty is? To do whatever the King needs of us? As soon as I'm able, I'll be there."

His mother softly chimed in, trying to disarm the moment. "The King's never gone without his supper, Charles. Don't think he knows what this empire costs us out here. Just as well you're only turning seventeen next week and not eighteen, the war will be over before you're able."

Charles's mind retreated. She was probably right. The war had been dragging on for three years now, and deep down he felt he was missing out; held back by nothing more than his age.

He went back to his breakfast, staring out the window. The view was almost therapeutic: rolling fields stretching into the distance, broken only by scattered trees and grazing cattle. This was home. It was all he had ever known.

Yet to him, this life his father had chosen felt bland, repetitive, each day a mirror of the one before. Wake early. Muster cattle. School. Chores. Dinner. Bed. Then do it all again. It felt as though he could already see the next thirty years laid out before him, unchanging. The thought deflated him. He wanted more, the mateship, the medals, the escape from the farm. The glorious adventure he imagined war to be.

"You're going to be late," his mother said gently. She was right again. He had plans to walk into town and should already be on his way to meet Billy at the gate.

As usual, Billy was already waiting with his cheeky grin, when Charles came wandering down the track, sweating from both the rush out the door and the blistering heat. Billy had been swinging from the gate, tossing stones at carriage wheels as they rolled by.

"'Bout time, Charlie boy; thought you'd gone and enlisted without me," Billy snickered as they met.

He lived on a farm further along the road, and though the same age, Billy was taller and broader in the shoulders, carrying a look far older than his years. The two had been inseparable since childhood, ever since Charles was first fostered. They'd grown up, side by side, best mates; and it was common to see Billy dropping in unannounced at the farm. He always seemed eager to escape his own chores, usually repairing yet another busted fence while cattle roamed free.

Billy was a real larrikin, recklessly confident and endlessly mischievous. Often, when Charles found himself in strife, Billy had been the one to lead him there. Yet Charles couldn't help but be drawn to his mate's rogue charm. Maybe it was Billy's cheeky bravado, his courage without caution, that made the world feel less dull. In some ways, Billy embodied everything Charles longed for: freedom, excitement, and a hint of danger.

They started down the rough, dusty road to Woodstock. The walk was a couple of kilometres, and by the time the boys usually arrived, they were already covered in dust from passing horse-drawn carts. If they were lucky, they might even catch a stray stone flung up from the rutted track. Not that either of them minded, a bit of dirt never bothered country boys. If it did, they were growing up in the wrong part of the world.

Billy could tell his mate was flustered, but he also sensed there was more on Charles's mind.

"Well, come on then, Charlie boy, let's have it. Move 'em to the wrong paddock this morning, did ya?" Billy teased, his booming voice cutting through the dry air.

He knew that wasn't the case. Charles was meticulous, almost systematic in how he handled his work. It was a discipline that didn't always carry over to school or other decisions, but on the farm, Charles took pride in doing things right. Still, Billy never passed up a chance to get a rise out of him.

Charles just shook his head. He was used to Billy's digs, but today he wasn't in the mood to give him the satisfaction.

"Nah. Just butting heads with my father again," he muttered.

"Ahhh, that old bother," Billy said, his tone softening. "What's he pullin' your chin over this time?"

Charles sighed and began recounting the breakfast conversation, the talk about conscription, his father's temper, and his own slip of the word cowards. Billy listened, surprised. He'd heard plenty of stories about Charles and his father not seeing eye to eye, but this was different. Part of him was taken aback by what Charles had said, yet another part was quietly impressed. It took guts to speak that way to his father's face.

He could see Charles was still agitated. Maybe it wasn't just about the argument. Maybe it was about being stuck in the life chosen for him. After all, it was his father who'd pulled him from the orphanage and brought him here. Sometimes Charles said he felt more like a farmhand than a son.

At that moment, a rickety carriage drawn by two horses thundered past, leaving both boys gasping for air as a thick cloud of dust enveloped them. The cloud was so heavy it felt impossible to breathe. They yanked their mud-stained shirts over their faces until the haze finally cleared, then dusted themselves off and looked around to find the world peaceful once more. At least they thought, there weren't many travellers on this road; they should be safe for the rest of the walk.

Billy was first to break the silence. "Well, your old girl might be right, Charles. That war isn't gonna last forever. Our boys'll have 'em before Christmas."

The thought hit Charles hard. If the war ended before Christmas, all his dreams of adventure would end with it. He didn't reply.

Billy spoke up again, ever eager to keep the mood light. "Reckon we should do somethin' for your birthday, eh? Get in early before school ruins it."

Charles hadn't given it much thought, but Billy had a point. By the time his birthday came around on the 29th, school would have started again, and between that and his chores, there wouldn't be much time for celebration.

"We'll talk to Frankie and Edna when we see 'em in Woodstock," Billy said.

Charles frowned slightly. He knew about the plans with Frankie, but Edna? That was unexpected. Sure, they were all in the same class, but he didn't recall any of them being particularly close with her.

Edna Price was from different stock altogether. Her family's property was the largest cattle ranch in the area, one of the few that could afford hired farmhands. She didn't seem the type to belong in a place like Woodstock, and you'd never catch her walking into town. For all Charles knew, the carriage that had just choked them in dust could've been hers.

He wouldn't admit it to Billy, but Edna had caught his eye more than once. During those long, dull English lessons, the sunlight would strike her flowing brown hair, and when she turned, her piercing pale blue eyes would meet his for a heartbeat too long. Still, it didn't make sense. Why would she meet up with them? And why would she care about his birthday?

"What's with Edna being there?" Charles finally asked.

"Dunno fully," Billy replied with a shrug. "Saw her trottin' past our lower paddock yesterday. We got to yappin', and she sort of invited herself."

Billy didn't think much of it, he rarely thought much of anything beyond the moment. Charles, however, couldn't decide if he was bothered or secretly pleased that Edna might be there. Either way, it wasn't what he'd expected.

For the next twenty minutes, Billy filled the air with nonsense chatter; clearly trying to lift Charles's mood and restore the boisterous energy he was used to. Eventually, the boys reached the underwhelming sight of Woodstock's main street.

There was nothing refined about the place. Harsh, rugged, and worn by the sun, it was little more than a dusty strip of road lined with a few tired timber buildings. The only structure with any real pride was the newly built railway station. Though made of wood like the rest, its bright white paint stood out sharply against the red earth and always caught Charles's eye as they entered town.

The rest of Woodstock was humble; a single main street, a handful of shops, and, at the far end, the small schoolhouse where they were headed. The Woodstock State School was a simple one-room building with faded blue window shutters and a small brass bell tower perched on top, as if to remind everyone what it was.

Frankie Doyle stood by the school fence, not much taller than Charles, but he liked to think himself a man. Unlike the others, Frankie was already eighteen and proud of it. He sported a thin moustache and always wore polished boots that gleamed in the sunlight, making sure everyone noticed.

He fancied himself an intellect, and to be fair, he was. He'd been top of their class at school, though that wasn't surprising given his upbringing.

His father, Dr Doyle, ran a small clinic just outside town. Charles suspected the doctor wasn't thrilled about his son keeping company with the likes of Billy and himself, but in a town as small as Woodstock, there wasn't much he could do about it. One thing was certain; Frankie would never risk disappointing his father. There was every chance he'd follow in his footsteps one day.

Further back, leaning lightly against the bell tower, was Edna. She stood out like a daisy in red dust, the only spotless dress in sight, with neat ribbons and sparkling shoes that looked as though they'd stepped out of a city catalogue. Petite and poised, she carried herself with a confidence that rubbed Charles the wrong way, too polished, too sure of herself, too perfect for a place like this.

"Frankie D, your moustache's lookin' mighty thin today, mate!" Billy boomed by way of greeting.

"If you can't grow one, you can't comment," Frankie shot back without missing a beat.

Charles couldn't help but grin. Frankie's wit always bested Billy's bluster. The two were opposites in nearly every way, yet somehow, they'd become fast friends; perhaps out of necessity more than choice, given how few boys their age lived around here.

"Nice of you all to finally arrive," Edna cut in. "I thought we agreed to meet at eight, not half past."

She always had to be the centre of attention. Then again, it was easier to be punctual when the horse did all the work. Charles felt a flicker of guilt, he was probably the reason for their delay, still shaken from the morning's clash with his father.

"Sorry, lass," Billy said with a grin. "We ain't as quick as that fancy carriage of yours."

"Yeah, sorry, Edna. My fault," Charles added, owning up.

Edna turned her blue eyes on him, a faint smile softening her expression. "That's okay, Charles," she said quietly. "So, what are we doing?"

Her tone caught him off guard. She was usually so distant, so hard to read. Yet here she was, not at school but standing before him, joining their plans uninvited; and not unwelcome, he realised with some surprise.

After a short back-and-forth, the group decided to grab a soda from the hotel. Being underage made it feel slightly rebellious, more grown-up than buying one from the store. From there, they'd wander to the railway station to watch the trains pass, as they often did. Something about the station, the noise, the motion, the sense of leaving, always felt thrilling, like a glimpse of the wider world beyond Woodstock.

As they set off down Main Street, the town revealed its familiar mix of dust and charm. The general store, with its red-and-white sign above a narrow veranda, was one of the few splashes of colour. Out front stood the latest newspapers, including The Townsville Daily Bulletin, its bold headlines taunting Charles with memories of that morning's argument.

Beside the stand hung the updated casualty list from the war. Charles's eyes skimmed the names. None he recognised. None that mattered to him. He moved on without a second thought.

Kicking up dust as they walked, the group made their way toward the centre of town where the main buildings stood; the simple timber church, a few weathered shops, and the beating heart of Woodstock: the hotel. It towered above the rest of the town, a two-storey structure with a wide veranda and balconies stretching across the front facade, directly opposite the railway station.

Though it was the largest and busiest building in Woodstock, the hotel was well past its prime. The once-yellow paint had blistered and peeled away under the relentless sun, and the hand-painted black lettering across the veranda had faded to a ghostly grey. Still, every traveller stepping off the train knew exactly what it was. If you wanted to find someone in Woodstock, this was where you went.

The group bought sarsaparilla sodas and sat along the edge of the railway platform. A soft fizz sounded in unison as they cracked open their glass bottles, the cold drink a rare reprieve from the stifling heat of this godforsaken town.

"Well, Charlie boy," Billy said, leaning back with a grin, "you've had plenty of time to think. What's the birthday plan, eh?"

Charles hesitated. Truthfully, he hadn't thought any further about it. His mind had drifted back to the newspaper they'd seen at the general store.

"I think we need to get out of here," Edna said suddenly, her voice bright and confident. "Let's go to the big city, see the new Townsville Railway Station, climb Castle Hill." She'd invited herself again, though no one seemed to mind this time.

Billy grinned. "Ah, the big smoke, aye? Don't mind that at all!"

Charles looked out across the tracks, his voice quieter, steadier. "Well, that's exactly what I plan to do next year; head to the big smoke and volunteer for the war."

Before anyone could respond, a piercing whistle split the air. The sound grew into a deafening screech as a train rounded the bend, brakes squealing, sparks flashing along the rails. The group stepped back from the platform edge as the carriages thundered past, finally grinding to a halt.

It was one of the newer passenger trains, painted deep maroon, the polished brass catching the sun. The first-class carriages gleamed, the kind Charles imagined Edna might be accustomed to. Behind them came the second-class cars, crammed full, faces pressed to the windows, the doors swinging open to reveal a sea of khaki uniforms.

Dozens of fresh-faced AIF recruits poured out onto the platform, laughing, shouting, shoving one another with the energy of boys who hadn't yet seen war. They looked barely older than Charles himself, baby-faced, clean-shaven, not a hint of stubble among them. Their excitement was infectious, echoing down the street as they crossed straight toward the worn-out hotel across the road.

"Look at them," Frankie said, analysing the recruits as they streamed past. "Half of them look as young as you, Charles, though maybe an inch taller. Billy, you tower over them all."

"He's right, you know," Edna added, crossing her arms as she looked Charles up and down. "Clean shave, tidy clothes, you'd fit right in. I've heard my father say that half the volunteers these days are lying about their age. The AIF doesn't care. They'll take anyone to make up the numbers."

Normally so composed, Charles felt something shift, an epiphany. It was as if the whole day had led him here. His mother's warning about the war ending, his father's disdain for it, Billy's talk of adventure, Frankie's offhand comparison to a soldier; even Edna's presence. She usually made him feel beneath her, but this time her words landed differently. Maybe she was right. Maybe this was the answer he'd been searching for.

"That's it then," Charles declared, his voice firm. He stood taller, almost commanding. "I'm moving next year's plans up. This year, for my birthday; we'll go to the big smoke, and I'll enlist."

"Hi-ho! Here we go, Charlie boy!" Billy cheered, his pitch rising with excitement. "You can't go stormin' across the world without me."

Frankie chuckled. "Well, my father would kill me if I followed you fellas to war; but I'll come along for the trip to the big smoke."

"That's fair, Frankie," Charles said with a grin. "You've got a different path. You'll be another Dr Doyle by the time we get back."

"I guess that settles it, then," Edna said, a small smirk curling her lips. "Let's do it tomorrow, while we still have a day off. Clean yourself up, Charles, I'll bring some of my father's clothes for you."

Billy laughed. "What about a nicer fit for me, lass?"

Edna shot him a glance. "I don't think you'll have any trouble, Billy. You already look like you've been there and come back. Besides, none of my father's clothes would fit you."

She had a point. At least Charles was about her father's height.

And just like that, it was settled. Tomorrow the 21st of January 1917; the four of them would travel to Townsville. For some, it would be a brief escape from Woodstock. For Charles and Billy, it would be the start of something far greater.

Chapter 2

The Big Smoke

Tomorrow had come. Charles found himself back on the platform just as the sun climbed higher into the sky. The crowds were gone. In place of squealing train brakes, only the birds sang from the bushland across the tracks.

He'd barely slept a wink, most of the night spent tossing and turning, caught between bursts of excitement, waves of anxiety, and brief, restless moments of sleep. He'd told his parents about the plans to go to Townsville for an early birthday celebration but had carefully left out the real reason for the trip.

Now, standing on the platform, his stomach twisted with nerves. Was he really going to follow through? Was he truly turning his bold words into action?

His thoughts were interrupted by Billy, who had been standing quietly beside him the whole time.

"Don't fall asleep, Charlie boy," Billy chuckled, giving him a nudge. "Reckon you'd miss Edna's grand entrance, and the train'll leave you behind."

Almost on cue, Edna's carriage rattled up the road, kicking a cloud of dust straight over the boys. Charles muttered under his breath. So much for a grand entrance. But then the carriage door creaked open, and out stepped Edna, fresh, immaculate, as though the dust hadn't dared touch her.

She wore polished high brown boots and a crisp white dress made from the latest fabric, standing in the sun like a figure of light while the boys were still brushing grit from their hair.

Charles wasn't sure what stirred more excitement in him, the sight of Edna herself or the neatly wrapped suit she held in her hands.

"I thought you two were going to clean yourselves up," Edna chuffed as she approached, clearly amused to know she was the cause of their filthy state. "At least you sorted that stubble out," she added, reaching out to run her hand along Charles's freshly shaven cheek.

Caught off guard, Charles stiffened and gently directed her hand back down.

"Morning to you too, Edna," he muttered. "We cleaned up as best we could. Shaved, like you told us. I see you brought an outfit for me." His eyes widened at the bundle in her arms.

"The face will do," Edna replied, her lips curving into a smirk. "The suit is one of my father's best. Should make you handsome enough." Her eyes flickered over him, assessing.

"Good luck tryin' to polish this one, lass," Billy laughed, gesturing toward Charles.

They all turned as the sharp clack of Frankie's polished shoes echoed across the timber platform, followed by a thud as he dropped a briefcase beside him.

"Filled with bricks, is it, Doyle?" Billy asked.

"It has books in it, for the train," Frankie snapped back.

That line hit both Billy and Charles like a jab. Frankie had always been the reader. His father had encouraged it from a young age, and while Billy and Charles could manage the basics, it was Frankie who usually read the war news aloud to them.

The four were now assembled as planned when the first train of the day rolled into the station, the steam engine shrieking as smoke billowed from its chimney. The working-class carriage stopped directly in front of them, a converted goods wagon, its weathered exterior scarred by years of use. Crude holes cut into the sides served as windows, with small sliding panes for ventilation.

They climbed aboard, stepping onto the mud-stained floor, immediately hit by the sharp mix of sweat and tobacco. The wooden benches were hard and worn, and though most were empty, the stale smell of years past clung stubbornly to the air. They spread out across a couple of seats.

The engine rumbled, steam funnelling through the gaps around the windows. A bell rang. The carriage jolted forward. The journey had begun.

Ding.

Charles's eyes snapped open. The toll of a church bell drifted through the carriage. St James Cathedral. That meant they were pulling into Flinders Street Railway Station.

After such a restless night, he must have drifted off somewhere along the way. It amazed him he'd managed any sleep at all on those back-breaking benches; though the warmth of Edna's shoulder had likely helped.

Realising where he'd been resting, Charles straightened abruptly, rubbing his eyes and turning away in embarrassment.

Opposite him, Billy had his arm stretched out the window, waving at passers-by, while Frankie calmly packed his book and glasses back into his briefcase.

Looking outside, Charles was in awe. So much of his life had been spent staring out at paddocks, but now the view was filled with buildings; not timber, but solid brick and mortar. The faint smell of seawater drifted through the air, unlike anything back home.

Edna crept close to his ear. "Not in the bush now, are you, stockman? Or should I say... soldier," she teased softly.

Surprisingly, her words brought him comfort. In that moment, the anxieties of the night before melted away. He felt at peace with his decision again.

By now, the train was packed shoulder to shoulder. The whistle shrieked, the doors flew open, and the four were caught in the surge of bodies. They were shoved and jostled, feeling coarse wool coats brush against their arms and the jab of a tin lunchbox against Charles's ribs as the crowd spilled out onto the platform.

Flinders Street was alive with noise. Hawkers shouted their wares, a gramophone cracked from a shopfront, and the four pushed through the tide of people, down the veranda steps and onto the bitumen street.

Charles looked around. Through the sea of workers, soldiers, and porters, he took in the wide street lined with timber and brick buildings. Towering in the distance, Castle Hill dominated the skyline, impossible to miss. Above the train station, freshly painted signs screamed for attention: *"Join Now"*, *"Do Your Bit"*, *"Enlist Today – Tomorrow May Be Too Late"*. The words might as well have been aimed straight at him.

"That's the ticket, Charlie boy," Billy jabbed with a grin. "Best keep them lanky boots close. City'll chew ya up quicker than a bush steer."

As they weaved their way through the crowd, the city's soundscape surrounded him; horse-drawn carts clattering on the street, children darting between veranda posts, the sharp clang of a blacksmith's hammer ringing from a nearby forge. Charles winced, covering his ears for a moment. As excited as he was, the noise was overwhelming. For a boy used to quiet paddocks, this was another world entirely.

A crisp ding-ding split the air. Iron wheels screeched along a track as a tram cut straight through the crowd, forcing people to scatter. A boy stumbled, narrowly missing the tram's path. As it passed, its electric hum faded, revealing a sign ahead as if it had been waiting just for him:

AIF Recruitment Centre.

The words stood bold in green paint against a white background.

He was here. At the doorstep of the adventure, he'd been dreaming of.

"Better clean you up then, Charles," Frankie said with mock seriousness.

"We can try," Edna chuckled, patting the folded blazer in her hand. "I think the suit will do most of the heavy lifting."

Next to the centre stood a handsome two-storey brick hotel with Great Northern Hotel painted in neat letters across its corrugated tin roof.

"Go on, Charles," Billy teased, clapping him on the shoulder. "Trot in and get yerself dolled up, don't want Edna thinkin' she wasted a dress."

At six-foot-seven, Billy stood tall above the bustling crowd, utterly unconcerned about looking older. Charles, on the other hand, felt the weight of what lay ahead pressing down on him.

While the others waited outside, Charles entered the hotel with his head down, hurrying straight to the restroom. He turned the creaking tap and splashed cold water over his face, then ran his hands through his hair to rinse out the dust.

Wrestling with the wool serge suit, he finally managed to get it to sit straight on his slender frame. When he glanced up at the mirror, a stranger stared back. His baby face was still glaringly obvious, but the itchy, hot, and restrictive dark navy suit did give him a hint of maturity. There were flaws, of course, a missing waistcoat, a stained white worker's shirt underneath; but it might just work.

Stepping back outside, he was met with Billy's reaction.

"What's this then, aye?" Billy roared with laughter. "A half-polished turd! And what's with them mud-caked boots?"

"Billy's right, mate," Frankie chimed in. "The top's passable, but the shoes are cactus. Here, take mine. They'll be loose, but at least you'll look the complete package."

Even if the rest of the outfit didn't convince, the shine from Frankie's shoes might just blind the recruiter anyway.

"Well... almost complete," Edna added.

She stepped forward, closed the gap between them, and began fussing with his blazer. Her fingers moved deftly as she buttoned it up, then did the top button of his shirt. From her pocket, she produced a matching tie and looped it around his neck. With careful precision, she tied a Windsor knot, one of the few Charles had never mastered; and pulled it snug.

"Now you're polished for the ball," she declared, stepping back to admire her work.

Charles straightened his shoulders. Edna's approval steadied him in a way Billy's teasing never could. He was ready. It was agreed; Charles would go in first, with Billy right behind. Frankie and Edna would wait outside the hotel until the pair returned.

He crossed the street to the recruitment centre. Inside, the air was thick with the smells of sweat, ink, and tobacco. The rhythmic banging of stamps and the clatter of typewriters filled the room. Men laughed and talked loudly, their energy feeding off the charged atmosphere.

Charles joined the line. There were only a few men ahead of him, but the closer he got, the heavier the air seemed. His collar felt tighter with each breath. Was it the heat trapped inside the suit, or the surge of nerves? His heart thumped against his ribs.

"Next!" boomed an officer at the front.

Charles froze. The man's eyes raked over him, head to toe. Sweat beaded and slid down Charles's cheek as his throat clenched shut.

A hard shove from Billy behind sent him stumbling forward.

"Name?" the officer barked.

"Char... Charles... Young... Charles Young Watson," he stuttered.

The officer snorted. "Young's right. You look like you've just come out of the womb."

Charles felt as though he had shrunk. The suit now seemed to float on him, as if the officer's judgemental stare had sucked a few years off his frame.

"When's your birthday?" the officer asked.

"Twenty-ninth of January," Charles muttered.

"What year?" the officer pressed.

Charles's lips trembled. His train of thought had completely derailed.

"What's the holdup, Charlie boy? War ain't waitin' on ya!" Billy's voice boomed from behind.

The officer lifted his head, gaze locking on the towering figure behind Charles.

"And what's your name?" he asked.

"Billy Carter, sir," Billy replied, flashing his trademark grin.

The officer gave a faint nod of approval. "This lad with you?"

"Known him since we were nippers," Billy said easily. "Always the runt, scrawny as a roo tail, and too bloody stubborn to quit."

Charles stood frozen, caught between elation and dread. The room felt distant, muffled. His mouth moved before his mind caught up, reciting the oath, the pen scratching his name across the page as though guided by someone else's hand.

Then THUD; the approval stamp came down.

He blinked. It was done. Just like that, he was in. The escape he'd longed for... and the plunge he'd feared.

Outside, Frankie sat perched on the edge of the hotel veranda, nose buried in *Treasure Island*, off on his own adventure while the city swirled around him. His legs swung idly as people squeezed past.

Further back, Edna leaned against the brick facade, arms folded, watching the flow of Flinders Street. She was growing impatient; while the recruitment stop had been the point of the trip, the city was calling her name.

Then the veranda thundered under Billy's boots. He burst out of the recruitment centre loud and proud, snatching Frankie's book and swinging it above his head as he strutted past.

"Oi, have a gander!" he crowed. "Stockmen yesterday, soldiers today! And better lookin' for it!"

Charles followed, a wide grin stretching across his face, though more reserved than Billy's roar of triumph.

"The great escape is on," he said.

Frankie leapt up, ecstatic for his mates. He wrapped his arms around them, pride clear on his face. He already knew the consequences back in Woodstock, his father would be pleased.

Edna approached more elegantly, smoothing her dress as she stepped forward. She reached up and straightened Charles's collar, smiling softly.

"I suppose you can thank me for the suit," she said, brushing a bit of dust from his lapel.

Billy let out a bark of laughter.

"Ahh, that suit didn't save him one bit, near carked it on the spot, he did. Lucky, I butted in, or we'd still be waitin'!" Billy crowed, barely containing his laughter.

"It's true," Charles admitted. "Billy did save my skin in there." He turned to Edna, "But thank you, your encouragement helped too."

He caught himself smiling at her. It felt strange. A day ago, she only managed to irritate him.

"Guess I've got a soft spot for stubborn boys," Edna teased, her tone softening. "How about we celebrate your birthday, Charles? If you're brave enough, we could test your new elevated status by going up Castle Hill. See the big smoke from the top."

Castle Hill had loomed in the background since they'd stepped off the train, as if it had been waiting for them. The boys all agreed without hesitation.

They left Flinders Street behind, boots crunching on the red-dusty surface of Denham Street. The crowd thinned as they moved further from the station, but their spirits stayed high. Now their obstacles weren't bustling people but ruts, puddles, and the occasional horse dropping.

Ding.

The bell of St James Cathedral rang out, louder this time, echoing down the street. The church soon came into view on Melton Hill; its tall, sharp roofline cutting into the sky, its red-brick walls resembling a prison. Stained-glass windows stared down like watchful eyes.

As Frankie and Billy argued about brains versus brawn ahead, Charles drifted behind, his gaze fixed on the cathedral.

A shiver of unease slipped through him. It felt as though the building itself was taunting him with every step.

Edna noticed. She reached out, placing a hand gently on his shoulder. The touch lingered; steady, grounding. Their eyes met for a moment. Charles managed a small smile, though the shadows behind his eyes betrayed that the church still held its grip on him.

He pressed on, silently grateful for her quiet support.

Soon, the group stood at the base of Castle Hill. The red stone glowed warm in the late sun, streaked with shadows, broken by the rough lines of the steep, rugged goat track ahead. The climb awaited.

"Well, come on, soldiers. You can't let me beat you to the top," Edna teased, breaking into a run.

The boys laughed and followed. They caught up quickly, but the goat track soon revealed its true horns; steep, uneven stone and narrow switchbacks forcing them to grab at roots and rocks for balance.

"Not even a hill, boys!" Billy boasted as they neared the halfway point, chest heaving.

"I didn't come to Townsville for goat tracks," Edna shot back, breathless. She wasn't used to walking, let alone climbing in the heat, and struggled to hold up the hem of her dress as she climbed.

Frankie moved with slow, steady determination, his face twisted between a grin and a grimace. Charles grew quieter the higher they climbed, his thoughts tightening like a knot in his chest.

By the final stretch, even Billy had gone silent, their heavy wool clothing and boots dragging at them. The sun beat down, sweat prickled under their collars, and every breath came heavier than the last.

After thirty long minutes, they reached the peak. The boys stood with hands on their hips, gulping air as if it were gold.

"Thought you soldiers were meant to be fit," Edna wheezed, still refusing to let the opportunity pass.

"They haven't got a soldier's body yet," Frankie managed between breaths.

Below them, Townsville sprawled out in the afternoon sun; a patchwork of timber and brick buildings, the rail yards and port reaching toward the shimmering Coral Sea. Magnetic Island floated on the horizon like a painted backdrop. It was the first time any of them had seen the world laid out before them like this: wide, open, and full of promise.

For Charles, though, one blemish marred the view, St James Cathedral, stern and unyielding on Melton Hill.

"Oi, if I don't come back, tell the sergeant I died a hero!" Billy called, already running off to explore the hill.

Frankie crouched near a ridge, pulling out his small sketchbook and pencil. "Reckon that spots got the best angle," he said. "Perfect for a quick sketch."

That left Charles and Edna alone on the peak. He dropped onto a patch of dry grass, and she lowered herself beside him without asking. It was the first time they'd ever sat together like this, though he barely noticed; his gaze was fixed on the distance, weighed down by something heavier than the view.

"What's with that building then?" Edna asked quietly.

Charles blinked, startled. "What building?"

"The cathedral. It seemed to knock the wind right out of you," she said.

He turned to her. The wind tugged at her wavy brown hair, and her clear blue eyes held a steady, comforting gaze. He inhaled slowly, gathering the courage to let his walls down.

"That church is where my parents were married," he said.

"Oh. Why does that bother you? Your parents' marriage seems happy," Edna asked softly.

"No... I mean my real parents."

Edna fell silent. Few people in Woodstock ever spoke of Charles's past. Her family had only moved from Rockhampton after his fostering, when her father purchased their cattle station. She'd never known his history; or cared to ask, until now.

"My father, Charles Senior, and my mother, Mary, were married there in April. The year before I was born," he continued, voice low.

Outside of Billy and his foster parents, no one else knew these details. Edna could see how hard this was for him. She reached for his hand and gently rested it on her lap. The gesture disarmed him completely, the distance between them vanished.

"Can I ask what happened to them?" she whispered.

"My father died a couple of months before I was born," Charles said. "He was a Scottish sailor. Or at least, that was his job title. Truth is... he was an alcoholic. Drank himself to death."

"I'm so sorry, Charles. It sounds like a love story turned tragedy. Your poor mother," Edna said softly.

"My poor mother," Charles repeated, then paused. "I haven't seen her since I was four. I can barely remember her touch... and her face is fading."

"Did she pass too?" Edna asked gently.

Charles gave a short, hollow laugh, the kind people use to keep from breaking. His eyes reddened, moisture gathering despite his best efforts to fight it.

"There's another side to that church most don't know about," he said.

Edna leaned forward, sensing the weight of what was coming.

"There's an orphanage attached to it," Charles continued. "My mother abandoned me there to run off with a man to South Africa." A tear slipped down his cheek. "I spent most of my childhood trapped in those walls before finally being fostered to the farm."

He clenched his jaw, holding the rest in. A lifetime of suppressing emotion had made him good at it, but that single tear embarrassed him.

Edna pulled a handkerchief from her pocket and gently wiped it away. Her hand lingered against his cheek for a moment, warm and steady.

"That church has been haunting me," Charles said, his voice lower now, surer. "It's like it's stirring up the reasons behind every choice I've made. Am I escaping the farm? Am I really a stockman's son... or just another farmhand?"

His breath trembled. "Would my father even care that I'm leaving? Or will he just hire, or foster, another one?"

The confusion spilled out in waves. Edna tightened her grip on his hand, listening without interruption.

"Maybe I'm not running at all," Charles said. "Maybe I'm searching. Searching for adventure to feel closer to my real father, the sailor who saw the world. Or maybe I'm trying to prove my worth to the mother who left me behind. I don't know. I just..." His voice caught. "Sometimes I feel invisible."

He fell silent. The weight of his words seemed to lift slightly now that they were no longer trapped inside him. The wind whispered through the grass. A soft stillness settled over the hilltop; not awkward, but peaceful.

Then Edna spoke, her voice quiet but steady. "I know what that feels like. I, too, sometimes feel invisible." She hesitated. "I'm the youngest of nine on the busiest ranch in the district. I'm just another number, not a daughter. My parents are alive, but I could disappear, and they wouldn't even notice."

Charles turned to her, fully focused now. He'd always assumed her wealth meant happiness. He'd never thought about the weight of being unseen in a crowded house.

"I would notice," he said with a small smile, giving her hand a gentle squeeze.

The sun dipped lower, the sky awash with orange and gold. For a moment, neither of them spoke.

"Oi! You lot miss me?" Billy's voice boomed across the hill. "Reckon I found every bloody ant on this hill, tougher than the goats!" He came bounding over, grinning from ear to ear.

In the distance, Frankie carefully brushed the dust from his sketchpad and tucked it under his arm. The warm dusk wrapped around them like a soft blanket, a quiet reminder that the day was ending, and soon they'd have to return to the world below.

The last train to Woodstock wouldn't wait.

Chapter 3

Marching Orders

It had been a few days since their cheeky run into the big smoke, and Charles had spent them working the farm as if nothing had happened. To his parents, the only odd thing was Billy's visits now included Edna. They knew who she was, of course, but couldn't quite fathom why the well-groomed station girl kept making eyes at two filthy farm boys sweating through the blistering summer heat.

"No wonder you two spend all day doin' chores. No haste about ya," Edna observed as the boys wrestled with a fence between their properties.

"No haste?" Billy grinned. "We're just givin' the termites time to pack their bags proper. Don't want squatters in me hard work."

"At this rate, you'll still be fixing fences when the train leaves for Enoggera," Edna teased.

"You might be right. Too bloody hot anyway," Charles smirked, wiping sweat from his brow. "Maybe I should just sit back and let you boss me 'round the last couple of days."

"Speakin' of bosses," Billy cut in, "you told your old man you're shippin' off yet? Or waitin' for him to read it in the paper?"

He had a point. Charles had been dreading the conversation since the day he enlisted. The last talk about the war had gone south fast. His father would be furious. His mother, heartbroken.

"I'll tell 'em at supper," Charles said finally. "It's mutton stew. Father's favourite. Might lighten the mood."

They battled the fence another hour, the summer soil like stone under their shovels. When the work finally beat them, blisters burning and shirts glued to their backs with sweat, Edna still sat spotless on a downed log, cool beneath the wide brim of her straw hat. The horses grew restless; hooves stamped; tails whipped. It was time to call it a day. Charles knew supper awaited. And with it, the reckoning.

"Supper, Charles!" His mother's voice carried through the homestead.

He'd been rehearsing the lines alone in his room, searching for the perfect way to soften the blow. As he shuffled into the dining room, the heavy, gamey scent of mutton stew wrapped around him. His father sat opposite, his broad frame filling the chair, while his mother bustled with the ladle, dishing generous helpings. Each clang of metal against iron rang in Charles's head like a drumbeat before battle.

"And who's this pretty young lady keepin' you boys from their work?" his mother asked brightly. "That'd be Edna, wouldn't it?"

Charles flushed. Not this conversation.

"Edna? She just likes bossin' us around. Reckon she thinks she runs both farms," he said with a strained grin.

"I think she's more interested in the company than the fences," his mother teased, clearly pleased with herself.

His father barely looked up, already shovelling stew into his mouth. Charles's heartbeat thudded in his ears. He hadn't rehearsed for small talk.

Then, before his nerves could talk him out of it, the words burst out.

"Pa, I ain't askin'. I've joined up. The train to Enoggera leaves soon, and I'll be on it."

For a moment, all he heard was the wet sound of his father chewing. Then,

SMACK.

The spoon slammed onto the table like a gunshot. His mother shrieked at the suddenness.

"Don't you go makin' fool decisions without this family, boy!" his father barked. "You think runnin' off to war makes you a man? All you'll do is break your mother's heart and leave this farm to rot!"

The room tightened around them. The stew sat untouched in front of Charles, congealing. His father's nostrils flared, eyes burning across the table.

"It's not about makin' fool decisions, Father," Charles snapped, his voice shaking. "It's about doin' my part. You reckon this farm's all I'm good for? I'm not just your workhorse."

His father leaned forward, voice low and dangerous. "Workhorse? You ungrateful whelp. This farm fed you, clothed you, made you the man you are. You think playin' soldier makes you better than your own blood?"

"None of my blood, anyhow."

The words cut the air like a blade. Charles hadn't even meant to say them.

His mother froze. The chair screeched back as she stumbled up, tears welling fast. The chair hit the wall with a crack as she fled the room, sobbing.

His father stared after her, then turned back, voice cold and steady now. "You'll leave your mother in tears and me to break my back alone, all for some fool's glory."

He stood, pushed his chair back with a scrape, and left to follow her.

Charles sat alone at the table, surrounded by the wreckage of the moment; congealed stew, overturned chair, his father's words still hanging in the air like smoke after a shot. His stomach twisted, appetite gone. He dragged himself to his room, the sound of his mother's sobs spilling down the hallway.

The war had already reached their home.

Over the next few days, Charles dodged his father's hard stare across the yard, mended fences in silence, and offered quiet acts of kindness to ease his mother's weeping heart. When he could, he escaped to Edna and Billy. Frankie appeared more often too, his usual sharp wit dampened; the looming departure beginning to settle over them all like a slow, heavy fog.

Before long, the time had come. All four of them stood on the same platform where the plan had first been hatched.

"Wonder if I'll get meself a medal or two before the year's out," Billy beamed, nudging Charles in the shoulder. "Might have the King shakin' me hand while you're still polishin' your boots, Charles!"

Charles rolled his eyes, standing stiff in his khaki kit. The fabric scratched at his neck, the jacket hung loose, and the slouch hat seemed determined to sit crooked. Still, it was nothing compared to Billy's uniform, which ended awkwardly above his ankles and looked ready to split at the seams.

"You'd embarrass the King wearin' that," Frankie teased.

"That kit's the fanciest thing these boys ever owned," Edna smirked. "Better not wrinkle it, Charles."

"Don't worry," Charles shot back, "I'll bring it back wrinkled and covered in medals."

They all tried to keep the mood light, but the truth pressed in around them. This was goodbye.

The train hissed at the station; cattle bellowed as stockmen loaded them up the timber ramp. The delay before departure was a small mercy. Charles's mother busied herself rummaging through the canvas duffle bag she'd packed for him, hands working to outrun her heart.

"Charles, are you sure you packed enough underwear?" she fretted.

"Don't worry, Mother. The Army'll see me right," Charles muttered, scratching the back of his neck.

"I'm your mother. I'm allowed to worry. Your father worries too, Charles... he just don't know how to show it."

His father wasn't there. He was out tracking two missing cattle from that morning's muster. Rare enough to feel deliberate. The hurt sat heavy.

His mother let the bag drop with a dull thud, sending a puff of dust across the boards.

Charles's gaze drifted to Frankie, who stood with quiet steadiness; the group's voice of reason. Saying goodbye to him would sting. Edna was harder still. She'd arrived in his life unexpectedly, but exactly when she needed to.

A sharp whistle sliced through the humid air. Steam rolled across the platform, swallowing the world in a veil of white. Charles blinked through it, heart pounding.

Edna's hand brushed his sleeve, grounding him without a word. Then she stepped closer and wrapped her arms around him. Her lips brushed his cheek as she whispered, "I'll write to you. You'd better read every word."

She lingered, unwilling to let go. "And try not to scuff those boots too much, soldier. I'll be watching for the shine when you march me through town after."

"Don't go makin' a scene with long goodbyes. Boots up, lad, we've got a war to win!" Billy barked, smacking Charles between the shoulder blades.

Frankie gave them both a nod, the corners of his mouth tight.

"Cheerio, Frankie, next time we see ya, you'll be wearin' a stethoscope and tellin' us to cough," Billy added.

They climbed aboard, squeezing past the cattle as their boots clanged on the iron floor. His mother clung to the strap of the duffle bag until it slipped from her fingers and disappeared between the shifting bodies of beef. The doors clanged shut behind them, sealing Charles into the unknown.

After a long, hard slog battling the smell of dung, sweat and tobacco, they arrived at Enoggera Army Barracks on the outskirts of Brisbane. The bus jolted to a stop on the parade ground, a wide, sun-scorched square beaten flat by thousands of boots before them.

"Fall in, you scoundrels!" a voice boomed, cracking through the humid air like a whip.

The boys stumbled into two crooked lines. Standing before them was a lean lieutenant with sun-leathered skin, a stiff posture, and a perfectly waxed moustache. His name patch, frayed with age, read McCorley. A walking stick smacked the dirt as he strode down the line, his limp faint but his glare sharp.

"Name?" he barked at the first boy, a pale, pimpled recruit.

The boy gulped. "Chook."

"Chook? What kind of farm animals have they sent me? It's Sir to you, maggot!" McCorley bellowed, flecks of spit dotting the boy's cheeks.

"What's your name, soldier?"

"Henderson, sir!"

Charles and Billy stood shoulder to shoulder, their new uniforms already clinging to their backs with sweat. They exchanged a glance; half grin, half disbelief. *Get a load of this bloke.*

The lieutenant continued down the line, barking, swearing, and straightening the men with his stick. Whatever grand adventure Charles had imagined, this wasn't it.

After the interrogation, they were dismissed to collect their stretchers.

On the right of the square stretched neat rows of khaki bell tents, their guide ropes cutting sharp shadows in the dirt. On the left, a long timber shed spilled the rich scent of boiled mutton and tea into the air. The sound of clanging tins and laughter rolled out the doorway. A hand-painted red and white sign stuck in the earth read simply: Mess Hall.

"Smell that, Charlie boy?" Billy drawled, licking his lips. "Beats eatin' dust and Mum's stew. Reckon I've signed up for the Ritz!"

"That'll turn your broad shoulders into a round belly in no time," Charles smirked.

They continued towards the edge of the camp, to a row of weatherboard huts capped with corrugated iron roofs. Inside, stretchers were lined along each wall, half the timber floor caked in dirt, the air thick with the must of too many boots. Compared to the crisp khaki tents they'd passed earlier, the huts looked more like a bush pub after closing time.

"That's the go, Charlie boy," Billy said, tossing his duffle bag onto the first stretcher. "Dibs the closest bunk, don't want to be trippin' over you mob on my way out."

Charles claimed the one next to him. Within a minute, the scrawny, nervous recruit known only as Chook poked his head around the doorway.

"Can I... can I bunk in here? I'll take any bed. Don't mind where," he stammered.

Charles glanced up. Shirt half untucked, belt clip skewed; the kid looked like a lost goose. He'd need a bit of guidance before the officers chewed him up.

"Come on in," Charles said with a grin. "I'm Charles. That's Billy. Don't listen to him, he'll roast you, but his insults are ice cold."

Chook managed a sheepish smile and took the bed next in line. He opened his duffle and promptly spilled its contents across the stretcher.

"Making yourself at home already, Henderson?" Charles chuckled.

"Call me Chook," he replied. "Mum packed this, so I got no idea what's in it."

"Reckon she tucked a rattle in too?" Billy snorted, leaning over to rummage through the pile.

"What's your story, Chook? And why the name?"

"Chicken farm. Kedron," he said proudly. "Never missed a dawn feed. Been watchin' the soldiers train here since the war broke out. Joined the day I turned eighteen."

He puffed his chest like a bantam rooster, though he barely looked the part.

The door slammed open, the hinges groaning. A stocky man, broad as a gate, broader than anyone but Billy; filled the doorway.

"Afternoon, soldiers. Jack O'Donnell. Mates call me Snow," he announced.

The boys almost stood to attention before realising he was just another private.

"How we all likin' the festivities? Chook, you clean that face up yet?" Snow barked, half-laughing.

"I, uh... not yet. Lieutenants got it in for me already," Chook admitted. Everyone at Enoggera knew his name by now.

"Reckon McCorley's moustache has more authority than the man himself," Billy quipped. "Wouldn't wanna cross them whiskers."

"Word is he's the only officer here with real war under his belt. Boer War," Snow replied casually.

"Explains the limp," Charles muttered. "Waiting to use that stick for more than pointing."

"Correct," Snow nodded. "Shrapnel wound, they say. They call him Iron Jack."

Snow claimed his bunk with the precision of someone used to structure, folding his kit with sharp corners.

"Two Jacks in one pack?" Billy said. "We'll stick with Snow, wouldn't want Iron Jack dealin'."

"Better a Jack than bein' dealt a joker like you," Snow shot back.

"Already figured you out, Billy," Charles laughed.

They settled into their new quarters, stowing kit in wooden cases at the foot of their stretchers. Billy's method involved more scrunching than folding. Between jokes and stories, they learned Snow was twenty-one, a wharfie from Sydney Harbour. He had a fiancée waiting at home; a reminder that they all came here with different reasons to fight.

That evening, Iron Jack barked orders for their first night march. Chook groaned at the thought. The recruits filed out into the dark, the creaky hut door banging behind them.

Weeks passed in a blur of dust, heat, and shouted orders. Iron Jack's stick seemed to be everywhere; whistling through the air, smacking boots, tapping helmets. Charles gritted his teeth through the tirades; years on the farm had prepared him for men who barked orders. Billy and Chook were less fortunate; they drew his wrath like lightning rods.

The recruits were pushed hard: endless drill, obstacle courses, rifle practice, bush survival. The sharp crack of Lee–Enfield rifles filled the air, the smell of cordite hanging thick over the range. Their shoulders bruised, their legs ached, their nerves toughened. Charles even caught himself noticing muscle where there hadn't been any before; sometimes wondering if Edna would notice too.

The pack marches were gruelling for the city boys, who stumbled over rocks and cursed the Queensland heat.

"Townies trippin' on pebbles," Billy laughed, nudging Charles.

For Charles and Billy, it felt like walking home from school; hot, dusty, and familiar. Charles often found peace at the head of the line, the rhythm of his boots pulling him back to memories of Castle Hill and Edna's soft hand on his sleeve.

The best part of the day, though, was always the mess hall.

"March all day, feast all night; tell me again, Charlie boy, how this ain't a vacation?" Billy crowed, dropping his tin plate down with a clatter, peas and gravy spilling over the edge.

By late May 1917, the entire 1st Division crowded into the mess hall for lunch; a rare sight. The air was thick with sweat, smoke, and roasted beef. Even the officers were eating with the men, a sure sign something big was coming.

"Pass the spuds, quick, before Snowman weighs 'em like cargo," Billy said, jabbing Charles with his fork.

"Never seen the whole lot here at once," Charles muttered through a cough. "Feels like the walls are closin' in."

"Must be somethin' brewin'," Snow said, scanning the room.

"Attention!" Iron Jack's voice boomed through the hall. Every fork hit the table.

Heavy boots struck the timber floor as a grey-haired officer with a thick moustache and immaculate uniform marched in. Brass stars caught the sunlight, blinding half the room.

Major General Walker.

"At ease, men," he commanded, his voice carrying like a church bell. "Your training at Enoggera nears its end. In three weeks' time, you will embark for England. Unit assignments are posted outside this hall. Study them well. Prepare yourselves, you will soon serve King and Country. Dismissed."

For a moment, there was silence. Then the hall exploded. Cheers roared. Hats flew. Tin cups clanged. A sea of khaki surged toward the door.

Charles elbowed his way through the crowd, ducking and weaving between taller shoulders until he reached the wall of typed lists. His heart hammered in his ears.

PTE Watson, C.Y. – 12th Machine Gun Company.

A grin tugged at his lips. Machine gunner. Better than being a runner. He scanned down the list. Carter. Henderson. O'Donnell. All together.

Reunited outside, the four of them strolled down the dusty lane back to their hut, spirits blazing.

"England, boys!" Billy whooped, leaping into the air and kicking up a cloud of red dirt. "Dust and dung for castles and cobblestones!"

"Machine gunners? I can barely shoot a rifle," Chook groaned.

"Probably why they're giving you more bullets," Charles said with a grin.

"You'll shoot yourself before the Hun!" Billy piled on.

Their laughter carried across the camp.

"Save some of that cheer," Snow said quietly. "You'll need it when the guns start."

"Don't be a downer, Snowman," Billy shot back. "The real adventure starts now."

Three weeks later, they were packed like sardines on a long-haul train bound for the docks of Melbourne; and the war beyond.

Chapter 4

Suevic to Suez

The 1st Division had arrived in the city, early morning on the 21st of June 1917. They disembarked at Spencer Street Station and were ordered to march straight to the docks at Port Melbourne. Blue cobblestone roads crunched beneath their boots, a far cry from the red dust of Enoggera. The streets were lined with elegant stone and brick buildings, their ornate facades towering above like sentinels.

"Boots sound strange on these stones... back home it's all dust an' gum roots," Charles observed.

They marched in perfect time, their heels striking the cobbles as Iron Jack would have demanded; though, to Chook's relief, the officer had remained behind at the barracks to torment a new batch of recruits. Trams clanged past, and office workers streamed onto the footpaths to watch the soldier's pass.

"Get a load of this, Charlie boy. We're famous now. Never goin' back to the farm," Billy grinned.

He gawped at the tall buildings, cracking jokes about the city girls and waving like he was in a parade. For Charles, the atmosphere was overwhelming: the cheers, the boots, the city noise pressing in from all sides. Chook tugged nervously at the cord of his duffle, forever adjusting it. He stood out in the march; the only man out of time.

"Why are they all so interested?" he muttered.

Snow, on the other hand, was in his element. He pointed out buildings like a tour guide, tossing out trivia no one had asked for.

"That's the old Customs House, every crate comin' in or out of Melbourne's passed under that roof since the gold rush," he said, nodding proudly. Years working Sydney's wharves had taught him a thing or two about Melbourne.

As they neared the port, the salt tang of the bay and the sharp bite of coal smoke filled the air. Then they saw her.

The HMAT Suevic loomed above the docks, its steel hull towering over every other ship. To the farm boys, it looked more like a floating city than a vessel.

"Fair dinkum, reckon that thing could swallow Woodstock whole!" Billy hollered.

The once-white hull was painted wartime grey. Four tall wooden masts bristled with rigging, red ensigns with the Union Jack snapping in the wind. At the centre, a black funnel belched thick smoke into the crisp Melbourne sky.

"The adventure starts now, boys," Charles said, unable to hide his excitement.

They tramped up the long wooden gangway, the boards flexing under the weight of boots and kit, eager to claim a spot for the long voyage ahead. Inside the converted passenger liner, the glamour was long gone. Khaki-clad men filled every corridor, and the air grew thick with engine oil and damp wool. Rows of hammocks sagged from steel beams, condensation dripped from the bulkheads, and the heat intensified with every step deeper into the hull.

They passed the mess hall; a cavern of bolted tables and the smell of boiled mutton and cabbage. Finally, at the end of a narrow corridor deep in the ship's belly, they found four hammocks together.

"Home sweet home, boys," Snow sighed, sweat staining his armpits.

The heat grew worse as a deep rumble shook the walls. The engines were firing. A moment later, the ship's horn bellowed across the bay, rattling their chests. The Suevic lurched forward. They were on their way.

The first days were filled with laughter, jokes, and war songs. But the excitement faded fast. The endless ocean, the heat, and the constant sway of the hull turned enthusiasm to exhaustion. The crowded decks meant most of their time was spent below, fighting for fresh air. Whenever they did reach the surface, it was for drills or route marches around the deck.

The confinement gnawed at Charles. Sweat poured from him as the boiler room baked the walls. The Suevic's steel ribs pressed in on him like the red-brick walls of St James's had once done. The swaying hammocks were no different from the iron cots of the orphanage: boys packed in, restless, unseen, forgotten. The ship wasn't just carrying him forward, it was dragging him back.

"Get a load of him, roasted Chook for lunch. Reckon we're in for a feast!" Billy heckled one sweltering afternoon as they queued for food.

"Another day of this and I'll be overboard. Just to cool off," Chook muttered, fanning himself with a copy of the week's mess menu.

The mess hall was the day's main event. Utensils clattered and voices rose, almost drowning out the boiler's steady thrum. Outside of meals, most of their time was spent battling boredom and seasickness. Charles was hit hardest; the endless swaying had stolen his appetite.

"Just bring me a couple of biscuits, Billy. Stomach's not up for more than that. I'll join Snow next to a bucket," he muttered, one hand clutching his gut.

"Biscuits'll break your teeth before they fill your belly; but sure, Charlie boy," Billy smirked, waving his tray.

Snow could usually be found in the mess, either playing cards or writing letters to his fiancée. Billy loved to tease him about his "carrier pigeons."

Charles slumped down at the table mid-hand. The cold metal top against his forehead gave him a moment of relief from the queasiness. The stench of grease and tobacco quickly took it back.

"Welcome to the game, Charles. Have a sip of water, clear your head," Snow said, plonking a canteen in front of him.

Charles took a small sip. But it wasn't just his stomach turning. The iron walls pressed memories out of him; the orphanage, the church, everything he'd buried. He kept thinking if Charles Snr was alive, what he would make of it, the son of a sailor, and yet the sea felt like a stranger.

Around him, the card game carried on. Blackjack, if he could focus long enough to tell. Snow seemed to win more than his fair share.

"Fill ya pie hole with this, Charlie boy!" Billy cackled, lobbing a hard tack biscuit at him. It bounced off his head with a crack.

"Ouch. Feels like these things are baked harder than stone," Charles winced, rubbing the spot. He nibbled the biscuit, anyway, chasing it down with another small sip of water.

Snow leaned closer, voice low. "What's going on, mate? Haven't been yourself since we left the dock."

"It's just... this ship. Takes me back to places I'd rather forget," Charles admitted. He'd never told them about the orphanage, or his parents. What he carried wasn't just seasickness; it was the weight of who he was, and who he wasn't.

Snow nodded with a soft smile. "Hold fast. We'll be off soon. Open sky will do us all good."

"Thank God for that!" Chook chirped as he slid in beside them with a tray of pumpkin soup, bread, and tea.

"Pumpkin soup today! Least it's not mutton again."

"Best eat it while it's hot, Chook. You'll miss even this soon enough," Snow remarked.

The clink of Chook's spoon against the cup tugged Charles's thoughts back to Woodstock, the farm, his mother, Edna. He missed her teasing warmth, the way she could cut through the noise in his head.

"Long as they keep the tucker comin', they can ship me to the moon for all I care," Billy quipped, scraping the last of his bowl.

"Well, maybe not the moon," Snow said, smirking. "But I've heard the Suevic's stopping in Cairo on the way through the Suez Canal."

Charles's head lifted. "Fresh air at last, even if it's hotter and sandier than the Enoggera square."

"Sand or no sand, beats sweating in a tin can," Billy said.

A few more sweltering weeks passed in the ship's bowels. Then one morning, the Suevic's horn bellowed again: this time for land. Egypt.

Chapter 5

Night with the Pharaohs

Charles squinted against the haze as Cairo's dry air filled his lungs; sharp with dust but fresh compared to the ship. The 1st Division tramped to the army camp at Heliopolis, just beyond the city, every step on solid sand a relief after months of swaying decks. Then came the news they hadn't dared hope for: the officer barked that they'd be released in groups for a few hours' leave. Billy practically bounced on the spot, already tasting the adventure.

"Fair dinkum! This is what we signed up for! Coupl'a hours' leave; may need to stretch that one, aye," Billy grinned, slinging an arm around Charles and Snow.

"We should keep an eye on the clock, wouldn't want to be crucified," Chook said.

They headed back to the centre of the city, Charles still squinting against the haze but thankful to have traded the ship's stale confines. Cairo was alive with the aroma of spiced meat sizzling over charcoal and rich coffee drifting from the cafes.

"Well Snow, what's there to do other than dodge donkeys in this place?" Charles asked. He was far from the big smoke and knew little of the world.

"Can't come to Egypt and not go to the pyramids. Plenty of sailors showing off their Giza photos when they docked in

Sydney. I reckon we get one ourselves to send back home," Snow replied.

"Photos at the pyramids? Fair go, Snow, wait till they see my mug back home. Mum'll think I conquered Egypt meself!" Billy boasted.

They all agreed and headed for the nearest tram station, bound for the Pyramids of Giza. When they arrived, they stood in awe. Before them rose ancient, immovable giants; larger than any cathedral they'd ever seen.

"Would you look at that! Blocks the size of wagons stacked up to the heavens," Snow admired. "And over there's the Sphinx; half buried, its face worn by time," he continued in his makeshift tour-guide voice.

The boys really did feel like they were on holiday. Charles took it all in, beginning to understand the appeal of seeing the world. The clash of ancient history and their present reality felt surreal.

As they approached, the peaceful moment was broken by the groans of camels and the calls of hawkers. Local guides hustled for business, offering rides, postcards, and every souvenir a soldier could want. The desert stretched endlessly in every direction.

"Sun hits the stone like fire this time of day; perfect for a photo, lads," Snow insisted.

"Photo'll go nice on Edna's mantelpiece, Charlie boy. Frame me up beside the Sphinx, I'll outshine it," Billy teased.

As if on cue, Charles thought of Edna the moment Snow mentioned the photo. She hadn't seen him since he'd left Woodstock, but maybe this picture would bridge the distance. The Suevic had worn him down, but the army had also begun to harden him; filling out his frame and sharpening his stance. Edna had always teased him about the uniform. Perhaps now she'd see him not just as the boy from the farm, but as a soldier standing before the pyramids. The thought made his chest tighten with a mix of pride and longing.

Snow flagged down one of the street photographers, who dropped a large wooden box camera onto its tripod in the sand. A soft haze drifted on the breeze as the boys took turns posing, with Chook, of course, as the guinea pig.

"Do I... do I salute or somethin'? Don't want to look like a goose," he muttered, fidgeting with his hands.

Snow clapped him on the shoulder. "Just stand tall, mate. The pyramids'll do most of the impressing."

The boys clowned around between flashes, throwing sand, pulling faces, and doing their best to sabotage each other's photos. Snow's shot for his fiancée nearly ended in disaster when Billy managed to stick his hand in the frame. A few retakes later, Snow finally got his perfect picture.

"Won't be able to see the Pyramid behind these shoulders, boys," Billy boasted as his photo was taken with his trademark grin.

Then it was Charles's turn. He stood dead straight before the camera, hands behind his back, chest puffed out and offered a small smile. The photographer fussed with the box camera, then pulled the plate from the back and swirled it through a tray of chemicals beneath a canvas awning. Minutes later, he handed Charles the still-damp print.

Charles stared at it; his figure sharp against the pale desert, slouch hat tipped just so, jaw set firmer than he'd ever seen in the mirror. The uniform made him look older, surer, almost like the soldier Edna had teased he'd become. He tucked the photograph carefully into his breast pocket, suppressing the smile that tugged at him, already imagining her holding it back home.

The four wandered among the ancient monuments as the sun dipped behind the sands, casting the sky in orange light. They took a tram back to the centre of Cairo as night fell.

The city was even louder after dark, alive with colour and sound. They walked down a wide boulevard lined with palm trees, the facades around them European style, plastered in white and faded pastels. Market stalls spilled into the streets, selling everything from postcards of pyramids to brass trinkets and beads.

The crowds were intense, illuminated by streetlamps and lanterns strung along ornate balconies draped with rugs that stirred in the warm night breeze. Soldiers and sailors mixed with city folk, filling crowded cafes and bars. As they pushed through the throng, they caught scenes of roasted lamb sizzling on spits, cardamom and cloves rising from street-side coffee stalls, and the tang of tobacco and sweet molasses smoke drifting from hookahs lined up outside the cafes.

Charles and the others stopped in the middle of the main square of the party district.

"This is something else, boys… never thought the world could look like this," he said, wide-eyed.

Entertainment tugged at them from every corner; the beat of drums from music halls, cabaret singers spilling their songs into the streets. It was all foreign to him. Starry-eyed as the sky above, he was eager for what awaited. All thoughts of home and Edna seemed to vanish as the sound of intoxicated soldiers laughing and shouting pulled him further in.

"Bit loud for me. Don't think I've seen this many people in one place ever," Chook said.

"Loud's the point. The city wants you lost in it, cheap drink, loud music, easy company. Just keep your wits about you," Snow warned.

The crowds shifted constantly, hawkers enticing them into venues with happy hour specials and belly dancers swaying their hips. One whispered promise of dice games, cheap liquor, and girls leaning from doorways.

"Cheap drink, loud music? Now you're talkin'! First rounds on Cairo, seconds on Charlie boy," Billy declared, already sold.

A hawker led Billy down a narrow alleyway. Charles was quick to follow the more daring Billy, with Chook and Snow dragging behind. The alley grew tighter as they passed women dressed in bright, revealing gowns, their soft touches and confident smiles pulling the boys deeper in.

They were guided to a simple plastered grey facade with heavy stone trim around the entrance and a single window. A hand-painted sign in Arabic hung above the door, and another read "Stella", which they assumed was the local word for beer. The place was buzzing, packed with soldiers and the same type of women who had lined the alley.

Inside, Billy nearly took out the low ceiling with his head. The narrow bar ran down the left; locals hunched over their glasses. The boys perched on crooked wooden stools as the bartender slammed down four opened Stella's, beer droplets splattering their faces. The yeast smell was thick in the air, mingled with hookah smoke.

Billy raised his bottle and took a huge gulp, grinning. "Bloody 'ell, that's smoother than a freshly sheared sheep. Give that a go, Charlie boy," he jeered.

Neither Charles nor Billy had much experience with alcohol. Woodstock was too small to sneak into a pub underage, and though Charles's father drank, he wouldn't dare pinch his stash.

"Bottom's up, Billy," Charles said, clinking his bottle against his mate's. He took a sip, grimaced, and smacked his lips as the bitter beer coated his tongue.

"Don't worry, mate, first one always tastes like camel spit. By the second pint, you'll be singin' love songs to it." Billy laughed, clapping him on the back.

Snow slouched forward on his stool, comfortable and measured; already of age and well used to the drink. Chook, on the other hand, was nursing his bottle and shrinking into the bar, the energy of the room making him uneasy.

The place was packed tight. Elbows knocked together as voices rose to be heard over the gramophone crackling foreign music in the corner. The air was thick with the scent of sweat, spilled beer, and clouds of perfume as women brushed past.

Charles kept drinking, the thrill of the night washing away the bitterness. He scanned the bar: cracked plaster walls covered with hand-painted artwork and hieroglyphics. Lanterns swung gently, their light dancing across mismatched tables and chairs crammed into every corner.

As the night went on, the Stella's continued to flow. Even Chook was starting to loosen up. Billy and Snow were handling the drinks well; Snow keeping a steady pace, Billy's sheer size absorbing whatever he threw down. Charles, smaller in stature, began stumbling over his own words, grinning wider than he realised.

The beer blurred his edges; the worry, the homesickness, until all that was left was the giddy sense that this was freedom. This was how he imagined Charles Snr must have felt in his youth: untethered, bold, an adventurer on distant shores.

It was at that moment that two local women approached them. They were petite, with kohl-darkened eyes that shimmered under the low lamps. Their short, glittering dresses looked as though they'd been sewn from starlight. Hair waved and pinned in soft curls framed their faces as they moved; laughter already on their lips, as though the night belonged to them.

"You soldiers look like you own the place already. Big man, how many beers is it gonna take before you start singing?" one teased, eyes on Billy.

Billy grinned. "Only two more an' I'll sing loud enough to shake the pyramids."

The other woman's attention turned to Charles. "You're quieter than your friend. Too shy... or just saving your charm?"

Flustered by her beauty, he felt heat rise in his cheeks, his smile stretching without him meaning to. "Maybe I just haven't met the right company till now," he said, the liquid courage loosening his lips.

"Ah, he does have charm. The uniform suits you," she teased; the same kind of flirtation Edna had once thrown his way.

"Suits me better, though, don't it?" Billy cut in, flexing his shoulders to draw her attention back.

"You both look fine, and so do your other two friends. Which one of you's buying the next round?" the second woman laughed.

"Not me. Got a date with my hammock," Snow replied. He knew all too well these women wanted more than just a round of drinks.

Chook tugged at his collar, clearly out of his depth despite the alcohol. "Yeah... I'll leave you two heroes to your glory," he mumbled.

"Let's leave them to it, Chook. Stay out of trouble, you two," Snow said, his eyes narrowing more at Billy than Charles. He knew where trouble usually started.

They stepped out and headed back to the barracks, leaving Charles and Billy with the women at the bar. Conversation flowed easily, the flirtation thicker with every drink. Billy was thriving in it. Charles, on the other hand, was starting to slur. As the Stella's disappeared, so did his charm.

The first woman leaned in, grinning. "You boys know you can't come through Cairo without trying Arak. Stella's just for children."

"Stella's treatin' me fine, lass. What's this Arak though?" Billy asked, raising a brow.

"Only the strongest drink in Egypt. Clear as water, but one glass and you'll be dancing like a fool," the second teased, brushing Charles's arm.

"Dancing sounds harmless enough..." Charles mumbled, already blinking tipsily at her smile.

The women giggled and motioned to the bartender. Two cloudy glasses of Arak arrived, the sharp scent like liquorice and fire. The bartender set them down sternly.

"Careful, soldiers. Arak's not beer. Too much and you'll be on your back," he warned.

The first woman waved him off. "Oh hush. They're strong men. One glass won't hurt," she said, eyes sparkling.

"Reckon that's what she tells all the mugs. Bottoms up, Charlie boy!" Billy nudged.

Charles hesitated before knocking the whole shot back. His face twisted. "Sweet Jesus, burns like boot polish," he groaned.

The women laughed and leaned closer. More shots followed. The Arak hit fast; the liquorice fire sliding down his throat, his legs turning to jelly, his grin stretching wide as his laughter turned aimless. He leaned against the woman beside him, and for the moment, she was the only thing keeping him upright.

"You – yer me best mate, y'know that? No medals, no king, jus' Billy!" Charles slurred, pointing at him.

"Bloody hell, Charlie boy. You're three sheets to the wind. Can't take you anywhere," Billy snorted, steadying him on the stool.

"See? Strong as a lion, until a kitten drink topples him," the first woman teased.

"Reckon he'd sleep sound in your bed, love. Better than the barracks floor, aye?" Billy joked.

"Maybe next time, soldier. Off you go before you end up with him in the gutter," the second woman laughed, patting Charles on the cheek.

Charles tried to stand, but his knees buckled, nearly sending him under a nearby table. Billy caught him under the arm just in time.

"Told you, one glass too many. Get him out before he redecorates my floor," the bartender called out.

"Right, Romeo. Adventure's over for tonight," Billy grinned, hoisting Charles over his shoulder.

The journey back to camp was a blur for Charles. The next thing he remembered was flashes of white bell tents lined in perfect rows. Billy lowered him gently into his hammock, his head lolling against the canvas.

As his senses slowly returned, the guilt crept in. He lay back, peering through the open canvas flap that let the desert breeze cut through the heat. Above him, the night sky was astonishing; sharp and clear, the Milky Way flowing like a river of light. The stars seemed closer here than in Woodstock, brighter and endless.

Charles reached into his breast pocket. His fingers brushed the photograph meant for Edna. The guilt twisted tighter. The thrill of the bar; the drinks, the women, the recklessness; had pushed his real feelings aside, even for a moment. He wondered what she might be doing at that very hour, and the thought carried him into unconsciousness.

Dawn brought the end of the Egyptian holiday. Charles's first action of the morning was to post the pyramid photo to Edna, as if trying to scrub away the night in between. His head throbbed with the sharp hangover of Arak, but the ache inside was heavier.

His once romantic idea of a sailor's life had soured with the taste of liquor and regret. The struggle over who he truly was; farm boy, soldier, or something in between; continued to simmer beneath the desert sun.

Chapter 6

Salisbury Mist

The terror on board the Suevic dragged on for another few weeks before the 1st Division finally set foot on English soil at Liverpool, on the 26th of August 1917. Charles, like most of the men, staggered ashore with pure relief. To this point, the voyage had been the toughest challenge the AIF had thrown at them.

They were herded straight into troop trains, crammed in alongside horses and crates of supplies, the smell of coal smoke clinging to their uniforms. The countryside rushed past, patchwork fields hemmed by hedgerows, slate-roofed villages with church spires, and manor houses tucked behind stone walls.

To Billy, it looked like toy farms compared to Woodstock. To Charles, it felt impossibly old, every hedge and field marked by centuries.

By late afternoon, the rolling chalk downs of Salisbury came into view, bleak and treeless under a low mist. The train screeched into the station near Salisbury, and the boys were herded off into the damp English air. The sky was a dull grey smudge, the kind of drizzle that seeped into their collars before they'd taken a dozen steps.

Charles had imagined green fields like back home, but instead there was nothing but vast paddocks, flat and colourless, stretching on in silence.

"Bloody hell... feels like the whole place's been bleached," Billy muttered, stomping his boots in the mud that clung like glue.

They were marched up toward the camp at Larkhill; a maze of long rows of timber huts, canvas tents sagging under drizzle, and endless parade grounds beaten into chalk. The buildings looked plain and temporary, a far cry from the grand stone facades of Melbourne or even Cairo's humming streets. Smoke from coal stoves hung low in the mist, mixed with the tang of wet wool and horses.

Waiting for them was a row of British sergeants, buttoned to the throat, moustaches trimmed sharp as bayonets. Their polished Sam Browne belts and clipped accents stood in harsh contrast to the slouch-hatted Australians stumbling off the train.

One of the sergeants barked, "Right, line up! Quick smart, none of your colonial slouching here! You're in His Majesty's Army now, not back on the sheep paddock!"

Billy leaned toward Charles, voice low but cheeky. "Reckon his boots've seen more polish than his teeth."

Charles smirked but stayed silent. The sergeant's icy stare was already sweeping down the line.

Snow, ever the measured one, muttered, "Best keep sharp, lads. They don't take kindly to our ways here."

The men were marched into the heart of the camp; past trenches under construction, stacks of barbed wire, and gas mask drills already underway. The British officers carried themselves with the cool detachment of men who thought the war theirs to win, while the Australians shuffled in with a mix of curiosity and unease.

For Charles, the feeling was clear: Egypt had been strange, but Salisbury already felt like a different kind of battle; a fight to prove themselves. The honeymoon was over.

"This isn't the outback, straighten those lines!" the sergeant roared.

"I'm Sgt. Archie MacRae. You can call me Sergeant or Sgt. MacRae. Not Archie. Not MacRae. Not mate. Clear?" he continued.

What was clear was that the boys were far from the dusty parade ground of Enoggera. The 1st Division had been split into platoons, each with a British lieutenant and sergeant assigned to oversee training. MacRae was here to stay. His bark was like Iron Jack's, but his stance was solid as a bull.

"Reckon ol' Archie's practised that speech more times than we've fired our rifles," Billy whispered, grinning sideways at Charles.

Charles stifled a laugh. Chook tried to hold his grin.

"You there!" MacRae snapped, his hearing as sharp as the ends of his moustache. "Carter, is it? You've earned you and your 'mates' a special privilege for the company's first exercise," he barked, now grinning back at Billy.

"Orders from above, this platoon has a forty-kilometre pack march through the plains. Upon arrival, you will dig a defensive position and spend the night. You three, leave your water bottles here. No men in this company are to share with them," MacRae smirked.

Of course, Billy's the one getting us into mischief, Charles thought. It was sinking in now; Salisbury wasn't the England he'd imagined. The "Pommy way" was stricter, sharper, like the war was pressing against their doorstep.

It was already mid-afternoon. The numbers were not in the boys' favour. Billy, Charles, and Chook handed over their water bottles and began stomping their boots in time with the man in front.

They marched for hours through the rolling fields, the mud growing heavier with every step. The company, already exhausted from the long journey from the docks, was silent and miserable. The only sounds were the sloshing of boots and the occasional owl hooting as night crept in.

"Pick your feet up!" one of the corporals barked every few minutes, as if repetition alone could make the mud feel lighter.

Every so often a soldier tripped over a rock or exposed root, sending them face-first into the sludge. Charles began to struggle. There was no stop for supper, and hunger set in as darkness thickened.

He remembered how marches at Enoggera had once been almost therapeutic; a time to reflect, when he'd outpaced the pack with ease. Now, he was fighting just to keep up.

"I swear this pack's gettin' heavier by the mile... or is that just me losing me bloody spine?" Charles panted.

He wasn't alone. His partners in crime were flagging too.

"If I trip again, just bury me where I land. Tell my folks I died a hero... in a puddle," Billy gritted through his teeth.

"My legs don't even feel like they belong to me anymore... they're just two logs I'm draggin'," Chook muttered.

Charles licked his cracked lips, trying to draw moisture from the cool night air. Billy tilted his head back, as if trying to drink the mist. Their bodies were heavy with sweat and mud, their packs digging into their shoulders, their muscles weakening with every step.

"Breathe, boys. One boot in front of the other. Don't look at the hill, just the heels in front of you," Snow came in with a low, steady voice.

It felt like they were walking in circles, and for the most part, they were. After such a long march, they could still see the faint smoke of Salisbury drifting in the distance from fires warming the men lucky enough to stay behind.

Snow reached into his tunic pocket. The crackle of paper and scrape of tin against biscuit broke the heavy silence of the march. He pulled out a few jagged pieces of hard tack, rough in the moonlight, and passed them down the line.

"Here. Won't taste like much, but it'll keep your guts from eating themselves," he muttered, pressing one into Billy's palm, then Charles's, then Chook's.

Charles noticed there was nothing left in Snow's hand. "What about you, Snow? Couldn't rob you of your own supper."

Snow shook his head, lifting his canteen instead. "Don't worry about me. Water'll do the trick. Hunger's easier to swallow than guilt."

The once-dreaded hard tack was now a saviour. The march continued through the fog as they gritted their teeth, battling thirst and hunger. Charles had never been in so much pain; his shoulders felt ready to dislocate under the pack's weight. Then MacRae's bark cut through the night like a whip.

"Final hill, boys! Don't you dare slack off, you've a trench to dig before you even think about resting!" he boomed, as if delivering a backhanded celebration.

"Dig a trench after this? Might as well bury me in it," Billy grinned, his body broken but his spirit intact.

Charles smirked. Having his best mate beside him gave him courage. He lowered his head and fought for every step as his boots suctioned into the mud. Together, they pushed each other to the hilltop, overlooking the dark misty plains of Salisbury.

Charles plonked himself down to MacRae's dismay.

"You got a hole to dig, soldier!" the sergeant barked, tossing their water bottles back at them.

Without hesitation, Charles grabbed his aluminium can and threw the contents down his throat. It felt like an act of kindness, briefly making him forget MacRae had caused their thirst in the first place. The moment was short-lived. A shovel followed next, clattering into the mud at his feet.

Back in Enoggera, the boys had never dug trenches. Tired and exhausted, Charles speared the shovel into the sodden hilltop. The mud clung to the blade, doubling its weight, each lift threatening to snap his spine.

"Feels like we're diggin' our own graves," Billy muttered.

"Least you're still alive to do it," Snow countered, pacing himself with short, neat digs. "Short bites, lads, not big swings, or you'll wreck yourself."

Surprisingly, Chook was making the best progress. For him, digging felt more like farm chores. Billy and Charles had always hated digging, stockmen preferred to let the horses do the work mustering cattle. Even Edna knew how they'd shirk setting posts for a downed fence.

The mist crept higher up the hill, chilling their sweat-damp backs. British sergeants stood over them like overseers, degrading the colonials as they worked in the mud.

"Speed it up, soldier. Trenches save lives, they don't need to look pretty," MacRae spat.

They lost track of time. Lanterns cast weak yellow light across rows of men digging in silence. The muffled rhythm of spades across the hillside was like a grim orchestra at a funeral.

Running on empty, Charles felt close to collapse. But when he glanced at Billy and Chook, both struggling but still digging, he knew he couldn't stop either. Their shared misery held them up as much as their shovels.

After an hour on the end of the handle, the trench was finally deep enough for MacRae to give the briefest nod of approval. The boys were thirsty, hungry, and cold. Mist clung to the trench walls as they slumped against the mud, rifles stacked beside them.

Charles prised open his tin of bully beef, the congealed fat glistening in the lantern light. Billy tapped his hard tack against the timber support.

Crack. A shard flew off.

"Bloody hell, stronger than the trench walls. Reckon I'll use it as a sandbag."

Chook tried gnawing at his own biscuit, jaw straining. "Think my teeth'll give out before Jerry does."

Snow handed over his enamel mug, steam curling from it. "Here. Soak it. Tea makes everything edible, even this stuff."

Charles sipped, the bitter brew cutting through the grease. He let out a long breath. "Not quite Mum's mutton stew, but... warm enough."

Billy shoved a lump of beef into his mouth and spoke through the chew. "Warm enough? Mate, it's fine dining. Candlelight, mud walls, company of gentlemen. A proper bloody holiday."

Chook rolled his eyes but cracked a grin. "Holiday where they pay you in blisters."

Snow leaned back against the parapet, quiet for a moment, then said, "Better get used to it, boys. This is supper at the front. Cold, wet, and never enough."

Charles stared into his tin, the grease pooling in the bottom. He thought of Woodstock; of the supper when he told his parents he was leaving. He never thought this was what he was signing up for. He took another swig and swallowed hard.

Billy nudged him with the biscuit. "Don't go soft on us, Charlie boy. First one to complain's gotta trade with me, I'll take your beef any day."

As the night wore on, the boys found comfort in each other's company. They huddled close, trading warmth the way they had traded rations, each shiver passing through the group like a shared burden. Charles slept in fragments, the cold teasing him awake, until the thin morning light finally brought the first mercy of heat.

With the light of day upon them, the boys could finally see their surroundings. The mist had started to fade, uncovering the army barracks they'd overlooked from the top of the ridge. It was clear they weren't a full forty kilometres from where they'd started the march. The muddy plain below was broken by rows of timber weatherboard huts with corrugated iron roofs, surrounded by sagging khaki tents. Smoke billowed from chimneys, and the boys could see roaring fires encircled by British soldiers warming themselves.

"Joined the wrong forces, lads, need to be under a British flag," Charles muttered.

"You ain't wound up tight enough to march under those snobs," Billy shot back.

Bleary-eyed, Charles scanned the ridge. To the left, he saw low barbed wire arrangements with thick mud pits underneath, wooden walls between long trench runs zigzagging across the skyline. Timber planks hung suspended over the slush, the whole site riddled with mud.

To the right, a row of Vickers machine guns stood silent and alluring. Mounted on tripods and aimed toward the open fields below, they gave off an aura of grim power. It was the first time Charles had seen one up close. Now, assigned to the 12th Machine Gun Company, the sight hit him with a strange weight. He stared at them, transfixed; until MacRae's bark shattered the quiet.

"On your feet, you filthy machine gunners!" his voice cracked across the morning mist. "You're no use to me if you can't work the bloody thing. From now on, you'll be in pairs; one gunner, one loader. Learn your role, know it backwards, and prove you're worth the rations!"

MacRae strode down the line, pointing like a drill bit. "Gunner, loader, gunner, loader." As he reached the end of the trench, the boys tensed in anticipation. He took one look at Billy, towering above the trench.

"Gunner."

Then he leaned over to Charles. "Loader."

Charles's disappointment was instant. The decision was clearly made on size alone. The Vickers, fully assembled with its condenser can and tripod, weighed nearly 45 kilograms. The loader's 250-round ammunition boxes were much lighter, at around 10. MacRae was clearly making the most of Billy's build.

The boys got themselves set up. Billy spread his legs around the tripod and plonked himself down into the mud. Charles crouched beside him, his job simple: keep the rounds feeding smoothly and reload fast when the box ran dry.

"Finally, a weapon fit for these shoulders. Told ya, Charlie boy, all that farm work was trainin' for somethin'," Billy boasted.

"Yeah, well, let's see who keeps you shootin' when your lunchbox runs dry," Charles snapped back, irritation simmering. He didn't want to be a bystander to Billy's glory.

"Enough chatter, you pair of clowns! Get that Vickers belt ready, I want to hear it sing before the hour's out!" MacRae barked from above.

After a scramble of hands and fumbling fingers, the belt finally fed through. MacRae's voice cut across the trench.

"Fire when ready!"

Billy's eyes lit up like a kid on Christmas morning. He gripped the wooden handles as if the gun might buck away, trigger trembling under his finger. For a beat he just stared down the barrel, teeth clenched in anticipation; then he squeezed.

The Vickers erupted. A tearing roar ripped through the air, brass casings spitting like hail onto the mud. The stench of cordite hit Charles before the ringing in his ears did. He clamped his hands too late; the crack of the gun seemed to rattle his bones.

Billy's grin was feral, shoulders shuddering under the gun's recoil. The ache from last night was nothing compared to this pounding. But he wasn't letting go.

"Bloody hell, Charlie boy, she kicks harder than a bull at branding!" Billy shouted.

"You call that singing? My ears are ringing like church bells!" Charles yelled back, barely hearing himself.

"If that's your idea of singing, Carter, you'll be scaring the enemy off before the bullets reach 'em," MacRae jabbed.

Charles smirked. The first hint of humour he'd ever heard from the man.

"Enough smiling you clowns, this isn't a circus act. Keep feeding that belt, loader!" he barked again.

The machine gunner training carried on late into the morning. With barely a break for lunch, they were herded into gas mask drills in cramped timber huts. The doors slammed shut. Acrid smoke seeped in as they fumbled to yank masks into place. The stale rubber stank, their lungs rasping through the filters while muffled shouts echoed in the dark. A few panicked, clawing at straps until corporals beat their hands away and forced them forward.

The "Pommy way" was relentless. The British, drilled by centuries of war, ran a tighter ship than the relaxed Aussie methods. A far cry from Enoggera, where the journey had

begun. Weeks at sea had already worn them down; Salisbury ground the rest away.

After gas mask training came the obstacle course, slogging through mud until dusk, followed by a shorter twenty-kilometre march that night.

The training at Salisbury went on like this for months. One day it was a dawn march through freezing fog; another, a midnight dig where their shovels struck frozen clay like iron. Sometimes the gas alarms shrieked in their sleep, sending the men scrambling out half-dressed, masks askew, bile burning their throats.

They rarely set foot inside the warm barracks; always outside, always wet, always looking in. Their bodies hardened under the relentless routine. Charles loathed MacRae's bark, but when he realised, he could march further, dig longer, and haul heavier loads than men twice his size, he begrudged the sergeant less.

MacRae's voice no longer stung like a whip. It drove him.

Then, in March 1918, came the announcement. MacRae climbed onto the fire step, chest out, moustache bristling. His voice boomed across the trench line.

"Men, we're bound for Amiens in France! The AIF has reorganised the 12th Machine Gun Company into the 1st Machine Gun Battalion of the 1st Division. From there, we'll be rushed to Flanders to show the Hun what Australians are made of!"

For a heartbeat there was silence. Then the trench erupted; helmets flew skyward, voices cracked with cheer.

Billy pumped his fist, shouting over the noise. "About bloody time! Thought we'd rot in this mud before we saw a real Hun!"

"France... never been further than Kedron. Now I'm off to fight in Europe. How's that for a leap?" Chook grinned nervously.

"Careful, Chook. The Hun won't scare as easy as your birds back home," Snow said with a crooked smile.

"If we can march through this muck, the Hun doesn't stand a chance," Charles added. The moment lifted him; flashing through everything that had brought him here, and everyone who'd helped set the course.

The forty kilometres back to camp felt lighter, boots slapping mud to the rhythm of victory chants. Even the drizzle couldn't dampen their spirits.

As they filed under the wooden arch, aching but grinning, a sharp cockney voice rang out from a hut marked POST.

"Mail call, lads! Grab it quick, might be the last love letter you read in a while!" the postie bellowed, waving a fistful of envelopes.

Charles found two letters pressed into his hand: one from his mother, the other from Edna. He opened his mother's first, already guessing what it would say. Her words spilled with worry, heavy with emotion, with a line or two insisting that his father, deep down, was proud of him. He read it quickly, barely taking it in.

The second envelope sat in his palm, hot and heavy. Edna's. Mail was slow, six months had passed since he'd sent her the photo from Cairo. He'd wondered ever since how she'd see him: the uniform, the adventure, the man he was trying to become.

"Better read it before the war, Charlie boy," Billy nudged.

His palms were slick by the time he broke the seal.

Dear Charles,

I nearly fell over when your letter came, and the photograph tucked inside, well, I must have stared at it for an hour. There you are, standing so straight and proud before that pyramid, trying your best to look the picture of seriousness. But that grin of yours gives you away at once, I'd know it anywhere. Mother says the uniform makes you look a proper gentleman. I think it makes you look older, though I can still see the farm boy under the hat.

Everyone in Woodstock has been fussing over the photo, passing it round as though you're some great explorer. Billy's mum said it ought to be in the paper. I tell them all you're still Charles Watson who once fell out of the hayloft and couldn't sit for a week.

I do hope you're eating properly, not living on nothing but biscuits and tea. I know you'll laugh at me fussing, but I can't help it.

Take care of yourself, Charles. I'll keep your photo by my bedside, and I expect you to bring that same grin home when all this is over.

Yours, Edna

Reading her words, Charles felt the ache of distance sharpen; but with it came a warmth that spread deeper than the cold mud ever could. Edna's teasing steadied him; her pride lifted him. The photo he had sent wasn't just proof of his adventure, it was proof that she still saw him, still waited for him. For the first time since leaving Woodstock, Charles felt not like a lost boy dragged along by war, but a man with someone to fight for.

He folded the letter with care and tucked it close to his chest. Whatever lay ahead across the English Channel, he carried her with him.

Chapter 7

Into the Line

In April of 1918, the boys set foot in France, jumping off troop trains as steam hissed and officers barked orders in French and English. They marched into the shell-shocked town of Amiens, thick with the smell of coal smoke hovering over the city.

The scars of conflict were clear; a place caught between a functioning French town and a landscape shadowed by war. The 1st Division stomped their feet down the main cobbled road, the sound of horse carts and military wagons rattling close behind. French civilians in dark worn clothes, children darting through alleyways, and soldiers of every uniform stared curiously at the fresh reinforcements heading into the centre.

"Not as much cheer here as Melbourne," Snow observed, scanning the quiet faces.

"Probably stunned by our military prowess," Billy smirked, puffing his chest. His eyes drifted toward the cafes, the women in shawls, and the scent of fresh bread.

"Reckon I'll swap trench stew for proper French tucker, if the ladies ever look my way."

Charles rolled his eyes.

"Only thing they're stunned by is you lurchin' through like an ogre."

The boots thundered on, past shuttered shops boarded with thick planks, open cafes with chalkboard menus, sandbagged machine gun nests, and patches of rubble where shells had struck. Much of the central city still stood intact, and as they entered the main square the Notre-Dame d'Amiens dominated the skyline.

It was the largest structure the four had ever seen; the facade scaffolded to protect its spire from shell damage, stained-glass windows hidden behind sandbags. Even Charles, no admirer of most churches, paused at its beauty. He felt an unexpected urge to protect it.

"The cathedral is one of the tallest in France. British officers practically worship its survival as a symbol," Snow said, sliding into his tour-guide mode.

"Crikey, Charlie boy, look at that church! Biggest shed I've ever seen," Billy nudged.

"Could fit my whole farm in there... reckon it's safer than the huts we'll be in," Charles replied.

The sight of local kids laughing in the square unsettled him; too normal, too cheerful, this close to the thunder of war.

As the final boot stilled on the cobblestones, a low rumble rolled across the distance. The first real sound of what awaits.

Charles felt a surge of excitement. Everything he'd trained for; the dreams sparked by Frankie's stories of Gallipoli splashed across the papers; suddenly felt within reach. Yet beneath it, something twisted uneasily. The thud of artillery tightened his chest. He kept glancing at the civilians' weary faces, as if they already knew the fate of every fresh unit passing through.

MacRae stepped before the 1st Machine Gun Battalion, his tone cold and matter of fact.

"Men... we'll be heading to the line this afternoon, to hold against a German offensive. This is the real deal. No warm-up. Welcome to the war!"

The cheer they once had at Salisbury felt out of place now. Amiens wasn't celebrating them. It was watching them.

Charles wrestled with the news. He thought of his father; of becoming a man of his word, proving he wasn't a coward, fighting loyally for the King. Deep down he prayed that when he returned, his father might finally give his approval, and that his mother's heartbreak wouldn't be for nothing.

They didn't linger in Amiens. An hour of French hospitality along the boulevard was all they received before being packed into open wagons with horses and supplies for a 120-kilometre journey north to Flanders.

After ten hours, they reached Hazebrouck. They stepped out into the darkness, stiff and groggy. Battalion NCOs distributed Vickers machine guns in pieces; bulky puzzles of steel and weight. Billy was lumped with the weapon; Charles carried the ammo boxes. The tripod and condenser cans were hauled by additional men. No part of the kit was light.

As they marched, the signs of war grew sharper. The small market town was half in ruins; rows of brick and stone houses with Flemish stepped gables boarded up or sandbagged. Many roofs were half-missing, walls pockmarked by shrapnel. An acrid tang of cordite still lingered in the air.

In the town square, the Eglise Saint-Éloi rose over the cobbles, a Gothic silhouette under the moonlight. It reminded

Charles of St James Cathedral, as if his past were still keeping watch.

Lanterns flickered dimly behind shuttered windows. A wagon creaked over the stones, hooves clattering softly as the company tramped through in near silence. A few French civilians lingered in doorways, shawls pulled tight, watching the passing column with tired, hollow eyes.

"Keep step, boys! Quiet in the ranks!" MacRae growled. His voice bounced off the stone facades like a warning bell.

Billy tilted his head toward a group of weary AIF men resting by a wagon; faces gaunt, uniforms crusted with weeks of filth.

"Bloody hell, Charlie boy… look at 'em. They look like the life's been wrung out already."

Charles gave the faintest smirk, though his eyes stayed forward.

"Probably city boys. Not used to gettin' dirty."

Billy snorted a quiet laugh.

"Yeah, well… give me dirt over that look in their eyes any day."

Snow spoke softly, steady as ever.

"Eyes like that don't come from dirt. That's the front, lads."

They continued through the square, packs heavy, boots scuffing across the worn cobbles as they headed toward the outskirts of town and the reserve trenches. Once the rubble of Hazebrouck faded behind them, Charles looked up to see a flat landscape spread out under the moonlight. Canals and dykes criss-crossed the fields, barbed wire tangled everywhere, and an endless thunder rolled from the east, accompanied by flashes in the distant fog.

As he stepped off the firm street and onto open ground, his boots sloshed into wet mud. The weight of the machine gun parts seemed to suction every man deeper with each step.

The 1st Machine Gun Battalion moved carefully through the field. The mud was unavoidable; where it grew deepest, they crossed wooden planks used as duckboards. The smell of stagnant water and manure thickened as they pushed on. Under the cover of darkness, they finally reached a shallow trench and dropped in behind MacRae.

The battalion zig-zagged through the maze of trenches as they descended deeper. After nearly an hour of slipping through mud and shuffling along narrow passages, they reached a wider section of the dugout. To the left, a small stone recess held an old door frame carved into the trench wall; a faint lantern glow inside revealing basic timber furniture, all caked in Flanders mud.

To the right, the trench wall rose higher, reinforced with corrugated iron and steel posts holding back the collapsing earth. Above them, dugouts with sandbags formed machine gun nests large enough for several Vickers each.

"Here we are, boys. Reserve trench," MacRae announced. "Get your Vickers in the bays, two to a nest. Even spread, barrels clean. You won't be called unless the Hun smash through further east... but don't let that fool you into gettin' soft."

Exhausted, the boys were eager to unload the machine gun parts and ammo boxes from their aching shoulders. Boots squelched as they clambered into the bays. Billy and Charles set up their Vickers beside Snow and Chook, the tripod legs sinking an inch into the wet dirt. Somehow Chook had been made a gunner; his thin arms trembled as he fought with the feed block while Billy fitted the water can.

Charles crouched beside them, threading the belt into the gun, his fingers numb with cold and mud.

Within minutes, the clatter of bolts and locking arms died down. The barrels sat ready; ugly silhouettes sweating with condensation in the lantern glow. The boys slumped back against the trench wall; the weight lifted from their shoulders but still pressed into their bones.

For the first time since leaving Hazebrouck, silence settled over them; broken only by the distant thunder of artillery, a constant growl somewhere beyond the horizon. It seemed impossible that men could sleep with such noise rolling through the earth, yet fatigue overcame them faster than fear.

Billy muttered something about his stretcher at Enoggera being softer than the mud here, but his head tilted forward before he finished. One by one they drifted off; helmets tipped over their eyes.

Charles was surprised at how quickly sleep claimed him. Even here, in the war, he wondered what Edna would make of it all as he drifted off to the distant rattle of guns. The trench smelled of wet sandbags and the ghost of cordite, but for now it was enough to rest.

Charles awoke at dawn. The sun crept over a flat, empty horizon riddled with duckboards and trenches. The only vegetation was shattered tree stumps blown to splinters by days of shelling. Barbed wire snaked everywhere, some of it half-sunken in the mud that dominated every inch of the landscape.

"Bloody hell... neck's more crooked than the end of Iron Jack's moustache," Billy groaned, holding his neck.

"Now you know how we all feel looking up to your head height," Charles replied.

"Slept pretty well considering we're on the line," Snow assessed. "Can see and hear it in the distance but not much going on here."

Chook was still snoring loudly enough to alert the entire German Army. MacRae climbed the timber ladder and whacked the side of his helmet.

"Stay alert, boys. Might seem quiet, but there's an entire army out there wantin' to hunt ya," MacRae barked.

The days rolled on. The four of them spent hours watching others fight the war in front of their eyes. The dull, endless artillery rumbled like distant drums, broken only by the sharp cracks of machine gun bursts from trenches further forward. At times the wind carried a smell none of them could quite place; a foul mix of stagnant water, manure, and something far worse.

Their eagerness turned to frustration. After a few days, the novelty of being so close to the line dissolved. This wasn't the heroic adventure Charles imagined when he enlisted.

Then, after a couple of weeks, the boys got their wish.

"Tonight, men, we're moving up the line!" MacRae's voice echoed off the trench walls. "Forward positions. Get your equipment ready. Disassemble and clean the Vickers, you're about to wage hell."

Darkness couldn't come soon enough. Though in Flanders, even night never truly fell, the sky flickered constantly with distant artillery bursts.

They clambered out of the trenches and trekked through sodden clay, keeping to duckboards whenever possible. Boots were sucked off feet by the mud, soldiers cursing as they lunged to pull them free. The closer they came to the line, the thicker and more treacherous the ground became.

The stench in the air grew stronger; unmistakable now. The rumble of guns grew louder, vibrating puddles of stagnant water at their feet.

"Crikey, that smells worse than the inside of your boot, Charlie boy," Billy whispered.

"Quiet, soldier!" MacRae snapped, eyes cutting straight through him.

MacRae's mood was different that night; sharper, heavier. His usual bark had stripped back into something cold and clipped as he led from the front. Every bend in the trench, every shadow, he scanned like a hawk. The boys behind him weren't nearly as sharp; their minds dulled by hours of hauling the Vickers, shoulders burning with every step.

BANG!

The world went white.

Charles was launched sideways, slammed into sucking mud, ears screaming with a piercing ring. His chest locked tight as if someone had punched the air out of him. For a moment he lay stunned, muffled voices drifting in like echoes underwater. Edna's face flashed across his mind like a ghost.

Rough hands grabbed his tunic and heaved him upright.

"You alright, mate? Loose shell; blew you clean off your boots," Billy puffed, panic and relief tangled in his voice as he patted him down.

Charles blinked through the blur, his hearing hissing back like static.

"I'm... I'm alright." His own voice sounded distant, hollow.

Then the smell hit him.

Sweet. Sickly. Rot.

His eyes dropped; and froze.

A trench-side pit gaped open beside him, heaped with tangled uniforms and pale, swollen faces. Dozens of bodies, Allied soldiers like himself, shovelled together into the earth as if they were debris, not men.

His stomach lurched.

The war was no longer somewhere ahead of him. It was here. Under his feet.

Snow came over silently, a steadying hand on both boys' backs, guiding them onward. No words; just a hard, empty look. Charles moved like he was underwater, MacRae's voice a muffled thud. They turned a corner and dropped into a deeper cutting. The walls barely held back the earth, sandbags slumping where shells had punched through, the floor thick with sludge.

The men already occupying the ditch looked broken; blood on their kits, mud caked up to their waists. Many sat slumped against the walls, their backs in the drenched earth, eyes hollow as they watched the new arrivals. The 1st Machine Gun Battalion was here to relieve them; these men would march back toward Hazebrouck the following evening.

No greetings. No nods.

Just the dead-eyed stare of the front line.

MacRae broke the tension with orders, pointing the Vickers crews to the ridges along the trench.

Charles moved on autopilot, the stink of chlorine, smoke, and decay hanging over everything. His heartbeat thudded in his ears, his mind numb. Billy watched him, worry tightening his jaw.

"Not much of a welcome party, ay, Charlie boy?" he murmured, trying to lift the dread.

But the mood didn't dampen the spirits of most of the 1st Machine Gun Battalion; after a year of training, they were finally on the front line.

It was early morning, just past midnight. Their routine from the reserve trenches returned, taking turns watching the silent, blackened field before them. Charles and Chook leaned into opposite sides of the gun pit, shivering against the cold sandbags, perched just high enough to peer over the rim.

Charles' mind replayed the bodies.

They weren't shapes anymore. They were men.

Men who had stood where he stood; until they didn't.

Regret flickered for the first time. He had enlisted at sixteen, believing if he kept his head down, nothing could harm him. After being blown through the air, that childish invincibility cracked.

A roar built in the distance.

Flashes lit the fog.

Then a long, screaming whistle ripped through the air.

"Take cover!" MacRae bellowed.

Charles buried his head into his arms.

BOOM.

The ground convulsed as explosions ripped across the trench. Mud rained down on them. The walls shook, sandbags bursting. Shrapnel hissed like angry hornets. Men screamed; raw, animal sounds swallowed by the chaos.

It felt like minutes. It was probably seconds.

Then silence.

Except for the groans.

Charles opened one eye. Their gun pit was still intact. They were shaken but alive. He scanned down the gully toward the source of the cries. One of the men they'd passed earlier clutched what remained of his left knee; nothing below it. His mate beside him was still, neck at an impossible angle.

The relief had come one day too late for them.

"Everyone okay, boys? Pat each other down, make sure there's no holes," Snow ordered, his voice hard, all softness gone.

"Still in one piece," Billy muttered. The grin had faded. "Can't say the same for them poor buggers."

"Eyes front. Hun won't wait for you to compose yourselves," MacRae snapped.

Charles wiped his face and turned to the field. Tears stung; quiet, uninvited. Not for himself, but for the memory of gum trees and warm sun, things impossibly far from this cold, endless nightmare.

The barrage continued day after day, all hours. Constant bursts answering each other like angry typewriters.

The artillery duels felt like a chess match, while the men in trenches were pawns.

After a week at war, they still hadn't fired a single round.

Late April arrived. The battalion began to break down. They now looked like the men they had once pitied; gaunt, pale, worn through. Rats gnawed at their kits at night. Lice spread through the ranks. Sleep was rare and shallow.

"These dang rats are the real landlords here, size of a possum back home," Billy muttered, a hint of humour creeping back.

"Almost look appetising," Charles said as his stomach grumbled.

"Disease-infested, every one of 'em," Snow added.

Chook hardly spoke anymore. The constant shelling had rattled him to the core; headaches and ringing wore him down. He'd sit clutching his temples until Snow forced water into his hands.

Then came the yell,

"Incoming!"

Shells clanged off the trench wall and disappeared into the mud. No explosion.

For a moment the boys thought they were duds.

Then the hissing began.

A high-pitched squeal.

A burning scent; garlic and horseradish.

Not supper. Poison.

"Gas! Gas! Gas!" Snow roared.

Charles dove for the timber box, hands shaking as he fought to untangle the masks. The air burned his face as the cloud rolled into the gun pit. He managed to seal his own mask and threw the others out. Billy and Snow got theirs on, but Chook panicked; fingers slipping, breath wheezing.

The fog rose around him.

Snow ripped the mask from his hands and slammed it onto his face, sealing it tight.

"Bloody hell, Charlie boy, thought we signed up to shoot the Hun, not sniff their cookin'!" Billy muffled through his mask.

The gas was thick, choking; worse than the dust from Edna's carriage on the way to Woodstock.

When the cloud drifted off, the screams began. Some men hadn't sealed their masks. Others had exposed skin. Mustard gas kissed neither gently nor briefly.

Six men were pulled out with severe burns, to be carted back toward Hazebrouck. Their cries lingered long after they were taken.

"This could become the new normal," Snow said firmly. "Good work, Charles. Next time, keep the masks untangled. Seconds count."

MacRae echoed the same message, pacing the trench like a wolf. Gas wasn't rare. Gas was war.

Chapter 8

Flanders Fields

By early May 1918, the Allies had fought bitterly through Flanders. Australian and British divisions had driven the Germans back past Strazeele and onto the edge of Meteren, six kilometres east of the 1st Division's position outside Hazebrouck. Each battered French village became another marker in the hard-won advance. MacRae gathered the men, all crouched low in the valley they'd called their hellish home for over a month.

"Men, the Hun won't stay on the run forever. They're dug in at Meteren. The 1st Division is holding the line here. Be ready for a renewed German counterattack."

The boys said their goodbyes to Hazebrouck.

"Glad to see the end of this crater-filled field," Charles said.

"Don't count your lucky stars yet, Charles. Who knows what's waiting for us," Snow warned, ever the realist.

When they dropped into their new sector, shock followed quickly. The trenches barely reached their shoulders; shallow cuts in the earth that left helmets and heads exposed. Across the mud and wire, Charles could see Germans shifting between shattered houses in Meteren, machine gun pits jutting like dark sockets. Between the two armies lay a dead sea of mud and barbed wire.

"Feels like they can almost see us blink," Charles muttered.

"Closer than I'd like," Snow replied flatly.

Billy grinned, hoisting the Vickers into position. "Well, Charlie boy, guess it's time we gave the old girl a polish. Hun won't like the shine off this beauty."

"Holding up all right, Chook?" Snow asked.

"Yeah, Snow... hanging in. Far cry from the chook pen," Chook muttered.

MacRae stomped over. "Hang in there, Chook. Boys, dig this pit deeper. Don't want the Hun watching what you eat."

The battalion set the machine guns on the trench lip, fully exposed. The Allies hadn't had time to fortify these newer positions. The boys dug, shovels squelching through soggy clay. Charles felt the weight of the German army massing in the town, eyes prickling as though every rifle was aimed at him. They couldn't dig deep; walls crumbled at every bite of the shovel.

"Are my arms still attached, Billy?" Charles groaned.

"Still there, mate. Can't say the same for your shovel swing; you look like you're tryin' to butter toast," Billy teased.

A low rumble shuddered across the field, stagnant puddles trembling. A harsh mechanical roar rose from the town. Chook's face drained of colour.

"What is that?"

"I'd hate to look," Charles said.

"I'll take a peek." Snow grabbed the trench lip and hauled himself up.

In the moonlight he saw metal tracks chewing at rubble, exhaust belching a black plume. A massive rhomboid shape crawled into view, iron plating glinting. The boys had heard rumours of these steel beasts, but nothing prepared them for the size or sound. German tanks, reinforcing the Meteren line.

One by one the others had to look.

"Fair dinkum, Charlie boy, looks like a steel cow with legs chewin' up the mud," Billy breathed.

"Reckon it's safer inside that thing than diggin' here," Chook muttered, clutching his head again as dizziness returned.

"Safer maybe... but imagine bein' cooked alive in that box," Snow countered.

Charles felt his stomach knot. It wasn't just the size of the thing; it was what it meant. His arms ached, eyes stung from smoke and mud, and now a metal monster joined the fight. He thought of Edna, of Woodstock, and how impossibly far away those simple things were.

Night fell. The boys huddled together, kits permanently damp, sleep shallow and broken by every distant sound. Until...

High-pitched whistles sliced the air.

Charles jerked awake, instincts taking over. He ducked, helmet pressed between his hands, curling against the trench wall. A falling whine cut through the night, then a deafening crump shook the ground. Shells erupted around them, showering dirt through the trench. Sandbags burst. Mud slumped into dugouts. Charles smelled hot cordite sting his nostrils. He curled tighter, praying.

"Bloody hell, they've found us," Billy muttered between blasts.

Snow shouted over the barrage, ensuring helmets and masks were ready. When the explosions eased, MacRae's voice boomed across the trench,

"On your guns! Eyes front! Loader, keep it clean! Gunners, keep it hot!"

Charles's pulse hammered. Sweat slicked his palms as he gripped an ammo box. He forced a breath, then scrambled up onto the firing step. Billy was already flat behind the Vickers, eyes wide, hands clamped on the handles.

Charles dropped beside him, trembling as he fed the first belt, fingers slipping on wet brass.

"Steady on, Charlie boy; feed her smooth, not like your lines to Edna!"

Before Charles could retort, the whistles started again; only this time they weren't shells. Guttural yells rose from the dark. Shapes broke through the mist, bayonets gleaming.

Then flashes.

Billy squeezed the trigger. The Vickers erupted, drowning the world in a tearing roar. German boots splashed through mud, their zigzag advance lit by muzzle flashes. Charles kept his head buried, lifting only when he felt the last round snap free. Mist thickened into smoke. The Hun were barely seventy metres out.

"Don't you bloody freeze; bayonets ready! If the gun jams, you fight with steel!" MacRae roared.

"Steel cow or no cow, Charlie boy, let's make the bastards dance!" Billy bellowed, lost in the trance of recoil and fire.

The advance slowed under the weight of the machine gun line. Some Germans fell; others dropped into craters for cover, muzzle flashes cracking back across the field.

"I can't hear myself think! Feels like the whole bloody world's on top of us!" Chook cried, his Vickers screaming beside them.

Charles reloaded again, hands shaking uncontrollably. He wished he could bury himself in the mud for an inch more cover.

Then he felt it; the rumble shifting into a living growl. The tanks.

"Don't worry; they can't get through this mud," Snow shouted, trying to anchor him.

Charles held onto that hope. Tracks clattered. Gears screamed. Billy didn't blink; just kept firing, rounds rattling from Charles's trembling hands.

"They're stayin' put," Charles said, half convincing himself. "Those cows are too afraid to get mud on their legs."

The tank's turret rose.

His smirk died.

Clack-clack.

Before he could pray, Chook's Vickers jammed. A twisted belt choked the feed. Chook yanked at it desperately, voice cracking. Snow yelled instructions from behind him.

Charles turned; just as the beast's guns spoke.

A blast hit close. The shockwave ripped through Chook and Snow's pit, spraying Charles with mud, blood, and splintered timber. His ears rang violently. When the haze cleared, he looked over.

Chook was slumped in the mud; helmet gone, eyes open but empty.

For a moment Charles froze. Not Chook. Not like this. His mind refused to process what his eyes already knew. Bile rose in his throat. The ringing in his ears broke only when Billy screamed,

"Charles! Feed the damn belt! Vickers is hungry!"

Dragged back into the living world, Charles forced himself to shove more rounds in, all while Chook's lifeless face hovered at the edge of his vision. Snow, shaken but moving, had already scrambled into the gunner's spot, taking over with trembling hands. The fight went on; the cost was real.

The Hun were still bogged down. The tanks had given them support, but the Germans stuck in the mire could not break through the Vickers line, every gun barking in perfect, deadly rhythm. Then came the blast from behind: friendly artillery zeroed in on the enemy armour, shells arcing overhead, tipping the balance. The German wave collapsed against the Allied line, bodies stiffening in the mud.

Again, whistles cut through the carnage.

The Hun withdrew as the Vickers barrels glowed red.

"Cease! Cease fire!" MacRae shouted as the assault faltered at last.

Charles slumped back, caked in mud and sweat. His eyes hollow, his face spattered with blood not his own. He dared one final glance toward where Chook had been. Snow had already covered him with a groundsheet.

Charles slid down into the mud; hand pressed to his breast pocket where Edna's letter sat. Then he wept.

Time slowed; memories flickering through his mind like a lantern slide: Iron Jack berating Chook on the first day of basics, their carefree days in Egypt, Chook's grin in the sun, his final terrified moment in the Flanders mud.

Two hands grabbed Charles by the shoulders. Billy and Snow dragged him back through the slop into the trench. Billy; mud-streaked, powder-burned; propped him against the clay wall.

"Easy, Charlie boy... fight's done. We're still standin'. That's more'n some can say," Billy panted.

"He's gone. Nothing'll change that now," Snow said quietly. "Best we can do is carry him with us."

"I should've... I should've done more," Charles whispered.

Billy shook his head. "No one could've. Not against that storm. Don't carry blame that ain't yours."

Charles felt like a fraud; Chook fighting to the last, while he'd been face-down in the mud, trembling over each reload.

"Get your breath, mate. Tomorrow'll come, whether we want it or not," Snow murmured, steadying him.

Charles's heartbeat slowly eased. The first red edge of sunrise crept over the blood-stained field. MacRae made his way down the line, assessing the battalion. He lifted the sheet covering Chook, sighed, and nodded once. When he spoke, the gravel in his voice had softened.

"Get a detail together, Snow. We'll see him buried proper before first light. He was green, aye, but he stood his ground when it counted. That makes him a soldier... one of us."

Charles heard respect in the sergeant's tone; more than command.

Billy and Snow wrapped Chook in the sheet, placed his helmet on top, and lifted their mate. Charles followed with a shovel, hands shaking as he trudged fifty metres behind the line where other details were gathering their dead.

Billy passed him the shovel. Charles dug the shallow grave, each scoop a reminder of the brutal truth. As they lowered Chook into the sodden earth he'd fought so hard to hold, Charles wrestled with the gulf between the noble deaths he had imagined back on the farm and the bleak reality of hurried burials in the mud.

He lingered, staring at the sheet.

"A mate deserves more than a few words over a hole in the ground… but this is all we can give him."

"We'll remember him, Charles. Even if the war don't," Billy said through clenched teeth.

Billy lifted the shovel again; a wet sucking squelch echoed as he filled the grave with waterlogged earth. Snow tied two sticks together, drove them into the clay, and placed Chook's helmet on top.

"He should be back on the farm… not lyin' here," Snow muttered. "Bloody waste. Bloody war."

They returned to the trenches. Every day began and ended in the mud. The smell of decay thickened as the weeks dragged on, and with it came more rats. Big ones. Brazen ones. Billy, usually broad and hearty, had begun to thin; meals nothing like the mess hall aboard the Suevic. They now resembled the hollow-eyed men from Hazebrouck: red-rimmed eyes, rotting boots, hands blistered raw. All of it forgotten the moment the next barrage began.

Weeks passed. The sky itself became a weapon, raining shells, gas, and soot at a moment's notice. Now and then an aeroplane droned overhead, scouting Allied positions. The Hun pressed hard to break the line, but the Vickers song held them back. The cost to the 1st Division was steep.

"The first death felt like the world stopped," Charles murmured. "Now it's just another shovelful of dirt."

Billy let out a low whistle. "Another day, another barrage. Jerry's got us on a schedule tighter than the bloody postman."

Snow slumped against the trench wall, eyes deadened. "Don't joke, Bill. We're losin' blokes faster than we can bury 'em."

Billy's grin flickered, then faded.

"Aye... I know. But if I don't laugh, I'll crack wide open. Chook wouldn't want that, would he?"

Charles stared at them both, mud streaking his face. "The war doesn't stop for grief. Not for Chook. Not for anyone. We bury one, and the next day the trench fills again."

"Feels like death's just part of the rations now," Snow muttered.

Billy forced a laugh that didn't quite land. "Well, pass the tin then. Might as well eat while the world ends."

The guns thundered again, steady as dawn. The sound had become background noise. Days blurred until whispers drifted down the line. Something big. Something different. For the first time in months... the mud felt restless.

"Fellas reckon there's a thunderclap comin'. Say the brass are cookin' up somethin' Fritz won't forget," Billy grinned.

"Heard that before. Always just more lads fed into the grinder," Snow said.

"Still... feels different this time. Like the air's holdin' its breath," Charles replied, noticing the shift in mood.

"Chook should've been here for it," Billy sighed. "He'd have wanted to give Fritz a proper hammerin'."

The rumours proved true; confirmed by MacRae the next day. The Allies had gathered their own armada of mechanical beasts near Amiens, and the 1st Division would be fighting beside them. The battalion was finally relieved from Meteren after nearly two months of hell. They hadn't gained even a metre; but they hadn't surrendered one either. The German counteroffensive had been stopped cold.

As the boys left the Flanders mud behind, Charles looked back one last time.

Chook's helmet still sat atop the makeshift cross. Their mate, forever part of that dreadful field.

Chapter 9

Battle of Amiens

The boys were rushed back by train to Amiens on the 8th of August. Rumours rippled through the carriages that the 1st Division had turned up late to the party. In the early morning fog, the Allies had already launched a massive offensive against the Germans. After months of stalemate and burying mates in Flanders, excitement finally stirred through the ranks.

"Here we go, Charlie boy, gonna have Fritz on the ropes this time!" Billy jeered, grinning as cheers echoed around the carriage.

Charles managed a faint smile. "I'm just glad to be out of that hellhole. Nice to see a town again before we're rushed back into another mud pit."

The brakes squealed, jolting the men forward as the train lurched to a halt. The doors creaked open, and the battalion spilled out onto a platform jammed with troops. Amiens rose around them; eerily quiet beneath a heavy blanket of fog.

Snow took it in with a long stare. "Been a tough few months here," he muttered.

The city was barely recognisable. Since they'd last marched through, Amiens had been hammered relentlessly. Facades were blasted open like rotten teeth, rubble choked the streets, and civilians had all but vanished. Yet somehow, the ruins hummed with life.

Soldiers from every corner of the Allied forces crowded the boulevards. Stone buildings had been patched with canvas; khaki tents sprawled across squares and footpaths. Carts, lorries, stretcher-bearers, dispatch riders, and columns of men moved in every direction. Amid the destruction, the cathedral stood defiant; a last monument to what the town had once been.

Billy sniffed theatrically. "Guess I won't be getting any fine French cuisine while we're here. Smells like bully beef stew again."

From behind them, a familiar voice cut through the din.

"Still thinking with your stomach, I see."

A figure pushed forward through the crowd, helmet gleaming white with a bold red cross painted across it. His uniform was pressed and spotless, far too clean for the trenches.

Billy's eyes went wide. "Bloody hell, Frankie Doyle!"

Charles beamed, reaching out. The three clasped hands, the reunion feeling like a piece of home suddenly dropped into the middle of the war.

"You shouldn't be here, Frankie," Charles said.

Frankie gave a tired grin. "Been thinking the same thing. But once I got into medical school at the start of the year, I couldn't dodge the call-up. AIF's been screaming for medics... and I couldn't stop thinking of you two twats stuck out here."

Billy barked a laugh, clapping him on the shoulder. "Ha! Didn't I tell you, Charles? Back at Woody, this bastard swore blind he'd be a doctor one day. Looks like he kept his promise; just picked the worst bloody place on earth to do it!"

"Didn't picture the classroom looking quite like this," Frankie said, eyeing the wreckage.

Snow lingered a step back, taking in the scene. He didn't know Frankie, but he saw the way Charles' face lit up, the way Billy's grin turned genuine for the first time in months. For a moment, the war loosened its grip.

The boys caught up quickly, though Billy and Charles didn't say much about their time on the line. Half of it was a blur, the other half they wished they could forget. Charles especially struggled for words; his emotions had numbed, as lifeless as the men left behind in the mud.

MacRae gathered his platoon on the cobblestones of the main square, his voice rising above the rattle of boots and shifting kit. Word had come down: reinforcements, reorganisation, and fresh orders for the 1st Machine Gun Battalion.

"Listen in, lads. We've taken losses, and we're not going back in half-strength. The brass wants every section sharp before we move again. Couple of changes to square us away."

His gaze fixed on Snow.

"Snow, you've stepped up when it counted. From today, you're a corporal. You'll take charge of your section and keep them squared away. That means discipline. That means steady hands when the lead starts flyin'."

He turned to Charles, giving him a hard stare that softened just a fraction.

"And you, Watson, you've proved you can keep your head under fire. From now on, you're on the trigger. You're gunner, not loader. Don't waste it."

He let the words settle before snapping back into command.

"Replacements are joining us, so make 'em fit quick. We move out soon, and I'll not have green lads dragging us down. While we're in town you may want to check your mail and send a letter home. Dismissed."

A gunner now. No longer Billy's shadow. Charles should have felt proud; he'd survived Flanders, held the line, seen more blood than he'd ever imagined. But instead of triumph, he felt an ache. Back in Salisbury he had wanted nothing more. But after Flanders... things felt different. What he did know was this: now it was his job to keep Fritz out of the fight.

"Come on, Charlie boy, better go collect my fan mail," Billy jeered, already making a beeline for the mail post.

"Wasting your time, I'd say," Frankie cut in with a grin.

Charles hung back, the weight of his new assignment pressing on him. Billy had one letter: from his parents. Snow carried a thick stack from his fiancée, one a week whether he had time to read them or not.

Billy slapped two envelopes into Charles' chest.

"Somehow double the amount of me," he smirked.

The same two names as always.

Home felt impossibly distant, and Charles felt trapped in a bed he'd made for himself.

"Well go on then, let's see that love letter of yours," Frankie teased.

Charles lingered on Edna's letter, running his thumb across the familiar handwriting. Her encouragement had once carried him into this hellhole, but now the thought of opening it twisted something in his chest. He slipped it to the back and tore open his mother's instead.

He scanned the words:

Dearest Charles... The calves are coming on well, though the fences need mending after the winter storms... I keep your room tidy, though it feels empty without you here... Everyone speaks proudly of the ANZACs. People say the end of the war must be near... Do not fret about us at home. We manage, though it is not the same without you... I pray each night for your safety... Your loving Mother.

The affection was there, but it felt far away, distant, muffled, like a voice calling from another world. He folded the letter and slid it back into the envelope, bringing Edna's to the front. After a breath, he cracked the seal.

My dearest Charles,

It lifts my heart to know you are doing your duty, though I wish I could see your face just once more. The papers say our boys are pushing the Germans back, and I cannot help but think it will all be over soon. Hold fast a little longer, and we will be together before the year is out.

I went walking by the river last Sunday and thought of you there in your uniform on that bright day you left. Everyone still speaks proudly of you, and I always tell them you are strong and brave, though I miss you more than words can say. Stay safe, Charles, and remember I think of you every day. Write soon, for your letters are my greatest comfort.

Yours always, Edna.

"She's clueless. 'Pushing the Germans back'? We were in a stalemate for months. 'Be together before the year is out'? It's already August. 'Strong and brave'? I've had my face buried in mud with the Hun firing over my head," Charles scoffed.

Frankie placed a hand on his shoulder. "Fair go, mate. We weren't getting much back home besides what the papers report."

"Bet they don't report on the slosh pit we've been living in," Charles snapped. "Or the lice that never leave. Or limbs getting ripped off. Or Chook's face getting blasted…"

"They're sheltered from it all," Snow cut in gently. "We signed up to keep it that way."

Frankie nodded. "And it's true, mate. You don't want her living the war with you. Since you left, she's been missing you like crazy. Best thing you can do is swallow your pride and give her hope."

"I'll write her back if you want, Charlie boy," Billy smirked. "Pretty sure I can swing a romantic line or two."

Before Charles could retort, MacRae stormed across the cobblestones.

"Moving out in ten minutes! Corporal, get your men ready!"

"You heard him. Finish up and get back to the square," Snow echoed.

"Yes, Corporal," Billy grinned with a half-salute. Snow whacked him on the helmet.

"Get moving, you buffoon."

Charles swallowed everything he'd been about to say and quickly pencilled a letter to Edna; thin on detail, thick on reassurance.

That night the 1st Division was put up in a barn. Excitement mixed with frustration in the air. Billy joked they'd missed the fun, Snow warned the fun was still coming, and Charles lay on a mattress of straw listening to the thunder of guns, heavier than Flanders. Yet somehow the soft itch of straw felt like home. He stared at the stars beaming through a shell hole in the tin roof. For a moment, he felt peace.

The sun rose on the 9th of August to heavy fog. Their task was to relieve the 5th Australian Division and continue the push towards Lihons.

"Say your goodbyes to Amiens! We won't be back till we've won the war!" MacRae bellowed, his voice echoing through the rafters.

The men shouldered their kit. Frankie fussed over straps, checking and rechecking, patting the boys down like a nervous mother.

"Managed to come through alright," he said with a forced grin, tugging Billy's webbing. "Might have to patch you up later if you keep this sloppy."

Billy barked a laugh. "Don't worry, Doc, I'll give you plenty of practice."

Frankie chuckled, but his hands trembled as he tightened Charles' belt buckle.

"Just... don't go catching bullets just to keep me busy, eh?" he murmured, licking dry lips as the rumble of guns drifted through the fog. "Textbooks didn't cover this part."

Snow glanced over. "Less talk, Doyle. Just keep your hands steady when it counts."

Frankie nodded quickly and returned to fussing with straps that didn't need fixing.

The battalion had a lot of ground to make up. Boots thudded along muddy roads in a dull, endless rhythm. Lorries rattled, horses snorted, and mess tins clinked with every shake of the march. After a few kilometres, a deafening metallic roar cut through the fog.

The march slowed to a crawl as the road ahead shook. Out of the grey mist, steel beasts lumbered past in single file; tanks, iron tracks chewing deep ruts into the road.

Engines bellowed. Exhaust belched. The ground trembled beneath them.

Billy let out a whistle. "Bloody hell, Charlie boy, looks like the circus is in town!"

Charles squinted after them, awe colouring his voice. "Never seen so many moving at once. Feels like they're dragging the whole war forward."

Snow sniffed. "They're loud enough to wake the dead. Fritz'll hear them coming long before they arrive."

Frankie gave an uneasy laugh. "Steel coffins, if you ask me. God help the poor sods locked inside when one gets hit." Snow smirked, as if hearing his own echo.

"Ha! Don't be such a funeral dirge," Billy shot back. "Reckon Fritz will leg it as soon as he hears that racket."

Snow shook his head slowly. "Don't count on it. They break down half the time. In the end, it's still us poor bastards bleeding in the mud."

The tanks rumbled away, swallowed by fog and smoke, leaving the infantry to tramp behind them.

After a day of marching through wrecked villages, abandoned trenches, traffic jams, and waterlogged roads, the battalion finally reached their assembly point on the outskirts of Lihons. Artillery boomed in the distance as the boys dropped their heavy gear onto a dry patch of field.

"My boots are crying for mercy. If this war doesn't end soon, I'll be marching barefoot," Billy groaned.

"Never thought stopping could hurt worse than moving," Charles muttered.

"Thought war would have toughened you two up," Frankie jabbed.

"In many ways, but not all. Keep the fluids up, lads," Snow smirked, raising his canteen.

The landscape was open farmland turned battlefield: smashed wheat, dusty tracks, shell holes, and a peaceful-looking town in the distance.

"So that's Lihons? Marched us all this way for a handful of rooftops," Billy jeered.

"Looks quiet... too quiet," Charles replied.

Snow scanned the horizon. "Don't trust the silence. Fritz is up there watching."

"Hope they left a pub open," Billy sighed.

"First round's on you," Frankie grinned.

"Focus. No trenches here. We're exposed," Snow warned.

"Should we dig in?" Charles asked.

"No time. We push to Lihons. Dig in after the next advance," Snow said.

MacRae barrelled in, full of fire that the march hadn't dulled.

"Let's get moving, men! Into the plain, we storm the hill at dawn!"

Charles gathered what strength he had left, hauled his kit up, and trudged into the open field, the ridge looming as a dark shape against the fading light.

Early hours of the 10th of August.

The battalion was already awake, gear rattling as they prepared to move.

"All right, men, small groups, stay low. Once you reach the forward line, find a spot to set up," Snow whispered.

Charles' new loader, Anderson, was sweating. The ammo boxes shook in his hands. He wasn't the only replacement fumbling; half the battalion had never seen a shot fired in anger.

Charles went over, tightened his straps, and steadied his boxes.

"You'll be alright, Anderson. Stay low and keep moving."

They set out, hunched low, boots whispering through the grass. Each step cranked the tension tighter. Charles led, hauling the Vickers, Anderson breathing down his neck. When they reached the forward position, Charles scanned the ground.

"That shell hole looks good, will give us some cover when the rounds start raining in," Charles said, signalling to the crater carved into the open field.

"Okay, Charles... whatever you say," Anderson panted, breath hitching with nerves.

Charles dropped the Vickers with a heavy thud, dust spitting up around them. He drove the tripod legs into the hard chalk until they bit. With a solid metallic snap, the gun locked into place. Dropping behind the butt, he swung the barrel left and right, testing the traverse, lining up the faint horizon through one narrowed eye.

Behind him, Anderson lingered awkwardly, dust clogging his throat, eyes watering as he fumbled with an ammo box.

"Come on, Anderson, let's get this gun ready," Charles said, nodding at the belt box.

Anderson's fumbling echoed Charles' first day in Flanders. Charles reached out, steadying him with a hand on his shoulder.

"You're alright, mate. Just breathe. Remember your training."

As the sun climbed, the German positions took shape; machine gun nests, shallow trenches, Feldgrau helmets piercing the skyline. Before Charles could zero the sights, the whistling of shells sliced overhead. Anderson clamped his hands over his ears as artillery crashed down on the German line. The ground trembled beneath them, dust and acrid smoke rolling low across the field.

That was the signal.

The machine gun battalion unleashed hell.

Charles wasn't accustomed to being the man on the trigger, but he didn't hesitate. The Vickers erupted into its steady, brutal hammering, spewing suppressive fire onto the German

MG08s. The air filled with the stink of burning metal, hot oil, sweat, and cordite.

Their orders were simple; pin them down while the Division storms the field.

Charles had imagined this moment for years; pulling the trigger, playing an active role; but now he felt nothing. Numb. Hollow. The recoil hammered through him, shaking bone and muscle with every burst.

The field lit up from both sides, but his finger stayed firm.

The hammering of the Vickers became a relentless song, drowning everything else. His world narrowed into a tunnel, just the front sight and the enemy trench. He stopped seeing soldiers, only shapes. Targets. Helmets toppled, bodies crumpled, but none of it registered. He swept the barrel across the parapet, stitching death in a methodical line.

Anderson blurred into the background, doing enough to keep the gun fed. The barrel began smoking. The belt rattled. Brass clinked and piled.

A few mounted Germans appeared behind their line; horses snorting, riders shouting. Something in Charles seized. Horses had once been mates, not enemies. He jerked the barrel aside, trying to spare them, but a few wild rounds struck. He heard the guttural cries of the animals as their riders toppled.

Still, the gun hammered on.

The suppressive fire maintained the Allied advantage until whistles shrieked across the field. The storm of infantry surged past. A thousand boots drummed the earth, rifles clattered, voices roared as they rushed the shattered German line.

The air grew thick with cordite, hot oil, and the sour stench of torn flesh. Charles saw men falling, stumbling, crawling through open field and bodies; but his perception had shrunk. Ricochets sparked off the shield, sharper each time.

Then something wet struck Charles' cheek.

He looked right.

Anderson was folded over, hands clawing at his chest, screaming.

"Medic!" Charles roared, voice cracking in the chaos.

Frankie scrambled through the dust, kit slung over his shoulder, the red cross stark on his helmet. He dropped beside Anderson, cutting open the tunic, hands working fast; too fast for how terrified his eyes looked.

"Chest wound; bad. We can't hold him here."

Snow fired his Lewis in a steady rhythm nearby, covering the position. He crouched low, face twisted in a grimace.

"Get him out, Frankie!"

Frankie hooked an arm under Anderson and dragged him upright. Anderson wailed, thrashing weakly. Frankie's jaw clenched as he hauled him toward the rear, bullets snapping overhead.

"Hold the line!" he shouted back. "I'll get him clear!"

Charles pressed his face to the sights again. The Vickers resumed its brutal rhythm. Anderson's screams faded behind him.

Snow dropped into the shell hole, slotting into place like he'd always belonged there.

"I'll keep you loaded. You keep your eyes front."

Charles continued firing, the barrel sweeping over a sea of khaki and blood. Smoke rolled thick across the fields, the stench of powder and flesh hanging heavy. Men pushed forward through torn wheat and broken bodies, their shouts swallowed by the storm of guns.

The line surged. The 1st Division poured through the breaches, bayonets catching the light as German fire faltered. The trenches were taken in violent bursts of mud and steel. Germans scattered, some fleeing into the town, others falling where they stood.

Charles lifted his finger. Reality slammed back in.

He stared at the bloodshed, eyes wide. His hands shook uncontrollably. His stomach twisted. He lurched left and vomited.

"No shame in it, Charles," Snow said softly, placing a hand on his back. "If you didn't feel sick, you'd be a monster."

Lihons loomed through the smoke, the broken roofs, the battered church spire. By afternoon the Australians were inside the town. Rifles cracked in narrow streets. The last machine gun nests fell silent.

The ridge was theirs; at a cost written across the fields.

The survivors gathered in front of the red-brick church, its stained-glass window glinting faintly through the soot.

Billy wiped sweat from his brow. "Fair dinkum... what a fight. Never seen so many bullets flyin'."

"I've never seen so much blood," Charles whispered.

"You did well," Snow said.

"Taught him everything he knows, I did," Billy added with a weak grin.

Frankie dropped beside them; kit soaked in blood and mud. "So that's what it's really like?"

"Pretty much," Snow said. "Though we're not used to going forward and taking a town. Price of that's high."

"How's Anderson?" Charles asked.

"He was in a bad way when I left him. They're taking him back to Amiens," Frankie said.

"Poor sod didn't last an hour," Billy muttered.

"Luck of the draw," Snow said quietly.

"Surprised they missed you, Billy, target the size of a tank," Frankie smirked.

The men laughed weakly, the sound hollow in the ruined square.

MacRae strode up, face grim, eyes proud.

"You did well today, lads. Damn well. The ridge is ours thanks to you. Now get your shovels. Dig in and hold it. You've earned this ground, and we're keeping it."

Chapter 10

The Long Advance

The boys had been dug in at Lihons for two days, the Germans launching multiple counter-offensives to try and claw back the tiny village. The fighting was intense; the stink of death clung to the air, thickened by the August heat. But the line held firm, securing the high ground and forcing the Germans to keep retreating. With the position secured, the Allies looked to continue the advance.

Snow had just returned from a briefing. He slid down into the shallow trench, dust rising before his boots settled into the mud.

"Alright, boys. Word is the brass reckon we've softened them enough. Lihons was only a small prize, now they want us pushing toward Chuignes, right up by the Somme," he announced.

"Chuignes? Never heard of it. Must be bloody special if we're meant to die for it," Billy chuffed.

"It's a rearguard strongpoint," Snow replied. "Likely where half the artillery that's been giving us hell is sitting."

"Lot of open fields between here and the river," Charles added. "If they're dug in, it won't be easy."

"Then we'd best keep moving. Can't let the infantry have all the bragging rights," Frankie chuckled.

"You're both right," Snow said. "Long march, plenty of Fritz waiting. Keep sharp, we'll need every man steady."

"You got it, Corps," Billy grinned, already unclipping the Vickers from its tripod.

The battalion pushed east, the ground churned by days of shellfire. Dead men and horses lay bloating in the sun, flies thick over the carcasses, the stink of rot hanging over the march.

"Poor sods," Charles muttered. "None of those beasts signed up for this. Just slaves to the Hun."

They trudged past shallow trenches and scraped firing pits dug by the retreating Germans. Progress was slow, but eventually the land began to breathe again. Shell holes thinned; stubbled fields rolled out ahead as if the war had only just begun to gnaw at them.

Every village, though, was a ruin; houses smashed, roofs collapsed, windows blasted open, their glass long gone . The heat was punishing; the smell of sweat settled over the battalion as they slogged through open ground.

"Keep your wits about you," Snow warned. "Never know if an obstacle hides a rabbit or a machine gun."

"Well, if there is a rabbit, I claim it. I'm getting over these lack-of-ration days," Billy smirked.

"Mate, I'd take army rations over your cooking any day," Frankie jabbed.

Just as the words left his mouth, cracks of rifle fire snapped across the field.

"Medic!" came the cry from further up the line as the battalion dropped flat into the dirt.

Charles lifted his head just enough to spot muzzle flashes in a distant hedgerow.

Then came the hammering of a German machine gun. Rounds sliced across the field, whistling through wheat stalks, catching the battalion by surprise.

Snow sprang into action, firing back in controlled bursts.

"Need those Vickers up! The rest of you, covering fire!" he shouted.

Frankie was already sprinting; sixty metres across open wheat as bullets chopped the stalks around him. The screams ahead had drawn him like a magnet.

Charles froze, watching Frankie's reckless dash; until Billy smacked him as he ran past.

"Let's get in that shell hole, Charlie boy!"

They kept low, pushing through the wheat before dropping into a crater. The two Vickers teams soon clicked into position and opened up, unleashing hell into the hedgerow. Branches, leaves, splinters; and blood; burst into the air as the muzzle flashes went out one by one.

The Hun and the hedge were obliterated, though the battalion had still taken casualties.

"Think they could take us on with only a dozen men?" Billy muttered, staring at the corpses.

"They weren't trying to beat us," Snow said. "Just slow us down. Every minute we stop, Fritz digs in tighter ahead."

"Guess that's why we've gotta keep pushing," Charles nodded. "Don't give 'em the time."

"That's the plan," Snow replied, just as Frankie staggered back, tunic streaked with blood, chest heaving.

He wiped sweat from his brow. "They got another couple. Boys'll be okay, but they won't be marching on with us."

The silence didn't last. Small detachments kept harassing them as they pushed forward. After months of trench warfare, the open-field skirmishes took them off-guard; exposure made everything feel dangerous.

"Bastards can jump out from anywhere," Billy panted as they neared another tiny town; little more than a battered church spire and a few broken buildings.

"We'll be on top of it soon," Snow said. "Let the riflemen lead. If we need the big guns, we'll bring them up."

MacRae stomped over, dust puffing at each step. "Something to be concerned about, Snow?"

"Town's close. Want to keep the Vickers back, safer that way."

MacRae nodded curtly. "Expecting trouble?"

"Always."

"Good. That's how you stay alive. Carry on."

Billy smirked at Charles, shifting the Vickers off his shoulder. "See that? Old Snow's calling the shots now."

The battalion moved in staggered columns, riflemen on point. The ground began to rise toward the ruined town. Charles slowed, scanning the hedges and broken walls.

Then, a sudden crack of light from the church spire.

The lead rifleman dropped, blood oozing from the base of his helmet.

"Sniper! Take cover!" MacRae bellowed.

Snow slammed his fist into the dirt. "Dammit! Our rifles won't reach him. We need to push up and get a Vickers on that tower."

"How about artillery?" Charles asked.

"Too slow. And they'll level the whole church for one man."

Snow turned to Charles, eyes hard. "Right, drop your gun. I want my best two men pushing up. You and Billy will get a Vickers on that tower. We'll draw his fire from back here."

Billy grinned. "Best two men, hear that, Charlie boy?"

Charles shoved him. "No time, Billy. Move."

The church spire loomed over the ruined town, its shadow stretched thin across gutted rooftops. The place was deathly still. Every man hugged cover, certain the sniper's glass was sweeping for the slightest twitch.

Snow gave the signal.

The rear Vickers opened up, chattering short bursts, bait for the Fritz marksman.

Billy and Charles sprinted low, zigzagging through broken fences and collapsed walls. Dust and shards of brick showered around them.

Charles pressed himself against a wall, breath ragged. His hand brushed his breast pocket; Edna's letter still tucked inside. He cursed her for urging him on, yet needed her more than ever.

Billy nudged him. "Don't stop now, Charlie boy. We're not dead yet."

They pushed on, praying the sniper hadn't seen the movement.

Sliding in behind a jagged wall just below the spire, Charles dropped to his knees, unhooking the tripod and slamming it into the dirt. Billy fed the belt through with quick, tense movements.

"Come on... come on..."

The Vickers locked into place. Charles pressed his cheek to the iron sight.

Through the shimmer and smoke, he spotted the glint of a scope high on the spire.

"Got him," he hissed.

The Vickers roared, recoil shuddering through him. Stone exploded from the tower, half the spire collapsing in a cloud of dust and slate. The sniper never moved again.

Billy whooped. "That'll learn 'em! Knocked him straight outta his bloody pulpit!"

But Charles didn't cheer. His chest heaved, acrid smoke curling into his nostrils. His hand brushed his breast pocket again, feeling Edna's letter through the sweat-soaked fabric. Because of her, he'd spilt more blood than he ever thought he could; but the hope of getting back to her kept his finger on the trigger.

The push toward Chuignes tested Charles in ways the mud of Flanders never had. The German rearguard made them fight for every mile; snipers, machine gun, the sudden thump of scattered bombardments.

It was less terror now than a grinding frustration, casualties mounting with each day. By the time Chuignes finally came into sight, Charles no longer felt like a boy playing at war; he was a soldier, worn thin, but every bit as committed to seeing it through.

The battalion were nestled in a tree line southeast of the village, crouching low amid the smell of sap bleeding from torn branches and damp earth under their kit. Distant artillery rumbled as murmurs threaded through the ranks.

Charles lay prone, Vickers tripod splayed in front of him as he sighted through gaps in the branches. Beyond the trees, between them and the smoking roofs of Chuignes, lay stubbled wheat fields, wrecked fences, and battered farm buildings.

The Hun had amassed the largest armament they'd seen since Lihons. Machine gun nests jutted from hedgerows and shallow pits, their arcs overlapping every approach. Streets were barricaded with carts and rubble; smashed walls turned into kill zones, the church spire half-ruined but still looming over the battlefield.

The civilians were long gone. Only khaki and feldgrau shapes remained, darting between the ruins.

Billy dropped his Vickers down beside Charles' position with a grunt.

"Bastard's heavier than my sins. Hope we don't have to drag her far," he panted, adjusting the gun.

"Your sins wouldn't reach this far, Billy," Frankie jabbed, checking his kit.

"Cut the chatter. Soon as the rifles go, we open up. Keep the bastards' heads down," Snow cut in.

Then came the stampede from the east. The 1st Division's riflemen stormed up across the open ground, boots drumming through the field. The Fritz MG08s answered from their nests, hammering the advance.

"Suppressive fire! Keep the Hun in their holes!" MacRae bellowed, his voice echoing through the trunks.

The Vickers awoke, tat-tat-tat ringing in their ears. The Hun returned the favour, bullets whining through branches, snapping twigs overhead.

Snow shouted arcs over the din. "Left hedge! Centre street! Keep it moving!"

The rapid calls were hard for Charles to keep up with.

"Steady arc, Charles. Don't jam her!" he barked.

Charles braced hard against the butt, finger white on the trigger, traversing left to right.

Billy was in his element. "That's it, girl! Sing 'em into the dirt!"

The sharp tang of cordite thickened as bursts cracked through the trees. The 1st Division were making ground now, storming up the main road into town, their ranks thinning as casualties mounted.

"Looks like I'm up, boys! Give 'em hell!" Frankie yelled, leaping from the tree line and running straight into the action.

"Bloody hell... I feel like the war's made him lose all sense, running across there," Billy said, stunned.

"Men like him are the ones who save lives," Snow nodded.

Frankie had mastered the zigzag in his first weeks of battle; there wasn't a man in need he couldn't get to. The Vickers kept singing. The riflemen had now pushed into the town and were on top of the Hun. The tide turned as feldgrau began streaking back out of Chuignes, faint German shouts echoing across the fields as they bolted for cover.

"Gunners, sweep the rear!" MacRae commanded.

"Let's not waste it. Reposition and cut 'em off from the woodline!" Snow yelled.

Charles and Billy broke down their Vickers, brushing leaves from the belt. Charles scanned the ground ahead.

"Let's move it, Billy. Lug the bastard to that farmhouse," he said, grabbing the gun by the tripod while his loader hefted the water jacket.

Under covering fire, half the platoon pushed out to the right. The barrel was already smoking, the water jacket boiling over. The sharp stink of cordite rode over the deeper reek of rot as they pushed forward.

Charles reached the farmhouse first, Billy lagging behind. The place was mostly ruin apart from the remnants of a kitchen. He dragged a wooden dining table to the window and slammed the tripod down on top, his hands red and raw.

The Vickers still hissed as it threatened to overheat. Through the broken pane, Charles spotted a German crew in the distance, struggling to haul back a field gun as the rest of the Fritz fled.

Without hesitation, Charles swept bursts across them. After a few sprays and splatters across the gun and its team, the survivors broke and scattered under the fire.

Billy finally stumbled in, breathing hard as he slapped Charles on the shoulder.

"Keep runnin', Fritz, Charlie boy's got your number!"

The Hun were in full retreat now. With no organised resistance left, the Aussies burst through the town. The fight turned into target practice for Billy and Charles, like plinking tin cans back on the farm.

Billy grinned. "Bloody hell, it's like shooting ducks on a pond!"

Snow burst through the back door with the rest of the platoon.

"Keep it steady. Don't waste rounds just because they're running scared," he snapped.

The town roared as the infantry surged in. Grenades boomed in windows, rifles cracked in alleys, timbers splintered under the blasts. Then, as quickly as it had begun, the firing ebbed away.

Chuignes lay broken at their feet.

On the outskirts, the battalion slumped into the dirt. Their bodies ached; uniforms blackened with sweat and grime. Compared to some, they'd come through lightly, though it hardly felt that way.

"Fair dinkum fight today. You held firm. Now dig in, if Jerry wants it back, we'll give him another hiding," MacRae barked, pride buried beneath his usual growl.

Billy nudged Charles with an elbow. "If he don't make us dig, he doesn't know what to do with us."

The adrenaline bled away, leaving only the weight of ten days' marching and fighting. Charles hefted his shovel, arms trembling, sweat stinging his eyes as he tried to bite the blade into the dirt.

Frankie stumbled in, kit streaked with grime and blood, the metallic stink clinging to him. He dropped into the churned trench beside them, shoulders slumped.

"What a blood bath," he muttered, head bowed.

"How'd the infantry fare?" Snow asked quietly.

"Heavy casualties," Frankie said. "Might be called a victory, but the cost..."

Billy let out a long breath, reaching for humour but sounding hollow. "Reckon we'll be seeing that mess in our sleep tonight."

Charles leaned on the shovel until the colour drained from his face. Frankie eased it from his grip and sat him down.

"You alright, Charles?" he asked, crouching beside him.

"Just... exhausted. Light-headed," Charles panted, chest rising and falling too fast.

Frankie pressed a hand to his forehead. "You're burning up. Here, get some water into you." He shoved a canteen into Charles' hands, scanning him with a medic's eye.

"These conditions'll wreck you quick. Keep drinking, keep warm, get food in when you can."

Billy cut in with a smirk. "Food? Bloody sign me up. Haven't had a decent feed since England."

Snow chuckled as he dug. "With that enthusiasm, you can finish Charles' hole."

"Well, someone has to. Charlie boy looks ready to nap in it," Billy shot back.

The boys kept at the earth, carving their nests for the night. Vickers were mounted, arcs set, ready if the Hun wanted another dance.

That night, the trench gave no rest. Charles lay curled in the shallow scrape, every joint aching, skin clammy though he shivered under the blanket. A dull hammering throb pulsed behind his eyes, making even the stars blur.

When he forced his eyes to focus, the heavens were startlingly bright; thousands of pinpricks hanging over the churned fields.

For a moment he could almost imagine himself back on the farm, lying under the southern sky with Edna's laugh in his ears. Sleep came in fragments, broken by shivers and distant guns, until he was jolted awake by Billy stamping and hollering at the edge of the pit.

"Charlie boy! Wake up, you won't believe it! Word is the boys bagged some giant Fritz gun, biggest bloody cannon you've ever seen!"

Billy grinned, panting with excitement. "They say it's so big it could shell half of France. And now it's ours! We gotta go see it!"

Charles, half-dazed and wiping drool from his chin, blinked up at him. "What are you on about, Billy?"

"A big bloody gun, size of a train!" Billy chuffed, eyes wide.

Charles turned to Snow. "Corps, we good to go see it?" He couldn't deny a flicker of excitement of his own.

Snow weighed it a moment, then nodded. "Alright, but only a small detachment. We still need eyes on the line."

The four stepped out of the trench as the dawn haze lifted. Smoke still drifted from the ruins of yesterday's battle. Boots crunched in the churned dirt. Engineers hammered and shouted as they cleared booby traps and secured the town.

They followed the rail spur east of Chuignes.

Billy was still grinning. "Wouldn't miss this for the world. Bigger than a bloody pub, they say."

"Rumours grow larger than guns, Billy," Frankie muttered, rolling his eyes.

Along the railway line, the aroma of scorched oil and singed timber was thick. Flies swarmed around the bodies of horses and men. They passed abandoned German positions and shattered trees. Charles lagged, vision hazy, every ache tugging at him.

"Don't wander. Fritz could've left traps," Snow cautioned.

Charles looked up and nodded. "I'm alright, Snow. Just didn't sleep right."

Billy smirked. "Didn't sleep right? You were snorin' like a brass band, Charlie boy. Kept half the trench awake."

Frankie frowned, studying him. "Snoring's the least of it. You're running yourself ragged, you look pale as death. Maybe you should head back."

"Not now, Frankie. Sounds like we're here," Billy lit up.

Laughter and swearing grew louder as they came through a stand of trees, boots clattering on metal carried on the air. The boys rounded a bend, and there it was.

"Bloody hell, Charlie boy, they weren't kidding. Big enough to knock the moon out of the sky," Billy breathed.

"Doesn't matter how big it is now," Snow said with a crooked smirk. "It's ours. That's one less hammer Jerry can swing."

The gun sprawled along the railway like a beast slain in battle. Its barrel clawed high into the sky, absurdly long, now pointing at nothing but clouds. The carriage beneath was immense, as big as the rumours. Steel wheels taller than a man, plates riveted like a factory wall. The closer they got, the harder it was to believe men had ever moved it at all.

Dozens of diggers from the 1st Division swarmed over it. Men clambered up ladders and rungs, crawling along the barrel, some carving their names into its skin. A slouch hat dangled from the muzzle, drawing jeers and roars of laughter. Others grouped below, shaking their heads as they talked about how it had shelled Amiens from miles away.

The whole place crackled with energy: relief, pride, disbelief.

Charles hung back a few paces, catching his breath, watching. The noise of his mates blurred into a distant hum as he tilted his head back. The gun was enormous, but silent now. Neutered. Just iron and rivets.

His fingers brushed the letter in his pocket. For the first time, the thought of home didn't sting; it steadied him.

This wasn't just another captured trench or ruined village. This felt larger. Like history itself had shifted.

A turning point.

Chapter 11

The Price of War

The Somme valley was burning again. For weeks the Germans had been giving ground, but never without blood, and now the Australian commander, General Monash, had set his sights on Mont St Quentin; a steep rise looming over Péronne, the key to the river crossings and the retreat beyond.

The men of the 1st Division trudged east from Chuignes on the 26th of August, worn to shadows of themselves after a month of advancing and fighting. Dust clung to their sweat-soaked faces, boots scuffed on broken roads lined with smashed wagons and bloated carcasses, and the dull thunder of artillery rolled across the valley without pause. Every farmhouse was rubble; every hedge scarred with wire.

The wide, marshy Somme River was another challenge, zigzagging through the countryside and forcing the Aussies into its swampy ground. Half the bridges, broken by shelling to slow the Hun's retreat, now caused chaos for the advance.

Sergeant MacRae's voice cut through the trudge, gravelled but urgent.

"Keep your heads up, lads. This isn't just another push. Monash says if we take this hill, Jerry's finished. History's turning here, you'll want to be part of it."

Their target at Mont St Quentin would push the Fritz squarely onto the other side of the river. Charles, coughing into his sleeve, barely lifted his gaze. His head throbbed with fever, each breath a weight, his appetite fading, but he clung to his place in the line.

Beside him, Frankie marched steady, eyes scanning the men, checking their pace like he always did.

"Don't burn yourself out, mate," Frankie said low, so only Charles heard. "You're burning hot as it is. Just get through this one, that's all you have to do."

Charles gave a faint nod, but the words stuck in his chest like ash. The hill waited ahead, and with it, another storm.

The resistance stiffened as they got closer, a mix of fatigue and frustration. Hours of slogging were punctuated by bursts of chaos when an MG08 nest opened up. The road east was no victory parade. Rearguard machine guns and stray shells bled the column mile by mile. The heat, the stink, and days of fighting bent every back.

By the time Mont St Quentin rose from the mist, the men looked more like silhouettes than soldiers.

The ragged 1st Division connected existing shell holes with shallow trenches on the outskirts, tasked with covering the flanks while other divisions stormed the low but dominating hill. Its position overlooking the Somme valley gave the Germans a commanding view. The slopes were riddled with barbed wire and trenches, split by machine gun posts covering all approaches.

Charles hadn't seen such a fortress before, the same gut punch he'd felt taking his first steps into Flanders. Smoke hung low in the valley after days of Allied shelling. The barrage still whistled overhead; the falling shells crashed everywhere yet seemed useless against the dug-in Germans, making their objective even more imposing.

The attack was set for dawn. After another night fighting fever, Charles woke to more artillery as the light crept in through smoke and dust. MacRae stood behind the trenches, voice carrying over the shellfire.

"Those posts up there look ugly, aye, but they'll break just the same as they did at Lihons. Keep your heads down, work the guns, and we'll give the infantry the gap they need."

Billy muttered through a grin, "Well, if it's the turning point, Charlie boy, maybe we'll be home by Christmas... again."

Charles briefly looked up and gave a small smirk.

Snow chimed in, "Don't start counting chickens, Billy. Just keep your belt steady and your head lower."

Frankie leaned toward Charles. "Don't push it too hard, work the gun and leave the rest to us," he said quietly.

MacRae's bark snapped them back to the line.

"Right then. Rifles forward, guns in position. When the barrage lifts, I want the Vickers spitting before the smoke clears. Make Jerry know the 1st Division's watching him!"

The artillery intensified, smashing the roofs of the town, the smell of acrid cordite sweeping down the ridge. War cries and rifle cracks rose in the distance as soldiers from the 2nd Division leapt from their dugouts and swarmed.

"Let 'em have it, boys!" Snow shouted as he opened up with his own rifle.

The Vickers put the hammer down. Charles's eyes were stinging, his vision blurred, but he forced the trigger down, tracing bursts across the German lines. A bloodbath emerged in front of him. The method of advance was more hope than strategy; the Allies trying to overwhelm the Hun, leaning on the Vickers to keep the Fritz in their holes.

Billy glanced over. "Keep your head straight, Charlie boy. She don't need fancy aimin', just keep singin'."

Charles' breath came ragged as sweat dripped down his face. The deafening noise of war and suffering all around barely registered.

Then came another sound, distant but distinct, the grinding rattle of gears, the cough of exhaust. Tanks. Their hulks strained forward through the smoke, tracks clattering as they tried to climb the battered slope.

Billy smirked bitterly. "Hear that? Sounds like Fritz won't need to aim; those things rattle louder than a bloody marching band."

Snow shook his head; eyes fixed on the shapes in the haze. "Won't matter. Ground's too torn up. They'll bog down before they get near the wire."

Sure enough, one lurched sideways into a crater. Shellfire walked its way in until the iron beast shuddered still, smoke curling from its plates. Stuck like pigs in mud at the base of the hill, they could do nothing to change the nightmare unfolding above them.

Frankie muttered, voice tight, "Steel coffins, the lot of them. Poor sods inside never stood a chance."

Then another voice cut through; a wounded infantryman crying out between the lines, rolling in the dirt of no man's land as his blood seeped into the ground.

The Hun on their high ground were decimating the advance. Frankie froze, eyes wide as he saw the man, jaw setting. Without a word, he leapt from cover.

"Christ, Frankie..." Snow grimaced under his breath.

"Frankie, you bloody hero, get back here!" Billy yelled.

"Don't..." Charles muttered through his sights, half delirious.

Their voices were swallowed by the hammer of the guns. Frankie sprinted side to side across stubble and broken earth, kit bouncing, like a horse at a gallop. MG08 bursts ripped across the field, scything through as their spray flicked up dust around him.

Then one burst tore him down, just short of the man he was trying to reach. His body slumped, still.

Silence fell among the platoon. Billy's humour vanished; his face went hollow.

Charles kept firing, in denial of what he'd just seen. His colour drained, fever clawing at him, stomach heaving until he vomited bile beside the gun. He stared at his shaking hands.

"Man down. Nothing we can do for him now. Keep the line tight," MacRae cut in, hard as flint.

The rhythm of the Vickers started again, its familiar hammer masking the pounding in Charles' chest. His vision seemed to sharpen through the fever haze, not from clarity, but from rage. Frankie's fall burned in his mind, driving him into the trigger.

He squeezed. The gun bucked as he raked the line. The faint cries out in the field vanished under the roar, the world narrowing to targets in his sights. He wasn't fighting for the ridge anymore, or for Monash's grand plans; it was for Frankie, and the fury that he'd never walk back with them.

The Hun were trapped in their holes, dirt and splinters erupting around them as the suppressive fire finally pinned them down. The tide started to sway as the 2nd Division lifted their ferocity. Outnumbered, the Aussies kept charging through wire and trenches. A blanket of khaki engulfed the hill; they dropped into enemy trenches and took the fight into the Germans' own dugouts, catching them off guard.

The line buckled, bayonets flashing as men wrestled and fell in the smoke. Charles fired until the belt clattered empty, his ears ringing with the roar of rifles and the raw cries of men locked chest-to-chest.

And then; it shifted. The Germans began to slip back, one hole, then another, men abandoning their guns and scrambling for the riverbank.

Snow shouted over the din, "They're breaking! Keep the pressure on!"

Through the chaos, Charles saw it too; grey figures scattering, some with hands up, others running for the water's edge. Weeks of retreat had bled the fight out of them.

The offensive moved forward as the Aussies took over the town. The shattered morale of the Hun saw them forced across the river. Aussie engineers got to work securing the crossings as the 2nd Division formed a new line overlooking the Somme.

As the smoke cleared and silence settled, the men could circle back across the blood-ridden field, the smell of cordite and churned earth hanging thick.

Charles stared at the dirt, head spinning as he tried to catch his breath. Flashes of the burst tearing through Frankie's body taunted him; the blood spatter spraying out the back, a quick, clean kill by the Fritz.

"We... gotta... find him," he mumbled between pants.

Charles' legs buckled as he tried to drag the Vickers up, the fever twisting in his chest. Billy's arm slid under his, steadying him.

"Easy, Charlie boy. We'll find him. Frankie's not stayin' out here in this muck," he said softly, voice cracking just a little.

Charles blinked hard, his vision swimming, but he nodded. The two of them, with Snow close behind, moved across the torn ground until they came upon Frankie's body.

The noise of battle had drifted, replaced by the distant crack of rifles and the hum of flies. Frankie lay where he'd fallen, face half in the dirt, blood already drying into his tunic.

They knelt beside him. No one spoke at first; the war, for a moment, felt impossibly far away. Billy brushed mud from Frankie's shoulder, lips tight. Snow rested a hand on the lad's chest, bowing his head.

When they buried him, the three men stood together, watching the dirt settle. The Somme River shimmered beyond, the ruins of Mont St Quentin burning on the ridge. Smoke smudged the sky, but the silence was deeper than any barrage. Billy muttered, almost to himself,

"Bloody hell, Frankie... couldn't keep yourself safe, but you'd run for anyone else."

Charles swayed, shivers gnawing at him, but he stared at the firelight across the river. For the first time since Amiens, he felt the war turning; but it didn't feel like triumph. It felt like loss.

He looked at the fresh earth, bile rising with the fever. He'd manned the gun, he'd held the line, but he hadn't saved Frankie. No bullet haunted him as much as that truth.

After the burial, the men climbed to their new post on the other side of the hill, dirt under their nails and Frankie's face fresh in their minds. While the rest of the Divisions moved like clockwork; engineers setting charges, axes chopping wood, hammers pounding stakes; Charles watched through a haze. Across the Somme, tomorrow's target, Péronne, smouldered. The smoke looking like a funeral pyre, the faint stink of shallow graves drifting up the slope.

"Feels wrong... ground's not even settled over him, and they've already moved on," he murmured.

A crack in the dirt made him look up. MacRae crouched beside him, in earshot as he inspected the new line. He placed a hand on Charles's shoulder.

"I know what he meant to you. But look across that river, that's why we're here. We finish this for him."

Charles nodded, but deep down he'd lost all sense of why he was here. Adventure... what a lie. His father's words rang louder now; this war wasn't theirs. Blood spilled for a crown he'd never see. His will to push forward was deteriorating like his appetite.

That night brought flashes of fire across the river, reflections flickering off the water. Charles tucked into his kit and leaned into Billy's side. His body shivered, swinging between sweats and chills.

"You're alright, Charlie boy," Billy whispered whenever Charles jolted awake.

The night seemed endless. Charles placed a hand over his chest pocket, clinging to any comfort of home. Wishing he could escape; back to Woodstock and Edna, or even the orphanage at this point.

Daylight came, Charles barely registered it, as a sea of activity swelled around him. Men lugged crates of ammo, guns, water tins, and rations like ants to the forward positions. Snow slid into the shallow dugout, kicking up a dust cloud.

"One more day in this war is one more day he carried us. Don't forget that."

"Guess we got another fight with the Fritz on our hands?" Billy asked.

"Yep. Another push. We'll be keeping their heads down while the lads take the streets," Snow replied.

A flurry of noise and energy engulfed them; shovels scraping earth as trenches were deepened, artillery booming behind them.

MacRae added to the fury.

"Shift it, men! Mont's not ours till we've broken their backs in Péronne. This is Monash's hammer blow; don't you dare falter now!"

Charles, heavy-eyed, staggered to his feet as the 1st Division shifted positions across the river. He struggled to keep pace, coughing into his sleeve, drenched in sweat as the thump of gear smacked against his webbing. The clatter of boots on duckboards rang in his ears. His shoulders sagged until Billy nudged him along.

"Come on, Charlie boy, nearly there. Just point that Vickers where they tell us and the war'll be done."

They reached their forward position and collapsed into a shell hole. Snow handed Charles a canteen while he smacked his Vickers together.

"Don't think on it, just keep the hammer down," he said, slotting the belt into place.

The assault had already begun. The 2nd and 5th Divisions stormed the streets of the smoking town. Rounds flew through clouds of dust and smoke, lighting up like lightning.

MacRae roared over the chaos,

"Suppressive Fire!"

Charles gripped the handles. Sweat beaded, fever surging, he squeezed. The vibration shook through every bone, the recoil punishing his already aching muscles. Shell casings spun around his head as his vision tunnelled and adrenaline took over.

The battle swallowed the whole town. Hun fired from every crevice. Every doorway spat bullets. Every street was a killing ground. Charles drifted into another dimension. Training and instinct took over. Sound warped; too loud, then muffled. Time blurred. He didn't know how many belts he fired. He wasn't fighting the Hun; he was fighting his own failing body.

The fight raged past midnight into the 2nd of September. The Australians gained ground steadily; the Germans' will cracked. Charles didn't know any of it. All he knew was the ache, the heat, the rattling breath. He fought to keep his hands on the grips, but the strength bled away.

The Vickers sung until he couldn't.

"Charles! Hold it steady!" Snow yelled.

"He's burning up! Frankie was right, he's crook!" Billy shouted.

Charles's chest rattled, breath scraping. His arms refused to lift the gun. He coughed red into his sleeve, vision swimming. Then the weight of his body pulled him sideways. He collapsed beside the Vickers, the gun smoking in the dirt.

"Stretcher-bearer!" Snow's voice cracked through the thunder.

Hands grabbed him, dragging him backward, but Charles no longer knew if he was in the fight or already gone. The world pulsed between fire and black; until even the hammering of the Vickers slipped away.

Chapter 12

Bristol Fever

His ears rang as bright light poured through narrow slits. He half opened his eyes, blinking constantly, the white glare filtering in. His skin was clammy, his ribs aching as his senses returned one by one. A dry taste coated his mouth; tongue stuck to his teeth. A coughing fit seized him, rattling his chest and dragging him back into the living. The ringing faded as a stern woman's voice cut through.

"Don't fight it, lad. Fever's got you. Let it run its course."

"Where... where are... the boys?" Charles rasped, his voice broken.

"Somewhere safer than you. Now hush."

His eyesight adjusted. A lantern flickered. Canvas walls surrounded him. Nurses moved quickly between beds, the metallic clatter of trays and the clicking of their shoes on planks laid over mud filling the tent. The stench of antiseptic mingled with sweat and sour bodies.

Thud!

His stretcher shuddered as bearers rushed another man past, boots stomping as someone shouted, "Make way!" Moans and groans bounced off the khaki walls. Damp sheets clung to Charles's back as he rolled. He clawed at the frame, dragging himself half upright; only for the world to tilt sharply, sending him crashing back into the canvas.

"Take it easy, lad," the voice returned.

"Where... am I?" he managed.

"You're in France. A clearing station. You won't be here long if I've got anything to do with it. Now rest."

Charles tilted his head back into the sweat-soaked pillow. His body shivered as he surrendered again to the dark.

Flashes of consciousness followed over the next few days. Lantern light swung overhead, unmasking blurred faces. The smell of mud and iodine stung his nostrils as his body jolted, ribs flaring in pain while wheels bounced over cobblestones.

"Lift! Careful with his ribs!" someone barked as steam drifted warm against his cheek. Doors slammed open. Lanterns flashed off brass handles on weathered timber marked with a red cross. Black iron steps rose before him, swallowing him whole.

Then came the metallic rhythm of iron wheels pounding rails, the carriage shuddering in time. Coal smoke seeped through the cracks, mixing with the sweet-sour stench of sickness.

His stomach lurched as the movement shifted to a sway. He grasped at the stretcher frame, coughing bile onto the timber deck. Cold air slapped his skin; salt stung his lips. The nightmare of the Suevic washed over him as men all around coughed and retched.

"Keep breathing. That's it, lad," a firm woman's voice said over the throb of engines.

Buckets were passed frantically. Nurses murmured encouragement over the chaos. The smell of sickness and vomit made his stomach turn. Above, gulls cried unseen in the grey sky, their calls sharp and mocking.

A long, mournful blast trembled through his bones as the ship's horn announced its arrival. The ache of the note vibrated through him, pulling him back under until a gentle touch brushed his hand and a soft voice whispered,

"Charles... wake up."

He opened his eyes. Light seeped through tall windows, illuminating a high whitewashed ceiling that seemed to sway above him. A shadow leaned over; brown hair pinned back, loose strands catching the light. Cool fingers slid across his temple, soothing the fever's burn. Grey-blue eyes steadied on him, almost amused.

"There you are," she said with a small smile. "I was beginning to wonder if you meant to sleep the whole war away."

Charles tried to clear his throat, but only a rasp came out.

"Don't rush. You've nowhere to be but here," she murmured.

A faint scent of her soap lingered beneath the richer aroma of beeswax and clipped gardens; fresh air he hadn't tasted since leaving home. Charles placed shaky hands on the soft sheets and tried to push himself upright. The woman stood and gently propped him against the wall.

He looked around. A long corridor stretched out, lined with beds spaced far apart. It reminded him of the orphanage, though grander by far. Moulded plaster softened the ceiling, broken only by chandeliers dulled with dust. Tall sash windows spilled pale English light onto faded wallpaper and rows of iron bedsteads. Gilt-framed oil portraits looked down, their painted eyes watching silently over the wounded.

Unsure if he was awake or still dreaming, he whispered, "What... is... this?"

The nurse steadied him with a hand on his shoulder, voice calm with the faintest hint of humour.

"You're in Clevedon Hall, in Bristol. Once a grand house, now a hospital. Not quite what its owners had in mind for their chandeliers."

Charles blinked at the tall windows, the greenery beyond them. He swallowed, managing, "And... what are you?"

She let a small smile slip.

"I'm a nurse silly. And I'll be harder to shake off than the fever."

His voice cracked. "Where's... my division? How long... have I been gone?"

She adjusted his pillow before answering.

"Your division's still in France. Pushing on, so they say." Her eyes softened. "As for you... it's the first week of October now. You've been in our care nearly a month."

The words hit harder than any shell. A month gone. The boys still fighting, and he here; in a grand house.

He stared out the window at the manicured gardens, the lush lawn, the flowers in bloom. Hedgerows that hid nothing but branches. No mud. No smoke. No bodies. Just peace.

"When do I head back?" Charles asked.

"You've played your part, soldier. From what I hear, they're doing quite well without you," she teased gently.

"The fight's not done," he insisted weakly.

"Your fever only just broke. Go back too soon and you'll be waking up to me again," she replied.

Charles sighed, defeated by her wit. Trapped again; stone walls instead of mud, but a prison all the same.

"Well, if you insist on imprisoning me... what's your name then?"

"I'm a nurse, not a jailer," she chuckled. "And my name is Nancy Whitaker."

He smirked. "A pleasure to meet you, Nancy Whitaker."

"You're a bit cheeky, Charles. Rest now, you can't be using all your energy on me." Her touch brushed his sleeve before she moved down the hall, slim silhouette framed by apron and cap.

He lingered on her steps until distant groans and murmurs broke the moment. He looked back to the window. From the upper floor he could see rolling farmland; lush fields, quiet shrubs, nothing like the Somme.

He wondered what Billy and Snow were staring at now. Hopefully well past Péronne. Hopefully giving the Hun hell at the German border. Billy would be singing at the top of his lungs behind a Vickers; Snow turning the battlefield into a chessboard.

A weight settled on his chest. Frankie should have been there too; book in one hand, rifle in the other, ready with some clever remark to cut Billy down to size. Charles could almost hear his laugh: quick, sharp, swallowed by memory.

The polished walls and chandeliers blurred. Even Nancy's voice faded beneath the absence.

The days rolled on like the fields outside. His spirits lifted when Nancy was near: her touch, her wit, her scent. But when she wasn't, the guilt surged back. He had dragged Frankie into this. Dragged himself. Months of horror had broken him; flashes of battle played in his mind unbidden.

The window reminded him of the view from the kitchen at Woodstock. Not as rugged, but distant farmland all the same. Sheep instead of cattle. Manicured instead of wild. It made him ache.

He wished he had never left, his mother's heartbreak, and Edna of course. Had he abandoned them like his birth mother had done to him? Or had Edna pushed him toward a war he never should have fought?

Nancy's soft footfalls glided down the hall, her hair catching the morning light and giving her skin a warm glow. Her beauty distracted Charles as she approached, envelopes in hand.

"Good morning, soldier," she grinned, handing the letters over. "Seems we tracked down some fan mail, an Edna Price and an Agnes Dean. Girlfriends back home?"

Charles chuckled, though it caught painfully in his chest. "Agnes is my mother. Edna... she's more complicated than that." He dropped his gaze to the envelopes, avoiding Nancy's eyes.

"Would you like a moment alone with them?" Nancy asked.

"It's okay. You can stay," he said, running his thumb along the wax seal, shifting between the two letters.

Nancy moved around him with quiet purpose, checking his temperature with the back of her hand, adjusting the blanket that had slipped off his shoulder, smoothing the creases from his pillow. Her eyes flicked briefly to the letters in his hands.

He felt her gaze as he slid his mother's letter to the front, Edna's firmly beneath it. He broke his mother's seal.

My dear Charles,

It breaks my heart to tell you that your father has passed.

The first line flattened him. His jaw locked, his shoulders stiffened, but his eyes betrayed the blow. The ward around him seemed to hush.

Nancy was already close, steadying the water glass on his bedside table, her hand brushing his forearm. She said nothing.

He had been unwell for some months... the sore on his face worsened, and the doctor said it was cancer of the skin... he slipped away quietly at home.

Charles's grip bent the page, the fold creasing beneath his thumb. He pictured his father in the yard, sleeves rolled, always moving, always certain; now still, now gone. A sharp breath rattled out of him.

Nancy's hand lingered gently on his shoulder, anchoring him.

I know that you and he did not see eye to eye about the war... but in his last days he spoke often of you... I believe he was proud of the man you have become.

The words blurred. *Proud.* Too late; spoken only when distance and death made it safe. His jaw twitched, but he refused to break. He glanced up and met Nancy's eyes, no pity, just quiet steadiness.

The farm is quiet without him... I lean on the thought of you, my son... keep strong, Charles... your father would want that.

Your Loving Mother

He lowered the page. The chandelier above swam out of focus. The walls of the once grand hall seemed to lean inward. Only Nancy's hand, warm, firm on his shoulder; kept him from sinking completely.

He turned to the window. Beyond the glass, clipped hedges and blooming flowers stood in perfect order. It was too quiet, too neat. Nothing like Woodstock. Nothing like home. Nothing like him.

He had left the farm with his father's anger still fresh between them, convinced the war would prove him right. Now the war had stolen his chance to make anything right.

The letter sagged in his grip. The silence pressed heavier than fever.

Charles spent the next few days with little words. His chest ached, not from illness now, but grief. The hall seemed to press closer, chandeliers looming lower, rows of iron beds narrowing like the pews of St James Cathedral. His father had once pulled him back from that despair. Now, in his absence, Charles felt orphaned again.

Nancy came more often, fussing quietly.

"You feeling any better today, soldier? Can I fetch you something?" she asked, her smile warm but her eyes shadowed with concern.

"I'm fine," he muttered, staring out the tall window.

She followed his gaze. "Your fever's broken. Your strength is coming back. You could take a turn outside instead of staring at it."

He said nothing.

"Come along now," she urged, firmer this time. "Fresh air will do you good."

She slipped a hand under his arm and guided him up. He didn't resist as she steered him toward the doors, the perfectly kept garden waiting beyond.

Outside, Nancy released him to the garden's quiet. Autumn clung to the air. Roses still held colour, though fading. The clipped hedges and neat garden beds felt foreign beside the noise in his head.

He wandered until he found an empty chair beneath an ivy-covered arbour. He eased into it, the iron cold through his trousers.

After a long moment, his hand drifted to his chest pocket, brushing the folded envelopes. His mother's letter already lay heavy in him. Edna's waited like a wound yet to be opened.

He removed it, tracing the seal with his thumb. The paper was too clean, too untouched.

Finally, he drew a breath and opened it.

My dear Charles,

I hardly know how to begin... your mother has not been alone in her grief... I have been with her often... she misses you terribly.

He felt some ease at first, relief his mother was not alone.

Your father's passing has shaken us all... he thought of you often near the end.

His breath caught.

I have helped with the stock... though my hands are clumsy beside his... some nights I have stayed in your room... to keep your mother company... it brings me close to you.

His jaw tightened. She was stepping into a world she barely knew. It should be him. His duty. Not the war.

I will not pretend that words can mend such a loss... I want you to know that we are looking after one another... your duty is heavy enough where you are... remember you are not forgotten, and you are dearly loved.

Yours always, Edna

He gripped the letter until it creased. A tear fell onto the page, one he thought had been beaten out of him months ago. He wiped it away quickly. Breathing in the cool garden air, he caught the scent of cut grass and lavender easing his chest.

The moment lingered, birds chirping softly. Then...

Church bells.

One tower, then another, overlapping, ringing without stopping. Shouts rose from the streets beyond the hospital walls, cheers, whistles, even the distant blare of a brass band.

The garden trembled with the sound. The ward erupted behind him; patients cheering, clapping, some banging cups on bedframes. Nurses rushed to the windows, voices high with disbelief.

"It's over! It's over!"

Charles's eyes widened. His ears pricked.

The door burst open. Nancy ran toward him, skirt brushing gravel, cap askew, breathless, face flushed with joy.

"Charles, it's over! The war's over!"

Before he could react, she bent and kissed his cheek, swept away by the moment. Stillness lingered afterward; her hand resting on his shoulder, their eyes meeting, a spark held between them.

But the weight of Edna's letter lay heavy in his chest. The warmth of Nancy's touch collided with guilt; affection tangled with obligation.

Nancy stepped back, smoothing her apron, face flushed. Bells and cheers roared around them.

For Charles, the joy rang hollow. Frankie's laugh, his father's silence, and Edna's words pressed against him like armour he could no longer carry. The kiss only tangled the knots already pulling at him

Yet he knew the date, the moment, the sound of church bells piercing the English sky would stay with him forever.

11th of November 1918.

Armistice.

The day the world exhaled; and he could not.

Chapter 13

Lonely in Victory

His health strengthened with each passing day. Since the Armistice the hospital had grown lighter, laughter trickling through the wards, and Nancy's teasing had taken on a warmer edge.

"Well, soldier," she said with a sly smile, "seems my nursing has worked wonders. You've been cleared to leave."

Charles raised an eyebrow. "And where are they sending me now?"

"Weymouth," she said, pretending to sigh. "To embark back to the bush. But before that... you're owed a little leave."

"I've always wanted to see London," Charles replied, watching her reaction.

Nancy's eyes flickered, a grin tugging at her lips. "I'd quite like to see it with you."

"Then come," he said, half-challenging. "Show me your city."

She shook her head, though not without regret. "The war may be over, but these men still need me." Then, lowering her voice a little: "But if you ever find yourself in England again... you'd better look me up."

Charles smirked, though Edna's name weighed in his chest. "I'll hold you to that."

Before long he was back on a train, service dress pressed sharp, boots gleaming to a shine that would have made Frankie proud. The diamond patch on his sleeve marked his unit, and two blue chevrons stitched low spoke of the years he'd been away.

Outwardly, he looked whole again. But each tunnel cut across his reflection, and in the dark came the flashes; the two men torn apart at Flanders, Chook's blood warm on his face, Frankie falling flat in the mud, Fritz fire swallowing him whole.

The whistle's shrill cry split the air as the iron clatter of carriages ground to a halt. Coal smoke billowed; steam hissed beneath the vaulted roof of the station. For a moment it wasn't steam at all but gas, crawling low through a trench, men clawing at masks, eyes wild.

Charles blinked hard and stepped down onto the soot-stained concrete, boots clacking in chorus with the crowd that filled every inch of the platform; women in bright hats, soldiers grinning wide with ribbons on their chests. He had never seen a city so vast, so alive. Yet it slid over him like smoke, leaving nothing behind.

He pushed through the crowd, feeling swallowed, the press of bodies on the platform like a battalion clinging for cover. As he surfaced from the station the walkways were just as packed. Bunting hung from lamp posts, flags from every window, Union Jacks draped across buildings as bells clanged from every steeple.

Noise rolled off the Victorian stone facades. Charles struggled to take in the beauty with the ringing in his ears, the sound like the hum of the Vickers.

Newsboys wove through the throng, papers clutched high, ink still smudging on their fingers. *Peace Declared!* the headlines shouted, but Charles caught only the ghost of casualty lists, names tumbling back into mud. For a second he thought he saw Frankie's among them, sharp and black against the page, before the paper folded in the boy's hands and vanished into the crowd.

A gust of wind sent a loose sheet skittering down the street until it slapped against Charles's leg. The crack of paper snapped tight in his chest, too close to the slap of rifle fire. A boy darted after it, laughing, flag in hand, his voice bright as a bell.

In Charles's ears it twisted into a stretcher-bearer's cry: *"Make way!"*, boots hammering past his gun pit. He turned sharply, heart pounding, but there was only the crush of Londoners, faces flushed with excitement, eyes bright with relief.

The centre of the street was a churn of wheels and hooves. Motorcars honked as they shoved against horse-drawn hansoms, engines coughing and belching smoke that clung to the air. A driver shouted, reins snapping as a horse reared, and for an instant Charles was back in the lines at Péronne, a team of mules screaming as shells burst around them.

He blinked it away, swallowing hard, but the sound lingered.

Women in vibrant coats clutched parcels, their laughter rising above the din, too clean, too untouched. Shopfronts glared with polished glass and gold lettering; promising fashions and luxuries he'd never had reason to notice before. Charles slowed, watching the light play across the windows, wondering what price in blood each item on display had cost.

The streets of London flowed like a river, pushing and pressing him along, strangers' shoulders jarring against his own. His eyes scanned the crowd; nerves braced for a sudden rush that never came.

Then he saw it; Big Ben rising above the rooftops, its bells tolling deep and steady across the city. He paused, rooted as people jostled past, staring up at the vast clockface. For a heartbeat he marked it as a sniper's perch before the soldier's thought slipped away, and he found himself caught on time itself; on what he'd lost, and what still lay ahead.

Drawn by the noise, he drifted with the crowd. Streets narrowed then opened into sudden grandeur, until he was pushed out onto a broad avenue lined with tall stone buildings, clean and ordered, not shattered like Amiens.

It ran straight to high iron gates, trees standing either side like sentries. The further he went, the quieter it became; celebration fell away in scraps as he came to a huge pale-grey facade, stretching wider than any farmhouse he'd ever seen.

The stonework was immaculate, rows of tall sash windows reflecting nothing but clouds, like lifeless eyes watching him. No shell marks. No craters. No broken plaster. The kind of safety his mates never had in their shallow trenches.

He stopped at the cold metal gates, crowned with the royal crest, feeling firmly shut out.

He imagined the King's house full of life, but it stood eerily still; guards posted, windows dark. All that sacrifice to keep this safe. For a King he was not welcome to see, even on the doorstep. In the silent palace windows, he saw the faces of men lost.

"We fought and bled for this? For walls that never saw mud, for windows that never rattled with guns?" he thought.

He turned away, boots echoing on the wide avenue. As the streets narrowed again, they filled with voices and music spilling from open pub doors, leaving the silence behind for chaos ahead.

A cheer burst from one doorway; the clink of glasses carried in the brisk winter air. Charles hesitated. A pint, just to feel human again, he told himself.

He ducked inside. Warmth and cigarette smoke rolled over him, the noise swallowing his thoughts. Beer soured the air, wood polished by years of leaning elbows gleamed under yellow light. The room was packed with soldiers, their laughter loud as they slammed pints together. Voices hoarse from singing, the sound reminding him of Cairo; only here it was English accents instead of Aussies.

He slumped at the bar, its timber beautifully carved, shelves behind stacked with the finest whiskies. Barmaids wove between groups, tankards balanced in both hands, shouting orders over the roar. Khaki crowded the room, broken only by women in bright dresses and their painted smiles.

A pint was thumped down in front of him. He took a swig. The beer tasted flat on his tongue, no lift in his chest.

He felt more spectator than celebrant. The press of bodies made him uneasy, every shove a reminder of another advance, another scramble across no man's land, leaping over men left behind.

A woman a few stools away caught his eye and offered a warm smile. He didn't return it, gaze sinking back into his glass. His mind ran to Cairo, to the two girls laughing as Billy charmed them with his easy banter. Back then the future had felt wide open, the world one big adventure.

Now, surrounded by strangers, it felt hollow without him. Billy would have dragged him into the crowd, given it colour. Now it was just noise, clatter, and ghosts.

He stared at a group of soldiers nearby. The loudest of them broadened in his mind's eye until, for a moment, it was Billy; shoulders squared, arm hooked around a mate, eyes darting as he spun some tale only he could tell. Charles almost expected him to turn, grin, and wave him over.

But the figure blurred, shrinking back into a stranger, leaving Charles alone at the edge of it all.

Smash.

A glass hit the floor, shattering. Charles jolted, his pint spilling across the bar as the sound cracked like a shell burst. For an instant the cheers bent into screams, stamping boots into a charge. His ears rang with artillery as he shoved through the crowd and burst back onto the street.

Cold air slapped his face, clean but cutting. The noise of celebration still roared behind him like a war that refused to end.

The night pressed colder as he wandered the cobbled streets, boots scuffing on wet stone. The crowds thinned to soldiers stumbling toward their next destination and couples arm in arm, their laughter slipping down side streets.

Charles passed a boy tugging at his mother's hand, cheeky grin wide, and for a moment he thought of Billy and the childhood antics that always stirred trouble. He wondered where he was now; surely somewhere harassing Snow, pushing his buttons while they waited to be shipped off.

Coal smoke hung heavy, but beneath it he caught the sweet smell of chestnuts roasting on a brazier. It tugged at him;

sharp, unexpected; like woodsmoke over cow paddocks at dusk, his mother calling from the kitchen door.

His thoughts turned to her heartbreak, trying to hold the farm together alone, with Edna doing what she could to help. The ache of Woodstock lodged in his chest. London, with all its stone and grandeur, felt foreign, someone else's world. His own waited an ocean away; dust and warped timber, paint flaking under harsh sunlight.

As he walked, he found himself outside a church and sank onto the cold stone steps. He imagined the open fields back on the farm, wire fences rolling over dry paddocks, his mother waiting, Edna in the distance. The picture brought comfort and pain in equal measure.

Somewhere in the city church bells tolled the hour, deep and distant. Charles rose stiffly from the steps, the chill settled in his bones. London had given him its noise, its grandeur, its ghosts; but none of it belonged to him.

He turned back towards the station, boots striking the wet stone, and boarded the train south. Each mile carried him closer to the coast, and closer to the fields of Woodstock.

Chapter 14

Home Soil, Hollow Man

After months of delay; consisting of weeks in the Weymouth barracks, those days filled with hollow boasting and nights broken by screams; then the long voyage back across the oceans, rocked in the dark below deck with only his thoughts, Charles finally emerged. On the 24th of July 1919, he stepped onto the same creaking wooden platform he had left over two years before.

The town seemed smaller now, subdued, the wind pushing dust along the main street past weathered timber buildings. Charles felt older than it all, his youth swallowed somewhere far away.

The faint smell of gum leaves and the warble of magpies steadied him. This was home. As the steam hissed away and the smoke thinned, what remained was absence, no parade, no crowd. Only two figures waiting at the edge of the platform: his mother, and Edna.

His mother rushed forward, clutching him tight, though she felt fragile in his arms. Two years had etched themselves into her frame, the strain of the farm pulling down her health. He felt her tears soak his tunic as she cried out,

"Oh, Charles, I've prayed for this day!"

Over her shoulder he saw Edna, holding back, a quiet smile on her lips, eyes searching for his. She had changed; her hair pinned differently, her posture more assured; but her beauty remained. The flowing dress she wore, impractical for farm work, still commanded attention as it always had.

His mother's embrace lingered until Charles gently lowered her arms. She stepped aside. Edna approached, not rushing, almost hesitant, and laid her hand softly on his shoulder. The touch was restrained, but it lingered, sending a jolt through his chest.

"Welcome home, soldier," she said, her eyes holding his with steady warmth.

He took half a step back. Comforting, yes; but unfamiliar. He wasn't sure of himself in that moment.

"Home is what I'd like to see," Charles muttered.

"That," Edna said with a flicker of a smile, "is something I can help with. My carriage is at the end of the street, if you can manage the walk."

"Better riding in it than choking on its dust with Billy," he replied.

His mother's breath caught just slightly. Edna's smile faltered, but only for a heartbeat. The two women exchanged a glance, silent and weighted, before brushing the moment aside.

They stepped down into the dust bowl that was the main strip. Charles glanced across the road to the hotel; nothing had changed except for the paint peeling even more. "*How could it fade more than it already had?*" he wondered. The rest of the town was the same, leaning shopfronts, creaking verandas, a world untouched by the war. No bullet scars, no shell craters, no soldiers in sight. Just him, standing in his pressed uniform like a ghost who didn't belong.

He trudged down the street. Edna stayed close, guiding him with small gestures, her hands hovering, never quite touching. No crowds, only the smell of horse manure clinging to the dust. A couple murmured outside the post office, a signboard creaked above the store, and the rest was stillness; the rehearsed kind, a town holding its breath.

The general store drew his eye, unchanged except for the headlines pasted across the window; *Treaty of Versailles; The Full Details. The True Cost of Victory.* Charles barely skimmed them. He didn't need print to remind him what war cost.

Then he saw the casualty list. Longer now, the chalk thick and uneven where it had been rubbed out and rewritten. He froze. Edna shifted closer, slipping her hand lightly around his arm.

His eyes swept down, breath catching when they snagged on Frankie's name. The letters blurred, replaced by the image of Frankie sprinting across open ground, medical bag in one hand, rifle in the other, his spirit too bright to last. Charles pressed his palm hard to his forehead, trying to force the memory back, but it clung like smoke.

He forced himself down the page; then stopped again.

Billy Carter.

The world tilted. His jaw slackened, colour draining as though the name itself had struck him. The street noise fell away until only the thud of his pulse remained. His fist curled tight, white-knuckled, until Edna's hand slid into his. She steadied him with quiet strength. No words; just her touch, anchoring him, louder than his shock.

His mother touched his back, guiding him toward the carriage with gentle insistence. He followed, hollow and wordless.

Charles stared out the window as the fields rolled past, gumtrees etched against the sky while the wheels bumped along the rough road. The familiar sounds of cattle and kookaburras tried to ground him. The smell of sheep and hay mixed with the faint perfume from Edna as she rested a hand on his arm. He sighed just as his mother leaned across and placed a hand on his knee.

"Edna's been my right hand here, Charles. Truly. We'd have gone under without her."

"I did what I could," Edna said softly. "Fixed the books, kept the fences mended, even chased cattle once or twice."

"Chasing cattle isn't the same as keeping a farm alive." Charles's reply came out flat, bitter.

The smile vanished from Edna's face. "I know that. But I tried..."

"Tried," Charles snapped, sharper than he meant, "doesn't keep food on the table. Tried doesn't bring Father back."

Edna withdrew her hand. Her gaze dropped to her lap; lashes dark against her cheek.

"I wasn't trying to replace him," she said quietly. "I was only trying to help."

"Charles," his mother warned gently.

He swallowed hard, regret already rising, but stubbornness holding it in place.

"I just... it should've been me here. Not you," he said, softer now.

Edna looked up, her expression guarded, her voice clipped. "But you weren't. That's the truth of it."

The words stung, sharper for their calmness. Charles leaned back against the worn leather seat, staring out at the paddocks rolling past.

The wheels rattled on, each bump jarring the words he wished he could swallow back down. Edna's silence beside him was worse than any scolding, her hands clasped tight in her lap. He wanted to speak, to undo it, but the words stuck in his throat.

As they pulled up at the farmhouse, Charles was the first to jump out, the carriage feeling too tight, too warm. He scanned the horizon; the sun was sinking, the fields drier than Bristol yet dotted with cattle. It looked like home, but haunted.

Climbing onto the creaky veranda, he felt the house had shrunk. The wind rattled the iron roof as though trying to lift it clean off.

He pushed through the front door, the hinges groaning like they might tear free. The smell of mutton stew hit him; his father's ghost lingering in the air. The walls felt heavy with his absence.

Inside, the table was already set. A pot of stew steamed in the centre, the smell thick and familiar. They ate mostly in silence, the scrape of cutlery louder than words. Charles kept his eyes on his plate, chewing without tasting, while his mother tried now and then to smile, to coax something normal from the room.

Edna finally spoke, her voice low but steady.

"You'll get used to it again. Home's stubborn that way."

Charles glanced up, guilt softening his expression. He managed a faint nod, nothing more. The tension eased just enough for Edna to rise from her chair. She placed a hand lightly on his shoulder, not lingering, before collecting the plates. His mother disappeared into the kitchen, the clatter of dishwater masking the thick silence left behind.

He retreated early to his bed. The hallway was dim, floorboards squeaking beneath his steps. Edna passed him with a folded blanket in her arms, pausing as their shoulders brushed.

"Goodnight, Charles," she said softly, almost cautious.

He gave a faint nod and moved on.

His room resembled a child's shrine more than a man's quarters; walls lined with faded cricket posters, a shelf stacked with schoolbooks, dust thick in the corners. The narrow bed sagged in the centre; the same blanket sat neatly folded at the foot. Even the boots he'd outgrown years ago sat in the corner, stiff with cobwebs. Nothing had changed, yet everything had. He no longer fit the room, as though it had been waiting for someone else to come home.

Charles lay in bed, eyes fixed on the ceiling, moonlight leaking through holes in the rusted iron roof. Shadows stretched across the walls like steeples, watching, waiting to unleash a sniper round. He tossed and turned. The blanket felt heavy, suffocating like mud. Though winter cold seeped through the house, sweat pooled on his skin, dampening his hair. His eyelids sank despite himself, the ceiling blurring as the shadows lengthened.

Boots began to patter; faint at first, trampling duckboards. A whistle cut across the dark, thin and distant, clamping his chest tight. Voices swelled; men shouting, charging. The patter thickened, no longer boots but the rattle of the Vickers. His head was stuck, face pressed into mud, the taste of it thick on his tongue. Shapes swelled around him.

BANG!

A white flash. Chook's blood sprayed across him as the body slumped lifeless into the mire. Charles lurched upright with a strangled gasp, lungs clawing for air.

The door burst open. Edna crossed the room in an instant, pressing a cool hand to his drenched forehead.

"You're safe now," she whispered, voice steady. Her thumb brushed his temple, lingering longer than necessary. Slowly, the world shifted back; not blood, but rain; not gunfire, but drops drumming on corrugated iron. His breathing eased, though the ghosts still crouched in the corners of the room.

He spent the rest of the night tossing in shallow sleep, exhaustion finally smothering the worst of the terrors but never easing them.

At last, the sharp squeal of the billy boiling tore him awake. He dragged himself down the narrow hall, gloom clinging to him until the kitchen's morning light struck his face.

His mother and Edna were already at the table, the faint scrape of teaspoons stirring cups filling the silence. Charles dropped into his chair, the wood groaning, and his mother slid a bowl of porridge in front of him without a word; just as she had when he was a boy.

He stared at the lumpy surface, its craters and ridges blurring into a shell-torn field. His gaze stayed locked there until Edna's voice broke the quiet.

"Are you feeling all right?"

The question lingered unanswered. Then, still staring at the porridge, his voice cut the air,

"What happened to him? To Billy?"

Edna and his mother shared a glance, neither wanting to speak. Charles's spoon scraped against the rim, louder than it should have been.

"Just tell me," he muttered.

His mother's voice came first, soft and breaking.

"It was the Hindenburg Line. First of October. They pushed through the canal near St Quentin. Billy was... he was in it."

Edna swallowed, tightening her hold on her cup.

"They say he was hit in the chest, Charles. It was quick. He didn't suffer. At least..." her voice faltered, "that's what they told us."

Charles sat still, staring into the porridge until it blurred. His mind filled in the rest; the smoke, the roar, Billy charging with that grin... cut down before the finish line. Dead before Charles had even broken his fever in Bristol. He clenched his jaw until it ached, his spoon trembling against the bowl.

"He was a hero, Charles," his mother said gently. "They say that push convinced the Germans the war was lost."

Charles gave the faintest shake of his head; eyes fixed on the bowl.

"Some finish line," he muttered. He shoved the porridge away, the scrape sharp in the silence.

The room held still. Edna's hand twitched, as though she might reach for his, but she didn't. His mother's eyes glistened, searching him, but he stared past them both, past the kitchen walls, the table, all the way to a muddy field half a world away.

From then on, routine set in.

His focus shifted to his father's farm; once thriving, now only just surviving. He'd spent half his childhood shadowing the old man across these paddocks. What once felt like chores now carried the weight of purpose.

He rose early, before dawn, to kookaburras calling from the gum trees. Pulling on his boots, he stepped into the chill air, the smell of dew and manure grounding him. Taking the reins of his old horse; still patient, still steady; he was clumsy in the saddle at first. Flashes came quick: men dropping from their mounts under fire, jolts rattling his grip.

The herd had a mind of its own. His attention snagged on fences that blurred into barbed wire, his moment's lapse letting cattle drift loose. He snapped the whip to turn them back; only to flinch, ears ringing as though it cracked like a rifle shot.

Day after day he forced himself back to the task; sharp breath, stiff shoulders, and then on again.

By the time he drove the herd home, Edna's carriage often glimmered on the horizon. His mother and her busy inside, the smell of fresh bread drifting out the door.

Edna helped with chores. Mending a fence brought more frustration than comfort. Billy's easy humour; once enough to make the work pass, was gone. In its place, the taut pull of wire, the metallic twang when it snapped, sharp enough to stagger him.

Edna noticed. She didn't speak, only steadied the post and handed him the hammer. Their eyes met, his nod a wordless thanks, her silence a quiet anchor.

Evenings brought darkness, and with it the horrors he'd carried home. Only the fire gave peace; its flames dancing, warm, the crackle almost soothing compared to the thunder of a barrage. Still, he sometimes caught himself waiting for the heat to flare into something worse.

He worked methodically, oiling his saddle leather, the sharp smell numbing him. Each stroke of the cloth calmed him, a small defence against chaos.

Edna lingered often, a soft presence for him and his mother. She sat close, needle flashing in the lamplight as she hummed faintly. Now and then she drifted nearer, her hand brushing his arm. Charles looked up. Their eyes held for a breath before she slipped back to her chair. No declarations; just presence.

Later, when the fire had burned low, he found himself replaying that glance, the quiet determination in her eyes, the way her voice steadied the room without trying. He turned it over like a stone, surprised by the comfort it offered.

He often caught himself scanning the paddocks as though through the sights, waiting for the charge. But all he found was silence, the kind only home can give. The wind stirred the grass; the gum leaves whispered sharp and clean.

Sometimes the silhouettes of cattle shifted into Billy's shape, swaggering across the fields as he used to. Frankie would follow, laughing at his heels. Charles carried them both, their ghosts lingering in the tall grass, their shadows threading through his dreams. But here; this ground, he could stand on.

The grind of chores, the demands of the herd, the endless repairs; the very routine he'd once run from now kept him moving. Stepping into his father's boots, he wondered if the old man would be proud now.

He leaned against a fencepost, hands rough, breath steady, watching the cattle scatter across the twilight paddock. From the homestead porch came the faint clatter of dishes, and when he glanced back, Edna stood in the doorway, silhouetted by lamplight. She lingered a moment before turning inside.

Charles drew in the cool air, chest loosening.

Not whole; but no longer lost.

Chapter 15

Edna's Garden

The farm had settled back into routine, but Charles had not. His ghosts stalked him across the paddocks, slipping in with every snap of wire or crack of thunder. A stockwhip set his ears ringing like a shell burst; cicadas screaming in the heat became the rattle of machine gun fire. Even the sudden flight of magpies stiffened him, chest tight, waiting for a rush that never came.

When the images swarmed too close, the smell of cattle, the drone of insects, or Edna's hand on his sleeve would bring him back. She visited often; cooking beside his mother, keeping the farm accounts in careful order. In the evenings she hummed while she sewed, soft and steady, filling the silence with something warmer than memory. Sometimes, when the night terrors gripped him, she slipped into his bed; not as a lover but as a sentinel; stroking the sweat from his brow until his breathing eased.

Her affection was clear, and his mother adored her, but Charles kept her at a distance. His thoughts were closed off; his focus fixed on the land as if it alone might hold him together. Edna often watched him across the table, wondering if there was still a place for her in the life of the man who had come home.

One evening, as dusk deepened and the fire steadied, she spoke quietly.

"Your father always said this land would either make or break a man. Which are you, Charles?"

His jaw tightened, gaze on the darkening paddocks. "I'm still standing. That's more than some managed," he said, muted.

Her sewing paused. "Standing isn't the same as living," she murmured. He didn't answer.

His demeanour worried his mother. She fussed constantly; straightening his collar, tidying his boots, setting meals before him as if he were still a boy. Caught in her own grief, she buried herself in needless chores: folding the same linens twice, polishing crockery already gleaming; anything to keep her hands busy and her mind from wandering to the empty chair at the table.

One late afternoon Edna worked in the garden, pressing roots into the soil. The smell of cut roses drifted on the warm air. Charles paced restlessly nearby.

"Those roots are too deep," he muttered.

"Too deep for what?" she asked.

He didn't answer. Heat clung heavy. He leaned on the homestead fence, letting a broken post take his weight.

"You've had your head bowed at that post long enough," she said, tone gentle but edged with concern.

"I don't need lessons in mending fences, Edna." His voice was flat, hard enough to bruise.

Hurt flickered in her eyes. "I'm not trying to teach you anything. I just want you here. With me. Not always somewhere else."

He looked away toward the paddocks. A breeze stirred the trees. "You don't see what I see," he said quietly. "You don't feel what I feel every dawn when the world still seems broken."

Edna stood, brushing dirt from her hands. She crossed to him and laid a hand on his shoulder.

"Five years home, Charles... but sometimes it feels like you never truly left the war."

"I did what was asked of me. Isn't that enough?" His voice was clipped.

"I don't want enough. I want you," she pressed.

"I've got work to do. That should be enough for anyone," he replied, low with dismissal. He turned away, grinding his heel into the dirt.

Edna caught his arm, forcing him to face her. "You can't keep shutting me out. I stood by your mother; I stood by you. What more do you want me to prove?"

His mouth drew thin. "Maybe I don't want you to stand by me. Maybe I just need room to breathe."

The words came harsher than intended, but he didn't take them back. Her eyes stung, though her voice stayed level.

"If you want to be alone in this, then I'll leave you to it." She turned, brisk and unyielding, her back straight as she strode toward the house.

Charles didn't move. The urge to call her name burned in his chest, but pride sealed his tongue. The garden seemed suddenly too still, broken only by the distant low of cattle. He told himself it was better this way. The hollow ache spreading through him betrayed the lie.

The house grew colder without Edna. His mother lingered in her quiet fussing, missing Edna but never daring to push. Without the soft evening hum, Charles began reaching for the bottle. Each night the liquor burned his throat, a bitter echo of his birth father drinking himself into an early grave. Now the same shadow crept over the son.

The nights were worst. Without Edna's steadying hand, the terrors took him whole. He woke choking, tearing at his sheets, Frankie's name raw on his tongue. After weeks he looked worn; face lined, eyes sunken, the farm's labour carving him down until he resembled the gaunt figure he'd left behind in France.

Waking before dawn was easy; rising was not. Charles dragged himself upright, light-headed, body heavy from nights wrestling ghosts. By the time the saddle cinched tight, and he swung into the stirrup, the day already pressed against him, Queensland's heat burning through his shirt.

The horse shifted uneasily beneath him, ears flicking at every sound. Charles tugged the reins, but his hands weren't steady. A crack split the air; maybe a branch, maybe a distant stockwhip; but to him it was the whip of machine gun fire. Instinct surged; he ducked low, spurring the horse in panic.

The gelding reared. Charles lost his seat and hit the ground hard; the breath blasted from his lungs. His vision burst white, then black.

He didn't stir.

By the time his mother found him crumpled in the dust, she was already calling for Dr Doyle.

Charles came to with salts stinging his nose, eyes forcing open to the neat moustache of Dr Doyle, its ends pinched sharp as his suit collar. Doyle struck a match, the flare harsh in the dim room, and watched Charles's pupils shrink. He moved a thumb side to side.

"Good. They follow. No fracture, just a rattled brain," Doyle said briskly. "Rest. Dark room. Cold cloths. And if he vomits, send for me at once."

He scraped his chair back to leave, but Charles's mother spoke, voice taut.

"There's more, doctor. The night terrors. The emptiness. Charles is here but... not here."

Doyle turned, studying him. "Shell shock. War neurosis, some call it. What grips you, son?"

Charles stared at the floorboards. His throat worked. Silence stretched until he managed a single word,

"Frankie."

Doyle froze, the name landing like a blow. He cleared his throat. "What about him?"

Charles's voice faltered. "I saw it. That last day. He ran to save someone. Took it in the chest... the stomach. There was no chance. I see it every night. Not just him, others too. Always others."

Doyle's hand gripped the chairback until his knuckles whitened. His composure wavered.

"You were with him," he said quietly. "That's more than I was. More than his mother was."

He turned away a fraction, staring at the wall as though looking at Charles hurt. His hand brushed over his face, rough, trying to wipe the years away.

"When the telegram came," Doyle said, voice low, "I imagined him lying there alone. Wondered if he called for me. Wondered if he knew..." His voice cracked. He drew a breath, steadying himself.

Then he straightened, mask back in place though his eyes were rimmed with wet.

"You stayed. You saw him. For that, I'll always be in your debt."

For a heartbeat the weight lifted; not gone, but shared. Charles had feared Doyle's anger, but saw only grief.

"The terrors are common," Doyle said quietly. "A test of will. Work can steady a man, but don't carry it all alone. Speak when you can. Some use whisky for medicine, but I wouldn't prescribe it."

Charles nodded, though he doubted he could open up. The only person he wanted to speak to was Edna; and he'd pushed her away.

That night the house was too quiet. His mother retired early, her footsteps fading down the hall. Charles sat alone at the table, oiling saddle leather out of habit. But the silence pressed in; no hum, no needle tapping, no Edna. Only the scrape of cloth and the creak of the chair.

A low thunder rolled across the sky. He froze, heart hammering, the crack that followed like artillery. His hands trembled, the cloth falling to his lap. Instinct drove him toward the cupboard; the bottle waiting. He gripped its neck, Doyle's warning circling back.

"Some use whisky for medicine, but I wouldn't prescribe it."

He held the bottle a moment longer, then shoved it back. His hand lingered on the wood, breath ragged. He knew who he needed; the only one who had quieted the storm.

Pride told him to leave it be.

The silence told him otherwise.

By dawn he'd made up his mind. The saddle creaked beneath his hands, leather worn and familiar. His horse shifted, stamping in the chill. Charles swung up stiffly, tightening the reins with a grip that betrayed the shake in his chest.

The road carried him toward the Price farm. Mist curled across the paddocks, gum leaves dripping with dew. As the first light broke, the homestead rose ahead; white weatherboards bright against the sky, veranda wrapping it like an embrace. Roses bloomed along the lawn's edge.

Edna bent among the flowerbeds, hands deep in the soil.

Charles slowed, breath catching. He dismounted, boots hitting the earth. For the first time since France, he felt truly afraid. Reins still in hand, he hesitated; almost ready to mount again and flee.

She looked up; surprised, but steady. Kneeling among the roses, gloves dirt-stained, hair pinned beneath her hat, her white dress brushed with soil. The same effortless beauty he remembered from the schoolyard steeple.

He stepped forward, boots crunching along the gravel path. Edna rose, brushing her dress, keeping her distance.

"You remembered where I live," she said; calm but cutting.

"I should've come sooner," he murmured, guilt twisting through his words.

"What are you doing here, Charles?" Her tone firm, unflinching.

"I... want to talk," he managed.

"Well, talk." Hurt sharpened her voice. "I stood by you... through your silence, through nights no one else saw. And still you pushed me aside."

Charles dropped his gaze, jaw tight. Words tumbled out in fragments. "I wasn't whole. I thought I'd break you too. I thought you'd be better off."

"Better off alone than with the man I loved?" she shot back.

The words struck deep. He finally broke, voice raw.

"I can't outrun the ghosts. Every night I see Frankie fall. I hear Billy's laugh turn to silence. And worse than all of it, the thought of losing you."

Edna's eyes brimmed. She stepped closer, voice trembling but firm.

"Don't say it unless you mean it. Don't take me back only to cast me off again."

Charles hesitated only a moment, then reached for her hand, and for once, didn't let go.

"I don't want to survive without you anymore. I want a life, with you, Edna." His voice cracked as he pulled a small ring from his pocket, sinking awkwardly to one knee, a war-worn soldier kneeling among new growth.

"Marry me. Not to mend me, but to walk beside me. Please."

Edna exhaled, the years of distance and silence loosening at last. She nodded through her tears, placing her hand against his cheek.

"Yes, Charles. But this time, you don't shut me out."

They fell into each other's arms, rough, imperfect, but real. For a moment the world held its breath around them. Then the garden stirred; flowers shifting, kookaburras breaking the silence, life pressing forward.

The months that followed moved quietly, each week softening the edge between them. The garden grew wild with colour again, her laughter returning to the veranda like it had been waiting all along. Charles worked the land with a steadier rhythm, the weight in his chest lightening, though never gone. When they set a date, it felt less like a new beginning than the slow return of something that had always been meant.

After a short engagement, Charles found himself on the steps of St Joseph's Church in Townsville as it gleamed in the late morning of the 26th of April 1924. It rose high above the Strand, the sea breeze carrying salt and frangipani through the white arches. The church facade was freshly whitewashed; Roman, bright and clean.

It felt like a place of peace and new beginnings compared to the church of his boyhood, St James, with its imposing red brick and shadow, its Gothic architecture cold and lifeless. Edna had chosen St Joseph's for their new vows not to erase old pain, but to reclaim the act of standing at an altar; no longer as a boy abandoned, but as a man choosing.

Inside, sunlight flooded through tall arched windows. The air was warm but still, incense faint in the rafters as ceiling fans hummed lazily. He took his place at the altar, clean-shaven, hair neatly slicked back with pomade – the disciplined look of a man who'd learned precision the hard way. His dark wool suit, formal but plain, sat square on his frame, shoulders straight but no longer stiff. The line was broken only by a small boutonnière Edna had grown in her own garden, pinned carefully to his lapel.

Charles looked around. The quaint wedding party favoured the bride's side. The empty seats he wished he could fill were occupied only in his mind by men still resting in French soil. That thought drifted when, through the door and walking in late, came a man in a khaki service uniform; pressed but weathered; chevrons on his sleeve, medals gleaming neat on his chest. Upright, broad-shouldered and sharp, as if on parade.

He took off his hat at the door, looked up at Charles, and gave a smile and a nod.

Snow.

He took a seat beside Charles's mother, his presence reminding Charles of the past but grounding him for the step ahead. The rattle of a carriage wheel and the distant clip of hooves pulled up outside as the bell tolled and echoed down the street. Before the organ began, Charles thought of the first time he'd stood before a priest; a scared boy in stiff hand-me-downs. Now he stood on his own free will.

The doors swung open to reveal Edna.

Charles stared, awed. Light from the high windows caught her mid-length dress; graceful, with delicate lace trim that highlighted her undeniable beauty. The brightness from the high ceiling framed her elegance. She walked the aisle, steps soft against the dark timber floor, a large bouquet trembling slightly in her hands, filled with wild ferns and drooping sprays of her favourite flowers. The organ's sound was rhythmic and steady.

She took her place beside him, looking straight into his soul. Her smile was subtle, almost private, her gaze carrying the same hint of mischief that had first drawn him to her. Their vows were simple, unpolished, but raw; a deep love that filled the room. He glanced at the crucifix, not in prayer, but in thanks that this time he was not alone; his future stood right in front of him.

After the ceremony, out on the church steps, Snow found him. A new stripe gleamed at his cuff, Sergeant now. The tropical sun caught on his brass buttons as he gripped Charles's hand, firm and proud.

"Didn't think I'd see the day, mate. You've traded your rifle back for the saddle," Snow said with a smirk.

"And you? Thought you'd have hung up the khaki by now," Charles replied.

"Well, I'm back where it began, Enoggera. No Iron Jack breathing down my neck this time. The Army's home enough for me. Wife couldn't make the trip, kids kept her there; full house, full noise."

He paused, eyes softening. "You've done well, Charles. Not many can keep land alive after the mud we've seen. If you ever tire of the cattle, there's always a place for blokes who've been through it."

He meant it; not as temptation, but as respect.

Charles looked past him to where Edna laughed with her bridesmaids, hat tilted, sunlight catching her hair. He shook his head with a quiet smile.

"Think I've found my post," Charles said.

Snow grinned, clapping him on the shoulder. "Then hold it, mate. And hold her."

Before year's end, on the night of the 13th of December, the air pressed heavy, thick with the stillness before summer rain. The lamp's flame trembled, throwing long shadows over the walls as the old boards creaked and sighed. Sweat clung to Charles's back despite the open window, the faint breeze carrying the drone of insects and the scent of earth waiting for the storm.

Edna's breath came shallow and fast. She lay propped on pillows, hair damp against her temples, one hand gripping the sheet, the other reaching for him. Charles knelt beside the bed, useless but unwilling to leave. The midwife's quiet instructions blurred into the background.

"It's alright," he whispered, voice rough. "I'm here."

Then the cry came; small, thin, but fierce; cutting through the night like a flare. For a heartbeat Charles didn't move. Then he saw her, pink, slick, alive.

The midwife placed the child into Edna's arms. She wept, from exhaustion, from relief. "She's strong," she murmured.

Charles watched, the moment blurring through tears he hadn't felt since Bristol. The midwife turned to him.

"Would you like to hold her, Mr Watson?"

He nodded dumbly. Her weight was slight but comforting in his arms, warmth seeping into him. The ghosts went quiet.

"Lurline," Edna said softly. "It's just a name I love. No past. Just hers."

"Then it's perfect," he said. "Clean start."

Outside, thunder rolled, soft and distant. At dawn he stepped onto the veranda, shirt still open, daughter pressed to his chest as the world glowed pink over the paddocks. The air smelled of eucalyptus and rain.

For the first time in years, Charles felt still.

"Lurline," he whispered. "I'll keep you safe."

It felt like a vow; not just to her, but to himself, that the war would not be the end of him.

Chapter 16

Kennedy Calling

The years eased forward, not gentle but honest. The nightmares still came; the explosions, the gas, the muffled shouts; but mornings brought work that asked no questions. The land, rough as it was, gave him rhythm again; horses to shoe, fences to mend, calves to brand, daughters to lift high into the sun.

Lurline was soon joined by Margaret, Lucille, and little Clair, their laughter chasing the ghosts from the house. Charles found steadiness in the chores, pride in Edna's patience, and a strange comfort in the long, silent rides across the paddocks.

Yet some part of him; something he'd left overseas; stirred when he looked to the horizon, or across the dining table now in the place his father once sat. He caught himself reading the paper the same way, hearing the faint swirl of his mother's teaspoon, always present.

At that cramped table he often sat in proud misery. His family were his calm against the storm that never quite left his mind. And still, a quiet shame pressed at him; that he'd become the man he once swore he wouldn't be. The life he never wanted was now the one he'd built for his daughters; honest, harsh, predictable.

He pushed back from the table, the chair legs scraping the boards. Edna was already in the kitchen, sleeves rolled, steam rising from the wash tub. The scent of soap and boiled water filled the room, mixing with woodsmoke and the faint sweetness of baked pumpkin.

"They'll be tripping over each other soon," she said, half a smile, half a sigh. "Four girls and a house built for two."

Charles leaned on the doorway; thumb hooked in his belt. "Could always sleep the calves inside," he said dryly.

She glanced up. "Wouldn't be much noisier."

They shared a tired laugh, the kind that softened the air for a moment before the weight of things settled back.

"We'll need another room before next winter," Edna said, turning a plate through the water. "But the bank's already breathing down our necks. Wheat's down, beef's down, everything's down but the bills."

Charles nodded, watching her hands scrub the grime.

"Could stretch the veranda, put walls up maybe. Do the boards myself. Won't be pretty, but it'll stand."

"You'll need to find the time first."

"There's always time," he said, though they both knew there wasn't.

The wind stirred the lamp smoke. Outside, the dogs barked at something in the distance. Edna paused, wiping her hands.

"You've been quieter lately," she said. "Not the bad kind. Just... different."

He shrugged. "Guess I've been thinking."

"About what?"

"Just... ways to make things better," he said, then stopped there – not ready to name what was forming in his mind.

She nodded once, reading him as she always had.

"Whatever it is, make sure it doesn't take you too far from here."

"Nowhere far," he said, though the words didn't sit right in his chest.

The lamp guttered, the flame stretching tall before shrinking back. Charles looked at her, apron stained, hair loose, hands raw from soap; and felt the swell of something between guilt and gratitude.

"We'll work it out," he said. "We always do."

She smiled faintly. "Yea. We always do."

Outside, a breeze lifted the smell of rain from the paddocks; that sharp, metallic scent that promised change but never seemed to come. The Great Depression was settling over them; since the stock market crash of 1929, a year had passed, and the burden was beginning to bite.

Charles rode out alone, checking fences and water. The heat was building early, flies thick, the wind sharp with dust. The trough lay low, the drought was hitting hard. He came upon another dead cow from overnight, hide drawn tight over bone. The herd was scattering wider than usual, grazing whatever stubble remained.

With beef prices falling, they struggled to afford enough hay and grain to keep the stock alive. Charles counted heads as he rode, automatically calculating losses, each weakened beast another weight on his conscience. He'd been here before and knew the land owed no fairness. Yet there was still a fire in him, a quiet recognition that somewhere within all this dust and hardship, there had to be a way forward; a way to bring back pride to himself and his family.

Late day turned to dusk. The sky was a bruised blue and gold, fading as it brought the homestead into silhouette, smoke curling from the chimney. The horse's hooves landed hard as Charles made his return. He pulled up, wiped his face with his sleeve, and sat a moment in the saddle.

Laughter rolled down the hill, the girls playing outside, one chasing a chicken, another skipping rope. Lurline, the apple of his eye, wrangled the rest like a small mother. Spirited, just like her own.

Edna called from the veranda, hair tied up, hands on hips.

"Wash up before you come in."

Charles didn't answer right away. His eyes stayed on his daughters; he watched them, heart full and heavy at once. He saw how the light caught their hair, how their joy cut through the dry evening.

In that moment: the drought, the debt, the ghosts; it all faded. He was proud of the small world he'd built; strong, noisy, alive. But was it enough? Something stirred inside him, not ambition exactly, but a craving for significance. He wanted to be a father they could brag about, not just depend on. His thoughts drifted to the uniform folded in the trunk, the medals he never showed.

He finally dismounted, patting the horse's neck as the girls rushed him. "Daddy! Daddy!" they called, voices tumbling over each other. He smiled, placing his rough hands on their gentle heads.

Edna watched from the veranda, a towel slung over her shoulder, smiling in that knowing way. Charles glanced at her, nodded, and headed for the trough to wash up; the smell of stew heavy in the evening air.

The night was cooling now. After eating with the family, Charles slipped away, saying only that he was off to "check the lamps." Edna knew better, she simply nodded, eyes following him across the yard as lantern light flickered behind him.

His mother, now known as Granny Dean to his children, lived in a cottage a few hundred yards from the main house; close enough for supper, far enough for peace. A simple one-room weatherboard with a tin roof, whitewashed walls, and a veranda just wide enough for a rocking chair and a pot of geraniums.

She rocked slowly, shawl over her shoulders, a kerosene lamp burning low beside her. Woodsmoke curled from the small iron flue, mixing with lavender oil and damp earth after the faint spit of a storm that never bit.

In the distance, frogs croaked near the dam. A single kookaburra gave its clipped, lonely call. Her eyes sharpened as the crunch of Charles's boots moved through the gravel.

"You walk like your father when you're thinking too much," she said.

He chuckled quietly. "Could be. He thought plenty."

"Yea, but he never talked it. Sat there counting hooves and rain clouds. Thought if the herd was right, the world was right."

Charles sat on the step, elbows on knees. "Never worked that way for me."

"No," she said, smiling. "You were the one always looking past the paddocks."

The frogs started up louder now, the night alive with small, patient sounds. Charles watched the smoke drift into the dark.

"I've been thinking," he said finally. "About joining up. The Citizens Military Force in Townsville. They're calling for experienced men; sergeants, instructors." Snow's words from years ago rang through him.

She didn't move, just rocked once, twice.

"Feels wrong, does it?"

"Feels... disloyal. The land's been good to us, mostly. But it's not enough anymore. I want the girls to see me as more than a man fixing fences and counting losses."

Granny Dean exhaled through her nose, slow and steady.

"Your father measured life in head of cattle," she said. "You measure it in opportunities taken. Same grit, different stock."

Charles looked down, voice rough. "I'm not turning my back on the place, Ma. I'll still run it. Just... feels like there's more I could be doing."

"We brought you to this land, Charles," she said, eyes still on the paddocks. "But it was always too small for you, for that spark you've had. I'm just happy to see it back. You were never meant to stop at the fence line."

"It's home though. Always will be," Charles said, nodding.

A gust of wind stirred the geranium leaves as the kerosene lamp flickered. They sat in silence a long while; mother and son, the night thick around them.

Finally, she reached over and rested a dry hand on his forearm.

"Well, at least there's no war for me to worry over this time," she said, smiling faintly.

Charles smirked. "Not this time, Ma. Just drill and dust."

She nodded once, the rocking chair creaking softly. The frogs droned on. He rose and headed back toward the homestead, the glow of its windows soft against the dark.

He entered late in the evening; the house was settled, the girls asleep. Taking his place in his old armchair angled toward the fireplace, he let the warmth and flicker of the fire fill the room; the kind of silence that made him feel full.

The mantel was cluttered with family relics: a framed photo from their wedding, another of him before the pyramids, a small clock ticking unevenly, and a tin box never opened; his war medals inside. He felt calm, but weighted.

Edna sat opposite in her own chair, the rhythmic whisper of her needle sliding through cloth, the faint smell of soap on her hands.

Without looking up, she said, "You were out with your mother a while."

"Yeah," he said, chuckling. "She thinks I was never meant to stop at the fence line."

"She's not wrong," Edna replied, half-smiling.

Charles paused, watching the needle flash in the lamplight. Finally, he murmured,

"I've been thinking, the Citizens Military Force, over in Townsville. They're after men with experience. Bit of training, parades, that sort of thing."

Edna stopped sewing, placed the needle and cloth aside, and reached for a folded newspaper. She slid it across the small, crooked table between them, the CMF advertisement face-up.

"It'd mean time away from here," she said.

"Only a few nights a month. There's pay in it too. Would help with feed, maybe put something aside for the girls."

Edna studied him; looked him up and down, then to the mantel and its war memories. She knew the money wasn't the real reason.

"We'll manage," she said softly. "But I know that's not why you'd go."

Charles hesitated, defensive. "It's part of it."

Edna tilted her head, raising a brow. "And the other part?"

"Maybe the girls'll see more than a man with mud for dreams," he said.

Edna smiled softly. "They already do, Charles. They see a man who adores them."

He looked down, firelight flickering across his face. "Still... it feels like something worth doing. Feels like me again."

She nodded slowly, returning to her sewing. Her voice was even. "Then do it. If it steadies you, helps you feel whole again, and if it brings a bit more back into this house, I'm with you."

The fire popped. Charles leaned back, exhaling deeply. "You've always been."

Edna smiled faintly. "And I'll hold you to that extra money."

They shared a quiet laugh; small, genuine.

Soon enough, Charles found himself back in the big smoke. Enlisted with the 31st Battalion of the CMF, known as the Kennedy Regiment. He stood in the small room he'd been lent, his old khaki tunic laid out on the bed, the fabric rougher than he remembered. His fingers traced the WW1 ribbons on the breast pocket: faded, edges frayed; they hadn't seen sunlight in over a decade. They caught the lamplight and for a breath, he was back in France. He ran a hand down the brass buttons; their clicks echoed faintly like rifle bolts in his head.

He slid the uniform on, buttoned the collar, the weight of the cloth settling across his shoulders; heavier, but steadier somehow. He pulled on his boots, freshly polished to a clear reflection, the air filled with the sharp scent of linseed and effort. Charles turned to the mirror; three new chevrons stitched to his sleeve. The man staring back wasn't the boy who'd gone to war. The face was leaner, lined, but the eyes calmer.

He stepped out onto the parade ground after a late tropical storm. The air was thick; puddles reflected the lantern light. Sergeant Watson's boots sounded sure as they crossed the gravel. Rows of men were forming up, some in ill-fitting uniforms, boots in every shade of brown and black. The smell of oil and polish hung heavy. Young recruits straightened instinctively as he passed. This side of the parade ground was unfamiliar yet felt natural to him.

Charles took his place at the head of the platoon and approached his Lieutenant. A single nod passed between them, the officer's eyes flicking briefly to the ribbons on his chest, a quiet acknowledgement. He stood there, scanning the men staring straight ahead, some with sweat running down their faces. Charles wondered what they saw. Did they see him as he once saw Iron Jack; a strung-up veteran past his time, or as a leader like MacRae?

His eyes caught on two boys near the end, fresh-faced, awkward: one slender with a thin moustache, the other tall and broad. For a moment they blurred into Billy and Frankie. Not the dying versions from his nightmares; these two were alive, smirking, talking under their breath. The old ache flared, but it didn't hollow him. He felt still. Proud. As if the boys were standing with him, not behind him.

He lifted his chin slightly, voice firm as he looked their way.

"Straighten that line. You're soldiers now, act like it."

The words echoed MacRae's from years ago. The soldiers stiffened. Charles had never held this kind of command before, a power that felt both fragile and sure.

"Alright, lads, rifles at the ready. Let's look like soldiers, not scarecrows."

The ancient Lee–Enfield rifles, relics of the first war, clacked in rhythm as they moved. A few fumbled their grips; he didn't bark, he corrected. They drilled through the heavy night air, boots stamping, lantern light gleaming. Step by step, the line tightened, rifles lifted, their movements smoothing through the puddles, beneath his calm direction.

When the bugle finally sounded stand down, the men were slick with sweat, breath coming hard but steady. A couple of the younger recruits lingered, glancing up at him with a mix of curiosity and respect.

"You really fought in France, Sarge?" one asked quietly.

Charles gave a small nod. "A lifetime ago."

"What was it like?" another pressed.

Charles looked at them; too young to know, too eager not to ask. "Loud," he said. "Louder than you can imagine. That's why you drill. So, when it comes, your head doesn't fall apart."

The boys nodded, shoulders squaring just a little.

As the platoon peeled away into the warm night, their boots crunching on the damp gravel, Charles lingered. The lantern light wavered across the ground. He ran a thumb along his belt, listening to the quiet hum of the night. The faces of those young recruits gave comfort to the noise in his head. The ghosts didn't vanish; they simply fell into line. This wasn't the war. But if the past had marked him, then maybe it could teach them. Maybe that was enough.

The years that followed settled into a kind of rhythm, shaped by two worlds that never quite met but somehow held him together. By day he was a farmer: boots deep in red dust, hands calloused from wire and rope. By night, on drill evenings, he was Sergeant Watson.

In May 1934, Edna gave birth to their son, John. The house grew louder, busier; the kind of noise Charles never knew he'd come to treasure. Lurline hovered protectively over her little brother, and Edna took it all in stride, steady as she'd always been. The walls of the homestead seemed to settle more firmly into the earth.

The military promotion had come without fanfare, passed over in a clipped handshake beneath the lanterns on the Townsville parade ground. Warrant Officer Class 2. It wasn't the crown that mattered, but the quiet trust behind it; the nod from men who'd seen him lead.

His uniform, once stiff with disuse, had grown worn in again. The khaki darkened with sweat, the patches softened at the edges, the boots shaped to his step. Townsville had become a second home of sorts. The barracks always smelled the same, polish, linseed oil, and damp canvas after a summer storm. Bugle calls cracked the humid air before dawn, bouncing off tin roofs and gravel yards.

The young recruits listened when he spoke; not because he shouted, but because his voice carried the weight of something they'd only heard in stories. Billy and Frankie never truly left him, but their shadows softened with time. He could look at young lads, faces still soft, and feel calm instead of torn. He corrected their grips, showed them how to hold a Lee–Enfield like it mattered, drilled them until the stamp of boots fell like one heartbeat.

"Keep your chin up," he'd tell them. "The world's heavy enough without you helping it down."

Back home, the land didn't care for rank. The Depression still dug in its claws. Paddocks bleached under a punishing sun, troughs ran low, and bank letters piled like dust. But something in Charles had shifted. The discipline of the parade ground followed him through the gate. The fences held straighter, the shed was kept sharp, and the horses felt the steadiness in his hands.

Edna saw it too. She'd always known his weight, carried part of it herself. Now, when he rode off for training, it wasn't with worry in her eyes but a quiet, certain pride. She packed his kit without fuss, smoothing the fabric over the WO2 crown as if it belonged there. And when neighbours spoke of the uniform, of how far he'd come since the war, she never corrected them. She didn't need to. The girls watched him go; heads high, calling out promises for him to bring back stories.

Weekend bush training soon became part of the family's routine. These meant early starts and long days out in the scrub; rifles stacked by the fire line, canvas tents pitched under a restless sky. Smoke clung to their uniforms, and the air filled with the low murmur of men too tired to talk. Nights were spent on hard ground, the bush alive with the quiet sounds of boots shifting, gear settling, and breath turning heavy with sleep. It was rough living, but nothing like the sucking mud and cold of Flanders. This was Australia; and it felt almost kind by comparison.

And then came the ride home.

Coming back was its own ritual. After a long weekend, the house would be still, the kitchen lamp burning low, the fire banked to embers. The gate creaked. His steps on the veranda folded easily back into the heartbeat of the homestead.

"Daddy?"

Lurline's voice came before he saw her. She'd be barefoot in the doorway, nightdress rumpled, hair wild from sleep, small hands clutching the railing.

"You're up late," he'd whisper.

"I heard the horse."

He set down his kit. She'd wrinkle her nose at the smell of dust and leather, squinting up at him like a little sergeant.

"You're late."

"Exercise ran long. Some of the boys can't march to save themselves."

"You'll teach 'em," she'd say, sure as sunrise.

A quiet warmth settled in his chest. He'd scoop her up, her arms looping tight around his neck, and carry her inside. Edna would be waiting in the kitchen, hair tied back, the soft light of the lamp catching the corners of her smile. Pride didn't need words between them.

He tucked Lurline into bed, her small hand brushing the fabric of his tunic as though it were something magical. When he returned to the living room, he sat in the armchair that once felt too heavy to hold him. Edna handed him a mug without a word. Outside, cicadas hummed in the warm night. Beyond the fence line, cattle shifted in the dark. Somewhere back in Townsville, recruits were still snoring in their bunks. Between those two worlds; dust and drill, family and duty; he'd found a part of himself he hadn't known in years.

From down the hallway, Lurline's drowsy voice drifted out.

"Night, Daddy."

Charles leaned back, the fire snapping softly, smoke and summer rain threading through the room. The weight of old battles was still there. But it no longer pulled him off course.

Chapter 17

The King's Invitation

The sun hung low over the tin roofs, turning the red dust into a haze of gold. Boots were scuffed, collars loosened, sweat drying on khaki after another hard drill. Laughter and dry jokes rolled through the ranks as the men packed down for the day. Charles moved along the line, offering quiet corrections; elbows tucked, feet sharper on the turn. The men gave him the kind of ribbing only earned through respect.

The sound of boots on gravel broke through the chatter. His platoon commander strode toward him, cap tilted back slightly, a folded envelope in hand.

"Warrant Officer Watson, telegraph," he said, and there was a note in his voice Charles wasn't used to. Not the usual clipped efficiency; something closer to excitement.

"Telegraph, Sir? From whom?" Charles asked.

"Buckingham Palace."

Charles froze. Buckingham Palace. That grey, silent facade he'd once stared up at as a young, broken soldier nearly twenty years ago. What on earth would they want with him now?

The men nearby had gone quiet, sensing the shift. The envelope crackled in his hand as he tore it open, the snap of the paper cutting through the warm evening air.

WARRANT OFFICER CLASS 2 C. Y. WATSON

31ST BATTALION CMF

YOU HAVE BEEN SELECTED AS ONE OF ONE HUNDRED AND FIFTY REPRESENTATIVE VETERANS OF THE GREAT WAR TO ATTEND THE CORONATION OF HIS MAJESTY KING GEORGE VI AT LONDON ON 12 MAY 1937

STOP

YOUR PRESENCE IS REQUESTED FOR PARTICIPATION IN THE OFFICIAL MARCH AND INVESTITURE CEREMONY

STOP

FURTHER INSTRUCTIONS AND EMBARKATION ORDERS WILL FOLLOW

STOP

CONGRATULATIONS AND THANKS FOR YOUR SERVICE

STOP

For a moment, the parade ground felt distant, as if he'd stepped out of it entirely. London. The coronation. After everything.

"Everything alright, Warrant?" someone called from down the line.

Charles folded the telegram slowly, a small breath catching in his chest. "Yea," he said, voice steady. "More than alright."

He turned to his lieutenant, a boyish grin breaking through his usual steadiness. "My old man would choke on his tea," he said.

Charles folded the telegram carefully, the paper crisp beneath his calloused fingers, and slipped it into his breast pocket; the same place he'd once kept Edna's telegram all those years ago. It was where all his precious possessions went.

He didn't waste a minute. "Sir, requesting early leave," he said, already half-turned toward the station in his mind. The last train to Woodstock was waiting, and he couldn't imagine telling anyone else before Edna.

The night air was warm and still when Charles stepped off the siding, the last of the train's steam hanging low along the tracks. A buggies lantern bobbed at the edge of the road, casting a soft gold circle on the dust as Charles waved them down for a ride. By the time he pulled up at the homestead, the kitchen light glowed steady through the front window, moths dancing in its halo.

Inside, the house held the hush that followed supper. The old timber table bore the remains of bread and butter, the clock ticked steadily above the hearth, and cicadas droned through the open window. The curtain's edge lifted and fell with the warm breeze. Edna still wore her apron, a mug of tea, cupped loosely in her hands.

The family paused with the creak of the gate, followed by the footsteps on the veranda. Edna looked up, surprised as Charles steps in, dusty uniform, telegram in hand. The girls rushed to him, voices overlapping, Lurline the first to arrive, she always was. They all embrace, swamping him at the door.

Edna remained seated for a moment, John on her lap, taking him in; warm, honest pride. Charles comes and gives John a soft kiss on the forehead before he places the telegram on the dining table with the remnants of supper. Edna ran her fingers over the royal seal catching the lamp light. Her eyes flicked up to his. No words yet; just a shared question.

Lurline leaned forward until her chin nearly touched the table. "What's it say, Dad?"

Charles's mouth twitched into a grin. "It says your old man's been summoned to London."

Margaret let out a sharp gasp. Lucille clapped a hand over her mouth, wide-eyed.

Lurline blinked. "You went there before, didn't you, Dad?"

Charles's eyes softened. "Yes, my dear. But it wasn't London I saw back then, I couldn't see it for what it was" he said, his voice lower now, a quiet truth beneath the warmth.

Edna turned the paper slowly, as though the weight of the crest alone was something fragile. "The King's coronation," she murmured.

Margaret leaned closer. "The King? The King?"

"The King?" Clair copied.

"Seems so," Charles said lightly. "Someone must've made a mistake."

Lucille swatted her sister's arm, grinning. "He's serious!"

Lurline kicked her feet against the floor, beaming. "Dad's going to London! To see the King!"

Edna finally looked up at him fully, her eyes shining in that steady way she had; not loud or showy, just full. "Charles," she said softly.

He scratched at the back of his neck, feeling the heat rise there. "Never thought a bloke from Woodstock'd be called up for something like this."

The clock ticked. Outside, the insects kept their song. Around the old table, pride threaded through the room; quiet, and warm. It wasn't the telegram that made it real. It was the way their faces lit at the thought of it.

Within weeks, Charles was bound for Europe once more, following the same route he had taken as a boy in 1917. The long sea voyage carried him past familiar ports; Colombo, Port Said, through the Suez Canal; each stop stirring old memories of a time when he'd sailed off to war with Billy, Chook and Snow at his side. Now, nearly two decades on, it felt as though he carried them with him, their share of the honour stitched into his uniform.

On a foggy London morning in May, he stepped off the train into the heart of Trafalgar Square. The city was dressed for celebration. Bunting draped from lamp posts, Union Jacks snapping in the breeze, the lion statues at the base flanked by neat ranks of Royal Guards. Red double-deckers rolled steadily down Whitehall, their engines growling, black cabs weaving between them with the familiar rattle of fenders and tyres on wet cobblestones. The great column of Nelson rose into the soft haze, its stonework slick from an earlier rain, pigeons wheeling overhead.

Crowds moved through the square in a slow, excited current; women in vibrant spring dresses, boys in short trousers waving paper flags, vendors spousing their spoils, men in bowler hats clutching folded newspapers with headlines about the King's Coronation. The air carried a damp chill mixed with the smell of coal haze, sour cooking fat, and the faint tang of wet stone.

The last time Charles had stood here, the noise of London had pressed in on him like a storm; then it had been agony, too loud, too bright, too much. Now, it filled him with quiet awe.

He made his way through the streets slowly, letting the city wrap around him. Every sound, every colour, every detail; he tried to take it all in, something to carry home to Edna and the kids. The last time he'd walked these streets it had been a blur, swallowed by nerves and ghosts. This time, he saw it.

Charles had been summoned to a small photography studio just off the Strand. His kit was cleaner and stiffer than it had ever been, creases sharp as blades. His face was freshly shaven, boots polished so bright they seemed to melt into the floor beneath him.

The moment he stepped inside, the sharp tang of developing chemicals hit him; mingled with the familiar scents of leather polish and starch. He joined a neat line of men waiting their turn, each one standing to attention as the flashbulbs cracked and the photographer's voice ran like a drill sergeant,

"Chin up... good man... hold still."

An assistant approached, brisk and practiced, tugging at his belt, straightening his jacket, tipping the edge of his hat just so. Charles shifted, uncomfortable under the fuss. When it was his turn to stand in front of the painted backdrop, the bright light catching his ribbons, he held himself still, back straight, chin lifted.

As the camera clicked and flashed, a memory surfaced; the photos taken in front of the pyramids with Billy and Chook behind the camera, laughing like fools. They'd been boys then, playing at soldiers. Now, he straightened his shoulders for them. For what they'd done. For the war they never came home from.

The morning of the procession, Charles was formed up with the other 149 members of the Australian contingent, three columns wide in the middle of a broad avenue, he'd recognised it from before and now knew where he stood. The Mall; the great ceremonial road, stretched ahead like a polished red carpet leading toward Buckingham Palace, slick with morning rain.

The white stone facades of the buildings flanking the street loomed clean and sharp, trimmed with royal bunting that fluttered in the soft breeze. Above it all, the faint chime of Big Ben rolled across the city, each note deep and clear, threading through the murmuring crowd.

A brass band swelled in the background, the first notes humming through the cool, damp air. Drums began to roll; a low, deliberate thunder that vibrated through the soles of their boots; before a booming voice barked through the stillness,

"Quick march!"

The column moved as one. Horses clopped on the wet stone, their harnesses jingling faintly, the scent of damp leather and linseed oil carried on the breeze. A soft sprinkle of rain settled over the ranks, speckling the khaki uniforms and lifting the earthy smell of wet wool and sweat. The sharp snap of boots struck in perfect unison, echoing down the avenue like rifle fire on a parade ground. Medals flashed against tunics, catching the thin sunlight as the clouds began to shift and open.

The crowd was vast; a living tide pressed against the barricades on either side. Flags whipped in every direction, a sea of Union Jacks and Commonwealth banners waving above hats and umbrellas. Police in white gloves lined the road, holding the surge at bay with calm, practiced precision. Voices rose like a single wave, the roar of thousands greeting them with cheers and applause. From open windows, clerks leaned out, waving handkerchiefs and tossing flowers down onto the marching men.

Charles soaked it in. The colour, the noise, the weight of it; all of London seemed to rise up around them. He could feel the beat through his chest as much as under his boots. It was impossible not to think of that other march twenty years before; Spencer Street, Melbourne. Back then a boy in a brand-new uniform, marching toward the docks with Billy, Chook, and Snow, drunk on the noise of the crowd and the promise of adventure. Now, the cheers felt heavier; not naive or expectant; but earned.

He didn't grin or wave. He just marched; boots striking in rhythm, carrying not just himself, but the memory of those who'd never made it back to march again. Pride sat alongside the ache, and neither outweighed the other.

The parade came up to Buckingham Palace. The white stone gleamed in the morning light, its high windows catching and scattering the colours of the empire. The last time Charles had stood here, the place had felt cold, grey, unreachable.

Now it was light and alive; thousands of civilians crowding the streets, waving flags, children perched on shoulders straining for a glimpse. The noise of the crowd echoed off the palace facade as he passed through the iron gates, not as an intruder this time, but as an honoured guest.

The contingent reached the forecourt and fell into neat ranks, boots snapping into place. Charles stood at attention, eyes fixed forward. In the blur of his peripheral vision, a small procession approached; a man at its centre robed in deep crimson. As they drew closer, the figure sharpened into striking clarity, the morning sun catching the crown that glittered on his head.

King George VI moved down the line slowly, flanked by officers and guards, stopping before each man in turn. When he came to Charles, the soldier lifted his chin; not as a frightened boy, but as someone who had already given.

"Thank you for your service," the King said quietly and formally, pinning the Coronation Medal to his chest.

Charles responded steadily, "Your Majesty."

This medal felt different; not one earned in blood; but given in honour. His other medals had always hung heavy, like anchors. This one sat light, carrying more meaning than he'd expected.

His father's voice drifted up from memory, from the far end of the old dining table, *"Fight for a crown; or for a king you'll never meet."*

Yet here he was, in the flesh, standing before the very man his father said he'd never see. Charles wondered what he would make of it, or of him now.

The cheers of the crowd still rang faintly in Charles's ears long after the parade had ended. The pomp and ceremony bled into twilight, London softening as the day gave way to evening. He'd slipped away from the lingering chatter of officers and well-wishers, drawn by the city itself. The medal sat cool and unfamiliar against his chest as he walked, a quiet reminder of the moment trailing him like an echo.

By the time he turned off the main thoroughfare, the noise of the city had faded into a low, steady hum. Gas lamps cast golden pools across the slick cobblestones, puddles holding reflections of bunting and theatre lights still glowing from the day's celebrations.

Piano music drifted through an open pub door, warm against the cool air, carrying with it the rich smell of beer, bread, and tobacco. For the first time since he'd stepped back onto London soil, Charles felt something ease inside him. The rain had set in since the afternoon, the kind that blurred the city's edges into soft streaks of grey. His steps slowed, drawn to the soft light and laughter spilling from the doorway.

Charles pushed open the pub door, shaking the wet from his hat, boots leaving dark prints on the worn floorboards. Warmth rolled over him at once, gin, smoke, damp wool coats, the thick smell of roasted meat from somewhere out the back. Gaslight glowed low in pressed tin lamps, turning the wood-panelled walls a deep honey.

He'd come in for a quiet pint. Just to sit a while.

But then,

"Well now... bush boy in the big city."

The voice caught him before the barman did. Charles turned and saw her perched at the bar; elbow resting on the polished wood, gin fizz in hand, that familiar half-grin he hadn't seen in eighteen years. Nancy Whitaker.

She looked older, of course. Lines at the corners of her eyes, a more deliberate way of holding herself. But there was still that easy confidence, the same spark that used to light up the ward at Clevedon Hall when everything else felt grey. Her hair was pinned in soft waves, lipstick a little too bold for the hour, and somehow it suited her perfectly.

"Nancy bloody Whitaker," Charles said, a smile tugging despite himself.

She gave a mock gasp. "I was starting to think you'd made me up."

"I wasn't looking for anyone," he said.

Nancy leaned in just slightly, grin growing. "And yet here you are, I'd say London's trying to tell us something."

Charles laughed low in his chest, shaking his head as she slid the empty barstool toward him with the toe of her shoe. He sat, the medal on his chest catching a slant of gaslight. Her eyes flicked down to it, not lingering long, just enough.

"Medal and everything," she said, raising a brow. "You've gone respectable on me."

"Don't spread it around," Charles replied.

They found a small corner table near the window, fogged over from the warm air inside pressing against the cold outside. Rain streaked the glass. The piano in the corner rolled through some cheerful tune, just loud enough to soften the rest of the room into a murmur. Nancy's drink glowed pale in the lamplight as she leaned back, crossing her legs like someone entirely at home here.

"So," she said, swirling the gin with her straw, "what became of the lad who left my ward with mud in his hair and a grin too big for his face?"

"He went home," Charles said. "Married Edna. Built a farm. Ended up with five kids."

Nancy's jaw dropped dramatically. "Five? Lord above, I leave you alone for eighteen years and you turn into a one-man village."

Charles chuckled. "Edna was the pen pal, remember?"

"Of course I do. You used to talk about her like the sun rose and set on her. Guess it still does."

He nodded, the ghost of a grin there but quiet. She wasn't teasing now; she said it like a fact.

"And you?" he asked. "What's England done with you?"

Her eyes softened, and she swirled her drink again, slower this time. "Married a clever man. Lost him a few years back. Evelyn's sixteen now. She's got more fire in her than I ever did. Keeps me honest."

"You always did handle fire better than most," he said.

She laughed softly, tilting her head. "You used to say things like that to make me blush."

"And did it work?"

"Every time."

It hung between them for a breath; warm, familiar, easy. The kind of feeling that came from a place long before children and responsibility and the weight of years. But Charles didn't let it stretch too far.

"I'm still married to Edna," he said plainly.

Nancy didn't flinch. She just gave a small, lopsided smile. "Of course you are. And she's lucky."

The piano player stopped for a smoke break, leaving the air suddenly quieter. Someone opened the front door; a gust of cold wind curled through the room, rustling a newspaper at the bar. A headline stared out in bold print, *Hitler Defies Treaty as German Troops Enter Rhineland*.

Nancy's eyes flicked toward it, then back to Charles. The change in her tone was subtle, but real.

"You've come at a strange time, Charles," she said, voice lower. "London looks bright now; bunting, medals, all the show for the King; but it's just paint."

Charles frowned. "What do you mean?"

"Germany," she said simply. "Hitler's marching his men where they shouldn't be. No one here wants to admit it, but everyone can feel it. It's like the wind before a storm."

"We don't hear much about it on the other side of the world," Charles admitted. "Feels far off."

Nancy lowered her voice, leaning closer.

"That's the trick," she said. "It won't stay far. My brother works down in Whitehall; says they're all pretending it'll just… go away. But it won't. He's building something, Charles. Not just an army, a whole machine. Factories, soldiers, airfields, the works. And everyone here's whistling like it's nothing."

The rain grew heavier, tapping the window in sharp, rhythmic bursts. A man coughed somewhere near the fire. A few men laughed too loudly at a table near the door: soldiers, not so different to him.

Charles stared into his pint. "We thought the last one fixed it."

Nancy's fingers traced the edge of her glass. "So did we. But it didn't. It just pressed pause; they say Austria is next"

A long silence settled between them. Not uncomfortable, just heavy, in the way only war talk could be. Charles glanced at her and saw not the nurse he'd known in the soft haze after the Armistice, but a woman who'd lived with the world at her doorstep ever since.

"I came here thinking it'd be different this time," he said quietly. "Lighter."

Nancy gave a small, sad smile. "It is different, Charles. But peace... peace has a way of cracking."

She finished her drink with a soft clink against the table. The piano picked back up, a jaunty tune that didn't match the air at all. Charles leaned back in his chair, watching rain streak down the glass, Union Jacks outside hanging limp in the damp.

Nancy's laugh drifted over him, warm but distant, and beneath it he felt the weight of what she'd said settle in the pit of his stomach. London was still alive and bright; but somewhere, beyond the glow, something darker was stirring.

Chapter 18

Rising Tensions

Charles had returned from London, back amongst the smell of dry paddocks and bleached timber fences. A windmill groaned somewhere beyond the yards, steady and familiar, but the world didn't feel the same. The fields looked unchanged; the man walking them wasn't. He wore a worried look now, as if London had followed him home. He brought back more than a medal and a handful of stories; Nancy's words clung like a storm cloud on the horizon.

He threw himself into work, catching up on the maintenance that had piled up in his absence. He mended wire and adjusted tack, fixed the gate hinge that had been squealing for months. But he wasn't really present. A folded newspaper was always wedged into his back pocket; the one with Hitler's face and the word *"Reich"* stamped across the top.

Edna watched him from the veranda, hands wrapped around a chipped mug, her skirt blowing in the wind. She knew the signs: the quiet, the far-off stare, the way he checked the post each afternoon and buried himself in The Townsville Daily Bulletin. The headlines from Europe crept in a little louder with each edition.

"You've been pacing like a hound waiting for a whistle," Edna called out, leaning against the post with a sly grin.

Charles half-smiled back. "And you've been watching like a hawk."

"Only 'cause I know what comes after the pacing," she said, eyebrows up, tilting her head in that way she knew disarmed him.

She never missed a cue. He couldn't settle. London had lit something old inside him: a duty, a restlessness that wouldn't stay quiet.

As the months rolled on into early 1938 and the summer heat softened, distant news kept seeping into their evenings. Charles stopped fussing about fence posts at dusk and instead took to his armchair. The wireless hummed low in the corner, the announcer's clipped voice weaving foreign names through the croak of frogs and the tap of flies against the screen.

Clair perched on his lap, knees tucked in, her hair brushing against his chin. She was too old to need to sit there, but not too old to want to. Lurline sprawled on the floor in front of him, legs crossed, pencil tapping against her cheek as she worked through her schoolbooks in the golden pool of lamplight. Margaret and Lucille whispered in the doorway, their laughter sharp and quick, like flint strikes. John pushed his tin car along the floorboards, wheels rattling against the cracks in the wood.

Edna crossed the room with a steaming mug of tea, hips swaying just enough to soften the heaviness that hung around him. She leaned down and glanced at the headline in his hand.

"Another parade?" she asked, voice light but with that knowing edge.

Charles didn't look up. "Yea, another," he murmured.

"They must have sore feet by now," she teased, setting the mug down beside him.

He tapped the page with his thumb. "Big crowds too... all waving the same flag."

Lurline didn't look up from her book. "They're always marching somewhere. Do they ever stop?"

Charles huffed softly through his nose, not quite a laugh. "Not when they're getting ready for something."

Clair twisted on his lap to peer up at him. "What are they getting ready for, Dad?"

Edna cut in before he could answer, a touch of playful sharpness in her tone. "For another parade, love. Maybe they just like showing off their shiny boots."

That earned a grin from Clair, and a soft snort from Lurline. The air lightened for a moment. But behind Charles's eyes, the map of Europe was already unfolding. He heard the wireless, smelled the dust of the paddocks, and felt that old tug in his chest; the same one he thought he'd buried decades ago.

It was now the 12th of March, the midday sun bit through the dust like a blade, turning the main street into a glare of white and ochre. Charles walked in from the siding still wearing his CMF uniform, collar undone, hat pulled low against the heat. The town looked the same as always; horses tied to the hitching rail out front of the post office, timber boards bleached silver by years of sun, the pub's flyscreen door banging against its frame.

A cluster of men lingered under the post office veranda, hats tilted, pipes going. The air carried the mingled smells of tobacco, horse dung and dry dust kicked up by passing drays.

From inside the postmaster's office, a radio crackled to life; the sharp pop of static, then a clipped, measured voice.

"...reports from Vienna... German forces have crossed the border without resistance... crowds in Austria cheering the Anschluss..."

The men leaned in without moving, ears sharpening.

"Chamberlain's in talks with Berlin," the announcer went on. "No immediate plans for action."

A magpie called somewhere down the street. A horse shifted its weight and stamped.

"Bloody hell," one of the farmers muttered, knocking his pipe on the rail. "Didn't they learn their lesson last time?"

Another man spat into the dust. "Europe's problem, not ours. Let 'em sort their own mess out."

"You reckon Germany'll stop in Austria?" the first man said.

"Course they will. Just chest-beatin'. They all do it."

"Yeah? That's what they said about the last war, too."

A small, taut silence settled among them. The radio kept on, the announcer listing place names half a world away; Linz, Vienna, Berlin; names that suddenly didn't feel so distant.

Charles slowed his steps, pretending to check his bootlace so he could listen. The heat pressed down, sweat running between his shoulder blades. The back of his neck prickled.

Nancy's voice surfaced in his mind, as sharp as the day in London when she'd said it.

"It just pressed pause; they say Austria is next."

She'd been right. He stared at the dusty boards of the veranda, the worn post where men leaned every day to talk about weather and cattle prices. Now they were talking about war again. He didn't need to join in; the shift inside him was silent but certain.

The breeze stirred, carrying the faint scent of sun-warmed gum leaves. He straightened his hat, gave the men a curt nod as he passed, and kept walking.

But the weight of the wireless followed him down the street.

Charles had started spending more evenings in town, his focus slowly drifting from the farm toward the militia. Edna noticed it; the longer nights away, the way his hands itched for something more than wire and stockwork. She didn't press him. She just rolled up her sleeves and picked up the slack with the kids, keeping the place running the way she always did.

One evening he stood on the veranda, shoulder against the post, staring out over the paddocks. The last of the light bled gold across the fence line, the windmill letting out its long, weary groan. The stillness of it all pressed up against him.

Edna stepped out quietly, wiping her hands on her apron, the smell of bread and saddle soap hanging in the air. She came up beside him, sliding her arms around his middle and pressing her cheek against his shoulder.

"What's got you troubled, soldier?" she asked, her voice soft but with that familiar lilt; the one that could cut through any storm in his head.

Charles drew a slow breath, then pulled a folded letter from his pocket and set it on the veranda rail. The paper caught the last slant of evening sun. Edna didn't pick it up straight away. She let the quiet sit between them for a heartbeat, then finally lifted it, smoothing a crease with her thumb.

"Permanent?" she asked after a moment.

"Yep, Australian Instructional Corps" he said.

She tilted her head. "Brisbane's not round the corner."

"No."

"And this place?"

"We lease… or sell. Can't half do both."

She looked out across the fields; the weathered fences, the troughs catching the light, the place they'd built a life together.

"You've already gone in your head," she said quietly.

He exhaled, a tiny, guilty breath. "I have."

Edna set the letter down carefully, then nudged him lightly in the ribs with her elbow; a small, familiar gesture meant to break the weight of things.

"Well, Charles Watson, I didn't marry you for a quiet life."

A corner of his mouth lifted, just enough.

She straightened, brushing a loose strand of hair behind her ear. "Then we'll start sorting," she said, practical as always; but behind the steadiness was something warmer. She wasn't just going to follow. She was already moving with him.

Charles threw himself into maintenance on the farm, working from sun-up until the last light slipped across the paddocks. The sharp tang of kerosene clung to his hands as he oiled bridles. Fresh paint bled across the veranda posts, the old wood drinking it in. Up on the windmill, he oiled the groaning gears, the creak of the blades carrying out over the property like an old tune.

Inside, Edna moved through the house with quiet precision. Dust drifted in slow spirals through the lamplight as she opened drawers that hadn't been touched in years. She folded the same cotton dress over and over, the fabric catching between her fingers.

"Feels wrong folding it up like this," she murmured to no one in particular.

All their years together; their children's years; were being packed down into a few boxes stacked by the wall.

Granny Dean stood in the doorway, one hand gripping the frame. She didn't speak. She'd built this place with Charles's father, and now she too was preparing to let it go. Leaving with the family to help Edna while Charles did his duty.

Outside, the horses shifted in the yards, tails flicking at flies. The cattle stirred uneasily, hooves shuffling in the dust. Even the animals seemed to sense something was changing.

Charles saddled his gelding and rode the fence line, the leather creaking softly beneath him, the scent of warm dust and dry grass rising around. Beside him, Lurline sat straight on her pony, reins loose in her hands, heels brushing its flanks. She didn't speak for a while, just let the sound of hooves and the wind in the gums fill the quiet.

He scanned the paddocks as they rode, every post, every gum tree, every dry creek bed. All of it was etched into him as surely as the lines on his hands.

Lurline shifted in the saddle, studying him the way only a daughter could. She glanced sideways at him, her pony moving beneath her.

"You really love it here," she said.

"I do," he answered simply.

"It's like you know every inch of it," she added, not as a question but a quiet truth.

Charles let his gaze travel across the paddocks, over every blade of grass. "Reckon I do."

She rode a little closer, her voice softer now. "That's why it's hard, isn't it? Leaving."

"It's more than land, love," he said after a moment. "It's... everything that came with it."

Lurline lifted her chin, trying to sound braver than she felt. "We'll make new fences. New everything. Won't be the same, but maybe that's alright."

The words settled between them like a quiet promise. She had the same stubborn, steady warmth as her mother; the same way of finding the light in the middle of change. It was enough to ease something tight in his chest.

Later that evening, as the work light softened and the kids gathered on the veranda, the air hung still and warm. Edna wiped her hands on her apron, watching him with that quiet, knowing look she always had. Lucille leaned against the railing, practically buzzing with the idea of the move.

"Brisbane's got trams, right? And shops?" she asked.

Charles's mouth twitched into a small smile. "More than you can count, love."

"Can we ride on top?" Clair piped up.

Edna laughed, the sound soft and warm. "Not unless you want your ears blown clean off."

Lurline grinned at that, already picturing the city in her head; all bustle and bright lights, everything the farm wasn't.

The laughter faded into the evening stillness. The warm air, the smell of eucalyptus, and the soft whirr of the newly oiled windmill settled around them like the farm itself was listening. Charles let the sound sink into him, knowing it was the kind of quiet you only get once.

The stable glowed soft under the hurricane lamps, the light stretching over the dirt like a warm glow, the town had come to say farewell. Smoke drifted low from the fire drum where Dr Doyle and Billy Carter's father stood with Charles, their boots planted wide against the cold. The fiddle from inside rolled through a lazy tune, laughter rising and falling with it like the wind.

Doyle flicked his ash toward the drum. "Not many sign up to teach," he said quietly. "Everyone wants to be a hero in the next one. But teaching," he shrugged. "Might save a few of them."

Billy's father gave a short grunt. "Save 'em from what? War finds you anyway."

Charles shifted, warming his hands against the barrel. "This way, maybe it doesn't catch 'em off guard."

None of them rushed the silence after that. The embers cracked. The music swelled again inside.

"You'll be shaping green boys," Doyle said after the long pause. "That matters, Charles. Better they learn from someone who's seen the real thing."

Billy's father let out a dry breath. "Maybe this time they'll get to finish what you boys started."

Across the yard, Edna stood with the neighbourhood women, hands busy stacking plates and wiping crumbs. They didn't talk loudly, just the soft, steady way women do when they've known each other a lifetime.

"City'll drive you mad first week," one of them said, brushing sugar off her skirt.

Edna laughed, quiet but real. "Better the city than a herd of stubborn cows."

Another woman shook her head. "Hard thing, leavin' land that knows your name."

Edna glanced toward Charles, the lamplight catching the side of his face. "It's in him," she said softly. "This place. Always will be. But so's the fight."

Inside, Lurline sat cross-legged with a knot of kids, talking big with the bright certainty only fourteen can carry. Lucille perched beside her, chin in hands, hanging off every word.

"They've got bells," Lurline said. "And they're faster than horses. Way faster."

The neighbour boy smirked. "Faster than Snowy?"

Lucille wrinkled her nose. "Course they are. I'm sittin' right at the front."

Their laughter tumbled out the open doorway, catching in the night air.

Later, Edna's parents arrived, her father cutting through the crowd straight to Charles. No greetings, no fuss. Just a hand to the shoulder, the kind that said what words couldn't.

"You ain't one for adventure anymore, this isn't running," her father said, voice low.

"No," Charles answered. "It's getting ready."

Her mother pressed his hand in both of hers. "We'll keep the hearth warm if you ever want it back."

As the night stretched thin, neighbours began peeling away, boots crunching down the dusty track. Doyle lingered by the fire drum, smoke clinging to his sleeves. He clasped Charles's hand, firm.

"Don't carry it all yourself this time," Doyle said.

Charles glanced toward Edna, her laughter carrying through the open barn. "I won't," he said simply. "Not anymore."

When the last lamp burned low, only the two of them remained. Edna tucked her arm through his, leaning her head against his shoulder. The yard was quiet now except for the soft hiss of the coals and the groan of the wind through the paddocks.

The night held both weight and warmth; like the land itself didn't want to let them go.

Dawn the next morning. Frost silvered the fence lines, mist hung low across the fields. Boots creaked on the old timber platform of Woodstock Station, the sound sharp in the still air. The train whistle cut through the quiet; a clean, two-note call that carried down the main street like a farewell.

A trunk marked *WATSON* sat at the edge of the platform, chalk white against the dark timber, ready to be loaded.

Lurline almost vibrated with excitement, her coat too big for her narrow frame. "I can't believe we're actually going!" she said, breath fogging in the cold.

Clair tugged on Charles's sleeve. "Is it further than the trip to Townsville?"

"Just a touch longer, love," Charles answered, smiling despite the knot sitting low in his chest.

Margaret and Lucille were busy licking the last of the sticky toffee from their fingers, Edna gently trying to herd them toward the carriage. Granny Dean stood a few steps back, jaw set tight; the sentinel who refused to be left behind.

Charles brushed his hand against the cold iron rail of the train steps, a quiet, private goodbye.

"Will we come back?" Lurline asked.

Charles leaned down so only she could hear. "One day," he said softly.

As they boarded, the steam drifted low like fog, swallowing the platform. The paddocks blurred away behind them, fading like the edges of an old photograph.

Chapter 19

A House on Red Hill

The rattle of the train gave way to the buzz of the city as it slowed into Roma Street Station, steam billowing out and swallowing the platform in white. The crowd pressed close; men in felt hats, women clutching string bags of fruit, a newsboy weaving through with headlines about Czechoslovakia and Hitler.

Edna tightened her grip on John's hand to keep him from wandering. The girls huddled close, wide-eyed, and together they spilled out of the station and onto George Street, swept along in the tide of bodies.

The air was thick after a passing shower, the smell of hot tar rising off the road. River silt drifted in on the breeze, mixing with fried onions and cigarette smoke curling from a food cart. The noise of the city struck them all at once: tram bells, gulls, vendors shouting for attention.

Lurline turned in a slow circle, awestruck at the trams rattling past. Granny Dean stood a few steps behind, steady but wide-eyed, adjusting to the sheer volume of Brisbane.

"It's like the whole place is shouting," Lurline said.

"That's just Brisbane saying hello," Charles replied with a half grin.

"Where's the river?" Lucille asked.

"Where's the big bridge everyone talks about?" Margaret added.

Charles lifted his chin toward the horizon. Beyond the rooftops, the Story Bridge's skeletal frame arched over the river; an unfinished giant of steel and rivets, cranes perched like iron birds.

"Over there," he said. "Not finished yet, but she will be soon."

A taxi carried them through the steep, tram-lined streets of Red Hill. As they climbed, the city's roar softened, replaced by the smell of wet timber and woodsmoke drifting from the cottages. Their new house sat in a neat row of married quarters; weatherboard walls with white paint flaking at the edges, a corrugated roof dulled by years of storms. A wide veranda wrapped around the front, the leaning picket fence giving the impression it had been waiting just for them.

Edna traced her fingers along the doorframe, studying it with the same cautious hope she once used on new paddocks. Charles caught her eye.

"It's a start," she murmured.

He stepped beside her, placing his hand over hers. "A good one."

Below them, the city hummed; river steamers calling across the Brisbane River, trams clanging on the ridge. It wasn't Woodstock, but it was theirs.

On the brisk morning of the 1st of July, Charles stepped onto the parade square at Enoggera where he'd once stood as a recruit, a lifetime ago. The ground was the same but everything else had changed. Gravel now rolled firm beneath his boots; the old bell tents were replaced with timber huts, their fresh paint doing little to hide crooked frames. A bugle cut the air, followed by the faint clang of rifles somewhere beyond the ridge.

Charles marched past uneven lines of young recruits, boots too shiny and faces tight with nerves; just like Chook fumbling his first salute years before. A fresh-faced lieutenant stood where Iron Jack once barked. A few heads turned as Charles passed; his kit was immaculate, his war ribbons pinned firm, a duffle bag swinging at his side.

Inside one of the brick admin buildings, warmth struck him first: ink, paper, tobacco, and the faint clatter of a typewriter. A lieutenant looked up from a desk.

"Warrant Officer Watson?"

"That's me."

"Welcome back to Enoggera. Been a while, I hear."

Charles gave a thin smile. "A lifetime."

A chalkboard map on the wall behind the officer caught his eye. Europe was drawn in white, red arrows curling toward Austria. The chalk lines were just lines, but he knew the weight beneath them. He looked a moment longer before accepting his papers.

He didn't linger. After dropping his things in a hut, he strode back out to the parade ground. He adjusted straps, lifted chins, corrected elbows: efficient, quiet, precise.

"Shoulders back, lad. Life'll try to bend you soon enough."

Two recruits whispered at the rear. He let it go for three seconds before cutting it off with a single clipped word. Then he stepped forward and demonstrated a turn; slow once, sharp the second time. Boots struck gravel behind him, the rhythm tightening like a drumline.

By midday the sun burned high; recruits were flushed red, boots scuffed, shoulders aching.

The mess hall at lunch was the same one Snow once lectured in, and Billy cracked jokes through, where the orders to England had been handed down. Charles paused at the doorway for only a heartbeat; just long enough to feel the memory of his younger self at one of those narrow timber tables.

"How'd we do, Warrant?" one of the recruits asked, still catching his breath.

"You didn't fall over," Charles said dryly. "Next time you'll look like you meant not to."

Newspapers rustled across the room, NCOs murmuring over headlines. A map of Europe hung lopsided on the wall, fresh pencil lines creeping deeper into its borders. A radio hummed on low, talk shifting to the Sudetenland.

"Reckon it'll reach us, Warrant?" another lad asked.

Charles didn't hesitate. "It reached us once."

And that was all he said.

The afternoon smelled of cordite and warm earth. Lee–Enfield shots cracked across the range, brass casings pinging like tossed coins. Sergeants barked; Charles moved quietly between shooters; lifting barrels, adjusting grips, steadying tremors. His silence carried further than shouting ever could.

By sunset he stood alone on the parade square, breath fogging in the cooling air. Same soil. New boys. A familiar weight settling over him. When the tram screeched along the ridge, he boarded and let Brisbane swallow him into the night.

Their Red Hill home was warm when he stepped inside. Edna sat mending one of John's shirts by the fire. Granny Dean dozed in an armchair, book slipping from her hand. Lurline sprawled on the floor over a tram map; Margaret and Lucille whispered under a blanket.

"Long day," Edna said softly.

Charles hung his tunic over a chair and sat near the fire. "They've got spirit," he said. "Rough as guts, but keen. Reminds me of us."

"You came home with mud on your boots and something different in your face," she said quietly.

He huffed a tired laugh. "Maybe I just know the ground too well."

"Or maybe being back with the army isn't as strange as you expected."

He didn't reply immediately. A tram bell rang faintly outside.

"Strange, yes. But... familiar too. Like walking past a place where a younger bloke left his boots behind."

Edna crossed to him and touched his arm.

"Then let him stay there. You're not that boy anymore."

Half-asleep on the floor, Lurline murmured, "Did you yell at them, Dad?"

Charles smirked. "Didn't need to. Just walked past 'em."

Margaret giggled. Edna shooed them all to bed. The house settled again.

For a moment Charles watched the last tram glide along the ridge, its bell fading. In the glow of the fire, he could almost hear Billy and Chook laughing in their hut at Enoggera, young and loud and alive.

"You're home, Charles," Edna said quietly.

He nodded. "Yeah. I am."

The next year hardened. Dawn drills became fierce, convoys rumbled into the scrub, and lanterns bobbed like ghost lights in the night. Maps littered the tables, chalk dust hanging in the air. Every radio bulletin from Europe sharpened Charles's pace; Hitler in the Sudetenland, then all of Czechoslovakia, then Italy in Albania. The world was shifting again.

In the evenings he returned to the warmth of Red Hill; the clatter of dishes, children laughing, tram bells drifting. He'd sit by the fire while they slept, radio humming, training notes spread over his knees. Edna was always nearby, knitting or folding linen.

Then, on the night of the 1st of September 1939, the wireless crackled sharply:

"We interrupt this broadcast... Germany has invaded Poland. Britain and France have declared war on Germany."

Firelight flickered across the walls. Shadows lengthened. The room felt suddenly smaller.

Edna whispered, "It's starting again."

Charles stared at the radio.

"Yeah... but this time, I'm not the one they'll send."

"You were eager once."

He gave a half-laugh, weary and thin. "That was a boy talking. I'm not chasing another war. I'm here to get the young ones ready, not throw myself back into the mud."

Edna folded the cloth in her hands. "War doesn't always ask, Charles. Sometimes it just takes."

The silence that settled wasn't empty; it was old, familiar.

"Then it'll have to take someone else this time," he said.

Outside, the tram bell chimed; thin and steady.

The world kept turning.

The storm crept closer.

Chapter 20

Steady Hands

The war didn't arrive with a bang for Charles; it crept in like floodwater, slow and unstoppable. He was now with the 2/10th Field Regiment, 8th Division, an artillery unit. Bigger guns, louder thunder, a little further behind the line.

Brisbane shifted quietly at first; new enlistment posters plastered on tram stops, more khaki than suits filling the carriages. He'd step off at the platform and catch sight of the boys; eager, raw, all elbows and big grins; and for a split second, 1917 and the big smoke bled through the edges of the present.

Billy's jeering. Frankie with that thin moustache he swore made him look older and Edna on her platform, her ribbons pinned just so with the piercing pale blue eyes.

He could still feel the weight of the kit on his shoulders, smell the heat on the timber platform. Back then it had been a lark; a war they thought they'd conquer like a storybook adventure. He knows better now. And watching these new recruits pile into the trams with that same wildfire in their eyes only made it clearer why he stayed.

He wasn't here to fight; he was here to shape the ones who would.

Bugles still tore the morning apart; boots still hammered the parade square. The base now riddled with canvas, tents in rows like they once were, convoy drills ran down bitumen roads, not the dusty bush tracks of Salisbury. Recruits stumbled over their rifles, trying to look like soldiers before they'd even learned how to march. Charles didn't bark. A hard stare was enough to make their spines straighten.

"You'll thank me when the bullets start flying," he muttered to one, tightening a chinstrap.

The boy beamed, not understanding a damn thing.

"Most don't," a low voice said beside him.

Charles turned. A lean man in a faded shirt and battered slouch hat stood just off the line, chewing a matchstick like it owed him money. His sleeves were rolled, boots still crusted in red dust.

"Harris," he said, sticking out a hand. "Sergeant. Came down from Katherine."

"Watson," Charles replied, shaking it. "Warrant."

Harris's handshake was wiry and dry, like old rope. He nodded toward the recruits. "Look at 'em, all chest and no clue."

Charles didn't smile. "They don't know what they're walkin' into."

Harris glanced sideways, testing the water. "You do, though."

Charles let the silence answer for him.

Harris cleared his throat, a small sign he knew where the line was. "Well... guess it's a good thing they've got someone who does."

Charles adjusted his cap; eyes still fixed on the recruits. "Yeah. Let's hope they listen."

The mess hall became a revolving door. Every few months the band would strike up, speeches barked, and another batch of boys shipped out. North Africa, the Middle East. Their boots still shone as if the mud would never touch them. Charles clapped a few on the back, knowing their odds as he watched the train roll away.

At night, the wireless murmured low. France had fallen in weeks. Russia had shaken hands with Hitler. Britain stood alone. The young sergeants argued over the Japs; Charles just rolled a cigarette and listened.

When the bulletin came about French Indochina, Harris spat his matchstick into the dirt.

"They're inchin' closer."

Charles tapped a teaspoon into an empty mug. "And we're still teaching chinstraps."

Outside, cicadas sang in the dark, a long, relentless chorus that never let up. Down the hill, hammers struck timber as new barracks went up, the sound carrying through the warm Brisbane night like a heartbeat. The city was swelling, waiting.

Charles spent more nights at the base than at home. Edna ran the Red Hill house like a captain ran a ship; calm, steady, never showing the storm to the children. Granny Dean kept vegetables alive in the thin city soil like it was still Woodstock. And on weekends, when Charles sat at their table, the war sat with him.

Edna doing dishes in the warm kitchen light, the wireless murmuring in the corner.

"You're already marching in your head, Charles," she said softly. "I can hear the boots when you look at that thing."

Charles leaned against the doorway, arms crossed. "I'm not going anywhere."

She didn't look up. "Not yet."

A few weeks later, January 1941, the ceiling fan rattled like a loose canteen on webbing as Charles stepped into the admin hut. The place smelled of hot coffee, polish, and chalk dust. Outside, the parade ground thudded with shouted orders and the crunch of boots.

A knock on the door.

Lieutenant David Fraser entered; boots polished to a mirror, posture stiff as a rifle barrel. His Sandhurst accent was crisp, but there was a flicker behind his eyes; the nerves of a young man delivering something he didn't fully understand.

"Orders for our regiment, Warrant Officer Watson," he said, holding out an envelope as though it might burn him.

He placed it on the desk. Charles didn't move right away. He didn't need to.

"You're on the list too," Fraser added after a beat. "They want steady hands. Seasoned men."

Charles opened the envelope slowly, eyes scanning the neat type,

2/10th Field Regiment – 8 Division – Malaya

Reinforce British defences against the Japanese threat.

Departure to be confirmed.

Charles slid the paper into his breast pocket with two fingers. "Steady's not the same as ready, Lieutenant."

Fraser straightened a little too fast. "No one's ever ready."

Charles gave a dry, dismissive smirk; not cruel, just old. "You'll find that out soon enough."

Fraser gave a tight nod, but his jaw betrayed him; a tiny clench before he turned on his heel.

When the door shut, the noise of the base seeped back in. Shouted commands. Boots on gravel. The rattle of the fan overhead. Charles stared at the empty doorway a moment longer.

He'd known this was coming. But knowing didn't make the air any lighter.

Charles walked home slowly that evening, hat tucked under his arm, streetlights spilling small amber islands onto the road. The quiet let old pictures surface. Lurline was sixteen now; the age he'd signed his name the first time. She had Edna's spark, the same free spirit. Her arrival had been the moment that pulled him out of the dark.

He thought of Margaret, Lucille, and Clair; how their laughter had filled the farmhouse with life, bright noise poured into rooms hollowed by silence. It had layering warmth over everything France had broken. And John, only six; too small to measure a goodbye by anything more than the weight of a hug.

The guilt bit deep. His own mother had left him, a small boy clutching nothing but the wool of his jumper on the orphanage steps. That night never truly let go. He'd built a life on the promise he'd never do the same to his own children. Yet here he was, about to leave them all behind and call it duty.

There were no Japanese soldiers in Malaya. But the British were shoring up the line because the wind was turning that way. Malaya stood between the danger and Red Hill, between what might come and all he loved. If the darkness pushed south, someone would have to meet it before it reached them.

He tightened his grip on the hat and kept walking.

Edna was in the kitchen when the creak of the door cut through the quiet. Home on a weeknight. She didn't need to ask; she'd known it was only a matter of time.

The warm glow of the bulbs threw soft shadows across the room. Lurline sat curled up in her father's chair, chin on her knees. Margaret and Lucille sprawled on the rug, whispering behind cupped hands while John kept breaking their huddle. Clair was perched on Granny Dean's lap; her hair being brushed slow and steady.

Charles stepped through the door, boots heavy against the timber. Edna looked up, and the way his shoulders sat told her everything. He pulled off his boots, crossed the room, and wrapped his arms around her. His breath brushed her ear.

"It's come," he whispered.

Her hands tightened on the fabric in her fingers. "Where?"

"Malaya."

She drew in a sharp breath. "I thought…"

Before she could find the words, he gave the line he'd been rehearsing all the way home. "I won't be in the mud this time. I'll be behind the guns. Organising, not charging."

Edna's jaw trembled. "Behind the guns is still close enough to get hit."

"There's nothing to hit me," Charles insisted, forcing calm into his voice. "The Japs aren't even on the island. They'd be mad to try with the British and us sitting there."

Lurline had slipped off the chair without a sound. She came to stand between them, one hand on his arm, one on Edna's.

"Are you off to war again, Daddy?" she asked; steady voice, eyes shining.

"Yes, my love," Charles said, crouching a little to meet her eye. "But no need to worry."

"You'll write?"

"Every chance I get," he answered, smiling like it didn't hurt.

Edna's throat burned as she fought to hold herself together for the little ones.

Then Granny Dean spoke. No tears, no chair hitting the wall, no fleeing. Just one quiet line, heavy as iron.

"War doesn't care where a man stands."

The room breathed in the silence that followed. Lurline pressed closer. Margaret and Lucille had gone still. The warmth of the kitchen seemed to narrow around them, as if the war itself had stepped inside.

Before long, the time had come. Charles sat on the edge of the bed, ruffling through his kitbag, checking and rechecking everything as if a missed button could stall the inevitable. Outside, crickets hummed in the trees, and a dog barked somewhere down the street. Inside, Edna folded and refolded the same shirt, fingers pinching the fabric tighter each time. Granny Dean polished his buttons like she had the first time; not for shine, but because it was something to do.

Charles stepped out onto the veranda, needing space, needing air. The boards creaked under his boots as he leaned against the rail. Damp wood. Jacaranda. The soft night breeze.

He breathed it in like he could take the house with him; keep it tucked somewhere safe.

Edna followed quietly, no words at first, just the soft press of her arms slipping around his waist. She rested her cheek against his shoulder like she had since they were kids, when the world was smaller and war was just an adventure to be had.

"You'll send something home," she whispered. "Even if it's just a scrap of paper."

He exhaled slowly. "You'll hear from me. I swear it."

"I remember last time," she said, her voice catching. "I remember the silence more than anything."

He lowered his head, his cheek brushing against her hair. "This isn't the same war."

Her hands tightened on him. "No war ever is, Charles. And no promise can keep you safe."

For a moment, neither of them breathed. Then he whispered, "I don't want to leave you."

"I know," she said. "But you will anyway. And I'll be right here when you get back."

He almost laughed, but it wasn't a happy sound. "You always were the brave one."

"No," she murmured. "I just learned how to hold on."

They stood like that, holding on to the quiet, to each other, to the smell of home. Inside, their children's laughter rolled through the house, careless and bright, the way childhood should be.

Tomorrow, the sun would rise, and with it, take him away

The 2nd of February 1941, Roma Street Station was damp with early light, the timber platform slick under boots. Steam rolled across the tracks, thick and white, swallowing ankles as it curled and drifted. The military band played a march that sounded too bright for the hour, brass cutting through the chill like a blade.

The air tasted of coal dust and rain on iron.

Young soldiers crowded the platform in uneven ranks, faces shining with a nervous excitement they barely tried to hide. Some laughed too loud. Others whispered about the Japs; about how quick it would be over. Charles remembered that kind of talk. He'd spoken it once himself.

He stood straight in uniform, the greatcoat pulling at his shoulders, hat brim low. Edna stood beside the children, jaw set firm against the wind. Clair pressed her lips tight and tried to look braver than she felt. Lurline gripped his hand like she could anchor him in place. Margaret and Lucille shuffled at the edge of the crowd, clutching peppermint sticks from the station kiosk, the sweet smell sharp in the air.

And John, little John; had both arms locked around his father's leg, cheek pressed into the coarse fabric of his trousers.

Lurline's voice cracked through the hum. "You'll come back."

Charles leaned down, brushing a loose curl from her forehead. "I've got you lot to keep me honest," he said, forcing a grin that didn't quite reach his eyes.

Edna stepped closer, their eyes locking in that wordless way they'd always shared. "Don't make promises you can't keep," she said softly, her hand tightening around his sleeve.

Granny Dean's voice came next, steady and low. "You came back once. Do it again."

He pulled Lurline into his arms, held her tight, then went to each of the girls in turn. Clair met his gaze like an equal now, she was old enough to understand. Margaret and Lucille buried their faces against his coat, their small hands clinging.

And then John.

Charles knelt down fully this time, wrapping his arms around the boy, holding him so tight the world fell away. John's little fists balled into the fabric of his greatcoat, his breathing shallow against his chest. Charles pressed his lips to the boy's temple and whispered so only he could hear.

"You keep the fort for me, Johnny. You look after Mum."

The whistle blew. Steam hissed. Orders barked.

He straightened, found Edna's hand one last time, their fingers closing together like they always had: two halves of the same promise. Then he stepped onto the train, the crowd and the steam swallowing him whole.

Chapter 21

Into the Jungle

Charles found himself in the familiar stink of diesel, wedged below deck on another troopship. Iron ribs pressed in around him, the engine noise a constant hum running beneath everything. He followed the sound of a booming laugh down the corridor and paused at the NCO mess doorway.

Niel "Nugget" Morris was impossible to miss, leaning back on a crate, broad shoulders stretching the seams of his half-buttoned shirt, thick through the chest, arms like spanners. A quartermaster and another Warrant Officer, Nugget had a way of getting anything you wanted and making it look easy. Cards fanned through his fingers, his voice carrying over the engine's thrum.

"You know, boys," Nugget boomed, "last time I was sweating like this I was loading scrap steel off the bloody docks in Newcastle. Thought I'd escaped that life. Joke's on me."

Harris was there too, sitting on an overturned ammo tin, matchstick between his teeth. With his sun-worn skin and sharp cheekbones, the sort of bloke who didn't talk much because he didn't need to.

"Could be worse," he muttered, as Nugget's booming laugh rolled on.

Nugget was midway through another tale; a bar fight, growing taller with every retelling; when Charles walked over and dropped his kitbag at his feet, already soaked through with sweat. Nugget clapped him on the back like they'd served together for years.

"Welcome to the steam room, Charlie. Jungle'll soak you like a sponge," he grinned, the moustache bristling. He was supposed to oversee logistics, but he carried himself like the unofficial master of morale.

What threw Charles was the *"Charlie."* No one called him that. The closest anyone ever had was *"Charlie boy,"* and that was only Billy. Nugget reminded him of Billy in small ways; the big personality, the easy humour, the way everything seemed a joke until it wasn't. However, Billy could never grow a moustache, Charles always thought he would if he could, even though he'd given Frankie endless stick about it.

Maybe it was those little echoes that sat with Charles. Nugget's manner carried a kind of rough familiarity, a shape that fit somewhere Billy used to be. And with Edna so far away, that was... something.

He settled in amongst the tobacco smoke and damp canvas, the air hot and sour, thick with the hum of the ship. Men dealt cards and wagered coins, voices bouncing off the steel.

Fraser soon appeared at the doorway; back too straight, uniform too clean.

"Gentlemen," he said crisply. "Let's maintain standards."

Nugget smirked without looking up. "Oh, we're maintainin', sir. We're maintainin' a bloody good hand."

Charles added, dry as dust, "Yes, sir. We'll try not to sweat on parade."

The NCOs chuckled. Fraser stiffened but said nothing, stepping back into the corridor.

"Guy's as stiff as a rifle," Nugget jabbed.

"He ain't a fool, Nugget, just young," Charles replied, scanning the room. He was the only one there who'd already tasted war.

For a moment he just sat there, letting the noise wash over him. Nugget's booming voice. The rattle of cards. Laughter muffled against the iron hull. Sweat running down the back of his neck. The air was thick and close; too close.

The longer he sat, the more it felt like the walls were shrinking, the heat pressing in through steel. He needed air.

Charles pushed away from the table and climbed up the narrow companionway.

The deck greeted him with a hard slap of wind and salt. He leaned against the rail at the stern, staring back over the ship's wake. The sea stretched out in an endless blue, broken only by the black line of sewage spilling into the churn. The hull groaned as the ship rolled beneath him.

He thought of Red Hill, of Edna and the children. Of everything he was steaming away from, and everything waiting for him on the other side.

The voyage to Malaya wasn't long, but already it felt like a lifetime between here and home.

Before long the ocean turned to jungle on the horizon. The heat hit Charles like a hammer when they embarked into the city of Malacca. The scream of insects ringed in his eardrums as if it was the jungles heartbeat.

The 8th Division were loaded on to trucks as they lurched past the red Dutch facade reading Stadthuys, the air thick and heavy with the smell of river water, jasmine and charcoal smoke. For most of the boys from the dusty paddocks of Australia, this city of Malacca was a sensory assault; a tangle of narrow, crowded streets where the calls of Chinese merchants mixed with the chimes of a Christan church bell and the distant call to prayer.

Above the rows of carved wooden shophouses, where generations of Chinese families peered down at them, the Union Jack hung limp and indifferent in the humid stillness, a threadbare testament to a fading empire. It was a place of a thousand contradictory colours: the deep maroon of the old fort gate, the faded jade of tiled eaves, and the vibrant sarongs worn by the Malay women. The city hummed with a languid, oblivious calm that seemed as out of place as the khaki-clad troops that rolled on through.

Nugget leaned out the side of the truck, sweat already darkening his shirt.

"Bloody hell," he called over the engine noise, "I've had hangovers quieter than this place."

Harris squinted out at the maze of shophouses and prayer towers, chewing the stem of his matchstick. "Smells like the tropics and someone's cookin' at the same time," he muttered. "Can't tell if I'm hungry or sick."

Nugget laughed, loud enough to startle a rooster tied to a post they rumbled past. "Don't worry, Harris, I know where the good stuff's hidin'. Bet half these stalls've got something better than that bully beef."

Charles sat wedged between them, watching faces blur past; shopkeepers, kids barefoot in the mud, old men fanning themselves like they'd seen this before.

"They're not looking at us like an army," he said quietly. "More like a storm cloud that'll pass."

"Yeah," Nugget grunted. "Only question is what gets left behind after it does."

Harris adjusted his slouch hat against the dripping heat. "Jungle's waitin' out there. This..." he nodded at the chaos of the city "...this is just the warm-up."

Nugget gave Charles a sidelong grin. "Cheerful bastard, isn't he?"

Charles didn't answer. The sweat, the noise, the stillness behind the faces; it all felt like standing on the edge of something they couldn't quite see yet.

Sure enough, the vibrant colours of the city gave way to the pale green of rubber trees crowding the edge of town. The jungle thickened fast, branches clawing at the sides of the open truck as it rattled down the road. The men ducked and swore as leaves slapped their faces and shoulders.

The convoy turned through a tall wooden gate and rolled into the barracks on the outskirts of Mersing, their new home.

The back flap creaked open. Charles peered out at rows of long timber huts with thatched roofs, half-swallowed by the jungle around them. He jumped down straight into mud that sucked at his boots and didn't want to let go. The air smelled of earth, sap, and something faintly sweet, rot lurking just beneath the surface.

"Bloody sauna with teeth," Nugget muttered, wiping sweat from his forehead as he slogged through the muck.

Harris was already on a dry patch, squinting into the trees beyond the fence line. "Haven't felt dry like this since Darwin," he said.

Fraser marched over, back straight, voice clipped like he was reading straight from a manual. "Get the troops settled in. We're to hold the line here. Make it work."

Charles nodded, his reply flat. "Then we hold it."

Harris tilted his head. "Holding it against what, sir?"

Fraser hesitated, the question landing heavier than he expected. "When that order comes, I'll let you know, Sergeant." Then he turned and walked off.

"Great," Nugget muttered, heaving a crate onto his shoulder, "sent us to the only place on earth with no enemy, just playin' war games."

"Better this mud than blood-soaked," Charles cut in.

The men set to work. NCOs barked orders at privates as they dragged gear through the mud. Charles drifted between squads, lending a hand where he could, checking corners, making sure the place began to look like a camp instead of a mess. Nugget's booming voice carried above the noise, another story about the steel yards.

Harris moved quietly, fast, like the humidity barely touched him. Fraser kept to the centre of the yard, overseeing everything without stepping into the mud himself; standing just far enough apart to remind everyone he was an officer.

Days blurred into weeks spent grinding through the jungle in truck convoys. The canopy pressed low, the tracks dissolving into thick mud that clung to boots and tyres alike. Leeches rode the waterlogged ground like they owned it. The hum of insects was constant, a thin, needling sound that never stopped.

Nugget ruled the ration store like a petty king, wheeling and dealing with anyone desperate enough to trade.

"You touch the bully beef stash," he growled at one private, "and the mozzies'll be the least of your worries."

The poor bloke went pale, right before Nugget slapped him on the back with a booming laugh.

Harris took to the jungle like he'd been born in it, slipping down unmarked bush trails with quiet certainty. He and his men would reappear out of the tree line like ghosts, covered in mud but never lost. Years tracking pigs and cattle through the Territory had given him a sense for country no map could match.

Fraser lived in routine. He hovered over everything, making sure every tent was pitched to regulation and every truck parked square. Nights found him bent over a field table, tracing maps and murmuring lines from manuals like prayers. Studious, almost to the point of being brittle. Charles often worked late with him, talking logistics over kerosene lamplight.

One night, Nugget stomped up the steps to the admin hut, shaking rain from his shoulders.

"Evenin', sir," he called.

"Warrant Officer Morris," Fraser replied, formal as ever.

"Nugget's fine, sir. Even the mozzies call me that," he said with a grin.

"Alright then," Fraser said after a pause. "If that's what you request."

Charles handed over the report he'd been working on. Fraser nodded, eyes still on the paperwork, and Charles stepped back out into the thick, wet night.

By the time Nugget followed, the sky had opened. Rain crashed down in sheets, hammering the tin roofs and flooding the shallow trenches. Lanterns guttered in the wind.

Nugget ducked his head and sloshed his way across camp toward the mess. Inside, men huddled around enamel mugs of tinned tea. His booming voice was quieter tonight.

"Y'know," he muttered, "I figured I'd end up in Darwin at worst. Not bleeding out in a rubber swamp."

Harris chewed his twig. "You're not dead yet."

"Yeah," Nugget said. "But my bloody socks are."

Fraser passed by outside, hat brim slick with rain, giving quiet orders to a sentry. He glanced in through the flap but didn't step inside.

Charles slipped away to his tent, sat at the crate that passed for a desk, and pulled a damp envelope from his pack. The paper stuck to his fingers as he wrote:

Dear Edna,

I've never known heat like this. It hangs on you, thick and wet, until you can't remember what dry air feels like. The nights aren't cooler, just darker. The jungle never stops; mozzies whining, rain hammering, everything damp and close.

I keep thinking about the breeze on the veranda at home. About you making tea after the kids are finally in bed. About

Lurline's voice carrying through the hallway when she's meant to be asleep. I can see it all clear as day, even out here where everything smells like mud and rot.

He paused, the words catching somewhere between what he could write and what he couldn't.

Tell the girls I'll bring them something back from Singapore, something pretty. Tell John to keep an eye on the chooks for me. Tell mum that I am eating well and that I am far away from any harm. Tell them all that their dads still got both feet on the ground.

I miss hearing your voice. It's the quiet at night that gets to you most. Nothing but the jungle breathing.

I'll be all right. Just keep the home warm for me.

Love, Charles

He folded the letter carefully, slid it under a mug, and listened to the rain pound against the canvas. It was a sound as constant as the cicadas, the air always wet and heavy.

The division kept training, month after month, preparing for a storm that never seemed to break. Bayonet drills churned the ground into a reddish slop, the roar of artillery practise breaking the hum of the jungle as it pressed closer every day, thick and damp and alive. The waiting gnawed at everyone; privates and officers alike, twitching on the edge of boredom and madness. Holding the line in a hellhole with no enemy boots in sight.

Nugget was forever storming the ration line, swearing about missing crates like a king defending his throne. Harris pushed his platoon harder than anyone, slipping out of tree lines muddy to the knees, his soldiers trailing behind with the look of men who'd rather be anywhere else. Fraser's orders were sharp but carried an edge of uncertainty, like a man reciting someone else's lines.

Charles kept a steadier head. It was a different kind of hell than before, but at least the bullets weren't flying, and the shells weren't singing overhead. He moved through the camp with quiet authority, adjusting positions without asking, steadying the edges. Fraser had the rank, but Charles had the respect.

One morning, a runner stumbled out of the mist, soaked to the skin, clutching a bundle of letters tied with string. The chatter died. Mail meant home. Names were called out one by one. When Charles's name came, he stepped under an awning, out of the rain, closing his eyes for half a breath before tearing the envelope open with steady hands. Edna's familiar handwriting was a comfort; until it wasn't.

Charles,

I wish I could write this different. Mums gone.

She came down sick. The doctor said pneumonia. It was fast. I held her hand the whole time. She was talking about you, said you'd keep your feet, no matter what.

Lurline's taking it hard. The house feels too quiet. We keep waiting to hear her voice from the kitchen. It doesn't come.

I don't know how to make it make sense. But we'll carry on. We must.

She loved you. We all do. Come home safe.

Edna

The ink swam on the damp paper. The rain was only a hiss on the canvas, but it roared in his ears. The world seemed to tilt, a flash of Clevedon Hall, Nancy's face, that same hollow punch in the chest. All of them gone now. Every parent, real and foster, surely buried somewhere far away.

The noise of the camp slowly bled back in. Nugget was boasting about some half-remembered home triumph, privates jeered and swapped letters, a brief flicker of warmth in the mud. Harris, with no mail in hand, simply melted into the green.

Charles stayed where he was, frozen in the half-light. He folded the letter carefully, like it might break if he breathed too hard, then tucked it into his breast pocket. His hand lingered there, heavy.

Fraser caught the look on his face but said nothing. The world carried on around him; men laughing, boots sucking in the mud, rain drumming the canvas; but something in Charles didn't move at all.

The letter sat like a stone in his breast pocket, the weight of it heavier than any kit. Around him, the camp was alive; laughter, the slap of cards, the endless squelch of boots; but something in the air had changed. Or maybe it was just him.

Days rolled on, two signallers trudged past the admin hut, voices low but tense. One of them spat into the mud.

"...they took Kota Bharu, I'm telling you. Moved like bloody ghosts."

"Could be a rumour."

"Yeah? Then why are the Pommy officers buzzing around like kicked hornets?"

Nugget leaned on a crate, brow slick with sweat, listening without looking like he was. "If the Japs are moving south, it won't stay rumour for long," he muttered.

Harris appeared from nowhere, rifle slung over one shoulder, as if the jungle had spat him back out. "Tracks north of here are getting busier," he said quietly. "Locals are talking. They reckon the Japanese have landed, moving faster than the wet."

Fraser came out of the command post, starch still in his collar even with the humidity trying to crush it flat. "We don't deal in rumours," he clipped, a little too sharp. "Our job is to hold this line. Orders will come down from HQ."

Nugget snorted. "Yeah, and I'm sure they'll tell us nice and early, just like they did last war."

Charles didn't say anything. He didn't have to. He'd felt this before, not the jungle, but the pressure. A kind of stillness that settled right before things snapped. Back in France, the map lines had been straight. You knew where the enemy sat. But here... here the jungle twisted everything. There were no lines. No *"behind the guns."* The enemy could be anywhere.

The storm started again; soft at first, then relentless, hammering the tin roofs like a drum. Somewhere in the distance, a telephone clanged off the hook. Officers hurried past, their boots splashing through the slosh.

Something was moving. And it wasn't just the rain.

Chapter 22

Malayan Campaign

Orders came down on the 21st of January 1942, in the grey stillness before dawn. What had begun as whispers was now fact; the Japanese had been sweeping down the Malayan Peninsula for more than a month, moving fast, swallowing up towns before the British could even decide where to stand. Their advance had been so swift and precise it left the Empire's carefully drawn lines meaningless.

The 8th Division, too far south to be blooded in the first wave, had spent weeks training and waiting. Now, with the enemy closing, the men moved with a new edge; less talk, sharper eyes.

Fraser stood on the step of the admin hut, briefing sheet in hand, his voice clipped and formal.

"Advance to the road north of Mersing. We secure a perimeter. Guns set within the hour."

The words were steady, but Charles could hear the tension underneath; the young lieutenant's first real operation.

Engines coughed to life one after another. Trucks and gun tractors lined up in the mud, towing the regiments newly issued 25-pounders. Nugget charged between vehicles like a bull at a stockyard, swinging ammunition crates onto trays as if they were empty.

"Finally movin' instead of rottin'," he muttered, grinning through the sweat already on his brow.

Men clambered onto the trucks, strapping down gear, checking rifles. The air was thick and still; the kind of heat that stuck to your skin.

Charles swung up into the passenger seat of the lead truck. From there, he could see the column stretching back through the mist, steel and canvas ready to roll. He scanned the tree line as the engine growled to life. The jungle didn't move, but it felt like it was watching. The column crawled on, tyres slipping in the mud.

The brakes screamed as the convoy lurched to a halt short of the planned gunline. Diesel fumes hung under the canopy, drifting through the still morning air. The men stayed in their transports, shoulders tense, eyes flicking to the tree line.

Harris was the first down. He crouched low, fingertips brushing the mud, scanning tracks that disappeared into the scrub. He walked up to Charles's side of the truck, voice pitched low.

"Someone's been through here," he muttered. "Not locals."

Fraser's boots squelched through the mud behind them. He checked his watch like the timing mattered.

"Let's get those guns unlimbered," he said, a touch too sharp.

Charles lifted a hand to quiet him.

"Shhh. Listen."

The jungle had gone dead still. The kind of silence that pressed in right before it broke.

CRACK!

A single rifle shot split the air, a puff of mud kicking up near Fraser's boots. The men flinched as one, instinctively ducking behind the trucks.

Charles's voice cut through the confusion.

"Get the men unloaded and into the tree line, otherwise they're just bloody ducks on a pond!"

Fraser jerked back, startled by the edge in Charles's tone. Harris didn't wait; he was already moving. "Out! Cover!" Harris barked, dragging a small section forward into the scrub.

Charles's eyes narrowed, tracking the muzzle flash. "Japs," he breathed. "Scouts."

Fraser froze for half a second, fumbling with his map case. Charles didn't give him the chance to recover slowly.

"Guns hold position! Infantry forward, clear that tree line! Keep it tight!" he commanded.

"Lieutenant, get the gun crews under cover. This isn't the main show."

Fraser stiffly nodded, pale but moving. Then the jungle erupted. Rounds slashed through leaves, sending showers of green falling like confetti. Harris's men advanced through the mud, short bursts snapping back at the tree line. A distant moan echoed; a Japanese scout hit, and the rest of them melted into the green.

Nugget came up behind, dragging a crate of mortar rounds through the muck. "Want me to bring the bloody lot?"

"Hold it," Charles shook his head. "This is just a feeler."

A few more rounds cracked from a log bunker to the right of Harris's position. Sloppy aim, but enough to rattle nerves.

Charles jerked his chin toward them, sending a team around the flank. A burst of fire. Then silence.

In less than five minutes it was over. The men panted like they'd run a mile, fingers tight on their rifles.

"So much for an easy bloody morning," Nugget muttered.

Harris emerged from the brush; mud streaked down his face. "Tree line's clear. Barely a fight."

Charles glared at both of them, voice low. "They weren't here to fight. They just wanted to see what we've got."

The jungle seemed to inhale again. Insects began their song, as if nothing had happened.

"Let's get the tractors in. Guns on the rise. Ammo stacked. Arcs locked in," Charles ordered, wading through mud and smoke, checking on the men; some rattled, some stone-faced.

Fraser lingered at the rear, hands shaking despite himself. Charles walked up beside him, voice even. "This was the easy bit, sir. Next time, it won't be scouts."

Fraser swallowed hard, then nodded. He was learning, fast.

The convoy rolled to a stop at the end of Mersing–Endau Road, wheels crunching into soft mud as the early light filtered weakly through the trees. It was quiet except for the hiss of idling engines and the rustle of men climbing down from the trucks. Charles swung out of the cab, boots sinking into the muck, and surveyed the stretch of road ahead. This was it, their gunline.

"Guns up along the ridge. Keep it tight. We're not here to build a bloody garden," he barked.

The 25-pounders were unhitched and manhandled into firing positions, crews laying in with the kind of speed that comes from repetition and nerves. Far off, faint but unmistakable, the low rumble of artillery and small arms rolled down the coast; the 22nd Brigade was already in it.

Nugget heaved a crate of shells onto his shoulder, face slick with sweat.

"Reckon the bastards are comin' proper," he muttered.

Charles squinted into the distance, a dull red smear of dawn on the horizon.

"Yeah," he said quietly. "And we'll be here giving 'em hell."

Fraser appeared, breath short, map case clutched in one hand. His cap sat crooked as he rattled off grid references, the tremor in his voice betraying how green this felt. Charles listened, then started relaying clear, clipped orders down the line.

Then the guns opened.

A single blast tore through the stillness, then another. In moments, the barrage was alive; thunder rolling down the road in steady rhythm. The crews scurried between limbers and pits, mud flying from their boots. The shockwave from each round thumped through their chests. Smoke hung low, clinging to the tree line.

Nugget sprinted between guns, dropping ammo and swearing at the mud. Harris led a small section forward, taking a position on the flank, eyes scanning the dark scrub beyond the road. Charles moved like a conductor through the storm, taking Fraser's raw coordinates and turning them into precision, his voice steady above the din.

The radio cracked and screamed, new coordinates, shifts, adjustments. Fraser's face tightened with every call. Japanese seaborne landings were reported to the north. The barrage had bought time, but they were moving fast. The men knew it. The angle of the guns couldn't cover everything.

Nugget stumbled in beside him, breathing hard, a grin splitting his mud-spattered face. "They're bloody quick."

Charles didn't look at him. "Yeah," he said flatly. "Too quick."

The ground trembled again as another salvo thundered downrange. The sound of gunfire from up the coast was drawing closer now, faint bursts carried on the wind.

Charles snapped orders down the line. "Shift Gun Three thirty degrees north. Harris, eyes sharp on that flank. If they push through, I want to know before they breathe."

Fraser hesitated, glancing at the radio. Charles clapped him hard on the shoulder.

"Keep those bearings coming, Lieutenant. We're holding here."

And they did.

As the jungle hissed with distant gunfire and the battery thundered into the night, the 2/10th Field Regiment dug in at Mersing–Endau Road; their first stand against the Japanese advance. The line held, the guns roared, and the night was alive with the sound of war.

After the fight, the camp went through a wave of emotion. The adrenaline that had carried them through the day bled away with the fading light, replaced by a thick, heavy silence. Nugget's snores rumbled from the corner like a continuous drone. Harris smoked on the edge of the pit, ember glowing soft in the dark. Fraser scratched neat, nervous lines into a notebook, the tip of his pencil tapping like a metronome.

Charles lay on his back, staring through the sagging cam net overhead. The moonlight bled through in broken pieces, shivering each time the breeze caught the leaves. Edna's letter sat warm against his chest, the paper gone soft from sweat. Eventually, sleep dragged him under hard.

Before long he was in the jungle again; only it wasn't this jungle. Shellfire whistled overhead, explosions ripped the earth apart, and the mud of France filled his nose and throat. Chook's blood sprayed warm across his face, Frankie's laugh echoed somewhere in the smoke. And then his mother's voice; calm and gentle, calling him in for tea, as if none of it had ever happened.

Everything folded in on itself. France. Home. Malaya. No lines left between them.

He jolted awake, chest locked tight, breath clawing to get out. Sweat ran down his back in cold rivulets. For a moment he didn't know where he was, only the pounding in his ears and the phantom smell of cordite. His hand found the letter. He pulled it out, stared at his mother's name in the wavering lantern light. She was gone. He was half a world away in a steaming patch of jungle that didn't care who it took next.

Fraser stirred on the opposite side, voice thick with sleep. "Watson? You all right?"

Charles forced his breathing down, swallowing hard. A terror he hadn't felt in years. "Yeah," he said. "Just the bloody heat."

He folded the letter carefully and slid it back into his pocket. Outside, the jungle hummed like it always did; constant and indifferent.

Nothing had changed. To Charles, everything had.

After the skirmish, the men settled into a rhythm that almost felt like calm. The Japanese scouts had faded back into the jungle, and there was a growing sense; half belief, half hope; that they'd scared them off.

The gun pits were fortified further along the road north of Mersing facing Endau. Logs were stacked high, camouflage nets tightened, ammo boxes littered the ground. Days stretched into drills: ducking for cover during the afternoon storms, perimeter checks drenching them through the mud.

The smell of oil and cordite lingered faintly in the damp air as Nugget swaggered between positions, ration tin in hand.

"Told ya. Little nip scouts copped a fright. We'll be drinkin' in Singapore before they work up the stones to try again."

The men laughed; uneasy but wanting to believe him.

Harris led routine patrols into the scrub. They found nothing concrete: a few disturbed tracks, a cigarette tin, a hint of something moving too fast to follow.

"They're still out there," Harris muttered to Charles, eyes fixed on the tree line. "They don't just bugger off."

Fraser grew more confident in the lull, standing straighter in briefings, quoting maps and orders like they meant something solid.

"They've lost momentum. We've got them on the back foot," he'd declare.

Charles didn't say anything. He'd seen this kind of quiet; before the Somme, before Lihons. That false, waiting silence.

He noticed the jungle wasn't silent anymore; it was listening.

When the moment finally broke, it wasn't subtle. Charles jolted awake again, this time to another kind of terror.

Alarms tore through the camp just after 2 a.m. on the 26th of January; sharp, shrill, gutting the night. He was already on his feet before the siren finished.

In the distance, the thump of naval guns and the flat, hard crackle of automatic fire rode the wind. A runner skidded into the gunline, mud up to his knees, breath heaving.

"Japs landing at Endau, north of us! Naval support. Multiple boats. They're moving fast!"

Nugget yanked on his boots, muttering through his teeth. "Thought they'd buggered off. Stupid bastards."

Soldiers scurried like a hornet's nest being kicked in. Guns were set, ammo boxes dragged out. From the south came a new sound; a low, building buzz. Charles looked up to see RAF planes thundering overhead: Vildebeest biplanes with their Buffalo escorts. They looked delicate against the night, slow wings in a modern war.

The sky erupted a moment later. Black flak puffs bloomed, silhouetted by tracer fire. Searchlights clawed through the dark. Then the Japanese fighters came in low; fast, sharp, cutting through the night.

Nugget squinted up. "Bloody hell, they're flying museum pieces."

Charles didn't answer. One of the Vildebeest took a hit and bloomed fire mid-air, turning into a flaming arc that fell beyond the tree line. Another followed. The sky lit orange, their faces washed in it. The sound was low and heavy, like a distant rumble being torn in half.

The RAF put up what fight they could, Buffaloes twisting against the faster Zeros, but it wasn't a contest. The survivors banked south, engines limping. The gunline watched as the burning wrecks fell, one by one.

A hollow quiet followed; just the distant thud of naval guns and the first hints of machine gun chatter. Whatever cover they'd hoped for had been blown out of the sky.

Fraser came storming down the line, map in hand, shouting over the chaos. He jabbed a finger at a position further south.

"We hold here!" he shouted, voice cracking around the edges; too sharp to sound sane.

Charles stepped in close, voice low but cutting through the noise. "No, sir. We hold in this position if the guns can. Give the boys north as much cover as possible."

Fraser hesitated but nodded. Gun crews scrambled to redeploy 25-pounders and shift their arcs. The barrage was deafening; the ground thrumming beneath them as shell after shell whistled north. Ammunition crates were hauled through the mud under the pale light, the smell of burning fuel drifting down the coast.

Harris dropped into the gunline, breathless.

"They're already behind us," he growled.

A small team of Jap scouts; quick and silent; were threading through the jungle. Charles's mind raced. This wasn't France. There were no neat fronts, no safe rear. The jungle was too easy to hide in.

Nugget shoved a box of shells down next to him, panting. "This isn't a feint, Charlie. They're bloody everywhere."

Just as the words left his mouth, the orchestra arrived. Japanese machine guns raked the line, short sharp bursts probing for muzzle flashes. One round snapped through the corner of the sandbag wall by Charles's position, spitting mud across his face like Chook's blood once had.

For a heartbeat the world narrowed; silent, still; until another burst snapped him back.

"Gun Two, shift left! Keep those barrels cool. Harris, block that flank! Any man not on a twenty-fiver, get your rifle returning fire. We don't roll before dawn!"

The guns roared into the dark, lighting the jungle like a storm. Rounds pinged off barrels and sandbags, casualties mounting, blood mixing into the mud. Charles moved down the line, steadying shattered crews, dragging the shocked back into the fight. It was Flanders again; just hotter, closer, and meaner.

At the command post, Fraser's hands shook as he spoke, orders faltering as the line buckled. Hours passed in mud and smoke, the light shone bright as the Japanese pressed from every angle.

Fraser swallowed hard, his voice rough.

"Orders are in. We hold a few more hours. Then, in the dark, we send everything north. Full barrage. The division leapfrogs to Johore. Fighting retreat, no stragglers."

Charles had never retreated from the Hun. But this wasn't the Somme.

This was the jungle. And the war had truly arrived.

Those few hours were fought inch by inch; a wet, grey blur of sweat and gunfire. By midnight, the men of the 8th Division were filthy, red-eyed, and hollowed out by the fight. The gunline was ringed with churned mud and blackened tree stumps. Empty shell casings lay piled ankle-deep like brass gravel.

The firing orders were called in. It was time.

Charles stood in the gun pit, voice hoarse but steady. "Gun One, elevate two. Gun Two, repeat last. Make it count, boys."

The barrage opened like an eruption. Darkness lit up in a rolling thunderclap as the ground shuddered under them. Gun crews wiped grit and sweat from their eyes, blistered hands loading round after round. Nine hundred shells tore downrange in the first hour alone. When the Japanese finally answered, their mortars came shrieking through the air, splashing the gun pits with dirt and shrapnel.

Nugget sprinted through it all with ammo crates on his shoulders, swearing like a sailor.

"This is bloody stupid, Charlie! They're chuckin' these like cricket balls!"

A mortar landed close; enough to knock him sideways into the muck. He let out a shaky laugh, hauled the crate upright again, and kept running.

The pressure was tightening. Harris's section on the flank was the only thread keeping the Japs off the line.

"They're on us before the barrels cool," came his low voice over the radio.

"Then we'll just keep moving the barrels," Charles replied, flat as steel.

Fraser was beside him now, mud-spattered and hoarse, repeating fire adjustments without flinching.

"Gun Three, shift right! Keep your heads down!" he bellowed. No longer frozen; he was learning fast under fire.

Then came movement through the gunline: infantry columns, British and Australians, both stumbling through the half-light. Mud-caked faces. Blank stares. Uniforms stiff with blood and sweat. A Bren carrier coughed smoke as it passed. Stretcher bearers carried more men than they had hands for.

A platoon commander limped by, eyes hollow, giving Charles a grim nod.

"You're the last bloody wall now, mate. Make it sting."

"We will," Charles answered simply.

Nugget watched a line of trucks and carriers grinding through their position. "Poor buggers look like they went ten rounds with a goddamn storm," he muttered.

Harris's section held the flank as the retreating division bled past them.

The Japanese guns answered soon after. The air turned thick with smoke and cordite. Shells crept closer. One 25-pounder's shield was punctured; screams cut through the roar. Charles splashed through the trenches to the pit, still barking orders.

"Hold the line. Keep their heads down!"

He was too late. The pit was slick with red; the screaming had already stopped. Charles froze for half a heartbeat, boots sinking in the mud, the smell of blood cutting through. Another gun thundered somewhere down the line, snapping him back.

Fraser checked his watch, then looked to Charles, jaw clenched. "Rear says they're set behind us."

Charles gave a single, hard nod. "Then it's our turn to get out."

Harris's rear guard collapsed in just as the gun crews began limbering the twenty-fivers. Truck engines growled to life as the new defensive line behind them opened, their shells flashing overhead. Nugget staggered forward with one last crate: breath ragged.

"You know, Charlie," he panted, "I used to hate running. Now it's a bloody hobby."

Charles scanned the position for stragglers. He was the last off the line, mud to his knees, eyes hardened. As the trucks rolled, Japanese tracers slashed the trees where they'd just stood.

The leapfrog began, a punishing rhythm, day after day, of fighting and falling back. The Japanese pressed them relentlessly down the peninsula. There was no reprieve. Johore, once a supposed stronghold, was lost before they ever stopped fighting.

By the time orders came through to cross the causeway on the 31st of January, the division was running on fumes. The convoy crawled forward under blackout. Charles sat passenger in the lead truck, watching the dull red glow of Johore bleeding into the sky behind them. Fraser was silent in the tray. Nugget slumped against the side. Harris walked the roadside, eyes scanning the darkness for stragglers.

As the last trucks reached the Singapore side, explosions rolled down the crossing. The causeway behind them erupted, water and concrete leaping into the air. A great column of smoke marked the end of Malaya.

"Well... no way back now," Nugget said quietly.

Charles didn't look back. "Let's hope there's not for a while."

His hand found his breast pocket; Edna's letter, creased and damp with sweat. For a moment the roar of the guns and engines fell away. Lurline in his armchair, head tipped toward the wireless. Lucille and Margaret laughing near the hearth. Claire sitting cross-legged at Edna's feet while she brushed her hair smooth. Little John pushing his toy truck across the rug, making low engine noises with his lips. Safe. Whole. A world away from this mud and fire.

He folded the paper flat against his chest, as if it might hold the line for him.

Singapore loomed ahead: a place that promised safety but smelled like a last stand. Charles lowered his hand, the thrum of the truck engine dull against the weight in his chest. Behind them, another shell detonated on the far bank; a distant roar closing that campaign.

The Japanese were one step closer to home.

And he knew they wouldn't stop.

Chapter 23

Singapore Falls

The convoy of trucks and gun tractors rattled down the narrow laterite road, tyres hissing through the red dust. Coconut groves leaned in on either side, their fronds still in the thick, wet air. The humidity hung low and heavy, trapping the heat even this early in the morning. Sweat gathered under collars, sticking uniforms to backs.

As they rolled through a bend toward a sun-faded crossroads, Charles caught the signs nailed to a leaning post: *"Kranji Road"* and *"Tengah Airfield 3 mi"*. To the north, through the gaps in the palms, the Johor Strait stretched wide and shallow, its surface like glass. On the far shore, Johore burned; smudges of smoke smeared against a pale sky. The enemy was so close it felt like a breath on the back of the neck.

"Bloody hell, Charlie..." Nugget leaned out the back of the truck, grinning without humour. "You can wave at 'em from here."

"Let's just keep them on that side of the strait," Charles muttered.

The trucks shuddered to a halt in a churn of dust and exhaust. Charles swung down first, boots sinking into the soft verge, and met Fraser already striding up to the lead vehicle. The young lieutenant's face was flushed, his webbing banging against his hip.

"Let's check out the gunline, Warrant," Fraser said, a spark in his voice despite the long haul south.

Charles gave a short nod, and together they walked through the proposed battery position: a strip of slightly elevated ground skirting a rubber plantation. From the crest, they could see clear arcs toward Sarimbun Beach, the mangrove flats dark and tangled beyond.

"What are your thoughts, sir?" Charles asked, testing him.

Fraser's eyes narrowed as he studied the shoreline. "Mangrove thickets all along the front, excellent for concealment, terrible for defending."

Charles smirked, a dry flicker of approval. He crouched, running a calloused hand through the soil. It came up slick and dark, sliding between his fingers. "Soft. Wet. We won't get deep pits out of this." He glanced toward the narrow road that wound back inland. "And only one way out."

Exit plans already being spoken aloud. Not superstition. Just survival. Charles had learned that lesson the hard way over the past week; the Japs didn't hit you head-on. They slid around, found the soft spots, and left you choking on your own dirt if you hadn't already picked your escape.

Fraser kept scanning, pencil scratching over his notebook. Charles watched him for a moment, curiosity breaking through his usual silence.

"What brought you here, sir?" he asked quietly.

Fraser hesitated, then answered without looking up. "My father. He served at Gallipoli. Never talks about it."

"Duty in your blood?" Charles asked.

"Something like that." Fraser's voice lost its crisp edge. "We're not that close. Thought if I proved myself, maybe it'd change something. Or at least help me understand him."

The breeze off the strait was warm and damp. Charles felt something shift in his chest; not pity, but recognition.

"I can relate to that," he said softly.

For a moment, the noise of the trucks faded behind them. Charles was somewhere else; knowing his father had died while he was off fighting a war the old man never wanted him in. No chance for words. No chance for anything. He drew in a breath, forced the memory down, and turned his eyes back to the burning shore.

The position wasn't ideal, but it was theirs to defend. Gun tractors reversed into place with a grinding whine, engines coughing and popping in the heavy air. 25-pounders were unlimbered one by one, trails dug in, traverses checked. The men moved with the practiced rhythm of exhaustion; steady, automatic. Sandbags, coconut logs, bamboo; anything they could find went into shoring up the pits.

Cam nets sagged between palm trunks, heavy with humidity, dripping constantly like rain. Men swore as their boots were lost in the mud with every step. Fraser moved along the line, a stub of chalk in his hand, marking firing arcs on staked boards.

"This gun covers the strait. That one, north tree line," he called crisply.

"Won't stop 'em coming through the mangroves," Charles muttered without looking up.

"Right, then we'll turn Gun Three ten degrees east." Fraser adjusted without missing a beat.

It wasn't confidence, not quite, but it was getting close.

The men were weary, but at least there were no bullets overhead. Harris returned from a supply run to Tengah, his small detail grinning like they'd raided a king's pantry. They dumped half-empty ammo crates and a tin of weevil-riddled biscuits at Nugget's feet.

"Crunchy or wriggle?" Harris asked, shaking the tin.

"Both," Nugget shot back with a grin, already prying the lid open.

They scrounged whatever they could; water tins, sandbags, spare tarps; bartering with Indian troops bivouacked nearby or locals passing through. A slow trickle of Singaporean civilians moved down the road, pushing carts piled high with everything they owned. Smoke columns curled faintly across the strait. Children stared wide-eyed at the Australian guns, their faces pale in the dawn light.

From the command post; a raised wooden hut on a ridge; the entire shoreline lay exposed. Fraser climbed up first, binoculars slung around his neck, posture different now. Sharper. Charles followed, boots thudding on the steps. Fraser swept the shoreline through the lenses, noting fall-of-shot zones, issuing orders without the usual hesitation.

"About bloody time you looked like an officer," Charles jabbed lightly.

Fraser smirked. "Someone's got to keep up with you, Watson."

The division's defences were set. Anxious waiting was all that was left. The days became a staring match with the far shore, the nights restless and thick. Charles drifted in and out of sleep, some nights blank and quiet, others dragging him back to Billy's grin or a gun pit full of blood and limbs. The nightmares always ended the same way; with the jungle hum dragging him back to the present, clutching his chest.

Unable to sleep, he slid on his damp socks and boots, feeling the raw bite of hot spots on his heels, and walked the perimeter.

He found Harris on patrol, chewing his matchstick, rifle loose across his chest.

"Good evening, sir," Harris greeted.

"Evening, Sergeant. How do the lines look?" Charles asked.

"Straight as ever. Too quiet. It's coming, isn't it?"

"Yeah," Charles said softly. "It is."

Harris glanced out toward the black water. "Sir... you grew up on a farm too, didn't you?"

Charles gave a small nod. "That's right. Cattle farm. Father taught me all I knew." The words felt heavier than he expected. His father had been in his head more since Fraser's confession.

"Pig farm for me," Harris said. "Feel bad leaving. Hard work out there, just my folks and my little sister. Tractor carked it just before I shipped off. I'll rebuild it after the war."

Charles clapped him on the shoulder. "Nothing to feel bad about. The work you're doing here is keeping them safe. Just remember that."

He wasn't sure he believed it. But it was what he told himself too; every time Edna and the kids crept into the quiet corners of his mind.

The two men stood in silence for a while, the damp air pressing in around them. Midnight crept closer on the 8th of February. That's when they saw it: a faint lantern glow in the mist across the strait.

The jungle hum built for a moment; frogs, insects, the whisper of palms; then cut off, sharp and sudden. Even the air seemed to hold its breath.

"Now it's too quiet, Sergeant," Charles murmured, ears straining.

All along the line, men shifted in their pits, uneasy. Beneath the rustle of canvas and boots, a distant, low drone of engines drifted across the water like a promise.

At that moment, the searchlights snapped on; thin, wavering cones cutting through the darkness like scalpels. Black shapes slid across the water in their beams: Japanese landing barges, low and fast.

Alarms screamed. The gunline breathed into life.

"All guns, FIRE! Maximum rate!" Charles roared, voice shredded by the blast of the first salvo.

The night erupted into flame. 25-pounders spat muzzle flashes into the dark, the ground trembling beneath their boots. Explosions flared across the strait, geysers of water and fire tearing through the first wave. One barge bloomed into a fireball, orange and red licking the mist. The rest kept coming, relentless.

Enemy mortars answered almost instantly. The first rounds whistled in, splashing into the mangroves like thrown stones. Then the real barrage followed. Shrapnel ripped through the cam nets, punched into sandbags, and shredded palms into splinters. A direct hit on Gun Three; no scream, just a wet, sickening thud and two men erased in an instant. Their blood ran black in the mud.

"Shit, shit, shit, they're bloody walking it in!" Nugget barked, half a shout, half a prayer.

"Rear guns, two hundred left, five down!" Fraser's voice cracked through the chaos. "Fire!"

Charles swung his eyes to the shoreline. More barges slid into the shallows, black hulls scraping sand. "Harris," he snapped. "They'll flank us through the mangroves. Take your section, block them."

Harris didn't hesitate. He slapped a fresh magazine into his rifle, grabbed his men, and disappeared into the tree line; water up to their knees, shadows swallowing them whole. Charles caught glimpses through the muzzle flashes: movement in the swamp, shadows in motion. There were too many.

The jungle erupted with short, vicious bursts; staccato gunfire, grenades cracking like bones breaking. For a moment, Harris's line held. He could hear it in the rhythm of their fire; controlled, precise. Then the pattern fractured.

"They're flanking us, Jesus, they're quick–" Harris's voice rasped over the radio.

A roar of machine gun fire answered him. Then nothing.

Just static.

For half a second the gunline seemed to still. Nugget's head snapped toward the swamp, eyes wide. "I saw it. Flash right where he was," he said, voice low.

Charles stared into the black, jaw locking so tight it ached. Harris was gone. One more name that wouldn't make the roll call. One more man who'd never go home to a broken tractor and a sister waiting.

He drew in a breath; not deep, not calm, just enough to keep moving.

"Shift Gun Four north. Tighten the line," he barked.

The guns thundered again. The mangroves swallowed Harris whole.

Japanese mortars hammered the gunline, each impact closer than the last. The air vibrated with the thump and crack of falling rounds, pits collapsing under the pressure. Men yelled over the roar.

Fraser's voice tore through the chaos, hoarse and urgent. "Correct fire! Five left, four down, get those shells moving!"

But it was already too close. One gun lay silent, breech jammed, its crew pinned down. Another team broke under the barrage, abandoning the pit as the flank disintegrated. Aussie infantry and what was left of Harris's section streamed back through their line, stumbling, bloodied, shouting warnings.

"Pull the guns back! MOVE!" Fraser barked.

Gun tractors roared to life under fire. Charles and Nugget crouched behind the last firing gun, working the traverse, the barrel glowing faintly in the dark.

"Gun Two, last shot!" Charles bellowed.

The gun slammed one more shell downrange. He jumped onto the limber just as tracer fire chewed through the ridge where he'd been seconds earlier. Nugget scrambled after him, breath ragged, mud streaked across his face.

The convoy rattled down Kranji Road, engines growling in the night. Burning positions blurred past in flashes; gun pits gutted, palm fronds aflame, the sky behind them streaked red with fire. The men sat silent in the back of the trucks, blackened faces catching stray bursts of light. Somewhere behind, the Japanese pushed hard.

They didn't stop until the trucks rattled into Bukit Timah, near the perimeter of Singapore City. It wasn't a fortress; just another patch of ground that needed holding.

The 25-pounders were unhitched with tired, clumsy hands. Gun crews set up where they could, intersections, gardens, schoolyards, even between abandoned houses. Cam nets were strung across verandas. Shells stacked against walls like sandbags. One crew set their gun up on the edge of a cricket oval, aiming down a suburban street.

Charles jumped down from the limber, crunching into damp soil and gravel. For the first time in hours, there was no incoming fire. Only the ragged sound of men breathing.

Nugget leaned against the side of a truck; shirt plastered to his back with sweat. "This is a bloody mess," he muttered, eyes scanning the empty street.

"Mess is better than dead," Charles replied. He wiped a streak of blood from his cheek, unsure whose it was.

Nugget let out a sharp laugh; humour with no joy in it. "Never thought I'd be firing a twenty-fiver next to someone's bloody rose bushes."

Charles sat on an ammo crate for a second longer than he should have, letting his lungs catch up. "War doesn't care where it lands," he said flatly.

Nugget kicked at the gravel. "Harris should've been here."

Charles's hand tightened around his knee. He didn't look at him. "Yeah. He should've."

For a heartbeat, the city was quiet. In the distance, tracer fire arced faintly over the northern skyline, like lightning crawling across a storm front.

"Get some water in you," Charles finally said, standing again. "They'll be coming."

Nugget straightened, rolling his shoulders, as if the weight might slide off. "Yeah. And we'll be ready."

The men moved through the night, resetting fuses, stacking shells, building gun positions out of whatever the city gave them. Above, searchlights swept the sky, and somewhere out there, engines droned in the dark.

The morning of the 10th came heavy and still, broken only by the distant groan of machines and the smoke columns rising from the docks and fuel depots. Black pillars twisted skyward, blotting out the sun like funeral pyres. Singapore was burning.

Along the road, streams of civilians shuffled past their positions; carts piled high, bundles clutched to their chests, eyes hollow. To the troops, it felt like they were digging in to defend a city already lost.

Charles and Fraser walked the new perimeter together, over broken brick and gravel. They moved between half-built pits and half-broken houses, helping site the guns where gardens and intersections became fire points. Fraser spoke in short bursts, tight and controlled, the kind of command voice that gave structure to fear. Charles moved quieter, steadying men with a hand on the shoulder or a sharp nod. Neither of them truly believed they'd hold this line. But the men needed to.

Fraser climbed onto the bonnet of a truck, briefing sheet in hand, voice carrying down the line.

"We're the last guns between here and the city," he said, louder than the engines. "They come through us, they take everything."

No one cheered. But no one turned away.

The air itself felt tense; a stretched cord waiting to snap. The distant cracks of small-arms fire echoed like warning shots, and the lazy circling of Japanese Zeros above made the perimeter feel smaller with every pass. Charles thought of the Somme; the way the Fritz must've felt, waiting for the hammer to fall.

By evening, the tension finally snapped.

Smash!

Roof tiles shattered as the first shells walked down the street. Windows blew in like sheets of ice. Men flinched with each impact, ducking behind walls and sandbags. The Japanese artillery wasn't wild. It was measured. Systematic. They were zeroing in.

Charles pressed into the sandbags beside Gun Two, watching tracer fire crawl down the street like glowing fingers. The radio hissed, spitting out confirmation of Japanese armour advancing down Jurong Road.

Fraser slid down next to him, wiping sweat and brick dust from his forehead. "They're getting bolder," he muttered.

Charles leaned out just enough to scan the horizon. "They're creeping it in nice and slow. Softening us up."

From behind the gun, Nugget appeared, shirt half undone, covered in grime. He hefted a shell from the crate, grinning in that grim, stupid way he always did when things got ugly.

Charles jerked his chin at him. "How many rounds we got left, Nugget?"

Nugget gave the crate a pat like it was a loyal dog. "About a hundred and fifty per gun. Give or take what the weevils didn't eat."

Fraser snorted. "That's not going to last long when they hit us proper."

"Then I'll just start throwin' the bastards," Nugget shot back, sliding a shell into Gun Two with a satisfying clunk.

A fresh impact shook the street, dust raining down over them. A tile smashed beside Fraser's boot.

Charles met his eye, voice low. "They're close, Lieutenant. Real close."

Fraser nodded once, jaw tightening. "Then we make 'em pay for every inch."

The bombardment rolled on through the night, the rhythm of artillery like a slow drumbeat. The Australians crouched in the dark, hands-on hot steel and worn rifles, waiting for the storm to come down the road.

Just before dawn on the 11th, the shelling began.

Mortars slammed into intersections with the steady rhythm of a metronome, Type 92 machine guns hissing from the tree line beyond the western approaches. Shutters exploded from windows. Street corners vanished in splinters and smoke.

Charles was already at Gun Two when the first shells fell short, his palms black with grease and grit. Nugget slammed another round into the breech and snapped the block closed.

"Gun Two, point-blank! Give it everything!" Fraser bellowed, his voice hoarse but steady.

The 25-pounder barked again and again, recoil slamming through its trails, barrel already glowing a deep metallic red. The men worked with machine precision, sleeves slick with sweat, shirts sticking to their backs.

"Hotter than the bloody sun," Nugget muttered as he slammed the next shell home.

To the west, a column of Japanese tanks nosed through the gaps in the Indian unit's position. A burst of flanking fire stitched across the gunline, smashing into sandbags and brick. A man went down screaming. Fraser didn't even flinch.

"Shift Gun Three, west corner! I want every shell in their guts!"

The Japanese troops came in close behind the armour; lean shadows slipping through gardens, hedges, narrow lanes. Charles heard the crack of rifle fire from the rear flank, then the flat bark of a Bren.

He ducked as tracer rounds skimmed low over the sandbags. A figure burst through the hedge line ten paces away; a Japanese soldier with a bayonet raised high. Nugget spun and fired from the hip, the muzzle flash lighting the hedge like a camera bulb. The man dropped, smoke curling from Nugget's barrel. He didn't say a word. Not a single joke.

A truck loaded with wounded barrelled through their position, brakes screaming, scattering hot casings under its wheels. Blood smeared down its side panels. The driver didn't stop.

By late afternoon, the gunline was barely holding. Two 25-pounders were already gone; one silenced by a mortar burst, another by a tank's machine gun ripping through the crew. The smell of burned cordite and blood hung thick in the air.

Fraser slammed the wireless handset down and barked,

"We're pulling back to the reservoir road! All crews, limber what's left and move!"

Charles looked at the remaining gun, their gun, its barrel blackened and blistered from hours of non-stop firing. Nugget met his eyes and nodded once. They both knew the drill.

"Last bursts, mate," Charles said.

They held that position for five more minutes; long enough to let the others fall back. Shells cracked against the walls, as a house behind them caught fire, throwing orange light against the night sky. Nugget's face flickered in and out of the glow like a man already half a ghost.

They hit the firing lever one last time, then leapt onto the limber. As the gun tractor roared away, the position was instantly overrun.

No one mentioned Harris. Nugget just said his name once under his breath, then fell quiet.

By the next morning, the Japs had taken Bukit Timah Hill. That gave them the high ground, the water mains, the pipeline.

The bombardment never stopped. Day and night blurred into one endless barrage. What little food was left came in cold tins or mouldy biscuits. Water was a few canteens swallows a day. Men stopped shaving. Fraser's voice, once sharp, rasped like sandpaper now.

On the 15th of February, they crouched under the cam net at the edge of the new line, the city to their backs, the sound of tanks grinding somewhere out of sight.

Nugget flicked a cigarette from his ration tin. It was bent and damp but lit anyway.

"Reckon this is it?" Nugget asked, voice low.

Charles stared out at the darkness. "Reckon it was it two days ago."

Neither laughed. Neither needed to.

When the shelling stopped, it was like the world had gone deaf. No distant impacts. No tank engines. No gunfire. Just a kind of stillness that didn't belong to war.

The men looked at each other across the pits, as if waiting for the punchline to some sick joke. Then a runner appeared from Brigade HQ, clutching a single crumpled sheet. White cloth tied to his rifle butt.

Fraser met him halfway, his hands shaking before he even read the words.

"Ceasefire," he croaked.

"All guns to be spiked or abandoned. White flag orders."

For a second, no one moved. The silence was heavier than the bombardment.

Nugget let out a breath that sounded more like a laugh but wasn't.

"They've bloody done it," he muttered. "We've bloody lost."

Charles stood by Gun Two; what was left of it. The paint blistered, the barrel scorched black. He ran a hand over the steel.

Fraser's shoulders sagged as if someone had cut his strings. He wasn't shouting now. No one was. A few men stared down at the ground. One cried without sound. Another threw his helmet into the gutter.

Charles pulled his bayonet from its scabbard, drove it into the breech, and snapped the firing mechanism clean. The gun they'd held for weeks; the one that had roared down the peninsula with them, was dead.

Above the burning skyline, a strange stillness settled. No glory. No triumph. Just the sound of boots shifting in the dirt.

Charles felt the weight of the silence. Harris's absence. Nugget's trembling hands. Fraser's hollow stare. And beneath it all, the steady ache of Edna and the children, waiting somewhere he might never reach again.

The war had swallowed Malaya. Now it was swallowing Singapore too.

Chapter 24

The Surrender

Japanese soldiers bark orders, short and guttural, as they shove the prisoners into columns on Bukit Timah Road. Bayonets glint in the slanted, late-afternoon light, the air tastes of smoke and wet metal. The heat has settled over the city like a damp shroud.

The Australians of the 8th Division are pushed shoulder to shoulder with British and Indian troops. Thousands of men in silence. Boots coated in mud. Uniforms stiff with soot, sweat, and blood.

There were no Union Jacks now. No marching band rolling down The Mall, no cheering crowds waving flags, no polished boots striking cobblestone in time to a brass fanfare. Just the steady creak of webbing and the soft squelch of a beaten army shuffling through the heat.

On either side of the road, Japanese lined the route, motionless except for their eyes. Bayonets fixed. Machine guns on tripods. Bamboo poles poised like shepherds herding cattle. Any man who slows receives a shove or a jab to the ribs. Some stumble. No one dares speak.

Civilians gather in the skeletons of their ruined homes; small figures framed by splintered doorways and collapsed walls. Women clutch their children. Old men stand hollow-eyed. No one cheers. A few avert their gaze. Others can't look away. Their silence pressed against the column like a weight.

Ahead, in the dull gold of the fading light, the piles of rifles and Bren guns gleam like a field of broken bones. Stacks and stacks of steel, bayonets catching the sun. A forest of weapons about to be silenced.

Fraser fumbles with the clasp of his map case. His hands shake, the sweat on his fingers making it harder to work the buckle. For the first time, he doesn't look like an officer; just a boy wearing too-big boots. Nugget holds onto his rifle too long, jaw tight, eyes locked on nothing. When he finally lets it fall, the rifle hits the pile with a dull, metallic clatter that seems to echo forever.

Charles undoes his webbing slowly. Not because he's reluctant, because each buckle is an act of finality. Each strap peeled away is one less piece of the man he was this morning. When the last buckle gives, he feels stripped, bare. He presses Edna's letter into his tunic, tucking it flat against his chest; the only piece of home they can't take.

And then comes the sound.

The rifles fall. One after another. Then hundreds. Then thousands.

A cascading wave of iron and defeat that builds until it's louder than anything else, louder than the trucks, louder than the jungle. A single, overwhelming sound that will carve itself into the memory of every man on that road.

Japanese officers stand on the backs of lorries, binoculars glinting. They don't cheer. They just watch. Clinical. Detached. Victorious. A guard shoves Charles with a bamboo pole when he slows to look back. He doesn't react. He turns his head just once and sees the smoke curling up over Kranji and Sarimbun, soft against the setting sun. Their gunline is gone. Everything they held has been erased.

The column begins its slow march east. The humidity is suffocating. It crawls down their throats and sticks to their skin. The weight of sweat turns uniforms into wet canvas. Boots squelch in the thick, red mud. Every few minutes, someone stumbles. And every time, a guard is there with the bamboo, barking an order and beating them back to their feet.

"Bastards," Nugget mutters without looking up. His voice is hoarse, but there's no tremor. Just exhaustion.

Charles glances at Fraser. The young officer stares dead ahead. His shoulders are hunched now. He's not leading anyone. He's just walking like the rest of them.

Singapore unspools around them like a film played too slow. Shattered shopfronts with twisted shutters. Craters where houses used to be. Burnt-out lorries. Bloated horses lying in the gutters, legs stiff in the air. A city beaten to its knees.

The air is thick with the smell of smoke and rot. Diesel. Burnt wood. Blood.

Near a stretch of fence, a woman reaches through with a dented canteen, eyes wet. A guard steps forward and smashes it from her hand with the butt of his rifle. The children behind her shrink back into the ruins. More hands appear further down the road; small acts of mercy met with hard steel. One boy tries to pass a bucket of water. He's shoved to the ground.

The column marches on.

Charles's breath comes shallow and hot. His vision swims a little. The road ahead bends east toward Changi. His body moves, but his mind drifts somewhere else entirely.

Woodstock.

The air is bright and sharp and full of birdsong. A breeze moves through the gum trees like a soft hand through hair. The war is a distant rumour; not real. Not here.

Lurline rode circles through the paddock on her little bay pony, hair flying loose behind her, the hooves kicking up clouds of golden dust in the late afternoon light. She leaned low in the saddle, practicing her gallop the way she'd seen her father do, a fierce grin on her face.

Margaret and Lucille tore barefoot across the yard, squealing as they tried to chase her, their laughter ringing over the fences. Claire stood in front of Edna, who sat perched on the veranda chair, gently brushing her youngest daughter's hair and humming a tune Charles could almost place.

John, still just a baby, was tucked in Edna's arms. His cheeks were warm from the sun, his tiny feet kicking against her hip as he reached out toward the noise and movement of his siblings. Edna looked up, caught Charles watching, and gave him that quiet smile; the kind that felt like it held the whole world steady.

The laughter of the children rings across the field, clear and bright.

It's everything the march isn't.

The memory fractures like glass when another guard shouts. Charles blinks hard. The sound of boots in mud replaces the laughter. The field becomes the road again. The children are gone.

By the time the sun begins to sink, the sky is the colour of bruised red and smoke. The column turns through the battered outskirts of the city, moving toward Changi Barracks. The gates loom ahead, rusted iron and brick, ugly and final.

Japanese soldiers funnel them inside. No water. No food. Just more shouting. Men are forced down into the dirt of the parade ground. No one speaks above a whisper.

Guards patrol with bayonets at the ready. One prisoner, a young Brit who stumbles out of line; is struck in the back of the head with a rifle butt and dragged to the side. The message is clear.

Fraser looked around, rasping through cracked lips. "Feels like we've stepped into someone else's world," he murmured.

Charles felt the same chill.

Nugget doesn't bother speaking. His face is slack, streaked with grime and sweat. Around them, thousands of men hunch in the dirt like pigs, backs curved, eyes fixed on nothing.

The flies come first. Then the smell. Then the dark.

Night falls hard.

The jungle hum rises in the distance. For the first time in months, there are no more orders to give. No more guns to man.

Just silence.

Chapter 25

Changi

Dawn breaks grey and sticky. A wet, heavy haze clings to the parade ground, carrying the reek of body odour, blood, and stagnant water. Men stir where they dropped, slumped in the mud, faces streaked with grime, hair matted flat. Their uniforms have stiffened overnight, mud crusted thick around their boots. Mosquito bites swell in red constellations across their skin.

A low chorus of flies hymn over the ground, settling on open sores, cracked lips, the dead weight of men who hadn't woken. The sound is constant. Inescapable.

Japanese guards move through the broken line like wolves through sheep. Their bamboo poles slap boots and backs; sharp, cracking reports that cut through the morning silence. Orders snap out in short bursts of Japanese, fast and hard.

"Tenko. Roll call."

The prisoners drag themselves upright, shoulder to shoulder, swaying in the heat that hasn't even peaked yet. A British private, buckles forward; his knees fold, chin dropping.

SMACK!

The bamboo pole smashes into his jaw with a wet, hollow thud. Blood spatters the dirt. He doesn't get back up. No one moves to help. No one even blinks.

Beside Charles, Nugget rasps through a dust-dry throat. "Reckon they'll feed us today?"

Silence.

Fraser stumbles along the line, voice cracking as he counts. "Thirty-one." The number's wrong. Charles can see the empty spaces. Another quiet subtraction from what's left of them.

The sun climbs higher. The smell of rot thickens, crawling into their clothes, their mouths. Humidity presses down like a wet sack, sweat soaking through their kit. Charles squints at the glint of bayonets in the haze, at men who once wore the same uniform but now look like strangers.

Yesterday we were soldiers. Today we're nothing.

A barked order. Shoving starts. The men are herded into the long wooden barracks; seventy crammed into a space built for twenty. The air inside is worse than outside. Still, wet, unmoving. The smell of old timber fuses with mildew, sweat, and latrines, into something rancid and heavy.

Mosquitoes whine in Charles's ears like sewing needles. The barred windows let in only slivers of light, cutting across the room in thin white lines. Dust floats in the shafts like falling ash.

They try to lie down, but there's no space. Bodies press together, slick skin against slick skin. Boots knock into ribs. Every breath tastes of the man next to you.

Nugget mutters, voice low but sharp enough to cut through the noise. "Smells like a bloody stockyard."

Charles answers without looking at him. "At least stock gets fed."

A few men chuckle; short, dry sounds that don't quite make it to laughter. Fraser doesn't join in. He lowers himself against the wall, still in his boots, arms wrapped tight around his knees. He doesn't say a word. Doesn't take them off. As if unlacing them would mean surrendering the last thread of who he was.

Charles presses his shoulder against Nugget and looks up. The rafters hang low, streaked with mould, cobwebs sagging like lace curtains. For a moment, the past slips in like a draft through a crack.

St John's. The dormitory rows of narrow beds, the smell of damp wool blankets, whispers in the dark. Boys shifting on their mattresses, breath shallow, too scared to sleep.

Back then, those walls had felt like a cage.

Now, these were one.

The weight of that realisation settles somewhere deep; not like a sudden blow but a slow, cold seep, working its way into his bones. The room fills with breath and heat, and for the first time since the surrender, it feels permanent.

The barracks settled into a ruthless rhythm. Tenko at dawn. Every dawn.

They were driven out into the parade ground and made to stand for hours beneath a white, blinding sun. Any movement; a shift of weight, a twitch, a falter; brought punishment. Bamboo cracked against shins with a sharp, wet snap. A man sagged to his knees in the heat, and a guard kicked him back upright as if adjusting a piece of furniture.

The heat pooled between the barracks like an oven, thick and unmoving, baking everything beneath it. The air reeked of old sweat, cooked skin, dust and latrine stink, so heavy it stuck to the inside of their mouths. Men swayed on blistered feet, dizzy with thirst, the sun drilling into the tops of their skulls.

The only reprieve came once a day, if you could call it that. A single rice ball and a ladle of thin, greasy soup poured into dented tins. Men crouched in the dirt to eat it, backs hunched, heads down, the way animals feed.

Fraser's voice, hoarse from sun and dust, rasped down the line.

"Discipline's all we've got left."

Charles didn't lift his head.

"Discipline doesn't fill bellies."

He scanned the thinning ranks. Cheeks had hollowed. Shirts hung loose. Shoulders caved in under the weight of heat and hunger.

The same routine bled from one day to the next, until the days lost their edges. They spent hours standing and staring at the same patch of dusty ground, the same high wire fences, the same guard towers with rifles watching like unblinking eyes.

Even a glance the wrong way could bring a blow. Guards didn't need reasons; the bamboo poles spoke faster than words.

It felt less like a camp and more like a holding pen. As if the Japanese hadn't decided what to do with the thousands they'd captured. So, they left them to stand, to sweat, to starve; and wait.

For better or worse, mid-March brought a shift. Tenko now came before dawn, the world still dark and heavy with fog.

Men were herded out barefoot into the half-light, the road burning against their soles as soon as the sun broke the horizon. Humidity clung to their skin, slicking through their clothes before the day had even begun.

They marched east toward the docks, past skeletons of bombed-out buildings, piles of rubble and twisted rebar. Once, these had been warehouses and cranes. Now they were labour yards.

Charles's body ached long before the work began. He could feel the weakness settling into his bones now, a kind of hollowness that didn't go away. He'd grown up working cattle and digging fence posts, but this was different. Starvation took the strength out of every lift. Every breath.

They were made to heave broken concrete, steel beams, sandbags, anything the Japanese pointed at. Guards patrolled the line with bayonets fixed and rifle butts ready. Any man who faltered was punished on the spot, no words, no warning, just the crack of wood on bone.

It happened before breakfast. A young British soldier, barely more than a boy, bent low near a supply truck. Charles saw his hand dart out; a grain sack, maybe two handfuls of rice.

The guard didn't shout. He just raised his rifle and shot the boy in the stomach.

The sound was flat. Final.

The boy collapsed in the dust, twitching and choking, blood leaking into the sand. No one moved. No one was allowed to. A second guard dragged the body aside like a sack of cement.

Behind a half-collapsed truck, Nugget doubled over, retching nothing but bile. Charles gripped his shoulder hard.

"Don't draw their eyes," he whispered.

The work continued.

By the time the sun set, their feet were raw, backs flayed, hands shaking. The march back to Changi was silent. No songs. No talk. Just the shuffle of skin on gravel and the smell of blood in the heat.

The rations waiting were the same as always, a rice ball, watery soup. It tasted like nothing.

Charles sat in the dirt with the others, staring at the horizon where the sun had gone down. The boy's blood was still on the dock. And tomorrow, it would be someone else's.

The days bled together. The only thing that changed was the worksite, sometimes an airfield, sometimes a cratered street, sometimes the docks again. Always under the same relentless sun.

Each day stripped a little more from them; a handful of strength, a slice of dignity, a voice that stopped bothering to curse. Rations shrank as they did. A full rice ball became half. The soup turned to tepid, cloudy water that left their mouths dry.

"Lost a stone and a half, mate," Nugget rasped, rubbing the hollow where his ribs showed through. "Great bloody diet." He coughed midway through the sentence, a wet rattle that ended in blood.

Charles gave him a flat look. "Just keep scooping in what you can."

It wasn't advice anymore. It was ritual, something to say that sounded like leadership.

Around them, the men thinned out, bones showing through their sleeves, faces all angles and shadows. They weren't prisoners so much as walking outlines of who they'd been.

By April, the latrines were overflowing. The stench clung to everything: the air, their skin, the wooden walls. Buckets were hauled out by hand, sloshing through the mud to the shore, their contents flung into the tide that always brought it back.

Dysentery swept through the camp like smoke. Men folded into the dirt, clutching their bellies. Fraser burned with fever for three nights but refused the *"hospital hut."* Everyone knew why. You went in and never came back.

During the day, they trudged through mud laced with excrement and blood, sores spreading up their legs. At night, they were packed tight in the barracks, the air hot and wet like a damp rag over the mouth. Charles lay awake, listening to the wheezing, coughing, quiet whimpers that filled the dark.

As bodies break, minds start to slip, staring at the ceiling, moonlight seeping through the bars, he would drift into memories of home. Each time getting harder to hold the images sharp.

One always stayed clear.

Edna leaning against the bell tower, sunlight catching the dust around her hair. In her spotless dress, eyes bright and piercing; the look that started everything.

It hurt to hold onto it now, too vivid against the grey.

Across the hut, Fraser sat hunched against the wall, knees drawn up, a stub of pencil shaking in his hand. He wrote by the dim light bleeding through the slats, tiny letters on scraps of scavenged paper. When the guards' footsteps neared, he'd pause, sliding the paper under the loose plank near his feet.

Charles watched once, pretending to be asleep. "What's that you're writing?" he asked quietly.

"Something to remind someone we were here," Fraser murmured, not looking up. "If they ever find it."

Nugget rolled onto his back beside them, staring at the ceiling. "If?"

Fraser gave a thin smile. "Just in case."

Outside, the guards laughed again; sharp, careless, human. It sounded like music from another world.

"They want us to stop being soldiers," Fraser whispered after a while.

Charles didn't turn his head. "Then we hold on in defiance," he said. "Even if it's just inside."

Fraser gave a slow nod and went back to writing, the pencil barely moving.

Charles closed his eyes, feeling the breath of men all around him, the stifling air heavy with rot and fear. Somewhere below the floorboards, Fraser's little pages waited; words sealed in the dark, a fragile kind of defiance that might outlast them all.

As he drifted off, the darkness came alive again. The nightmares never really left; they'd only grown older with him. In his sleep, memories bled together: the crack of shells from the Great War, the sound of stretcher barriers over duckboards, the cold eyes of his father who'd never wanted him to enlist.

Now those ghosts walked beside the newer ones; Harris's voice on the radio, the burning shoreline at Kranji, the faces of men he couldn't save and a mother he'd never see again.

His world had become one long nightmare, whether his eyes were open or closed.

By early May, the morning tenko brought more men to their knees each day. Heat shimmered off the ground. One corporal swayed, then dropped face-first, kicking up a cloud of dust. Charles flinched but didn't move. None of them did anymore. They'd learned what that brought.

A Japanese guard stalked over, bamboo pole in hand. He prodded the fallen man's ribs, nothing. The pole slid beneath the body and lifted; the man sagged like a sack of wet grain before hitting the dirt again. Two prisoners were ordered to drag him out, his ankles leaving twin grooves in the dust.

Later that day came another; Private Jennings, dysentery. Days of fever and gut-cramps, too weak even to lift his tin when the bucket came. Charles found him upright against the wall, eyes open but gone.

The stench of sickness clung to everything: sweat, rot, the sweet metallic tang of blood. Even the flies seemed slower now. That night, the guards came with ropes. The bodies were dragged beyond the wire. A faint splash followed; the sound of them dumped into a pit or creek. No prayers. No words.

Fraser sat by the doorway, scribbling names into his notebook, hands shaking so badly he nearly tore the page.

Nugget's booming voice had fallen silent. For two days he stared at the same patch of wall. Didn't eat. Didn't speak.

"This isn't war anymore," Fraser murmured.

Charles stared into the dark. "No. It's what comes after."

Outside, thunder rolled. It didn't rain.

The storm dragged on for weeks; heat, rot, men dropping one by one. Then came the whispers, an escape attempt in the night. British prisoners, caught near the fence. By dawn, the rumour turned real.

Rifle butts slammed into the barrack doors, splintering them from their hinges. The guards burst in, dragging men to their feet. Those too weak to stand were beaten forward until they stumbled outside.

Barefoot. Gravel biting. The parade ground shimmered with heat.

"Kneel!"

Thousands dropped as one. Stones dug deep into skin. The sun climbed higher, the air thick as boiling tar.

Hours passed. Lips split. Men swayed. Some toppled forward, only to be kicked upright again. Charles felt sweat run down his spine, pooling in the dust. The smell was unbearable: salt, blood, dust baking into flesh.

A Japanese officer strolled the line, boots crunching on stone. Every so often he stopped, picking a man at random. The crack of bamboo echoed down the ranks. Nugget took a kick to the ribs, grunted, but stayed kneeling.

An Indian soldier near the front collapsed, trembling. A guard beat him across the back until the trembling stopped.

"Don't move," Fraser hissed. "Don't draw their attention."

Whispers drifted through the line; fragments of prayer, a bar or two of a hymn; cut short when a guard stamped on a man's neck.

When it finally ended, dusk had fallen.

They crawled back inside, knees shredded, skin blistered, lips cracked from thirst. No water. No relief.

Charles sat against the wall, watching the dark ripple with torchlight. The air stank of blood and fear. He thought of the horses back home, whipped for slowing. At least they'd been put down clean.

The days that followed blurred together: too hot, too long, too cruel. Every dawn felt the same: the bark of orders, the shuffle of bare feet, the smell of rice water and rot. Time stretched, empty and endless, until even pain became routine.

Then, one evening, something small shifted.

After roll call, as the guards paced outside the barracks, a faint rustle moved through the gloom. Men began to trade scraps; a chipped biscuit, a threadbare rag, a twist of tobacco paper smoothed flat again. Small things, worth nothing anywhere else, became treasure here.

Charles knotted two frayed bootlaces together to hang a ragged mosquito net near the doorway.

"Still a stockman at heart," Nugget rasped, his voice rough but faintly amused.

"Just doing what keeps the flies off," Charles said, the ghost of a smile flickering beneath the grime.

Fraser sat nearby, fixing a spoon handle with a bit of wire, the movement delicate, almost reverent. "We keep mending things," he murmured. "Because that's all we can still do."

From somewhere down the row, soft as breath, came a sound. A single voice humming Waltzing Matilda. Off-key. Thin. But real.

Another joined in. Then another. The tune spread, carried along the bunks in whispers; ghost voices from a world that felt centuries away.

For a heartbeat, the barracks sounded like soldiers again. Not livestock. Not ghosts. Men.

Charles stared at the rafters, at the dust drifting in the moonlight. He could almost smell the dry paddocks of home, hear his children laughing in the distance.

Then the butt of a rifle slammed against the wall. A guard barked a warning. The song snapped off mid-note.

The silence that followed was almost holy.

For a single moment, they'd remembered who they were; and that memory was something the Japanese couldn't beat out of them.

Then June crept in, stealing that warmth bit by bit, until tenko brought a twist of its own.

The guards came with clipboards, not rifles. The interpreter read out numbers in a flat, nasal rhythm. Each call made the crowd flinch. Men stepped forward, blinking in disbelief, some crying softly into their sleeves. There were no explanations.

The Japanese divided them into groups. Those called stood to one side, those staying on the other. Fraser's number was called first. His face didn't move, but his hand twitched at his chest, where the small notebook lay hidden beneath his shirt. Charles's came next. His stomach dropped, but he straightened his shoulders before stepping out. A habit from another war; if you look calm, the men might believe you are.

Nugget's number never came.

The three men locked eyes for a heartbeat; the only exchange they dared. Then the guards barked orders; those leaving were to clean the barracks. Sweep. Burn waste. Scrub the floors.

Preparing their own cage for the next batch.

The timber walls were etched into Charles's memory now; sharper, somehow, than the red brick of St James Cathedral.

As they packed their meagre belongings, Nugget shuffled over, his hands trembling.

"Don't die without me, Charlie."

Charles gave a faint nod. "Wouldn't dare." He placed a steadying hand on Nugget's arm.

Nugget pressed a single cigarette into Fraser's palm. "For when the bastards stop watching."

Fraser managed half a smile. "If that day ever comes."

Charles looked between them; the last of his mates, worn to ghosts. "We push on for Harris," he said quietly. "We don't let him die for nothing."

They all agreed, though no one said it again.

That night, the air in the barracks was still and thick. Sweat glued shirts to skin; the sound of coughing and shifting bodies filled the dark. It reminded Charles of the orphanage, the same restless breathing, the same waiting for a morning that never seemed to come. Only this time, there'd be no bell, no breakfast.

He lay awake, tracing the folds of Edna's letter, whispering his children's names like a prayer. Not for hope; just to remember them as real.

"Think we'll ever see home?" Fraser murmured from beside him, voice weak.

Charles didn't answer. He just stared at the ceiling, the faint drip of rain tapping the tin roof. Somewhere down the line, a man began to sob quietly. No one told him to stop.

Dawn came pale and wet.

Guards stormed in before first light on the 7th of June, barking while they cracked bamboo poles against the boards. Men were herded outside barefoot, the mud slick and cold underfoot. The line formed quickly, those marked for transport.

Charles gripped his pack, the weight pitifully light. No one knew where they were going, only that it wasn't back to the barracks. Rumours flickered like sparks: Sumatra, Thailand, maybe Japan itself. Each guess ended the same, silence.

Fraser walked ahead, his uniform hanging loose from his frame. Nugget stood behind the wire, gaunt and blank. He raised a hand in farewell, lips pressed tight.

Charles didn't wave, just nodded once.

The guards started shouting, pushing the column forward. The air thick with the smell of rain and unwashed bodies. Beyond the wire, the jungle waited: green, wet, endless.

Charles pressed his hand to his chest, feeling the outline of Edna's letter beneath his shirt. He didn't take it out this time. Didn't need to. The words were already part of him.

As they marched east toward the docks, he glanced back once; the barracks fading into the mist, Nugget's shape shrinking in the haze.

"France had a line," he thought. *"Singapore didn't. And Changi was just the waiting room."*

The sound of bare feet in the mud carried them away, swallowed by the jungle.

Chapter 26

Sandakan

The prisoners were marched from Changi in silence, bamboo strikes waiting for anyone who spoke. No orders, no destination; just the steady shuffle of loose stone on the road. On the horizon, the docks appeared through the haze, where an old freighter waited like a rusted carcass. Its funnel coughed thick black smoke that drifted low across the water.

When they drew closer, Charles could just make out the faint lettering on the hull: *Ubi Maru*.

The men stood at the base of the gangway, hesitant to move. No one knew where they were bound or if they'd ever return. The first few who lingered too long were clubbed with rifle butts, blood bright against the rusted metal. That was enough to get the line moving.

Charles was shoved forward and down into the hull, iron walls pressing in on him like the Suevic once had; but tighter, darker, hotter. There was no mess hall here, only a cargo hold turned cage. Men packed shoulder to shoulder, the iron door groaning before it slammed shut. The last slice of light disappeared, the air instantly thick and sour. Diesel fumes mixed with body odour and the rising stink of fear.

The only comfort was Fraser's voice somewhere nearby. The engine coughed to life, vibrations running through the bodies in the dark. The ship began to sway, a motion that never stopped, rolling men into each other until the word space lost its meaning.

Within hours, the first wave of seasickness hit. The Japanese had left two wooden buckets in the corner; mockery, not mercy. They filled fast, slopping over as the ship lurched, bile and waste sloshing across the deck. The sound of retching never stopped.

The steel walls sweated with condensation, dripping onto faces.

"You reckon this crate's seaworthy?" Fraser's voice cut through the darkness.

Charles felt the hull shudder beneath him. "Doesn't matter if it is. We're not the cargo they care about."

"Bloody feels like we're cargo," Fraser muttered. "Haven't breathed proper air since Changi."

"Keep it shallow," Charles said. "Use up too much and you'll steal the next man's breath."

Someone nearby heaved again, the sour reek of vomit mixing with the diesel fumes.

Fraser coughed into his sleeve. "Hard to believe we're even moving. Feels like we're sinking already."

Charles gave a dry laugh. "You should've seen the Suevic in the canal. Thought that was hell till now."

"First war, right?" Fraser asked quietly.

"Yeah," Charles said. "Different war. Same stink."

The engine droned on, a heartbeat they couldn't escape.

By the third day, Charles had lost all colour, dizzy and sweating through his rags. Every breath burned like hot oil. He coughed up bile and prayed for air that didn't reek of death. No Snow offering his canteen, no Billy throwing a hard tack at his skull. On the Suevic, there had been songs, banter, sunlight; here there was only darkness, the constant pitch of the ship, and the sound of men breaking.

The heat became unbearable. A man near the wall went quiet mid-breath, dead from exhaustion. The guards ignored the shouting from below. The body lay there for hours, eyes open to the dark.

When the hatch finally creaked, a blade of white light sliced through the hold. Guards barked orders, pointing to the corpse slumped against the bulkhead. Two men dragged him up the ladder, arms dangling. The smell of rot lingered long after the hatch slammed again and the light vanished.

"That's number four," Fraser murmured.

"Number doesn't matter," Charles said. "He's gone."

"I'll still write it down when I can see again," Fraser replied.

From the gloom, a younger voice trembled. "What's the point, sir? None of us'll make it home to read it."

Charles turned toward the sound, Private Bluey Hargreaves, barely a man, voice cracking under the strain.

"Someone will," Fraser said hoarsely. "Someone always does."

"Quiet, Bluey," Charles said softly. "Save your air."

"Just saying," Bluey muttered. "Feels like they're takin' us to the bottom."

"Maybe they are," Fraser whispered. "Keep count anyway."

The ship rolled on through the dark, the engine thudding steady as a pulse.

Eleven days blurred together: no horizon, no sense of direction, only the endless roar of the sea and the stink of men rotting alive.

When the hatch finally opened on the 18th of July, sunlight stabbed down, blinding. Men blinked and squinted, shielding their faces as guards shouted for them to move. The air outside felt wet and heavy, thick with salt, rot, and swamp.

They stumbled up into the light, coughing and retching. Some couldn't move at all; they were beaten or dragged off by the arms. The stench of death clung to every man.

The jungle loomed ahead: green hills under a furnace sky.

The guards herded them down the gangway onto the wharf, rifles fixed. Charles sucked in air that felt no freer than the ship's hold.

"Another island," Fraser muttered beside him. "Same bastards."

"At least we're breathing again," Charles said, though the words felt thin.

The prisoners were split into columns and marched inland. The weakest were thrown onto the backs of trucks. Locals stood by the roadside, silent. One woman hid her face behind a shawl as the column passed.

Hours dragged by beneath a sun that burned the colour out of everything. The road narrowed to a dirt track, the jungle pressing closer on both sides until it felt like the world itself was closing in.

When at last they reached a clearing, a set of crude gates loomed ahead; timber posts lashed with wire, a guard tower squatting above. As they were herded through, Charles caught sight of a weathered plank nailed to the fence, black paint peeling from the letters. He read it under his breath:

"Sandakan."

The word sat heavy on his tongue.

He didn't know where it was, only that it wasn't home. The guards barked and shoved them deeper into the camp; past bamboo huts and barbed wire that gleamed in the sun like teeth. Somewhere beyond the perimeter, the jungle hummed, alive and endless.

Charles glanced at Fraser. "Well," he said quietly, "we've found the end of the map."

Fraser didn't answer. He just looked at the sign again, then at the men behind them, and started walking.

A murmur rippled down the line, low and uncertain.

"Sandakan... that's Borneo, isn't it?" someone whispered.

"Borneo?" another voice said. "Then we're closer to home."

Charles caught the words, felt them hit like a stone in his gut. Closer to home; but not in any way that mattered.

The heat hit like a wall inside the wire. The ground was baked hard and red, the air heavy with the stench of swamp and sweat. Around them, the camp stretched out; raw timber huts sinking into mud, a single water drum already buzzing with flies. The guards' voices cracked like whips, echoing off the jungle edge.

The prisoners were herded into ranks on the open ground. Dust lifted around their boots as the order came down in sharp, broken English; "Work. Build. Airfield."

No rest. No food. No medical checks after the voyage.

Charles felt it sink in; they weren't just prisoners now. They were labour. Builders for the very bombers that might one day find their own shoreline. He thought of Red Hill, far enough away to feel safe, Edna and the kids tucked behind their fence and garden. But even the thought of bombs falling anywhere on Australian soil turned his stomach.

He looked to Fraser again, who muttered under his breath, "God help the poor bastards in Darwin."

Charles didn't reply. The guards were already pointing toward the tree line, where the first clearing cuts for the runway awaited.

They dumped what little they had into a hut and were split into work details. Fraser and Charles ended up together with a handful of Australians and a few British men; faces hollow from the voyage, uniforms stiff with salt and sweat. Guards shouted orders, rifles raised, forcing them down a narrow trail that wound into the trees.

The heat was thick enough to drink. Flies swarmed their faces and necks, and the jungle pressed in so close it felt like walking through someone's lungs.

When they reached the clearing, it didn't look like a worksite. It looked like a wound, half swamp, half jungle, the air rippling over black mud and broken stumps. A haze hung low, turning everything the colour of rust.

The guards barked, "Clear jungle! Drain swamp!" and pointed toward a heap of tools; tin plates, rusted buckets, a handful of shovels with handles hacked short.

Charles stooped, picked one up, and turned the blunt edge in his hand. Its balance was off; the metal warped from years of use. For a moment, his mind slipped back; the red dirt of

Woodstock, him and Billy as boys, digging fence posts under a blazing sun. Billy leaning on his shovel, smirking.

"You're worse at this than the cows, Charlie-boy." They'd laughed, drop tools, and go swimming in the creek instead.

Here, there was no creek. No Billy. Just mud, orders, and a shovel that weighed like guilt.

The young private beside him was Bluey, red-headed and wiry, squinting at the tool pile.

"These bastards reckon we're supposed to dig an airfield with that? Might as well give us spoons."

Charles gave a half-smile. "You want to suggest that to 'em?"

Bluey glanced toward a guard snapping a bamboo pole. "Not today, sir."

They started digging. Hacking. Scooping. Every stroke sank into muck that filled back in before they could blink. The air shimmered, heavy as syrup, and the smell of rot crawled into their noses and stayed there.

Corporal McAllister; a broad-shouldered bloke from Wagga; hauled a basket of mud and staggered sideways, knees buckling. Charles lunged to steady him just as a guard's shadow loomed. McAllister straightened fast, mud dripping from his chin.

"Don't," Charles muttered under his breath.

"Wasn't plannin' to," McAllister rasped. "They'd only make me do it twice."

Hours passed in a daze of sweat and noise. Shirts turned to rags. Hands split and bled. The slap of mud, the crack of bamboo, and the bark of guards became their rhythm, a drumbeat of punishment.

Bluey wiped his face with a filthy sleeve. "Reckon this strip'll ever see a plane?"

Fraser squinted through the haze. "Only if hell's got runways."

That earned a grim laugh, but no one had the energy to keep it going.

By late afternoon, the sun hung low, a molten disk sinking into the jungle. The guards finally barked "Stop!" and beat them back toward the camp. The air shimmered gold over the swamp, and the ground steamed as they trudged through it.

When they reached the huts, a pot of rice gruel waited; mostly water, a few stray grains floating on top. Charles finished his in two gulps. Fraser chewed his slow, jaw working like a man gnawing bark.

"Good tucker, eh?" Bluey muttered.

McAllister gave a dry chuckle. "Had better muck on the dairy back home."

"You from Wagga, aren't you?" Charles asked, half-remembering from Changi.

McAllister nodded. "Yeah. Grew up baling hay, feeding pigs. Thought it'd toughen me up. Guess I was wrong."

"Could be worse," Bluey said. "Could've been a bloody post digger."

Charles's mouth twitched. "Don't get me started on that."

The laugh faded quick. They were too tired for more.

Inside the hut, the air was close and wet. Men lay shoulder to shoulder on rough planks, their breathing shallow and uneven. Outside, the guards patrolled with lanterns, shadows stretching and shifting across the slats.

Charles sat by the wall, listening to the storm gather. Lightning flickered beyond the trees.

Fraser spoke low beside him. "You ever think we'd end up building a Jap runway?"

Charles looked down at his blistered hands. "Never thought I'd fight a war twice."

Fraser exhaled slowly. "You reckon they'll use it?"

Charles nodded toward the darkness beyond the wire. "They wouldn't bleed us for nothin'. That strip's for bombers, and it's pointing south."

Neither spoke again. The rain started, soft at first, then harder, drumming on the roof until the sound swallowed everything else.

Charles lay back, eyes open, the rhythm of the storm matching the thud of his heart. Somewhere out beyond the fence, the jungle roared; ruthless, endless, and waiting.

The days stretched, each one identical to the last; sweat, mud, and the echo of shouted orders.

Tenko came before dawn, when the mist still hung over the huts and the men's breath fogged in the half-light. They'd stand barefoot in the slosh, bodies trembling from fever or hunger, waiting for the count to finish. Then came the work. Always the work.

Through the long hours, the weather turned on them like an enemy; blinding rain one minute, furnace heat the next. They hauled gravel, hacked at bamboo, drained swamps one bucket at a time. Bare feet split open on coral and wire; hands blistered from hauling timbers and slinging shovels that no longer had edges.

Guards lined the perimeter with bayonets fixed, rifles glinting like silver teeth. One pause, one stumble, one breath too long, and the bamboo poles came down.

Charles kept the men moving. Calm, steady, always watching. He spoke in low tones, enough to keep their rhythm alive, enough to give the guards no excuse. He'd learned that silence drew blood.

When Bluey faltered one afternoon, his shovel slipping from his hands, Charles caught him by the arm and steadied him.

"Keep your back straight, lad," he murmured. "Don't give 'em a reason."

"I can't..." Bluey's voice cracked, half from exhaustion, half from fear.

"You can. Just slower. Keep the line moving."

The nearby guard's eyes lingered on them for a moment before turning away. Bluey swallowed hard and bent back to work.

Later, McAllister tripped while hauling a log. The guard raised his stick, but Charles was already there, crouching beside the corporal, pretending to adjust the load.

"Shift your weight," he muttered. "Up on three. Don't look at him."

They lifted together, the guard hesitating before stalking off, unsatisfied. It was like that every day, small interventions, unseen mercies.

Fraser collapsed once, heat stroke dropping him mid-step as he carried bucket. Charles dragged him up by the collar before a guard noticed, pressing a handful of gravel into his palms.

"Hold this," he hissed, "make it look like you're working."

Fraser's lips were cracked and grey, but he nodded, eyes unfocused.

Their bodies were failing, starvation was constant. The single bowl of rice with its cloudy soup didn't keep pace with the labour. Some days, a bean or two floated in the broth; a cruel kind of joke.

Charles began quietly rationing. Counting. Trading mouthfuls between those who needed them most.

"You eat half," he'd tell Bluey, "And the rest goes to McAllister." No one argued; they just nodded, too weak to speak. An extra grain could be the difference between survival and death.

Even through the punishment, the airstrip grew; a scar carved deeper each day. Mile after mile of coral fill laid over the earth, the jungle beaten back until nothing lived on its edge.

By December 1942, it was finished.

That morning, the guards forced the prisoners to line the runway. The air shimmered in the heat, and then the sound came; deep, rolling, mechanical thunder. The first Japanese bombers appeared from the north, their engines droning low as they descended.

Twin-engine Mitsubishi Bettys circled once before landing, their wheels spitting gravel and coral like shrapnel. The guards cheered, clapping and shouting, forcing the prisoners to stand and watch the spectacle.

Fraser shaded his eyes, his voice hoarse. "That one could reach Darwin."

Charles didn't answer. He only stared at the runway: perfect, gleaming, deadly. The weight of it settled in his chest. Every shovel of dirt, every blister, every drop of sweat had built the thing that might bring death to their own shores.

Around them, the men were silent. The cheers of the guards echoed off the jungle, hollow and cruel. The prisoners knew now; they hadn't built survival. They'd built a weapon.

When the last bomber rolled to a stop, Charles turned away, eyes on his men. "Keep your heads down," he said quietly. "We live through this. That's the fight now."

The monsoon broke not long after; lightning splitting the sky, rain hammering the wings of death, as the airstrip gleamed white like bone.

As 1943 rolled on, the work turned meaningless. Orders came down to move gravel from one end of the airstrip to the other, then back again. Men who could once swing a pick now leaned on their shovels just to stay upright. The guards no longer needed a reason to hit anyone. Beatings had become routine, something to fill the hours.

Each time a Betty roared overhead, the sound split something inside Charles. He'd watch the bombers rise into the sunrise, heading south, and his thoughts would drift home. Lurline would be eighteen now; a woman grown. He pictured her helping Edna fill the hole he and Granny Dean had left, getting the little ones ready for school, cooking, mending, carrying on. Two years gone, half of it spent behind wire.

It wasn't duty anymore, it was survival. For him and for the men who still looked to him. Charles helped the weakest to their feet at roll call, steadying them with a hand on the shoulder. He traded spoonfuls of rice for a feverish man's share of water, rationing by instinct the way he'd once done feed back home.

They'd started calling him the old stockman.

"You reckon the cattle were treated better, sir?" Bluey asked one afternoon, his voice as brittle as the gravel they were shovelling.

Charles managed a half-smile. "They were lad. Least the cattle got a regular feed."

That drew a few hollow laughs before the guard's bark cut through again.

Fraser was fading. His body thin as wire, his skin grey. He spent most of his days hunched over what was left of his notebook; just a few scraps of paper, ink thinned with sweat. The names filled every inch now, no space for words, only lines. His hand trembled as he wrote.

Through it all, a fragile kind of comradeship grew in the cracks. Aussies, Brits, even a few local prisoners; men who shared nothing else shared what little they had. A cigarette butt passed hand to hand. A thread used to mend a torn shirt. A single dry joke that made the day a fraction shorter. They were all in the same hell, and somehow, that mattered.

Their humanity was being stripped, slowly and methodically. They spoke in whispers about food; roast lamb, cold beer, bread thick with butter; until the memories only made the hunger sharper. Bones pressed through skin, faces sharpened, eyes sank deep.

Sometimes, men hallucinated. They'd murmur to ghosts: wives, children, mates already gone. Charles wasn't spared from it. Each night, his dreams were a storm of blood and wire; Flanders trenches folding into jungle mud, Billy's laughter echoing through both. The ghosts of two wars now shared his nights. The men heard him wake, gasping, but no one asked. They all had their own ghosts.

By mid-1943, the camp itself seemed half-dead. The jungle crept back along the fences, swallowing the huts' edges. The airstrip lay gleaming and worn, a monument to their suffering.

Then the whispers began.

Something was happening among the officers, late-night movements, coded glances. Charles heard it first from McAllister while hauling gravel.

"Blokes up in the admin hut," the corporal muttered. "Say they've built a wireless. Hidden somewhere under the floorboards. Locals bringin' in parts."

Charles frowned. "You sure?"

"Sure enough. They're talkin' with the Chinese traders, maybe even tryin' to get word out." McAllister spat into the dirt. "Mad bastards'll hang for it."

Within days, guards were searching huts, overturning bedding, shouting in Japanese. Men were dragged out by the collar and beaten bloody for no reason given.

Then came the real terror; the Kempei Tai.

They arrived without warning, black uniforms cutting through the camp like blades. Someone had talked. Or maybe someone had been found. A list of radio parts, they said. Charles never saw it, but he saw the fear it left behind.

That night, the prisoners were forced to watch as one of the officers was marched through the compound, bound and bloodied, the guards shoving him toward the trucks. He didn't look at anyone. Didn't speak. Just stared straight ahead, face swollen beyond recognition.

Fraser whispered beside him, "He won't be coming back."

Charles nodded, silent. He didn't need to be told.

The trucks started. The guards saluted. And the officer was gone into the dark road toward Kuching.

No one slept that night. The jungle squealed, restless, and even the rain seemed afraid to fall.

Chapter 27

Breaking the Chain

The camp had changed. The air itself felt charged, heavy with unease. Guards barked orders with new edge, and bamboo rods swung for smaller reasons than before. Tenko was no longer just a routine; it was a performance of control.

Roll calls came at midnight, and again before dawn, sometimes in the middle of a meal, forcing the men to line up, silent and barefoot on the sloppy parade ground.

Whispers moved through the huts, low as breathing. Missing tools. Hidden tins. Men seen crawling toward the wire at night. Bluey stirred a pan of gravel for no reason other than to look occupied.

"Could be one of ours made a run for it," he muttered, eyes flicking to the jungle.

Fraser sat nearby, his skin ashen beneath the film of sweat, a damp cloth pressed to his forehead.

"No one escapes Sandakan," he said. "Not now."

The words came out flat, no malice, no hope. Just fact.

Charles had seen that tone before, back in Flanders. Men who stopped saying *when we get home* and started saying *if*. He kept his head down, shovel working the same patch of dirt until his palms split. Something was stirring under the surface, too much movement, too many secrets in a place where secrets meant death.

He knew desperation when he saw it. It wore the face of courage, but it was suicide all the same.

Over the next few weeks, the current running through the camp grew stronger. Locals were spotted near the fence line at night, slipping between trees like ghosts. Some of the Australians whispered about a plan: boats, rivers, the coast. A few groups made mercy runs, hoping to follow the Kinabatangan River through the jungle to freedom.

None made it out.

One morning a body was found hanging from the wire, blackened by flies. It wasn't a warning; it was a promise. The camp fell silent after that, the air thick with the smell of rust and blood.

Patrols doubled. Dogs arrived, snapping at shadows. Beatings became casual. Even when Charles kept his eyes on the ground, he caught bamboo across the shoulders for walking too slowly. He'd seen cattle in stockyards treated better.

The days blurred into one another: grey light, rain, heat, pain. The prisoners shuffled like broken men, hunger eating them from the inside, breath rattling like loose nails in a tin.

Then the Kempei Tai arrived again.

They came from Jesselton with trucks and neat uniforms, their boots polished, their eyes cold. Everyone knew what they were. The secret police didn't need names or reasons. They were the end of the line.

That night, distant shots cracked through the rain.

Bluey froze mid-step. "That'll be the last of 'em," he whispered.

No one answered.

By late September, the camp was a nest of fear. The Kempei Tai tore through the huts, overturning bedding, pulling out floorboards, searching for anything; maps, tools, the smallest sign of rebellion. Officers were dragged away for questioning. None came back.

"They're thinning the head, one by one," McAllister muttered, wiping mud from his chin.

Fraser's fever had worsened, his eyes bloodshot and glassy. He sat on his bunk, clutching his notebook like it held his pulse.

"They're going after command," he said quietly. "Cut it clean."

Charles sat beside him. "You reckon they'll take you too?"

Fraser gave a dry half-smile. "Wouldn't that make things tidy?"

Charles didn't reply. He knew the truth; Fraser was already halfway gone.

The tension built for weeks, each morning thick with expectation, until it finally broke.

Tenko came without warning on the 15th of October 1943. The sky was low and heavy, thunder muttering in the distance. The men were herded out into the rain, the ground dragged at them, heavy and spiteful. Guards shouted over the wind, the interpreter's voice carrying from beneath a soaked poncho as he began to read from a clipboard.

Names.

Captains. Lieutenants. Chaplains.

Then, Fraser.

He flinched when he heard it, a fragile scaffold against collapse. He turned in the rain, searching the ranks until he found Charles. Their eyes met across the line, just for a moment.

Fraser's expression said everything; weariness, resignation, and something else, a kind of peace that only comes when you've stopped expecting mercy.

Charles gave a single nod. No words. They would've cost too much.

Fraser squared his shoulders, lifted his chin, and stepped out of the line. He walked past Charles, close enough that their sleeves brushed, close enough that Charles could see the tremor in his hand. He wanted to say something, anything; but his throat locked tight.

A guard shoved Fraser forward with a rifle butt. He stumbled, caught himself, and kept walking toward the trucks. No luggage. No goodbyes. Just the rain and the hollow sound of boots in the mud.

"Where they takin' 'em?" Bluey whispered behind him.

"West," Charles murmured. "Kuching, maybe."

A prisoner further down the line muttered something under his breath. A guard spun and slammed his rifle stock into the man's face. The line fell silent.

Charles stood there as the engines growled to life. The convoy pulled away through the gate, headlights flashing briefly in the rain before vanishing into the mist.

The camp was still after that. No shouting, no movement. Just the steady drum of rain on tin and the low hum of the jungle beyond the wire.

When the silence settled, it was heavier than the storm. The last of the officers were gone. The chain of command was broken.

Charles didn't move for a long time. The rain rolled down his face, washing the mud from his kit, but the weight in his chest didn't lift. When he finally turned his back to the square, the men were watching him; Bluey, McAllister, the others; waiting for someone to tell them what came next.

He didn't speak. He just nodded once toward the huts.

"Inside," he said quietly.

And they followed.

The huts were half-empty now, rain dripping through the thatch and pooling on the dirty floor. Men sat in silence, not sure whether to stand or lie down. The air felt stripped bare, no orders, no direction, just the sound of rain and breath. Whispers rippled through the darkness.

"Who's in charge now?"

"What happens tomorrow?"

Charles sat on his bunk, elbows on his knees, head in his hands. Fraser's weary face was still burned into his mind; that last look before the trucks rolled away.

McAllister's voice broke the quiet. "You're the highest rank left, Charles."

Charles didn't look up. "Rank's just a word now."

"Maybe. But they'll listen to you. They already do."

Outside, guards moved with lanterns, light sliding across the walls like searchlights. Every cough drew a glare. Every whisper risked a beating. The Japanese plan to break the underground had worked; clean and absolute.

By dawn, Charles understood what he had to do. Without structure, the men would eat each other alive.

He stood before roll call, rain still falling, voice steady but low.

"We keep working. We stay together. No panics. That's the order."

He set new routines; ration checks, water turns, rotating night watches. Anything to give the camp a pulse again. He adjusted work details, spreading the load so no one broke too soon.

Bluey frowned as they filled buckets for the morning shift. "You reckon the Nips'll let that slide?"

Charles wiped the mud from his hands. "They don't care what we do, so long as we keep shovelling."

And strangely, the guards didn't stop it. Order made the labour run smoother. Efficiency was its own permission. Soon the men began turning to Charles before anyone else; even the Japanese looked his way when things fell apart.

The days regained shape, cruel but predictable. At tenko, Charles walked the line like the old captains had once done, straight-backed and quiet, offering words beneath his breath.

"Stand tall."

"Breathe."

"Eyes forward, lads."

He kept them moving, blending the calm of command with the steady patience of a stockman. Rhythm. Repetition. Endurance. The same lessons he'd learned driving cattle through the heat back home; keep them upright, keep them breathing, and they'll survive the journey.

He saw the men that way now. Not as prisoners, but as something he was responsible for keeping alive.

"You ever reckon we'll get home, sir?" someone asked one afternoon, voice dry as gravel.

"Home's still there," he said. "That's what keeps us going."

He had no idea if it was true. The bombers roared overhead almost daily now, silver crosses in the glare, but he couldn't tell where they struck. Still, he forced himself to believe; in a world outside the wire, in Red Hill's wide veranda, in Edna's face when she saw him walking up the stairs. He pictured Lurline grown, the children older, a life without fear. That thought was what kept him from falling to his knees.

One night, a loose board slapped in the wind and woke him from a terror. He reached under it and found the edge of a notebook, Fraser's. Pages damp and thin, the ink smeared from sweat and time. Names filled every line. No stories. Just the dead, written down so they wouldn't vanish completely.

Charles turned the book in his hands for a long while, thumb tracing the spine. Then he handed it to a young private.

"Keep it going," he said. "Every man deserves a name."

By mid-1944, the camp had ground them down to bone and silence. Charles kept them together; sharing his rice when he could, forcing the sick to rest, making the strong carry the weak. McAllister stayed by his side through it all, steady as a post.

"If we start thinkin' like prisoners," Charles said one night, staring into the rain, "we're already gone."

Sandakan had become a skeleton of what it was, the camp now a swamp of disease and skeletons. The men yellow skinned, bellies distended. Even the guards looked half-starved.

Rations fell again, half a rice ball a day, sometimes streaked with worms, sometimes nothing at all. Soup became a coloured water, a thin trace of green if they were lucky.

Charles continued the daily rituals; trying to keep the men anchored. Without it, they'd drift into madness. McAllister helped where he could, dragging bodies from mud when they collapsed, tying bandages from shredded shirts.

Sometimes seeming pointless as beriberi, malaria and dysentery ran wild. The air stank of sickness; latrines overflowing, the huts heavy with the sour tang of fever. Charles forced men to drink whatever boiled water they could scavenge.

"You can't fight if you're dry," he'd say.

Even so, deaths were constant, sometimes three of four a night. Charles insisted on naming every man in Fraser's notebook.

"Write it clear. Someone has to know they were here."

Morale bled away. No letters, no news, no hope of rescue. Even the jungle seemed to close in tighter around them, as though the world itself wanted to swallow the camp whole.

The airfield, once alive with shouted orders and engineers, now sat cracked and dusty under the sun. Work became absurd, maintaining an unused strip, moving gravel for the guard's amusement.

"Feels like they're waitin' for us to die so they can bury us where we stand." Bluey muttered one afternoon.

"Then we make 'em wait." Charles said.

That line stuck. Becoming a quiet prayer amongst the men – *make 'em wait.*

By October 1944, the sky changed. The air dense, heavy with tension. Even the guards seemed restless, their eyes fixed on the horizon instead of the men.

One afternoon the jungle went still; no birds, no insects, just heat. Then came a distant rumble, too steady for thunder.

A siren tore through the camp, shrill and alien. Guards shouted in Japanese, sprinting toward their posts, rifles waving wildly.

Charles froze mid-swing with his shovel. The men looked to him. Then the sound hit; high-pitched whines cutting through the clouds.

"Aircraft," someone breathed.

The first Allied planes, American P38 Lightings, appeared like slivers of silver, sun flashing on their wings. Charles's heart slammed in his chest. For months the sky had been silent. But today, it roared again.

The guards yelled, forcing the prisoners to the ground. A split second later, the ridge beyond the strip erupted; deafening concussions that flung coral and dust into the air like volcanic ash.

Men ducked, hands over their heads. Some cheered before they even realised it.

"Bloody hell," Bluey shouted, grinning through the dirt. "Those are ours!"

A rifle butt cracked across his face. "No noise!" a guard screamed.

More blasts rolled through the jungle, the earth trembling beneath them. Smoke boiled upward, black and orange.

When the sirens faded, there was only the roar of fire. The airfield burned; the coral runway split and bleeding with oil, flames licking the edge of the jungle.

Then came the orders. Guards drove the prisoners out with rifle prods, shoving buckets and tin plates into their hands.

"Move! Fire out! Now!"

Charles ran with the others, choking on smoke. They formed ragged lines, passing water from drums, slapping mud on burning fuel deposits. The heat blistered their skin, the air thick with kerosene and sweat.

He glanced toward the inferno; planes in pieces, craters gouged deep as graves. *This is what we built,* he thought. *And it's finally burning.*

By nightfall the fires still glowed red through the trees. The camp stank of oil and charred wood.

"Reckon they'll come back?" McAllister asked quietly beside him.

"They always do," Charles said. "Just takes time."

Over the next weeks the raids returned; sometimes daily, sometimes without warning. Each siren sent the men diving for holes; each blast reignited a fragile spark of hope.

But every cheer brought punishment. The guards beat anyone caught smiling at the sky.

One raid tore through a hut, killing three outright. Charles and McAllister clawed through the rubble with their hands, dragging out what was left. When it was over, Charles stood amid the wreckage, his voice low and hoarse.

"The bastards are hitting what we built," he said. "Maybe that's justice."

The guards grew meaner as their fear deepened. Supplies dwindled. Water became scarce.

Rations dropped again, less than a handful of rice a day. The men grew hollow, moving through smoke like ghosts.

The airfield, once a symbol of punishment, was now a cratered ruin; jagged coral, burned machinery, puddles of fuel shining in the rain.

At night the jungle glowed faintly from the smouldering wrecks, and whispers passed through the huts.

"The Yanks are close."

"MacArthur's landed."

"We'll be free by Christmas."

Charles didn't stop them talking. Hope, even poisoned, kept them breathing.

He'd stand at the doorway of his hut after roll call, watching lightning flicker over the black horizon, and imagine home; the veranda wet from summer rain, the scent of jacaranda, Edna's lamp still burning in the window.

And he'd wonder whether anyone there still looked north toward Borneo, waiting for him to come home. Did they even know where he was, or if he still existed at all?

By November, the raids stopped as suddenly as they'd begun. The silence felt wrong: heavy, unnatural. Whispers followed. Maybe the Allies had taken the island. Maybe the war was ending.

The jungle began to reclaim the strip, vines curling through cracks in the coral, roots pushing up through twisted metal. What had once been an airfield now looked like a grave; a memorial to every man who'd bled building it.

"If they've been bombing Borneo, the Yanks must be close," Bluey whispered one night.

"Close don't mean here," Charles said.

The rumours multiplied. The guards grew anxious, tempers snapping quicker. Locals stopped coming; the Chinese labourers, the Malay traders who once passed scraps through the wire. It was as if the world beyond the fence had gone silent.

Charles watched the guards more closely now. Fear was setting in. They argued among themselves, officers shouting in the compound late into the night, their voices carrying over the huts like thunder.

One morning, McAllister came to him, holding a half-empty sack. "Trucks haven't come in days," he said.

Charles nodded. "Means we're on our own."

The men took it as a sign; the Japanese were losing. They clung to that thought, even as the food vanished and the beatings grew more savage.

A new word began to pass down the line in whispers, traded like contraband.

"Evacuation."

No one knew what it meant. Some said liberation. Some, transfer to safer ground. Others, a death sentence.

The guards began burning records, tearing down structures, dismantling anything that could be used as evidence. Crates of documents went into the fires, their ashes drifting across the parade ground like dark snow.

Charles watched the airfield burn, black smoke rolling into the clouds. He realised the Japanese weren't preparing to surrender; they were preparing to vanish.

At night, guards moved through the huts, whispering to interpreters, pointing at lists by lantern light. The smell of kerosene and ash hung heavy in the air.

Bluey leaned close. "You hear that? They're sayin' we're movin' inland."

Charles didn't look up. "Then we move when they tell us. One foot in front of the other."

"You think it's real? Evacuation?"

"Doesn't matter what I think. Just keep your feet close."

By early January 1945, the camp felt hollowed out; no aircraft, no supplies, no noise but coughing and the crack of bamboo rods. The guards were thinner too, eyes sunken, uniforms hanging loose. The jungle was taking everything back.

The rumours came softer now, worn thin like everything else. Men said the Japanese were losing, that ships were coming, that help was close. No one believed it fully, but they needed to.

Charles felt it in his gut; that cold heaviness that always came before a storm. He'd felt it before; in the trenches of France, the gunline of Malaya, and now here.

McAllister said one night, low so the guards wouldn't hear, "If they're evacuatin', maybe they're savin' the fit ones."

Charles looked at him through the dark. "And leavin' the rest to rot."

Neither spoke again after that.

That night, the rain came down hard; heavy tropical sheets drumming on the tin roofs. Charles was half-dozing when the door slammed open and a Japanese corporal barked through the doorway.

"You! Warrant officer! Come!"

He rose, exchanging a glance with McAllister before stepping into the mud. A handful of other warrants followed; gaunt silhouettes, faces hollow, feet slapping through puddles. They were led across the compound to the old officers' hut, now half-burned and stripped of furniture.

Inside, a Japanese lieutenant waited, an interpreter at his shoulder. A single lantern hissed on a crate, throwing long shadows against the walls.

The lieutenant began speaking in clipped bursts. The interpreter followed,

"Tomorrow morning. Movement. Fit men only. March to new camp, west direction. You prepare groups. Five columns."

No destination. No supplies mentioned.

Charles stepped forward slightly.

"How far?" he asked.

The interpreter frowned. "Far enough. Men must walk. Those who cannot, stay."

The lieutenant's eyes swept the room like knives. None of the men dared ask more.

The briefing ended as quickly as it began. Guards waved their rifles toward the door. The rain hammered harder as they were marched back across the yard.

In the dark, back in his hut, McAllister whispered, "New camp? Maybe they mean Jesselton."

Charles shook his head. "They'd have said. This isn't a move, it's a clearing."

By dawn, he watched the guards ready their rifles, lists in hand, rain still falling. The first names were called; Bluey and McAllister among them. Charles stood at attention as the interpreter approached, a clipboard slick with rain.

"Warrant Officer Watson," the interpreter said flatly. "You lead first group. Keep order. Move west."

Charles felt it hit him like a weight. They weren't asking; they were ordering. He was to lead them out.

He gave a single nod, jaw tight, forcing himself to stand straight, to give no sign of fear. Around him, men adjusted what little they had; blankets, water tins, rags tied around blistered feet.

He knew what this was now. Not an evacuation. A final order.

Chapter 28

March to the Death

Rain drummed endlessly against the huts, pooling beneath the stilts and washing through the camp like it meant to erase it.

It was the 28th of January 1945. Nearly three years of captivity; of hunger, fever, and labour; had whittled Charles into a shadow of himself. His skin clung to his bones, every muscle stiff with exhaustion.

But this order, to lead his men west; felt like a challenge unlike any he'd faced before.

He was to command the first march column. Around him, fifty-five skeletal men waited in silence: Bluey, McAllister, and others barely able to stand, to be escorted by thirty ruthless guards.

"West, eh? Long way home that way," Bluey muttered, his voice brittle.

"Keep your head down and just keep moving," Charles replied, forcing calm.

The air reeked of oil smoke, sweat, and rot. Behind them, the camp itself was burning, flames curling through the huts as guards shouted over the rain. Ahead, the gates yawned open; an exit that had once meant freedom.

Charles felt the weight of leadership settle across his shoulders, heavy as the sky. But beneath it flickered something fragile; a thought, a hope – *If liberation's close, I'll get them there.*

He drew a slow breath.

"Forward march!"

The words carried through the rain. Men began to move, a ragged line of ghosts. Their bare feet slapped and sucked at the mud, each step making a dull, wet sound: slosh, pull, slap.

Charles walked through the gates first, past the weathered Sandakan sign and the sagging barbed wire that had hemmed them in for years. It faded behind him into the mist; like it had never been there at all.

The track quickly turned to swamp. The further they went, the more the jungle closed in, swallowing the path. The ground dissolved beneath them until they were wading knee-deep through brown water.

Mangrove roots twisted around their ankles like fingers; branches snagged at their clothes. The air was thick with the stink of stagnant water and decay. The hum of insects never stopped.

Every movement was a struggle; mud clutching their feet, rags peeling away until bare flesh met rock and root.

Charles drifted through the column, sometimes leading, sometimes moving to the rear, giving a hand over fallen logs or slippery ground.

"Step. Breathe. Step," he repeated, steady, measured; something to keep rhythm, to keep men alive.

The guards shouted over him; "Hayaku!" their bamboo rods cracking across backs and shoulders. The sound cut through the rain like whips.

Hours dragged on before the first man fell; a young private, too weak, too hollow. He stumbled once, then collapsed face-first into the mud.

A guard strode over, lifted his rifle, and fired a single shot.

Crack.

The body twitched, then sank into the water. The sound of the shot echoed through the trees. The column froze.

"Christ... just like that?" Bluey whispered.

"Eyes up. Keep formation," Charles said quietly.

He felt the shock hit him, but he didn't stop. There was no time to check the man, no strength to carry him. One truth carved itself into him then; if you fall, you die.

His duty was to keep the rest standing. So, he did.

They pushed on through the mangroves, the flooded track fighting them at every turn. Rain poured through the canopy; leeches clung to legs and bellies, drawing what little blood remained in them. The men grew quieter as the day wore on, not from discipline, but from sheer exhaustion.

When the sun finally began to drop, Charles tried to guess the distance. The jungle distorted everything, but by his reckoning they'd been marching fourteen hours; maybe thirty kilometres, though it could've been half.

It didn't matter. They weren't free yet.

At dusk, the guards called a halt. The men collapsed wherever they stood, finding what little dry ground there was; a root, a mound, anything above the waterline. There was limited food, half a hand of rice, slither of dried fish. No water.

"Chew the grass," Charles ordered softly. "There's moisture in it."

Around them, the swamp hummed with life: frogs, insects, unseen things moving through the dark water.

It was a cruel joke: surrounded by water, dying of thirst.

Charles settled into the mud, his back against a tree. He'd slept in worse; France, Malaya, Borneo; the same filth, the same smell of fever and waste.

Men coughed and groaned around him, clutching their bellies. The air was thick with sickness.

He tilted his head back and looked up through the canopy. The rain had eased; the stars burned faintly through the mist. For a moment, it wasn't Borneo he saw; it was home. Red Hill, the wide sky, the smell of wet earth after a storm. Edna on the veranda, waiting.

He closed his eyes.

"Hold on," he whispered. "I'll come home."

And in that whisper, beneath the weight of the jungle, he still meant it.

Day two began before sunrise, the rain easing to a heavy mist. The first sound was the crack of bamboo against tree trunks; guards driving the men awake.

Charles blinked against the dim light filtering through the leaves, forcing his body upright. Every joint screamed.

He moved through the column, counting under his breath.

"fifty-one... fifty-two... fifty-three..." He stopped.

One man hadn't risen. Their body lay half-buried in mud, face slacked, eyes already filmed with insects. There was no time for burial, no way to write his name. The jungle would swallow him.

The guards began herding the rest forward, rifles gesturing west. Charles turned to McAllister, who still had some strength left.

"Take the lead," he said. "Steady pace. Don't let 'em fall."

They moved out. The swamp thinned, the trees opening into harsh light. The air turned dry, biting their throats. Beneath their feet, the mud gave way to coral; jagged and white. Each step sliced into bare flesh. The sound changed from sloshing mud to scraping stone and pained gasps. The smell of salt burned their lungs.

A scream tore through the line. Charles pushed forward, stumbling over the stones until he found the source, a private crumpled on the ground, his foot a mess of blood and grit, a shard of coral embedded deep in the sole.

Charles knelt beside him, his knee crunching on rock.

"You're all right, private. Just a scratch," he said, though they both knew it wasn't.

He tore a strip from the hem of his trousers and reached for the wound; only to feel the sting of bamboo across his arm.

"No stop!" a guard barked, eyes narrow.

Charles steadied himself, looked up, and said quietly, "Then you'll carry him."

The guard froze, his expression hardening. For a moment Charles thought that was it; that he'd be shot where he knelt.

But after a long pause, the guard sneered, lowered the pole, and turned away.

Charles exhaled, quick and shallow, then ripped the coral free and wrapped the foot in one motion. The private hissed through his teeth but didn't scream.

Bluey limped up beside him, shaking his head.

"Old bastards got a taste for you, sir."

Charles gave the faintest smirk. "He's not the first."

Inside, though, he knew that comment might've cost him his life.

By midday, the sun was a hammer overhead. The air shimmered with heat, glare bouncing off the pale stone until every man's eyes ached. Sweat stung their open cuts; the air reeked of salt, blood, and human rot.

When they would reach a shallow creek, men waded through, cupping the water in their hands. The stones underfoot were sharp, but the cold water gave a moment's mercy; washing blood from feet that would start bleeding again minutes later.

There was no rest. The guards kept them moving, bamboo rods tapping rhythm. The only sounds were the scrape of feet, the hiss of breath, and the occasional gunshot when someone collapsed for good.

As dusk fell, the count stood at fifty-one.

They huddled under scrub, bodies trembling, too weak for speech. The jungle hummed with insects, the air thick and hot even in darkness. Then came the whispers, drifting along the line like fevered prayers.

"MacArthur's coming... Darwin soon."

Charles didn't silence them. False hope was still hope.

He lay back on the coral ground, staring up at the night sky, the stars veiled by mist. His chest ached with every breath. He prayed, not with words, just with the stubborn rhythm of his pulse.

Another day, he told himself. One step closer to liberation.

Day three brought a new kind of torment, elevation.

The men still shuffled through coral, but now the track began to rise. Their legs shook with each climb; the stones cut deeper into already torn feet. Still little supplies, food dwindling quick. Their lips split and bled from dehydration, their tongues thick as leather. Every breath rasped.

Charles's thoughts drifted, unwilling, but unstoppable, back to Salisbury Plains.

Billy's grin, that sideways smirk as MacRae gave his practised speech. The whispered joke that earned them the privilege of a forty-kilometre pack march without water.

And now here he was, driving starving, broken men across Borneo's ridges with none.

He could still feel that old English mud, the endless trudge through fog, the sting of thirst and mud up to the knees. The way their tongues swelled, and how Snow had quietly broken his hard tack, sharing it out between them.

"Won't taste like much," Snow had said, "but it'll keep your guts from eating themselves."

Charles could almost taste that dry, bland biscuit now.

Back then he'd thought the Salisbury march was hell. Now he saw it was training, necessary conditioning. MacRae standing there at the crest, unmoved but not cruel, teaching them to endure.

And here he was, the lesson made flesh, driving his own men forward through thirst and exhaustion.

The guilt burned deeper than the sun. He hated the sound of his own orders, hated that they came in MacRae's voice.

"One foot in front of the other."

"Don't look back."

As the coral hills rose, Bluey faltered. His knees buckled, body hitting the ground with a dull thud, the crunch of stone echoing across the ridge.

Charles was on him instantly, hauling him upright with both arms.

"On your feet! Move!" he barked.

The tone wasn't his; it was MacRae's, alive in him, cutting through weakness.

He caught himself mid-shout, a flicker of shame passing through him. But Bluey steadied, coughed, nodded, and kept walking. That was enough.

The climb grew steeper. The air shimmered with heat, the light off the coral white as fire. Around him, the men mumbled to ghosts, wives left behind, children now fatherless. Their eyes glassy, their lips cracked. Whispering names, half-dreaming as they walked.

Charles didn't stop them. He understood. He did it too.

The rain came before dawn, rolling in from the ridges behind them. It drummed across the coral hill where they'd camped, turning dust into paste, bleeding the white rock into grey. When the guards barked orders, the men rose stiff and trembling, their bodies raw from the night's cold.

Charles watched them scrape water from the coral in their hands, trying to catch what little ran off before it vanished into the cracks. Some used leaves, some just opened their mouths. It was never enough. The rain mocked them; endless, but undrinkable.

He crouched beside McAllister, who was sorting through the last of the rations; a small tin, a few spoonfuls of rice stuck together like glue.

"This'll be the last of it, sir," McAllister murmured.

Charles nodded. "Spread it wide. Give the weaker a touch more. I'll take a spoonful, give the rest of mine to the others."

Even divided, it wouldn't fill half a dozen mouths. Charles knew it. So did the men watching from the shadows of the hill.

He stared west through the mist. By his reckoning, they'd come close to a hundred kilometres; far past Jesselton; deeper into Borneo than any map he'd ever seen. There was no sense of distance anymore, only forward. Ahead, the coral faded into a wall of green; jungle thick enough to swallow them whole.

He moved through the line, whispering as he counted. "Fifty left."

A guard cracked his bamboo pole against a tree. "Hayaku!"

The column lurched into motion. The last stones of the ridge vanished underfoot, and within minutes the light changed, no more glare, just the dim, wet breath of the jungle. The air pressed close around them, heavy and still.

The smell hit first; rot and bamboo sap, sweat turned sour, the iron tang of infection. Cicadas screamed like metal saws; frogs croaked from unseen pools. The rain dripped endlessly from the canopy, loud enough to drown thought.

Charles kept to the middle of the line, steadying the rhythm.

"Forward."

"Upright."

"Keep your balance."

The track narrowed, roots twisting like ropes beneath their feet. Every few yards someone slipped, the sound of a body hitting mud followed by a guard's bark and the crack of bamboo. No one looked back.

McAllister stumbled, catching his weight on Charles's shoulder.

"Still good, sir," he said through a cough thick with mud.

Charles nodded. "Then keep close."

The hours blurred. Leeches clung to their legs, slick and black, swelling with blood. Even the guards began to stumble now, their tempers thinning with every mile. Two broke into a shouting match over a canteen, one striking the other across the face. The spilled water hissed into the mud.

Charles turned away, throat aching. He'd trade anything for a mouthful, his shirt, his last shred of pride. He thought of the creek near the farm, cold water glinting between gum roots, and for a second, he could almost taste it.

By late afternoon, the jungle grew darker still, a world of dripping vines and red clay. The men waded through knee-deep mud, the air alive with the buzz of flies and the sour stench of rot. Each step was a battle against the earth itself.

When they finally stopped, it wasn't from command but collapse. Men sank where they stood, too weak to move. Failure to get up would end in a bullet.

Night fell fast, and with it the temperature. No fires: the guards wouldn't risk the glow. Beacons for Allied reconnaissance or bombing missions. The men lay huddled beneath palm leaves, shivering, listening to the jungle's hum.

Charles lay awake, the rain cold against his face. In the dark he saw the railway station at dawn, steam drifting through the platform. John's arms locked tight around his waist, small hands gripping his belt, as he kissed the boy's forehead.

He shut his eyes against the memory, swallowed hard, and whispered into the night,

"Hold on, Johnny. Your old man's still walking."

Day five, the ground continued to claw at them, the canopy closed over like a lid, sealing out the light. What little air remained hung thick and wet, every breath a struggle. The men moved in single file, shoulders brushing vines, rifles of the guards glinting faintly behind them.

The ground turned treacherous; roots twisting through the mud like snakes, vines catching on ankles, tripping the weak. Each step was a fight to stay upright. The smell was unbearable now: mould, rot, human waste, and blood.

McAllister stumbled twice before noon, his skin slick and pale. Charles caught his arm, feeling the heat radiating off him; fever, the kind that burned men hollow.

"You're burning up, corporal."

McAllister gave a faint grin. "Feels like I'm standing in the bloody sun."

"Keep talking," Charles said. "Talking means you're still here."

The column pushed through a stretch of dark gully, waist-high ferns brushing their faces. It felt endless, the air so thick it swallowed sound. The usual jungle chorus had gone; no birds, no frogs. Just the slop of feet and the hum of mosquitoes.

Bluey muttered behind him, voice dry as paper. "Can't hear the birds no more."

Charles didn't look back. "They're listening to see who's left."

By midday, their tongues were splitting, lips blackened and swollen. The last of the rice was gone the day before; now nothing remained. Hunger clawed at their bellies, but thirst ruled everything.

When the path dipped toward a shallow stream, the men broke ranks, falling to their knees in the muck. They plunged their hands into the brown water, drinking greedily, some lying flat to slurp from the surface.

Charles shouted hoarsely, "Stop! It's foul, you'll sicken yourselves!"

But the guards didn't interfere; they only watched, amused, as men drank the filth. Within minutes, the sound of retching followed. McAllister wiped his mouth, shaking.

"Better dead from this than dry," he rasped.

Charles knelt, scooping a handful just to wet his lips. The water tasted of rust and rot, but the relief was instant. He spat most of it out, forcing himself to stand.

"Back in line!" he barked. His voice cracked, more plea than command.

The rhythm returned; a mechanical shuffle through the undergrowth, each man lost in his own silence. Charles felt his mind drift from his body. His legs moved, but they didn't belong to him. The world had narrowed to one thing, forward.

Then, a gunshot. A man had fallen; face-first into the mud, not even trying to rise. The nearest guard didn't pause; he lifted his rifle and fired. The shot echoed, flat and final. No one stopped.

Charles's voice came out raw. "One more step. Don't think. Just walk."

They obeyed, because thinking was death.

As the hours bled together, the jungle began to feel like it was closing in; vines tightening around them, branches reaching down. He could hear it breathing, mocking.

And then the voices came. Not the men's, the old ones. MacRae's bark cut through his skull, *"Final hill, boys! Don't you dare slack off, you've a trench to dig before you rest!"*

Billy's laugh followed, faint and fading, *"Dig a trench after this? Might as well bury me in it."*

Charles muttered the line under his breath, almost smiling through the exhaustion.

Bluey glanced at him, eyes hollow. "You say somethin', sir?"

Charles kept walking. "Just ghosts talkin'."

By the time the light faded, the air was so dense it felt like walking underwater. Men leaned on each other just to stay upright. McAllister coughed until he fell to one knee. Charles grabbed him again, dragging him up, whispering through clenched teeth,

"Not yet, mate. Not yet."

They stopped only when darkness made the track invisible. The men slumped into the mud, trembling, the smell of sickness thick as smoke. Charles sat awake beside McAllister, watching him shiver, whispering names under his breath; names of those already gone, and of those he refused to lose.

Above them, the jungle dripped and sighed, patient, waiting.

Chapter 29

Jungle Fever

McAllister saw the morning, wheezing through the night, swinging between shivers and sweats. When the guards started barking, he tried to stand, legs shaking, skin slick with fever. Charles pressed a stick into his hand, steadying him before the shoves came.

The slope ahead glowed red in the pale light; the smell of iron soil heavy in the air. The ground steepened, each step a gamble. Clay slick as soap. Roots tore loose under boots; every man slipped, cursed, and clawed forward. Even the air felt thinner here, cooler but fouled with the reek of rot and infection.

"Bloody hell!" Bluey grunted as he skidded sideways, hitting a trunk hard enough to split the bark and his knee in one go.

A guard raised his bamboo rod, eyes cold. Charles stepped in before the strike.

"He ain't collapsing, just clumsy," he said, voice flat but controlled.

The guard snarled, "Fast! Move!"

Charles met his gaze, steady. "He moves when I say."

For a heartbeat, the air between them froze. Then the rod lowered. Charles knew why; without him, the column would scatter. Even the guards could see who held them together.

He turned to Bluey. "You all right?"

Bluey winced, half-laughing. "Can't trust these bloody roots."

Charles tore a strip from his trouser hem and wrapped the knee tight. "Try and keep your footing."

Then came the rain: sudden, hard, cold. It turned the clay to glass and the air to steam. The drops stung their faces, but the men tilted their heads back, mouths open, catching what they could. It wasn't much, but it was more than the guards ever gave.

They trudged on, bent forward under the weight of wet rags and hunger.

His father's voice drifted through the downpour: *"Keep 'em standin' till the yard, son."*

Lines from another time, but nothing truer in this moment. He repeated it aloud, his voice rasping through the rain.

"One ridge at a time, lads."

The rhythm worked; a beat to march by, something that wasn't pain. They climbed for hours, the light fading until the ridge loomed above them like a promise. Near the crest, McAllister folded and hit the ground, by the time Charles got to him his body was burning hot and slick.

"You made the hill, Corporal," he whispered, lifting his head from the mud. "Save your strength for tomorrow."

But McAllister's eyes were already rolling back, his breath rattling in his throat.

The guards ignored him, already crouched under trees, tearing into their hidden rice tins. Watching them eat twisted

Charles's gut. If their numbers weren't so few; if his men weren't so broken; mutiny might have been possible.

As darkness closed in, Charles sat in the mud, the jungle thrumming around him, the distant thud of rain, the rush of a river somewhere below. Then, faintly, another sound crept in, the stuttering song of the Vickers. For a moment, he was back at Chuignes, the barrel shuddering under his grip, mud and blood spraying through the smoke.

He jolted awake with a start, clutching his chest, breath short. The usual terror, yes, but something else now. His legs were numb, heavy, a hollow tingling spreading upward.

The first whisper of weakness he couldn't afford.

The jungle was hushed; a suffocating quiet. Mist hung thick as smoke, coiling around the trees, heavy enough to taste.

McAllister's wheezing had stopped.

Charles turned. The old corporal was slumped against a root, lips grey, chest still. No strength left; he wouldn't see another dawn.

For a moment Charles just stared, the silence roaring in his ears. Then he dragged the limp body off the track, hands sinking into the wet earth. He pushed mud over him with a stick and his bare palms until the shape disappeared. The shallowest of graves; a mercy most didn't get.

He sat beside it, breath fogging, watching the mud slowly fill with rainwater.

"Rest easy, Mac," he muttered. "You've done your bit."

Then he stood and rejoined the line, eyes burning but dry. There were no tears left to give.

A week of marching. Time no longer meant anything. Every bog hole swallowed feet the same way, every ridge the same grind. The red-clay path bled men backwards: slick, bottomless. The smell was always there; wet earth, sweat, rot, the faint smoke of unseen villages.

The men staggered like drunks, muttering names: wives, dogs, children, ghosts.

Charles tried to count. "Forty-something," he whispered, not sure if it was men or hours.

His body was turning on him. Hands trembling uncontrollably. Lips cracked and bleeding. Tongue like sandpaper. But the legs; the legs were worst, glossy like soaked leather. Each step was a jolt of pain that no longer even felt human.

Then the fever hit. It came in waves; chills so deep his teeth chattered, then sweats that soaked his clothes. Every breath rasped; his vision shimmered at the edges. Bringing him right back next to Billy, nudging him across the duckboards to Péronne. The rain became light, then sound, then nothing.

And through it; the Vickers. The familiar rattle cutting through the storm.

He saw Hazebrouck again; flares bursting, mud exploding, the scream of the line. The mist rolled over like gas, and he stumbled, clutching at his face, choking for a mask. Then he blinked, and the jungle was back, steaming and endless.

He turned to speak to McAllister, out of habit; but the space beside him was empty. The memory of that shallow grave struck him like a rifle butt to the chest. The first of his right-hand men gone. Slumped like so many he'd seen before.

He kept walking. Legs moving, mind somewhere else. The thirst clawed at him, and the fever brought hallucinations that felt too real to fight. His mother's voice called supper from across the paddock. Billy's laugh, teasing him by the fencepost. Edna's soft scolding, her hand brushing his cheek.

They shimmered between the trees; ghosts of home leading him on. He clung to them because the alternative was to fall.

Weakness was death. He couldn't let it show. He forced his stride, barked orders when his voice worked.

"One ridge. One ridge more."

The words became rhythm, drumbeat, prayer. The men started to echo it: "One ridge. One ridge more." Between the words came the hacking coughs, the fevered moans, the wet breathing of lungs half-filled. The jungle echoed with the sound of dying.

"Hear that? Planes..." Bluey muttered, eyes wide.

Charles looked up, not sure if he heard anything at all.

"Yeah," he lied. "The Yanks. They're comin'."

Bluey's mouth trembled. "They'll find us, eh?"

"They will," Charles said. "Just got to hang on."

That's what he kept telling himself; hang on. Because if he stopped, even for a breath, they'd all crumble.

The smell of eucalyptus drifted in the rain; sharp, clean; gone before he could breathe it in. Night came with cramps that twisted his calves into knots. His feet ballooned, hard as timber, and the fever pulsed behind his eyes like a drum.

By the tenth day, only forty-seven were still standing.

The march blurred into a waking fever.

Rain came and went in bursts, the air heavy with the sour stench of their own bodies. The jungle pressed closer – vines coiling around ankles, roots like ribs in the mud. Each ridge looked like the last, each hollow reeked of the same stagnant pools.

Charles's legs were monstrous things now. He could feel fluid sloshing beneath the skin when he moved. The numbness crawled higher with every mile.

Still, he forced the pace. "Heel to heel! Keep your spacing!" His words slurred, but the men followed. Habit more than command.

The first to fall that day was a young private; bones showing through his rags, lips cracked wide. He stumbled mid-step and never rose. No gunshot this time; the guards barely glanced down. The jungle swallowed him whole.

The second went quietly at dusk; fever shaking him apart from the inside. Charles sat beside him, wiping mud from his mouth as he breathed his last.

"You did well," he murmured, though the man was already gone.

The third fell during the night storm. Lightning flashed white across the trees; thunder rolled down the valleys. By morning, the man's body was gone; washed off the track, carried into the ravine below.

Bluey said nothing. Just tightened his jaw, walking slower, limping on the knee Charles had wrapped days before.

"How's it holdin'?" Charles asked.

Bluey smirked, weakly. "Still attached, far as I can tell."

Charles nodded. "Then keep it that way."

The fever worsened. He stopped sweating; his skin burned without moisture. When he blinked, shapes followed, flickers of home behind the jungle haze. Lucille and Margret, laughing in front of the warm fires glow. Clair on Edna's lap curled up in the old armchair. His mother's voice through the mist,

"Dinner's gettin' cold, Charles."

He whispered back to the air, "Nearly there, Mum."

By the twelfth dawn, the ground began to rise again; the first hint of the highlands. The clay turned darker, firmer underfoot.

The guards whispered "Ranau" to each other, and the men caught it like a spark. The word meant salvation, or at least an end.

Charles stumbled but didn't stop. He could taste blood at the back of his throat, a sign his body was breaking. Still, he continued the beat. "One ridge more," he rasped, voice little more than air.

That night, the mist thickened until even the guards vanished. Charles sat awake, listening to the wheezing breaths of the men who were left; forty-four by his last count. The fever had settled deep in his chest; his pulse fluttered, irregular and weak.

He stared into the dark, feeling the jungle breathe around him. They were close now, he could smell it in the air: cooler wind, woodsmoke drifting from somewhere ahead.

But in his gut, he knew what was coming. He could see it.

The mountain.

The last climb.

And he knew not all of them would see the top.

A fortnight had passed. The light came dull and heavy through the mist, and with it the sight of the ridges ahead; near-vertical, red and unforgiving.

Charles looked around. He could see every rib of every man, skin pulled tight over bone, each breath a visible tremor. Ten days without rations. They'd lived off beetles, worms, whatever insects they could scavenge, catching rain off leaves to wet their tongues. Their bodies were devouring themselves.

The guards grew restless, snapping orders, faces drawn thin from their own fatigue. Their impatience boiled over in shouts and rifle butts. The message was clear: whatever waited above, they were to climb to it or die on the slope.

They were beaten into line, shoved forward. The jungle thinned into highland scrub as the earth steepened beneath them, a slick red vein of clay twisting up through dripping ferns. Every footstep slid half a step back. Breath came ragged; the air felt thinner, colder. Their ragged uniforms, soaked from days of rain, now stiffened in the mountain chill, freezing against their skin.

Even the guards struggled; muttering curses in Japanese, using their bamboo rods as walking sticks between strikes. The climb splintered the column. Men fell behind, some crawling on hands and knees.

Charles spotted Bluey, bent double, leaning on a branch like a crutch.

"Get up, mate. Nearly there!" he urged.

Bluey looked up, eyes wide and unfocused, then slipped, his weight dragging Charles down with him. They hit the clay hard. Charles rolled, grabbed his tunic, tried to haul him upright; but Bluey's body stayed limp. His eyes had already rolled back.

For a second, the jungle fell silent except for the rain.

Another man went down behind them with a sickening slap. A guard raised his rifle to finish it, but Charles stumbled between them, waving him off.

"Leave 'em," he said, voice hoarse. "I'll see to it."

The guard hesitated, then turned away.

Charles crouched beside the private, mud dripping from his face, whispering, "You're home now, boy."

He pressed his hand over the boy's heart, still warm; then forced himself to his feet.

His own legs barely obeyed him. The swelling had reached his knees; each joint a block of wood. Every step felt like walking on splints.

Then, through the fog, the ridge changed; the shape of Castle Hill rising in front of him, glowing red under a break of sunlight. Its steep, rugged lines cut sharp against the sky.

And there she was.

Edna. Her bright dress flowing in the wind, too clean, too alive to be real.

"Well, come on, soldier," she called, smiling. *"You can't let me beat you to the top."*

She turned, laughing, and ran up the goat track.

Charles summoned everything left in him; strength, stubbornness, madness; and followed. The track twisted in switchbacks, narrow and uneven. He clutched roots and rocks for balance, breath coming in sobs.

"Not even a hill, boys!" he shouted, the words bursting out in Billy's old tone.

The men around him, what few remained, grunted and stumbled, driven by his voice alone. He saw Frankie's face ahead, shifting between grin and grimace, a ghost flickering in and out of focus.

The sun burned through the mist, heat prickling under their collars. Every breath scraped. Then, slowly, the sounds of the jungle faded: no birds, no insects, just the rhythmic gasping of the men.

An eerie silence hung over the slope. The faint scent of woodsmoke drifted down from somewhere above.

Charles lifted his head; through the mist, the shapes of huts appeared, roofs glinting. A wooden sign stood skewed in the ground, its letters carved deep and dark: *RANAU.*

And there she was again, standing before it all.

Edna. Smiling, radiant, her eyes clear and piercing.

He blinked. She vanished. The vision burned away into fog, replaced by the silhouette of a gate.

"Hold formation," he rasped. "We walk in together."

The men shuffled the last hundred metres in silence; feet dragging, faces hollow but upright.

Fifteen days.

Forty-two left.

Chapter 30

Liberation

The column stumbled through the gate on the 12th of February 1945, 260 kilometres of jungle behind them.

No celebration. No relief. Just silence, and the sound of feet sloshing through wet clay.

The Ranau compound was smaller than Charles imagined; a ragged patch of earth carved into the slope; bamboo huts crouched under the dripping canopy like animals in the rain.

The air stank of rot and faeces, the open pits spilling down the hill like infected wounds. Beyond the clearing, the jungle loomed close and watchful, the thunder of a river rolling somewhere below.

No other prisoners. No sound of life.

Charles realised his men were the first; the first Allies to set foot here. The air felt too still, as though the jungle itself were holding its breath.

Forty-two.

He whispered the number like a prayer, memorising each face in the half-light. Pride tugged at him; they had made it; but guilt pressed harder. Thirteen gone under his command. Bluey's grin still floated in the mist, the rest little more than bones held together by willpower.

Then came the barking.

"You! Unload supply! Rebuild hut! Dig latrine!"

The dream of rest vanished in an instant.

Digging again; after marching near to death; felt like some cruel echo of MacRae calling down the line.

"You got a hole to dig, soldier!"

Charles drove his shovel into the sodden clay.

"Feels like we're diggin' our own graves," he muttered, hearing Billy's voice overlap his own.

The mist crept higher up the ridge, clinging to their backs, cooling their sweat to ice. The guards stood over them like overseers, shouting, striking, laughing. The wet thud of spades filled the air; a grim orchestra at a funeral that refused to end.

He could feel himself shaking; muscles hollow, chest raw; but when he looked around, the others were still moving. Broken men, yes, but moving. That sight alone kept him upright.

By dusk, the trench was done. The guards dumped a dented pot of rice on the crude table, a pale lump of life. The men fell on it like animals. It tasted of nothing, but after ten days of starvation, it was a feast.

That night, Charles lay beneath the slats of a half-built hut, legs swollen and burning. The rain outside came steady, soft, rhythmic. He stared up at the bamboo beams until they blurred, and in the hum of rain he could almost hear her, Edna; that soft tune she hummed while knitting by lamplight.

He let the sound pull him under.

For the first time since Sandakan, he slept without mud or gunfire; only the faint melody of home guiding him through the dark.

Morning came grey and shapeless. The mist hung low, the rain now a fine drizzle that never stopped. The air stank of wet ash and waste.

Charles rose to the guards' shouts. His joints screamed; his legs looked worse: stretched, shiny, alien. Still, he forced himself upright.

"Forty-two," he said out loud this time, as if the number might hold them together.

They were set to work before dawn's light broke. Some carried bamboo, others hacked at the sodden ground. The guards barked, struck, moved them like cattle. Every breath felt like dragging air through a wet rag.

By noon, one man collapsed in the mud, face down. Charles reached him first, faint pulse, glassy eyes. The guard laughed, nudged the body with his boot, told them to keep digging.

By nightfall, two more were gone. They buried them beside the latrine trench, no words, no crosses. Just a mound of earth that would soon sink and disappear.

In the evening, the jungle answered with new sounds, boots in the mud, shouted orders. Lanterns flickered through the mist. Another column stumbled through the gate, barely thirty men left. Some carried the dying over their shoulders; others simply dropped where they stood.

Charles watched them file in. His own forty-two looked like giants by comparison.

"Second march," someone whispered. "Sandakan."

He tried to count them but lost track. The world blurred at the edges, colours running into one another. His legs trembled, shining in the lantern light.

The fever continued.

The nights came without form. Rain seeped through the roofs. Men coughed, muttered, dreamed aloud. Sometimes Charles thought he heard the shovels again; that dull, rhythmic thud in the distance, the sound rising and falling like a heartbeat.

He didn't know if he was asleep or working. Time bent around him, a blur of rain, orders, and breath. The mist pressed in like a blanket, and the shadows moved through it, half real, half memory.

Then, a branch cracked.

He froze. Through the haze, Frankie stood there, boots catching the moonlight, that familiar smirk cutting through the rain.

"Thought the war would've toughened you up."

For a moment, Charles believed it. He could almost smell the oil and polish on Frankie's kit, hear that dry chuckle that always followed a smart remark. The ghost of a friend; or just the fever, he couldn't tell.

Then the shape dissolved back into fog.

Only the rain remained.

As time passed, more columns came through, each one smaller than the last.

Starvation set in. The rice rations shrank to almost nothing. Men scraped moss from logs, chewed bark, plucked beetles from the walls; anything that might fool the body into thinking it had eaten.

Food disappeared, but the work continued. Charles was skin and bone from the waist up; below, his legs had ballooned, the skin stretched tight as drumskin. He hid the swelling under strips of his own shirt.

He walked the line, counting survivors by habit, voice slurred by fever.

"Fifty-one... fifty-two..."

A private whispered, "We're ghosts, sir."

Charles didn't answer. He knew they were.

A shiver seized him. He crouched inside a hut, hugging his knees against the chill. The rain on the roof softened, shifted; became the patter of boots on timber.

He looked up and Billy was beside him again, grinning as he tossed a duffle bag on the closest stretcher. The bamboo walls hardened into weatherboard, the air thick with eucalyptus and dust.

Chook's nervous voice cut through: *"Can I... can I bunk in here?"*

Then Snow's bulk filled the doorway, booming, *"Afternoon, soldiers. Jack O'Donnell. Mates call me Snow."*

The laughter came easy, the warmth filling every corner of the hut; until Iron Jack's bark cut through it. The sound cracked back into a guard's shout. The laughter curdled. Bamboo walls sagged inward. He blinked; Billy was gone, only mist and the stench of death remaining.

The smell of decay crawled down; even the jungle no longer tried to hide it.

Bodies were wrapped in rice sacks and buried in shallow pits at dawn. Starvation, malaria, and beriberi did the work the rifles no longer needed to.

Of the 455 men who had left Sandakan, only 190 reached Ranau alive. Half of those were already dead. The guards stopped counting, but Charles did not.

Mealtime brought no relief. His heart thudded unevenly; his breath rasped, chest heavy with water. A dying boy beside him couldn't lift his head. Charles tilted the tin cup to his lips, forcing the watery rice down.

He stared into his own bowl; the grain shifting, softening; turning into porridge. The drizzle changed to morning light warming the kitchen window.

His mother in her apron by the hearth. His father behind the Townsville Daily Bulletin. The whistle of the billy mingled with the hiss of rain outside.

"Eat before it gets cold," his mother said.

Then a cough snapped him back. The warmth evaporated. The bowl was empty.

The guards paced nervously, barking orders at shadows. Something had changed in them; an unease that ended in more punishment.

"Reckon the war's over, sir?" a younger soldier murmured.

"Not till the last man's home," Charles replied.

But *"home"* wavered in meaning; sometimes distant, sometimes close enough to touch.

Some nights, the whimper of a man in fever echoed like laughter from another life. The hut melted away. He was back on his veranda, the scent of supper in the air.

He stood in the doorway; uniform dusty, telegram trembling in his hand.

Edna sat with John on her lap. Lurline first to reach him, arms tight around his waist, with Lucille, Margaret, and Clair close behind. He leaned down, pressing a kiss to John's forehead, the boy's hair soft against his cheek. The girls' voices tumble,

"Dad's going to London! To see the King!"

Edna looked up, eyes shining. *"Charles."* She smiled.

The lamplight faded. A guard's lantern flared in its place. The seal on the telegram caught the light, then dimmed to nothing.

He had made it to March. His skin shone with fever, each breath a rasp of tin. His head throbbed, his legs swollen beyond pain. Still, the guards drove them on.

Rumours of rescue drifted through the huts. The word liberation passed from mouth to mouth, fragile as smoke. Charles clung to it anyway.

He steadied himself, using the perimeter fence to shuffle toward tenko. The barbed wire bit into his hand; then straightened into smooth timber.

The jungle brightened into dry paddocks under a clear Woodstock sky.

Lurline rode beside him, chin up, sunlight in her hair.

"You really love it here," she said, smiling.

"Reckon I do," Charles whispered.

"We'll make new fences... maybe that's alright."

Her words glowed with her mother's quiet warmth.

The creak of saddle leather turned into the groan of bamboo. He blinked. The wire was barbed again. Blood slid down his wrist and vanished into the mud.

There were barely any prisoners left. The guards watched from a distance now, their brutality dulled by exhaustion.

Charles could hardly stand. Two men tried to lift him; he shook his head. He whispered roll call by memory, names fading between breaths. Skeletons and ghosts swayed before him, and behind them the jungle hummed a single low note, the river drumming beneath it all.

The 6th of March 1945, the morning mist was pale as milk. Through the broken wall he saw a hill-shaped cloud, gold in the first light.

And then he was there, on Castle Hill with Edna.

The wind played in her hair, the cathedral below gleamed red against the sea.

She looked up at him. *"What's with that building then?"*

"That church is where my parents were married," he murmured.

The words came freely now; the sailor father, the orphanage, the mother who left, the loneliness.

Edna listened, then reached for his hand, resting it gently on her lap.

A tear slipped down his cheek. Her handkerchief brushed it away, soft and warm.

She smiled, her eyes holding his.

"You're not invisible, Charles."

The words hung there, light and steady. For a moment, the world eased. The air seemed to lift him, weightless, as if the pain had finally loosened its grip.

Her voice carried through the mist: clear, sure, familiar.

The hut around him faded to white.

He drew one last breath: shallow, peaceful.

It left him as a breeze moving through the trees.

The sun was only just lifting over the horizon; the paddocks shimmered in the early light.

Alone on horseback, a slender stockman moved the herd with ease.

Sixteen-year-old Charles rode the ridge, fearless, free; boy and horse as one, the land unfolding gold before them.

This was his liberation.

The portrait of WO2 Charles Young Watson at the Coronation of King George VI, 1937, is reproduced courtesy of the Australian War Memorial, Accession Number P08681.001.

From The Author

Charles' story was one that I came across by accident, or perhaps by fate. One autumn afternoon at my parents' house, someone remarked that my first son, who was just one year old at the time, looked remarkably like my father when he was young. Shocking, I know! So out came the old, dusty photo albums as my dad set out to prove the claim.

As we flicked through the pages of my father's past, I agreed that the resemblance was striking. But that wasn't what truly captured my attention. Instead, my eyes were drawn to an old black-and-white photograph, slightly out of focus; a young soldier standing in front of the pyramids.

Being a history buff; especially when it comes to wartime history, I had to ask. Who was this man, and why was his photo in our family album? My father explained that it was my great-grandfather, Charles.

I began asking more questions. I had heard as a child that my great-grandfather had fought on the Western Front during the First World War but seeing that photo made the story real. In previous attempts to trace my family's military history, I had never been able to locate him; I'd always assumed he would have shared my last name, not realising the records were listed under my grandmother's maiden name. What was already an incredible family history becoming even more extraordinary when my father told me that Charles had died as a prisoner of war during the Sandakan Death Marches.

At the time, I didn't know what the death marches were. The more I researched, the more I was shocked; not only by the unimaginable horror of what happened but also by the lack of awareness surrounding what is arguably Australia's worst wartime tragedy. Of the 1,787 Australian prisoners held at Sandakan, around 500 made it to Ranau. Severely weakened, most died soon after. The only six to survive managed to escape from Ranau, the liberation of Borneo came a year too late for the prisoners.

Kokoda is rightfully well known and honoured, but how had the Sandakan Death Marches been pushed aside in the history books?

From that moment, I was hooked. My dad shared some old newspaper articles and books that mentioned Charles by name. I was astonished; why was he singled out? Reading on, I learned that at the time of his capture he held the rank of Warrant Officer Class 2. With limited officers left at Sandakan, he was forced to lead the very first death march, taking 55 men through the brutal 260 km march that ended in almost certain death.

Charles past on the 6th of March 1945. His death certificate recorded the cause as beriberi, though in truth it was the inevitable result of starvation rations and the relentless brutality of the guards.

That story was remarkable on its own, but combined with his World War I service, I knew I had stumbled upon something rare; something this generation might not fully grasp. Charles had lied about his age at 16 to enlist and was thrown into the bloodiest war of its time, enduring the brutal conditions of the Western Front. He survived that hell and became one of approximately forty thousand Australians who went on to serve again in World War II.

I couldn't let his name fade into history. I began gathering every family record, service document, and military file I could find to piece together a timeline of his life; his service divisions, deployments, and the historical context, including the coronation of King George VI. Of course, there were many gaps, so to bring his story to life, I blended historical fact with carefully imagined detail. The family members in this novel are based on real people; Lurline is my grandmother, and Edna was Charles' wife. His other children: Lucille, Margaret, Clair, and John; are also based on real individuals as well as Granny Dean, though their scenes, dialogue, personalities and interactions have been fictionalised to give the story depth and humanity.

The purpose of this novel is to honour men like Charles; those who fought in one or even two world wars, or any military conflict, who gave their lives or carried the weight of their experiences long after. It's also to bring the horrors of the death marches into greater public consciousness, where they rightfully belong in our shared history.

For his service, Charles Young Watson received the British War Medal and Victory Medal for World War I; the Coronation Medal 1937; and for World War II, the 1939–45 Star, Pacific Star, Defence Medal, War Medal 1939–45, and Australian Service Medal. His record stands as a testament to a life defined by commitment, endurance, and courage.

He is commemorated at the Labuan Memorial in Malaysia on Panel 20 and honoured on the Roll of Honour at the Australian War Memorial, Panel 85 for World War II and Panel 188 for World War I. He is also remembered on an individual plaque along the Samford Avenue of Honour near Brisbane. His name lives on through these memorials, the Virtual War Memorial, and now this novel. Charles was survived by his wife, Edna Clair Watson, of Red Hill, Queensland.

Charles's military career, spanning both world wars, and his leadership in the face of unimaginable suffering, ensure his legacy remains one of courage, resilience, and quiet heroism.

For me, this journey has been more than research; it's been a reconnection with a part of my family I never had the chance to know. I grew up with only fragments of his story, and now, through this work, I can give those fragments shape and meaning. It's a reminder that behind every name on a plaque or memorial, there is a life lived, a family left behind, and a story worth telling.

Thank you for taking the time to learn about Charles. If his story moved you, please consider connecting with the social media pages or leaving a review on Goodreads or any of the publishing platforms. Just search **Between Two Wars**.

Lest we forget.

Aaron Dryden